THE JOURNEY

The Journey

A novel

by

MARTA LEE

Adelaide Books
New York / Lisbon
2021

THE JOURNEY
A novel
By Marta Lee

Copyright © by Marta Lee

Cover design © 2021 Adelaide Books

Published by Adelaide Books, New York / Lisbon
adelaidebooks.org

Editor-in-Chief
Stevan V. Nikolic

For any information, please address Adelaide Books at info@ adelaidebooks.org

or write to:

Adelaide Books
244 Fifth Ave. Suite D27
New York, NY, 10001

ISBN: 978-1-954351-49-3

Printed in the United States of America

Contents

Acknowledgements

I would like to express gratitude to J. Singleton, Attorney at Law, for assistance during the writing and publishing of this manuscript.

I would also like to acknowledge the following web sites and books that I consulted while researching and writing about a family's migration from their German homeland to Russia and finally to America.

Map of Hess Region of Germany: http://en.wikipedia.org/wiki/Hesse

General information:
https://en.wikipedia.org/wiki/Germans_from_Russia

Volga River region:
German settlement map: http://www. rollintl.com/roll/grsettle.htm

I utilized the Kansas Historical Society web site for: A picture of representatives going to US: http://www.kshs.org/p/on-line-exhibits-from-far-away-russia-part-2/10680

Flyer: http://www.kshs.org/p/online-exhibits-from-far-away-russia-part-2/10680

County map pf Kansas:
http://www.kshs.org/p/online-exhibits-from-far-away-russia-part-1/15648

Housing illustrations:
http://www.kshs.org/p/online-exhits-from-far-away-russia-part-3/10681

Sod House:
http://specialcollections.wichita.edu/collections/ms/95-20/sh-La_Crosse1.JPG

Post Card:
http://en.wikipedia.org/wiki/Ellis_Island

Farm machinery:
http://www.kshs.org/p/online-exhibits-from-far-away-russia-part-4/10682

Dust Storm:
http://www.livinghistoryfarmorg/farminginthe30s/water_02.html

Pictures and diagrams of the dustbowl:
http://www.pbs.org/wgbh/americanexperience/films/dustbowl/

For a picture of Hussenbach I accessed the following site:
http://cvgs.cu-portland.edu/settlements/mother_colonies/colony_hussenbach.cfm

Most importantly I would like to provide heart-felt thanks to North Dakota State University and their Germans to Russia Heritage Collection:
https://library.ndsu.edu/grhc/history_culture/history/people.html

Burns, Ken and Dayton Duncan. The Dust Bowl: An Illustrated History Chronicle Books: San Francisco, CA, 2012.

Coan, Peter Morton. Ellis Island Interviews. Fall River Press, New York, 1997.

Massie, Robert K. Catherine the Great: Portrait of a Women Random House: New York, 2011.

Denver, Colorado
Autumn 1971

Ever since I can remember I, Dani Keller, was intensely interested in knowing where my ancestors had come from. My curiosity grew when I realized that my mother's family did not know where in Germany the maternal side of the family, the Funks, had once lived. More importantly, I wanted to know why the family had moved to Russia. A family 'rumor' that I was aware of indicated that the family had lived in Russia for a hundred years. I was curious to know if this rumor was true or not.

With my thumb and finger on my chin and jaw, I began to contemplate where I might begin a journey into this branch of my family history. The majority of what I knew about the Funks was a little fact and a lot of speculation. Between the 1600's and 1800's many people migrated as a result of unfavorable living conditions. I did know that these unfavorable conditions often consisted of both political or religious factors. It is possible that unfavorable conditions were natural causes like lack of rain.

In order to answer some of these questions regarding my German ancestors I needed to begin the journey by talking with my Grandma Anderson. When my Grandparents came to visit during the week surrounding Christmas, I began a conversation with Grandma regarding her family. I began asking Grandma several questions about her family. "Do you know where in Germany your family lived? Why did your family leave Germany? I heard they left Germany for Russia; is that true? I am not sure where I heard it but sort of remember someone saying that they had lived in Russia for a hundred years."

Thinking for a moment before answering, Grandma finally said "That's a lot of questions Dani! I do not know where they come from in Germany or why they left. I do know that they had moved to Russia but not when. I vaguely remember someone stating that the family had lived in Russia for about a hundred years but am not sure of this."

Hmmm…so Grandma had heard the same rumor that I had heard and she seems somewhat skeptical. I continued by asking her "When did they move to America?"

"My oldest brother and sister were born in Russia in 1899 and 1900." Grandma stated "My sister, Molly, was born in 1902 after the family had moved to central Kansas."

I asked if Grandma knew anything else about the family. It had been many years since she had thought about the family's history so she would have to think about it. Grandma said that she would get back to me with any additional information that she might be able to provide as soon as she could.

Several weeks later, a package arrived from Grandma. Instantly curious I could not wait to see what the package contained. Once the box was opened, I found a letter laying at the top. Sitting down, I began to read what Grandma had written….

Mid—January, 1972

Dear Dani,

The enclosed journal could have waited until we saw you next but I felt that you might want to start reading about the family as soon as possible. However, before you start reading this first journal, I thought you might like some background information. Years ago, my father gave me a set of old books which turned out to be journals. Without reading them, I thanked him and put them away to read later. Life got busy and I forgot about them until you inquired about the family. I remembered that I had placed them in my cedar chest years ago.

Looking at the journals I realized that they were written in German. As I began reading the oldest journal, I came to the understanding that during the writing of this journal the family was living in Germany. At this time, the family began considering moving.

I translated this first journal so you could begin the journey with the family. I will translate the remaining journals and get them to you as soon as possible. Grandpa and I send our love,

Love Grandma

My eyes sparkled as I considered this journal. Lifting it out of the box, I fingered the journal's soft, supple leather binding. It was hard to imagine that one of my ancestors had held and wrote in this journal. What were my ancestors considering as they wrote in this volume? Was it possible that the individual just wanted an outlet to express frustration regarding the living conditions of the time? Carefully opening the journal, I found a map along with two documents. Examining the map, I wondered if this is where the Funks had lived while living in Germany.

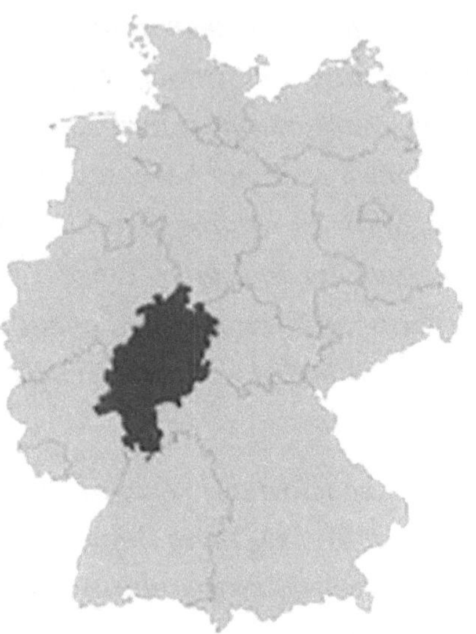

Hess Region of Germany
http://en.wikipedia.org/wiki/Hesse

Desiring to know which major cities were located in the Hesse region, I went to the book shelf to get an atlas. A detailed map of Germany showed the area called Hess. The largest city in the region appeared to be Frankfort. Was it possible that the Funks lived in Frankfort or possibility close by? Maybe, but I seem to recall that Grandma had told me that her family had been farmers for many generations. If this was true, then my ancestors most likely did not live in Frankfort or any other major city.

Knowing that the Hess region was probably the general area where the family had resided while living in Germany was better than not knowing anything. It did cause me to speculate about where exactly the family had lived and worked. The map seemed to create more questions than answers. I set aside the map, put the atlas back on the shelf, and then looked at the other document that had fallen out of the journal.

Manifest von 1763

Ausländern werden erlaubt, in Russland und zu klären wo sie es wünschen;

Russische Regierung Die Minister werden die Ausländer mit geld brauchte für die Reise wenn sie auswandern nach Russland;

Wenn fremde an der Russischen Guardian Office, die einwanderer hat anzugeben, welche lage sie niederlassen wollen;

Sie sollen auch erklären, ob sie im Handel oder Handwerk;

Ausländische einwanderer gilt den eid der treue;

Alle Ausländer die Freiheit bei der Ausübung ihrer Religion der Wahl;

Einwanderer werden befreit von tribute [Steuer] und Belastungen wie zum Beispiel Gehäuse Soldaten;

Einwanderer sind ausreichende Flächen für die Landwirtschaft, die Produktion oder die basteln;

Einwanderer werden mit benötigten Materialien für ein Haus zu bauen;

Einwanderer haben zum Schutz vor räubern.

Ausländer haben freie Einfuhr von persönlichen Gegenständen und -Effekte.

Zuwanderer werden nicht ernannt werden, die militärischen oder bürgerpflicht gegen ihren willen;

Die oben genannten Rechte sind garantiert der Zuwanderer und ihrer Kinder und nachkommen;

Nach der festgelegten Anzahl von Jahren die siedler den gewohnten Steuern bezahlen;

Ausländer, die sich in Russland sind frei, uns zu verlassen aber zahlt der Russischen staatskasse die folgenden perzentil:

Leben in Russland zwischen einem und fünf Jahren ein Fünftel ihrer Fülle gezahlt werden; Leben in Russland zwischen fünf oder mehr Jahren ein Zehntel ihres Vermögens gezahlt wird.

I speculated on what this document was about; did it have something to do with Germans migrating to Russia? I decided that the best thing to do is to begin reading the journal. Looking down at the package that the journal came in, I noticed some loose papers lying on the bottom. Placing the book on the table, I gathering up the papers from the box and began to read them. After a few moments, I decided that I would continue to read the papers the following day. I placed the journal and papers back into the box. The box was placed on the floor next to my bed.

Within moments of lying down I was sound asleep. Hours later, I woke up and looked out the window. Snow was gently falling softly to the ground. Snow wasn't surprising since it routinely fell during the winter in Colorado. Looking out the window, I noticed that the snow was not sticking to the ground which could only mean that the falling snow wouldn't accumulate or last long. Without the snow sticking to the ground it would make it easier to get to school or work in the morning. After an hour of tossing and turning, I turned on a light and reached for the journal's translation from the box. Laying on top of the journal's translation lay the English translation of the manifesto. In english the manifesto read:

The English version of the manifesto provided me a somewhat better understanding of why the people had been tempted to leave Germany for a new start in Russia. I, then, began my own journey with a portion of my family.

Manifesto of 1763

Foreigners are allowed to come to Russia and settle wherever they so desire;

Russian Government Ministers will supply foreigners with needed money for the journey when they immigrate to Russia;

When foreigners arrive at the Russian Guardian Office, the immigrants shall declare which location they wish to settle; They shall also declare whether they wish to be in trade or handicrafts;

Foreign immigrants shall take an oath of loyalty;

All foreigners are given the freedom to exercise their religion of choice;

Immigrants shall be exempt of tribute [taxes] and burdens such as housing soldiers;

Immigrants shall be given sufficient lands needed for farming, manufacturing or for producing handicrafts;

Immigrants shall be provided with materials needed for building of a house;

Immigrants shall have protection from robbers;

Foreigners shall have free importation of personal goods and effects;

Immigrants shall not be appointed to the military or civic duty against their will;

The above rights are guaranteed to immigrants and their children and

descendants;

After the established number of years, the settlers will pay the accustomed taxes;

Foreigners who settled in Russia are free to leave.

Journal One

Germany—1764

.

Conrad

Recent talk around Nauheim has indicated that more farmers than ever have chosen to move away. I, Conrad Funk, am positive that the reason the majority of farmers that are leaving is due to the drought that has been plaguing the region for longer than any of us care to remember. The drought resulted in fewer farmers selling their harvest for less money. This caused the region to experience a shortage of goods which, in turn, has caused the general store proprietor paying higher prices for flour, seasonings, coffee and other commodities. He has been forced to raise his prices in order to stay in business. Without enough money being earned from my harvest, how can I afford to purchase the supplies that I need?

Each year the droughts worsen and fewer crops survive. Just yesterday, I was forced to butcher three times as many pigs as I normally would at any one time. While the pork cured, I was forced to take the remaining pigs to market in order to obtain cash to buy supplies and pay my taxes. Another farmer, who lives on the other side of Nauheim, purchased my pigs at a price somewhat lower than what they are actually worth. I cannot continue selling off my livestock at such low prices. Besides, my family need the meat, milk and eggs that the cows, chickens, and other animals provide.

I am worried about how my family will endure through another year of drought. There is a real possibility that my entire family and I could be forced to stop farming; we could be required to move to a large city or, possibility, to a foreign country. I do not welcome the idea of leaving the land and moving to a city. We have heard that large cities are overcrowded and have high crime. Besides, what would we do for a living? Farming has provided us with many different skills but are these skills enough for us to make a living in a city?

Political unrest is wide spread in and around Hess. This unrest has caused territorial disputes to take place and for wars to break out. Many of the region's men have been forced into the army to fight these wars. Thousands of men have died over the past twenty to thirty years fighting wars that they do not believe in or even completely understand. This has left women alone to raise children and run a farm by themselves. My mother's sister was widowed last year due to her husband being shot in the chest because he refused to be drafted. My Aunt is now raising six children by herself. Both the Funks and the Mueller's, Mother's family, are helping my Aunt with the plowing, planting and harvesting of her crops. We all do what we can to help each other during tough times.

Eight months ago, Katherine and I were married. As a result of the long drought and recent war over who knows what, Katherine and I have discussed moving. As others in the area, I do not wish to leave my wife to fight in a war, or to change my faith to suit the winner of the conflict. Across Europe there seems to be a constant battle between the Catholic and Protestant faiths, at least among those in political power. The majority of the region's population live in religious harmony. Many of us have the belief of *live and let live* and do not wish to have the government tell them what faith to practice.

Sometimes my head swims as I consider the many possibilities of moving. I wonder if I should continue farming here or should we move westward to the British colony across the ocean? Should we move somewhere else on the European continent? If Katherine and I move, should we do so alone or should we convince the family to move also? Of course, I know moving a great distance with just Katherine would mean never seeing my family again. Farming does not allow men to travel great distances for a 'vacation' because feeding animals, milking, collecting eggs, and changing animal bedding is an everyday chore. Good neighbors help each other in a pinch but how long could a neighbor handle their own farm plus mine while I am having a leisurely visit with my family?

I know that Katherine and I could not survive without the possibility of seeing the family again. Being orphaned at an early age, Katherine was raised by her grandparents. Katherine's grandparents passed away four years ago causing her to be alone in the world until the two of us met. My family immediately fell in love with Katherine and has gone out of their way to make her feel like an integral part of the family. I know that I could move only if I can convince my family to also move.

One bright, sunny but chilly Saturday morning in late March of 1764, Katherine and I loaded our wagon with items that we planned on selling in town. In addition, Katherine had packed items to contribute to the family picnic that we shared with my parents and brothers. After the loading was complete, I assisted Katherine into the wagon and took one last look at the house. Last fall Katherine and I planted many different varieties of spring bulbs around the front of the house. It had been a big job planting all those bulbs but the work is paying off as the crocuses have already bloomed for the season and have begun their seasonal decline. The daffodils are in the process of sending their slim dark green leafs up towards the sun prior to blooming. The tulip foliage has just started to poke through the soil; in a couple of weeks they will provide wonderful color to the property. Knowing how Katherine loved lilacs, I am considering planting several bushes near and around the house. Maybe, I should wait until we decide about whether to move now or in the future.

The main reason that Katherine and I enjoy the shopping trip to Nauheim was because we would meet up with my family. Each week as we pulled up to my parent's home, Katherine and I would be greeted by either my father, Jacob, my mother, Maria, or one of my three younger brothers. Today my brothers and Dad were loading their wagon with items to be sold at market as Mom was leaving their cottage carrying a large picnic basket. Quickly, I climbed down from our wagon to assist Mom with her basket. After greeting each other, Katherine and Mom began to discuss the quilt that Mom was making.

Assisting Dad and my brothers was a welcome diversion for me as Mom and Katherine began their usual discussion about what type of quilt, they were either working on or planning on making. Mom asked whether Katherine had begun piecing her quilt top yet. Katherine replies by saying "No, because the majority of my material scraps consist mainly of yellows, blues and browns. I would like some greens, purples and reds prior to beginning the piecing process."

Maria agreed, stating that different colors and patterns made a quilt more interesting and beautiful. "Why don't you and Conrad come to supper tonight? Then, you and I can see what is in my scrap bag; you can select what fabric you would like to use for your quilt."

Katherine readily accepted the invitation because she loved spending time with the family and especially my Mom. In addition, she loved to see the different colorful fabrics Mom used in her sewing and ultimately in her quilts. Exchanging scraps of material with Mom or other women allowed Mom and Katherine to put into their quilt's subtle changes of color or just a splash of another color. I saw one of my Mom's quilts where it was mainly gray and white with just a few pieces of yellow and red; the quilt was beautiful.

Coming out of my thoughts I heard my Mom tell Katherine that she could help her prepare supper and they could discuss different quilt patterns. One pattern that Mom wanted to talk with Katherine about was a pattern that would utilize a red square of fabric in each blocks center. "I feel that the red square would represent the hearth of the home." Not having worked out any of the other details for the remainder of the quilt, Mom was open to suggestions from Katherine.

Considering the block thoughtfully before replying she finally said "If the quilt blocks were to reflect the family then wouldn't you want to select fabrics that would suggest the family members? Scraps from that blue plaid skirt of Jacob's or the green plaid fabric that you used for Charles's shirt would be perfect for that type of quilt. Do you have any material left from that beautiful fabric with the light rose pattern? That fabric would work well in this type of quilt."

As we neared Nauheim, I noticed that there was an unusual excitement among the people gathered near and around the general store. Dad and I slowed and eventually stopped the horses a short distance from the general store. "I wonder what is going on at the store." my brother, Johann, inquired to no one in particular.

Several people approached our wagons, exclaiming "Have you heard the News?"

"What news?" asked Dad.

Many began to talk at once which added to the confusion. Interjecting quickly, Dad said "Wait! Slow down, I am having trouble understanding with everyone talking at once."

Kieran Vogler began by stating that "there were some men from Russia on the porch of the General Store. These men have been distributing information on an immigration program. Their flyers claim that any foreigner who immigrates to Russia would be free from military service and be liberated from most taxes for a number of years. I am positive that I heard them say that assistance will be provided to those who desire to establish a farm in Russia."

[January of 1972: the journal talks of several flyers but I found only the Manifesto of 1763—Grandma]

I asked the group whether the men said how long these individuals would be free from taxes and conscription. Daniel Hemel said that they were not sure because of the "large crowd gathered around the Russians have made it difficult to get close enough to ask relevant questions. We did hear that we would have the freedom to practice any faith that we chose."

"The document being passed out states those choosing to move to Russia would be allowed self-rule and have political rights." Frederick Lies further pointed out that "at this time we do not currently live in a place where people have political or religious freedom."

Agreement arose amongst the men gathered around our wagons. Both religious and political freedoms were important for the majority of people living in Nauheim and the region. Dad and I decided that we would like to see the flyers regarding the Russian immigration program prior to continuing the conversation. "If you will excuse us," said Dad "we would like to see the flyers that we are discussing for ourselves so we can have a discussion with you and with others. We would also would like to ask a few relevant questions."

"Of course!" said several of the men in unison.

Someone else mentioned that "a meeting should be set up in order to discuss the prospect of immigration. The meeting could be held at the Lutheran Church after services on Sunday." Those around our wagons agreed that the meeting was a great idea. Other men that were gathered around said that they would spread the word so others could join in the conversation.

While we were talking, Katherine and Mom had walked towards the General Store. At the store's porch steps, they had to pick their way through a crowd in order to get inside. At the counter, Mom and Katherine sold eggs and butter; then purchased flour, sugar, seasonings, coffee, and tea. Bits of the conversations regarding the Russian Immigration Flyer were overheard by Mom and Katherine as they waited for their grocery items to be measured, bagged and gathered together. They looked at one another with interest but continued to quietly listen so they could learn as much as possible about what was going on in town.

The shop keeper turned towards Mom and Katherine and asked them if they "needed anything else before I ring up your order." Touching one of the light blue fabrics, Mom said that she would like a half yard. Katherine asked for two yards of a deep purple material.

Once finished in the general store, the pair headed towards our wagons to deposit their items. While waiting for us to complete our business the two settled on a bench just outside the general store. Since Katherine had always lived in the region, she said that it "would be exciting to travel to another part of the world and see new things."

Maria told Katherine that when she was younger, she lived in a region further north. "It was thrilling to see exotic boats journeying along the Baltic Sea and the region's waterways. As a result, I always dreamed of traveling by boat to new and faraway places. When I fell in love with and married Jacob, I realized that I needed to forget those dreams and begin a new dream; one where I would be loved and have many children. I have never regretted my choices but have often wondered where those boats could have taken me."

Dreamy eyed, Katherine acknowledged what her mother—in—law had said about a life where one was loved. Katherine said "Feeling totally loved by Conrad, I knew that we would have a wonderful life together and, hopefully, many children. However, I often wonder about those many exotic places that you talk about. I heard that the British colonies across the Atlantic Ocean can be an exciting place to live but there are reports of wars between these native people and the Europeans over land."

"Life's problems seem to be the same no matter where you live. The only thing difference is the characters and location."

"How true, how true. I wonder what life in Russia would be like."

Thinking for a moment before replying, Maria said that "life in Russia or in the British colony cannot be that much different than living in and around Nauheim. I have heard that as Russia expands eastward, Russians have had some bad encounters with the native populations. This is similar to what those in America, the British colony, are experiencing as they expand westward."

"I hadn't thought of that before. I never realized that you knew so much; have you ever considered being a school teacher?"

"When I lived near the Baltic Sea, I did work as a school teacher for a short time. I enjoyed working with the children. But after I met Jacob, I had to decide whether to continue teaching or to be married and raise children. You know what I decided to do." Mom said as a smile swept over her face.

Changing the subject, Mom asked Katherine if she had heard about Charles proposing to Molly Hoffman. Katherine replied that she had heard about Charles considering a proposal but had not heard that he had actually proposed. Thinking that her boys were growing up too fast, Maria said that she heard that "Charles and Molly were looking at having a December wedding. However, nothing is set in stone yet. Plans could change if decisions are made to move to Russia or elsewhere."

Recently, I read in a Swiss newspaper that many regions across Europe, such as Bavaria and Saxony, did not desire to lose population. As a result, laws were passed that prevented representatives from recruiting the region's population to move to Russia. The same laws prevented the distribution of documents or flyers dealing with migration. Effective, legal recruitment of immigrants became limited to free cities and states where such laws did not exist. I am positive that the Russians came to Nauheim because we did not have such laws.

When I first heard of these laws, I was outraged that any government would attempt to prevent people from freely moving. However, as I thought about it, I realized that if a large portion of the population left, a region would be negatively affected. I began to understand why these types of laws were implemented. However, if the family moved, we should do so before laws regarding migration were passed in Nauheim.

I was pulled out of my musings when Dad said that we should talk to the Russians about the program. Dad, my three younger brothers and I walked to the General Store. After climbing the porch's steps, I said to the men representing the Russian government "I understand that you have information about an immigration program."

Replying, the man said that they were passing out both a flyer and a copy of the manifesto. *[Spring of 1972: Again, there is no flyer with the journal, just the manifesto.]* These documents provided information regarding the Russian immigration program. After each of us were handed copies of the documents, I thanked the men and said that we wanted to look the documents over and to discuss the material amongst ourselves. We would then return to talk to them. We withdrew to our wagons in order to read and discuss the different points of the leaflets.

My brother, Henry, pointed out that the flyer stated that "crops grew in abundance in the region's fertile soil. Do they know this because people are already farming in the region? If so, how many people are currently living and farming in the region? More importantly will there still be enough land available for us and other Germans to farm?"

Dad said that Henry's points were valid and then asked if we wanted to move to an area that could be already overcrowded.

I thought a moment before I inquired about how much land each immigrant might receive. "There are many people in the Hesse region that only have a few acres; they are barely scrapping by and are on the verge of going under. We should have at least 75 acres along with a mild climate and an adequate water supply, including rain, in order to have a fighting chance at farming. The flyer claims that we would be tax free but is the thirty-year grace period stated in the brochure guaranteed?"

"Another point that we need to think about" that Dad debated "is that the manifesto declares that we would be able to practice the religion of our choice. On the other hand, it does not say there won't be any interference. Every time the government changes hands, the new rulers attempt to transform the regions religion to their religion. Because of this conflict there is tension between the Jews, Protestants and Catholics. This does not even take into consideration the Mennonites or any other faith. In an ideal world, everyone should be able to practice their faith in peace. But we know that we do not live in an ideal world."

The documents handed out also provided information about what immigrants could expect when moving to Russia. However, these documents did not answer all the questions that the Germans had, they only created more questions. Questions such as where in Russia they would be able to settle, how many acres they would be able to farm, and what the land would cost. The five of us decided to table further discussion until we could have a group meeting. I wondered if we could hold a meeting the next afternoon after church services. However, we decided to ask the Russians a few questions before going home. Walking back to the Russians, I realized that I had been seriously considering moving for quite awhile; this program might be the opportunity that I and the family needed for a fresh start.

As we approached the general store, we noticed that the crowd had thinned out somewhat. Dad, my brothers, and I walked up to the Russians and one of them introduced himself as Dmitri Antipov. Looking at his colleagues he said "This is Petr Bury and Ivan Brezhnev. We will be happy to answer any questions that you might have."

I shook their hands and said "It is nice to meet you. My name is Conrad Funk." Indicating my father and brothers I continued by stating "This is my father Jacob and my brothers Charles, Henry and Johann. We would like to know a little about the climate of Russia. Is the country experiencing a drought?"

Ivan began by telling them that the northern portions of the country experienced cold, severe winters and that the growing season was limited. However, since the Volga River region is located in the southern region it has a much milder climate. The region has numerous rivers and bodies of water to assist in farming. "Several years ago, I was told that the Volga River region experienced a very short drought. Since then the region has had an abundance of rain."

Dad inquired if the representatives could tell us more about how the program began and the reasons why the program began. Dmitri began by stating that "The Russian Empress wished to increase the population of the Russian empire, especially in portions of the country that are largely uninhabited. As a result, the Czarina opened an office called the Chancellery for the Guardianship of Foreigners. The Chancellery's main purpose was to direct the immigrant settlement in the Volga River region. The Czarina intended farming to be the programs main emphasis. But she also felt that artisans and businessmen were needed to help with the development of villages to support the region and its farmers."

Charles asked if we could get several additional copies of the two documents to pass out to friends and neighbors that we would see later that afternoon. Dad inquired whether the men would be willing to meet with the community the next afternoon following church to answer any questions the community might have. The Russians stated that someone else had invited them to a meeting tomorrow but had failed to inform them about the time or place. Dad said that the logical meeting place would be in the space between the Lutheran and Catholic Churches at one o'clock. He then said that we "would be happy if the three of you would share our lunch at noon. We will be eating a picnic lunch on the grounds between the Lutheran and Catholic Churches, at around noon." Pointing to the right, dad told them that "the church is just down the road on the left." The Russians thanked Dad and said that they would be happy to join us for lunch. We said our good-byes and told them that we looked forward to meeting with them the next day. We then selected a shady spot not far from the churches to eat our lunch.

After lunch we quietly headed home, thinking about what it would mean to not only move but to relocate to a foreign country. Where would this opportunity take us was on the minds of the entire family. Would we take the chance for a better life or stay where there were no surprises?

Gathering outside the church with a picnic lunch was a ritual for many of the region's population during the warm weather months of late spring, summer and early autumn. It was a time to sit quietly, to relax, and to socialize. Weather on this Sunday in late-April was rather balmy, windy and slightly damp. The three foreigners, attending the meeting, arrived a few minutes after we set up our blankets and had arranged our lunch baskets. Attempting to make small talk, I asked our three guests about the language spoken, the religious practices across Russia and about their culture. While the family continued the discussion, I silently ate and considered the possibilities of living in a place where the people spoke a different language and where the majority of the people practiced the Eastern Orthodox faith.

The representatives did not want to divulge to much prior to the official meeting but attempted to be as informative as possible during lunch. I wondered whether we would be able to continue to practice our faith and speak our German language in Russia? I know that there are no guarantees in life but I don't wish to dive in head first only to be sorry later. Mom always said that I had the wanderlust bug; desiring to see new things. Even so, I tended to hold back some because of not wanting to leave my comfort zone.

After lunch the men and a few women gathered in the Lutheran church for the meeting. At one o'clock, the Reverend, William Zeigler, rose from his seat and walked to the pulpit. He cleared his throat and waited for quiet to over—take the building before beginning the meeting. Reverend Zeigler began the meeting by introducing the three men; Dmitri Antipov, Petr Bury and Ivan Brezhnev. Reverend Zeigler shook the three men's hands, turned over the meeting to the men and then sat down.

Dmitri Antipov started the discussion by telling those gathered how the current ruler of Russia, Catherine II, desired to increase the population of Russia. He said that "Parts of the Russian Empire were largely uninhabited and unused but had the potential to be very productive agriculturally."

Ivan Brezhev stated that "the Manifesto was written and issued to encourage foreigners to come to Russia in order to take up residence in all provinces wherever it would be agreeable to both the immigrant and the Russian government."

Those in attendance had read the documents already and they had specific questions. David Mueller asked "What do you mean by taking up residence wherever it would be agreeable? Isn't all places agreeable to the Russian government?"

"Yes, I stated that all provinces will be open for immigration but there is a special emphasis placed on areas that that are less developed." replied Dmitri Antipov.

"Yesterday, you told the Funks that the main purpose of the Chancellery for the Guardianship of Foreigners was to direct the settlement of the Volga River region." David Mueller argued. "In addition, your flyer on the *benefits and advantages of settling in Russia* appears to be aimed at the Volga River region alone. So, which is it, the Volga River region or all portions of the empire?"

Dmitri Antipov, Petr Bury and Ivan Brezhnev looked at each other prior to replying. "Honestly," began Petr Bury "the Russians are looking at the empire as a whole for bringing in artisans and businessmen. Russia is attempting to improve Russia's industry by bringing in skilled labor from other parts of Europe. For agricultural purposes, the Russians are looking at portions of the empire that are largely unpopulated with great expanses of land available for settlement. Being under—populated and under—developed, the area of the Volga River has been targeted by the government for German settlement."

"Could you tell us more about the community that Russia wishes to develop along the Volga River?" asked Daniel Hemel.

The three representatives proceeded to discuss how Russia planned on expanding the region. The Chancellery of the Guardianship of Foreigners provided a second manifesto that would be used to protect any and all foreigners colonizing the Volga River region. This manifesto would allow immigrants the freedom to enter Russia from any border point. Immigrants will be guaranteed money from the government for transportation and living expenses. This monetary gift would be calculated from the point where the immigrants entered Russia until they reached their place of settlement.

Being somewhat confused by this concept caused me to ask "If immigrants were free to enter Russia from any border point, how would they obtain the money for living expenses and transportation costs?"

Dmitri interjected "A good point. Obviously, the Russian government is not going to have money floating around at every border point. So, immigrants will have to travel to St. Petersburg and go to the office of the Chancellery for the Guardianship of Foreigners. The Chancellery will provide the promised money and information immigrants will need for settlement."

Thanking Dmitri, I pointed out that it would be best to plan on entering Russia at St. Petersburg. Many at the meeting nodded their heads in agreement with my point.

Dmitri said that "any foreigner settling the Volga River region will be provided an additional six months of free lodging while establishing themselves. Assistance would be provided in the form of land grants and ten-year interest free cash loans."

Ivan stated that "During the early years of any settlement in the Volga River region, immigrants will be provided military protection. The entire time that any foreign—born immigrant lived in Russia they would have the right of self-government. Fairs and markets would be tax free. Immigrants would not be peasants or serfs but would be considered free men."

Once more conscription was brought forth by the Russian representative; Dmitri stated that any immigrant would be guaranteed exemption from military service. However, if an immigrant decided to enter the Russian military, he would receive a bonus of thirty rubles. Dmitri did not tell us that being free from conscription was for only ten years. Were we just told what the Russian Government thought would entice us to their country?

One issue on our minds was would we have the right to move if we so desired? Petr stated that "if we chose to leave Russia at any time, we were guaranteed the right to do so." At this point Petr thought that it was important to tell the us that "foreign immigrants would be allowed to form separate colonies where they would enjoy all the other rights plus be able to maintain our native language." I thought that this was very important which caused me to lean towards moving.

Wanting to know more about the land, Frederick Lies asked "Nothing has been said regarding how much land each farmer may obtain." Petr Bury answered by stating that each district had over a million acres and each married man would receive eighty—one acres. Under exceptional circumstances bachelors could also receive the allotted eighty—one acres but would have to be married within a year. Since we were able to obtain an answer to the number of acres available to each individual, I decided that it was time to ask about the cost of the region's acreage.

"The land in much of the Volga River region is allocated for foreign immigrants. The land is for the benefit and success of the entire village and not just for individual success. This means that the land will not be sold directly to the people; the acreage would be lived on and farmed by individual families for many generations." Ivan further stated "that farmers would not be allowed to sell, mortgage, or divide the land provided to them. However, the farm land may be passed from father to son to grandson as long as the family continued farming the land. However, if a family decides to leave the community, the land holding reverts back to the village to be used by others. So, to directly answer your question, the answer is there is no cost for the land."

Quiet came over the crowd as everyone attempted to digest all the information provided. The Germans thought that they would have many freedoms that they did not have in Germany but would still not own the land that they worked upon.

Reverend Zeigler stood up and went to the front of the room. "Gentlemen, we all have some thinking to do regarding the proposal. How long will you be in the area?" he asked.

"We are leaving tomorrow morning for the area just north west of Nauheim but we will be back in about two weeks. Anyone desiring to immigrate or want additional information should meet with us at that time. Could we arrange to meet here in two weeks at one o'clock?"

Everyone was in agreement about the date and time of the next meeting. Two weeks was more than enough time to discuss the situation with our families and each other. Ending the meeting, we began the journey home to consider the material presented to us by the Russian representatives. On the way home, my family considered what we heard about moving to Russia and about what we knew of life in our corner of the world. I knew that people suffered from forced labor and military conscription here; it probably happened elsewhere also. We knew that when wars occurred, people lost family members and often become destitute. Foreign occupations also lead to being politically oppressed by distant powers that were often strict and unjust.

I began to reflect on how people were forced to practice the religion of whomever their leader was at the time. Droughts caused crop failures, hunger and economic hardship. Droughts, political disputes and uprisings occurred anywhere, not just in the Hess region of Europe. However, having the freedom to establish self—government along with the freedom to practice the religion of choice is what most people desire. Recently, I heard that people living in the British colony, located across the sea, are unhappy about the taxes that they are forced to pay without any representation. I wondered how soon that there would be an uprising in this British colony.

Entire families are ready to make the move from Germany and go to a new place for a fresh start, that they just needed to hammer out the details. When it all said and done about forty percent of those living in and around Nauheim decided to take the chance and move to Russia between the years of 1764 and 1765. Over a hundred and twenty members of the Funk family gathered together to share a pot—luck style meal and to discuss being part of the forty percent leaving the region. The family knew that this might be the last time we gathered together as a large, extended family. As it turned out this was the last large family gathering of the Funk family. Two—thirds of the one hundred and twenty members of the Funk family decided on taking the chance on establishing a new life in Russia. A few family members, too old or sick to make such a move, decided to stay in Germany. While other family members considered migrating to the British colony in North America. Even with the rumblings about taxation without representation, family members are still considering moving there.

June 1972

Looking up from the beginning of my family's story, my left hand fell to the soft leather of the hand—written journal. I wondered who put the idea in Conrad's mind to keep a journal.

I am grateful for this because it has told me where the family lived in Germany and why they made the decision to move.

Glancing at the translated version of the manifesto, I realized that the document provided me a better understanding as to why the Germans were enticed to immigrate to Russia. During the 1760s people in Germany were looking for a better life which included more land, political and religious freedom. The manifesto stated that "immigrants shall be given sufficient lands needed for farming, manufacturing or for producing handicrafts" but as stated in the Conrad's journal the Russian land would not be sold directly to the immigrants. However, the land would be available to farm by a family for many generations. The people might not officially own the land in Russia but, it could stay in the family for as long as the family wished to work it.

I completely understand that the Germans and others did not want to be forced to fight a war that the population did not believe in. During Conrad's life—time many of the region's population decided to migrate to another country instead of being conscripted into the military to fight another war. The United States has been fighting a war in Viet Nam for what seems like my entire life. Every day people have been drafted and sent to Southeast Asia to fight in the war they don't believe in. Many soldiers have died or returned home permanently injured. Across the United States during the mid—to—late sixties and the early seventies there were many protests against the Viet Nam War. Over the past year or two I have heard that many people were leaving the United States and settling in Canada to avoid being drafted. Not wanting to fight a war that they do not believe in, like Viet Nam, is no different than how people felt in Conrad's time.

Conrad's journal also provided me the insight regarding the family's desire to have the right to practice the religion of their choice. Many different religions are practiced across America during the early 1970s. Conrad alludes to the idea that there was religious discrimination across Germany during the1760s; this bias still exists in the 1970s. I wonder if the world will ever have total religious freedom.

I cannot wait to read more about the family's journey that took them from Central Europe to Russia and, finally, to North America. I wondered how long it would be before I would get the next journal from Grandma. I didn't have long to wait as another package arrived in the mail within a week; the package contained two more journals.

Journal Two

Departure from Germany—1764

About two—thirds of the Funk family had made the decision to move to Russia. We intuitively knew that it could be impossible for eighty individuals to migrate together into Russia. As a result, the family broke up into several smaller groups for traveling. Traveling with the largest of the groups, I wondered how easy it would be for thirty—five people to travel the nearly two thousand miles together without getting lost or attracting undo attention.

Prior to leaving Nauheim, the family gathered to discuss our travel plans and settlement plans for the Volga River region. Our naivete showed as to the vastness of the Volga River region. We thought that settling in the Volga River region meant living within fifty to seventy miles of each other. The family wanted to be near each other so they could act as a support group for each other. We did not realize that living in the region could mean residing hundreds of miles apart. We decided that it would be best to wait until we got to the Volga River region to look the land over before deciding where to settle. During the late spring and early summer of 1764, the Funks concentrated on packing, saying farewell to friends, selling of household items and farm equipment.

Mom and Mrs. Hoffman were busy planning the wedding of Molly and Charles. Molly and Charles' had originally planned on marring in December but, since the Funks were moving sooner than that the wedding was moved up to the third Saturday of July. The wedding became a time to say goodbye to those family members that would were not immigrating immediately. Taking place in Nauheim's Lutheran Church, the wedding was moved outdoors due to the large number of people attending. The wedding ceremony would take place in the church's gazebo. Benches curved around the side of the gazebo that faced away from the Church.

From a man's point of view, I felt that the wedding was very nice. Molly was wearing a beautiful white gown and carried wild flowers as she walked between the benches to join with Charles in the gazebo. Being a male meant that I did not remember much about the wedding beyond what I have entered in this journal. A female could probably tell you every small detail. Don't tell Katherine, but I have a hard time even remembering the minor details of our wedding. All I was concerned about was finally having her as my wife.

Indian summer came upon north central Europe during the early autumn of 1764. Warm breezes, mild temperatures during the day and cool evenings settled over the region just as we were planning on starting our journey northward from Nauheim. I felt that the warmer, balmy weather was a sign that the family had made the correct decision to move at this time. We would be traveling northward, towards Lubeck; Lubeck is a port city on the Baltic Sea. Once we arrived in Lubeck, we would sell all of the wagons and horses; the new owner or owners would retrieve the horses and wagons at Lubeck's pier.

As we were readying to leave Nauheim, a distant cousin, named Anton, had heard about the immigration program and that a large portion of the Funk family would be emigrating. However, it appears that Anton did not have any firm plans about staying or moving. He was a mystery to many members of the family including myself. Through family stories, I had heard that he held many different kinds of jobs. But no one knew for sure what he did exactly. I thought about what kind of job would enable an individual to stay with family for a week or possibly two or three months before moving on. Anton might reappear after several years or he might never return. Hmmmm….I wonder if Anton could be a thief? I'd better keep that thought to myself because as of now it would just be considered a rumor.

Why did Anton select this moment to come back into the family? I might never know the answer because from what I have heard he does not share things about his life. When several other distant relatives heard that Anton had been hanging around Dad, they decided that it was time to warn us. Two of our distant cousins, Nicholas and Alexander Funk, approached Dad, Dad's brothers and myself. Nicholas began to tell us about his and Alexander's concerns regarding Anton. Rubbing his chin, Dad said "I have had concerns regarding Anton also. We," pointing to his brothers and himself, "have not seen him since we were teenagers. Somehow, he hears that we are moving away, and randomly, he shows up."

"I remember that during his last visit he attempted to blackmail a neighbor." Herman said "The neighbor told our father about the incident. Of course, our Dad confronted Anton and sent him packing."

Phillip pondered this and then said "I always wondered why Anton had left in such a hurry and why he never returned to visit."

Alexander, Nicholas, Philip, Herman, Dad, and I talked for a few minutes about the journey before Alexander and Nicholas excused themselves and left. Dad quietly said "let's hope that the family never sees Anton again."

Once in Lubeck, I was astounded by the number of people swarming around, especially around the docks. Someone in the crowd had stated that the population of Lubeck had quadrupled in size the past month alone. This had to be because the number of migrants flooding into Lubeck from the south, south—west and south—east.

I expected there to be just a few booking agents to aid in the migrants reserving passage but I was wrong. I heard that the number of booking agents had exploded over the past two to three years in order to assist the large number of people leaving the region. It was up to us to untangle the web of good agents from the bad agents. Many referred to the bad agents as crooks.

While on the docks, we heard rumors regarding shipwrecks and mutinies. Many Germans lost their money by booking and paying for passage on vessels that, unfortunately, did not exist. Because of these rumors we decided to ask around about reputable booking agents and the sailing records of the various vessels. A vessel was finally selected that could handle our large group of thirty—five people. Passage was booked on the vessel named *Katherine;* the vessel was scheduled to depart Lubeck in six days. *Katherine* was delayed because of a mutiny that had taken place on the way to St. Petersburg. The vessel had been diverted to Danzig where the unhappy crew was deposited ashore. The captain had to hire a whole new crew in order to complete the voyage and then had to spend an additional two days in St. Petersburg filling out several incident reports for the Russian government. After being delayed for eight days, *Katherine* was finally able to return to Lubeck. This delay did not ease the minds of the German travelers. I wondered if the family would make it to St. Petersburg safely or be sidetracked along the way. How would the family manage to get to St. Petersburg from Danzig or any other port where we might be stranded?

The delay in leaving Lubeck caused both Dad and I to feel uneasy about Anton and where he might be. We both felt that Anton was 'hanging around' close enough to follow our movements but kept just out of sight. Dad wondered aloud whether "Anton was somehow involved in illegal trade. If so, was he wanted by the police? Would he ask us to transport something for him and not tell us that it was illegal contraband?" There was no telling with Anton.

The day before the vessel was to leave port, Dad spotted Anton drawing near. Dad quickly told the family to go ahead, that he would catch up to us. I quickly convinced Dad that I should stay with him for added protection. Dad nodded his head in agreement as he greeted Anton. Anton told us that he had booked passage on the *Katherine* so that he could travel with us. Dad and I looked at each other wondering how he knew that we had booked passage on the *Katherine*. Before we could get an answer, five men quickly stepped up, surrounded Anton with their guns drawn and arrested him. Four of the men took him away while the remaining officer stayed behind to thank Dad for alerting them to Anton's attempt to escape the region. Dad asked "Can you tell me now what crime Anton committed? By the way, this is my son, Conrad."

Shaking my hand, the police officer said "Let's go over here and sit down." Sitting on a pier bench the officer began to tell Dad and me about Anton. "The man you call Anton is not your cousin. His real name is Andrew Koch."

"But I do have a distant cousin named Anton."

"You had a cousin named Anton. Anton was an innocent bystander when he witnessed Andrew Koch killing a man. Anton fled but Andrew tracked him down and killed him about twenty—five years ago." After a short pause, the police officer continued telling us that "Andrew knew that we were looking for him in connection to several other contract murders. We suspected that he killed Anton and another man but we had no witnesses or enough evidence to arrest him. After killing Anton, Andrew took his identity, leaving his own identity papers on Anton's body. He hoped to throw us off his trail."

"How could he have assumed Anton's identity without any relative noticing?" I enquired.

"Andrew has the same coloring, height and build as Anton so it was easy to begin the switch. He found out that Anton was a bit of a drifter; that he never stayed long in one place. Andrew decided to stay away from any close family, like siblings or parents that would know that he was not Anton, for at least ten years.

"When he returned, he could explain the slight change in the harsh conditions he went through living on the streets as a hobo. Andrew would visit for maybe two or three weeks before leaving for four or more years. Often, he would visit distant relatives who would not remember exactly what he looked like so he might stay longer before leaving again. Over the past twenty—five years Andrew has continued his 'killing for hire' business."

"What do you mean by 'killing for hire'?"

"It is where a man is contracted and paid to eliminate others. Andrew always carries a gun so you're lucky that you, your son or other family members weren't hurt. Again, thank you for your assistance in catching him. We will put him behind bars for a long time."

As the police officer walked away both Dad and I felt relief that the killer had been caught and that he would hopefully never bother the family again. There was several moments during our experience with Anton / Andrew that I felt that my life was close to being over. I never saw the supposed gun that he carried but just had a feeling that we were in extreme danger. I feel that the possibility of Anton / Andrew escaping was very slim but if he did escape, I hoped that he did not remember that we were immigrating to Russia. Dad wished to locate Nicholas or Alexander Funk to tell them what had happened with Anton / Andrew before we left Lubeck. However, we both suspected that they might have already left for St. Petersburg; maybe we would be able to locate them in St. Petersburg.

Living inland and away from large bodies of water, many Germans, including myself, had never learned to swim. I did not realize that I had a fear, although a slight fear but a fear none the less, of large bodies of water and the possibility of drowning until the family was ready to board the boat. I had to overcome this fear enough in order to travel to St. Petersburg. As my wife, Katherine, and I began to walk the gangplank to board the vessel, I momentarily hesitated. Looking at me, Katherine asked what was wrong. Feeling somewhat foolish about my fear, I told her that nothing was wrong, squeezing her hand, we boarded the vessel.

Less than a day out of the port of Lubeck a storm kicked up over the Baltic Sea causing torrential rains and choppy seas.

Over half of the passengers become chumming after the storm kicked up causing the vessel to rock and churn. Chumming or feeding the fish were the terms used by the crew about anyone becoming seasick. We had a good laugh over these words and would say to one another periodically: are you feeding the fish?

A day later, the *Katherine* came upon a ship wrecked among some rocks in shallow water. Seeing the name on the ship's bow, a few passengers realized that this ship had left Lubeck just a day prior to the *Katherine* leaving the same port. Hurrying to the captain, I insisted that we stop to see if there were any survivors. The captain insisted that "there weren't any survivors. Besides, I have a schedule to keep."

Standing up to the captain, I strongly insisted that we stop to make sure that there weren't any survivors needing assistance. Under stress, the captain backed down and agreed to stop. Dropping anchor, a safe distance away from the rocks, a group of rescuers consisting of the crew and a few passengers boarded a row boat. Two crew members slowly rowed around the wreckage.

On the far side of the wreckage, one of the rescuers spotted an exhausted man clinging to a rock. Those in the row boat assisted the man into the vessel. Wrapping a blanket around the man, a crew member asked him his name. Weakly the man told us his name was Nicholas Schmidt. Not finding any other survivors the group headed back to the *Katherine* where Nicholas' wet clothes were exchanged for dry ones. He was then given a small plate of food and some beer to drink. Many of *Katherine's* passengers and crew crowded around to hear what happened.

Nicholas began his story by stating that "The first day on the journey was fine. We did not experience any rough waters and we thought that we were off to a good start. However, on the second day, the crew appeared to be slightly drunk except for the captain who was extremely intoxicated to the point where he couldn't walk or think straight. Many of us wondered how he could run a vessel while his judgment was so blurred. Later that day, we were hit by an unbelievable storm. The crew was so drunk that they couldn't stop the vessel from hitting the rocks at twilight. Unfortunately, the majority of the passengers never learned to swim. I am positive that this contributed to two-thirds of the passengers drowning in the rough waters. The remaining passengers died when they hit the rocks; I am positive that I am the only passenger that survived."

Continuing with his story, Nicholas bitterly stated "Cowards that they were, the crew that survived swam ashore to save themselves. Once ashore they never looked back to see if they could assist anyone. Like the majority of the passengers, two crew members died when they hit the rocks. I clung to the rock where you found me for what seemed to be an eternity. I felt that I was going to die until I saw your vessel. I prayed that you would stop and search for survivors. I cannot tell you how grateful I am that you did stop,"

I turned and looked at the captain who was blushing the deepest shade of red that I have ever seen. I knew that he felt ashamed that he did not plan on stopping. In the future, I am positive that he will stop to provide assistance to those in need. As I was looking at the captain a bible verse came to mind:

> *I was a stranger and you welcomed me. Just as you did it*
> *to one of the least of these who are members of my family*
> *you did it for me.   Matthew 25:35—36, 45*

Being a stranger, Nicholas Schmidt was provided love and care when he was rescued, clothed, and provided food and drink. I wondered if it was God's way of letting me know that we did the right thing by stopping and looking for survivors.

Having listened to the horrible story, many of the passengers and crew instantly decided to stay away from alcohol. I wondered how long the groups pf people would stay away from alcohol before they once again began partaking of beer or any other alcoholic beverages. It was best to not get a taste for alcoholic beverages in the first place. Many of the family members attending Charles and Molly's wedding drank too much alcohol during the reception which caused them to act differently and their family to be embarrassed by their drunken actions. All the more reason that I vowed to stay away from spirits; I wanted to be in control of my actions.

Arriving in St. Petersburg, late one autumn day, our family and other passengers gathered on the dock to say a prayer of thanks for surviving the voyage. Being safely in St. Petersburg, we were provided directions to the Chancellery for the Guardianship of Foreigners where we began the registration process. I wondered why Germans had to take an oath of loyalty to Russia; it didn't make sense. I was hesitant to ask why we had to take the oath and I did not want the family to be turned away at this point in our journey. I decided that it was best to just take the oath and not rock the boat. I wondered whether we were making the wrong decision about moving to Russia but quickly put the thought out of my mind. The Chancellery provided the family additional information about the Volga River region along with directions on how to travel there from St. Petersburg.

While waiting for next portion of the registration process, my thoughts ran over how Russia expected the majority of the German immigrants to settle in the Volga River region. I thought about how the Chancellery instructed us to travel to

Saratov where we would be directed on how to move outward from there to settle the region. At face value, this sounded wonderful but, I began to have a few doubts; something just did not seem to be right about the entire thing. Several of us felt that the Russians were not telling us everything about this migration / settlement project. I just hoped that we were not encouraged to go to this region and then be stranded with no support. I attempted to put these nagging thoughts out of my mind as we continued the registration process.

Finally, we made it to the line where we would be given money for travel. The Chancellery stated that they would provide all immigrants enough money for the final leg of the journey. The money granted to foreigners was based on the cost of living back in Hamburg, Germany. Noting that the money was to be used for traveling expenses and would not have to be paid back, most of us took it. Men were to be provided fifteen kopecks per day while women would receive ten kopecks. Those between the ages of two and fifteen would receive six kopecks per day and finally those younger than a year old would receive two kopecks.[1]

While in line to receive the promised money, I saw a few German immigrants being cheated of the correct number of kopecks that Russia promised them for the journey; maybe this was part of what I felt was not right. Doing a quick calculation, I figured that a family of six, a man, a woman and four children between two and fifteen, journeying fourteen days should receive 686 kopecks. However, the Chancellery workers would not give a family of six 686 kopecks; they might be given six

---

[1] The Russian immigration program was so successful that Russia registered over 30,000 colonists between the years 1762 and 1775. This caused the immigration program to have a shortage of money and accommodations for those moving into Russia.

hundred kopecks and the remaining 86 kopecks would line the pockets of the worker.

The amount each family received varied and it never was the correct amount. As they handed the money to the immigrants, they would say to each other in Russian "Immigrants are so easy to cheat. They do not know how much they are entitled too so it is easy for us to take a cut from each group." Their co—workers agreed and felt that they would be wealthy within six months.

Stopping the last three groups of immigrants that had been cheated, I asked them to wait a moment. Stepping up to receive our money I said, in Russian of course, "There are fourteen men, twelve women and ten under fifteen but older than two. That means we should receive 5,460 kopecks for a two—week journey. Don't plan on cheating us like you did them."

The workers that had been cheating the Germans were deeply shocked that I understand them and that I had caught them red—handed. After receiving the correct amount of money, I then said "Don't you owe these people some money?" Embarrassment caused the workers to hand over the additional money to those immigrants that they had just cheated. I hoped that they would never try to cheat anyone ever again. However, it would probably take more than one German catching them in order for them to change their ways. But to ensure that they mend their ways I interjected "Maybe I should talk to those in charge about how you are cheating innocent people." Immediately, the workers pleaded that I not talk to their bosses. I agreed not too if they promised that they wouldn't cheat their 'brothers or sisters' in the future.

Again, the same bible verse flashed through my mind causing me once more to think about how God wished me to live.

*I was a stranger and you welcomed me. Just as you did it
to one of the least of these who are members of my family
you did it for me.   Matthew 25:35—36, 45*

While going through the registration process, immigrants were
provided lodging near the Chancellery's office. The family as a
whole was anxious to arrive at our destination and begin our
new life. While in waiting in various lines regarding registration, obtaining money, or for general directions some of fellow
travelers were moved to the back of the line. This was due to
many immigrants being impatient and often rude to the Chancellery's Workers. Not wanting to be delayed any further, Dad
encouraged the family to be patient and to not be rude, even
if we felt that way.

While patiently waiting, I watched people hurry off to
begin their final journey to the Volga River region. I wondered
how many of these individuals would live in our new home town.
Since I did not know the answer to that question, I thought that
I should remember to be polite and respectful to all.

During this time of waiting and wondering, I also saw
some people riding in fancy carriages. These individuals were
wearing elaborate hats and, from what I could see, dressed in
fancy clothing. I am assuming that these people were wealthy
and led a life of leisure. I wondered what they were doing in this
part of St. Petersburg. Maybe they were attending to business
at places near the Chancellery.

The people that I found most interesting were those individuals wearing clothing that was filthy and ragged; these
people had a look of near starvation. As they walked by, a sour
smell drifted towards me that made me think that they probably

hadn't bathed in weeks or maybe longer. I wondered what had brought them to wearing rags and being unwashed. Being brought to tears, I felt that the children begging on the streets were the saddest group of people in St. Petersburg. Over the many days of waiting, I had even seen some of the children stealing food. I knew from the looks of these children that they stole for survival. Silently, I prayed that God would forgive those who resorted to stealing in order to stay alive. Being still, a bible verse sprung to mind about speaking up for those less fortunate:

Speak up for those who cannot speak for the rights of all who are destitute.   Proverbs 31:8.

I wondered what I could do to help those in need here in St. Petersburg. As in reply another verse came to mind:

I tell you the truth that whatever you did not do for one of the least of these, you did not do for me.   Matthew 25:45

I did not have to solve all the problems of those in need. Providing for a momentary need would help those in need. When we went to obtain supplies for the mid—day meal, I saw a bushel of apples at one marketplace. I pondered a moment then suggested that we purchase a bushel of apples to distribute to the needy. One family member argued that a bushel of apples could be costly and it would take away from paying for the needs of the family.

"God has always provided for our needs." I began. "In the past when we have given to those in need we received more in return, haven't we?"

Being embarrassed, the family member agreed and we purchased the bushel of apples. Sitting down to eat our lunch in the park, we could almost see many of the cities starving drooling as they paused to watch us eat. We would pick up an apple or two and offer it to those so disparately hungry. Often the people would only momentarily hesitate before they took the fruit, telling us thank you before heading off. Some even gave us a hug before they began to devour the newly acquired apple. I am positive that these individuals repaid the kindness forward in the future.

During our time in St. Petersburg, Dad and I both felt blessed that we were able to locate Nicholas and Alexander Funk along with a few other distant relatives. We were able to tell the relatives what happened back in Lubeck with 'Anton'. Saddened, Nicholas said "I am sorry that his mother and father are not alive to hear what really happened to Anton. They thought that their son had become a criminal. We are all glad that you had the foresight to go to the authorities and had him captured."

Alexander told us to always remember to be aware of what is going on around us. We would never know if and when Andrew might escape. Dad thanked him and said that "it was a team effort that led to his capture; you both helped me in questioning myself about Anton / Andrew. I know that he is furious about being arrested and that he blames me for his arrest. It is true that I contacted the police but they were already looking for him."

"If he manages to be released or escapes, it is guaranteed he will come looking for you and possibly Conrad." Alexander further said that "I sincerely hope that he doesn't remember that the family was moving to Russia. We are planning on settling in the Volga River region; where are you headed?"

"We also are moving to the Volga River region. Hopefully, we will see more of you and the family once we are all settled in." At this time, we parted with the promise to remain in touch.

Our family began the next leg of the journey by traveling overland from St. Petersburg to Lake Ladoga. Arriving at the lake, I silently groaned just to think about another water voyage. We did not experience a mutiny or ship wreck during our voyage across the Baltic Sea so we considered it a success. I attempted to reassure myself that this portion of the journey would be a triumph. At Lake Ladoga, we were able to book passage on a river vessel named *Jessie* and would sail Russia's waterways for Saratov.

Living abroad a floating vessel meant that household chores would be accomplished differently than how they were done on dry land. For example, laundry was washed in tubs as usual but hung to dry on lines strung between masts. Inclement weather that lasted several days caused clothes lines to be stretched below deck.

Already having one sea voyage under our belts, many of the passengers expected the tough salted pork and beef. However, none of the passengers liked the dried, salted fish that we were served. We do like fresh fish which caused the passengers and the crew to take advantage of any stop to drop a fishing line into the water. During an early stop, the crew caught enough fish to feed themselves and the passengers for one wonderful banquet. As many of the passengers as possible went ashore to assist in building a fire and to fry the fresh fish. Those left abroad the vessels helped prepare side dishes and desert.

Always interested in food preparation, both Uncle Benjamin and I aided in making meals while sailing southward towards Saratov. Early on during this leg of our journey, Benjamin and I offered to make supper. We used some salted beef which the crew called Uncle Sam's mahogany. Then added some dried peas along with some fresh carrots, potatoes and onions that we obtained from our last stop. The fresh vegetables helped make a delicious stew. Having an oven to make fresh baked bread would have added the final touch to the stew but there was nothing we could do about the situation.

Abroad ship, the crew and passengers ate a lot of sauerkraut, dried anchovies, dried peas, cheese and extremely dry raisins. Bread was provided in the form of hard tack. Hard Tack was often referred to as a biscuit.[2] Vessels carried a limitless supply of beer for drinking instead of water. Water stored in barrels often went bad before it could be completely consumed. Many vessels traveling interior waterways stopped often to obtain a fresh supply of water.

Tainted food often caused illness and death among the passengers and crew. We prayed that everyone abroad the *Jessie* would survive the trip. However, several of the passengers, including myself and my brother Johann, fell ill due to the tainted water and bad food. For almost a week, Johann and I lay on our bunks because we were too ill to move. Katherine brought two buckets for when we felt the need to throw up what was or wasn't in our stomachs. Charles and Henry provided assistance when we needed help getting up. After about a week I started to feel better and attempted to pull myself up into a sitting position. However, the bunk above me did not allow me to sit straight up. Something was different but I was unsure what was different. Looking around I finally realized what was wrong: I did not hear Johann's labored breathing anymore. As quickly as my trembling

---

[2] Often hard tack was baked years earlier and would often be infested with weevils.

legs could take me, I went to my brother's bunk. Feeling his cold hand caused me to finally understand that Johann had passed away sometime during the past several hours. Sobbing, I laid my head down on his chest.

As I grieved, I was unaware of the other passengers gathering around me until a hand touched my shoulder. Looking up, I saw Uncle Phillip with tears in his eyes. He then said "Let's say a prayer for his soul." The *Jessie* dropped anchor in order to bury Johann and another passenger who had also died from food poisoning.

The two were buried side by side in a cemetery that sailors used to bury passengers and crew that had passed away. The captain began the service with a prayer, and then talked about the heavenly lives that the two were now beginning. He asked those gathered to say the Lord's Prayer with him. During the burial, Mom cried softly and had to be held up by Charles and Henry. The captain reminded us of a story in the bible where a woman's seven sons were all killed because they refused give up their faith and obey the king. He pointed out that as her last son faced death, she said

> *Do not fear this butcher, but prove worthy of your brothers. Accept death, so that in God's mercy I may get you back again along with your brothers.* 2 *Maccabees 7:29.*

During the next several days, Mom seemed to be in a constant state of exhaustion and would cry at the drop of a hat. Dad was holding up better than Mom but still was not doing well. He tried not to show his grief but I knew that he missed Johann greatly. What could I do or say to help them with their grief? I knew that they would see Johann again in heaven but would saying this help them in their moment of grief? I knew that a parent should never outlive a child; Johann's passing reinforced this idea.

Within a week of the burials, a sudden storm caused the ship to pitch back and forth uncontrollably. Five people were swept overboard during this storm. Three of the five were rescued within moments but one of my female cousins and another male passenger drowned. Once again, the vessel dropped anchor and my cousin and the other passenger were buried on a hill that overlooked the river.

Finally recovering from the shock and death of both Johann and a young female family member, Mom knew that she and others needed to help keep their minds and hands busy. Mom and Katherine discussed establishing a non—traditional quilting bee abroad the *Jessie*. Instead of working on a quilt from beginning to end, the women would exchange fabrics, piece quilt blocks together, discuss quilting techniques and in general discuss quilts. Women who did not know how to quilt joined the group so they could learn the craft.

Men did not have as easy of time staying occupied while on board the *Jessie*. Several men had offered to assist the crew wherever possible. Henry, Charles and a few other male passengers became a lubber; a lubber was a term used by sailors when talking about an inexperienced seaman. They learned how to properly raise and lower sails, how to swab the deck and to fish off the side of the vessel. Some of the younger men were allowed to take the spy glasses to the bucket, which is located near the top of the ships mast. Once in bucket, the lubbers would use the spy glass to see what was ahead.

After a long journey, the captain finally told the passengers that in about an hour the *Jessie* would arrive in Saratov. We began to gather our possessions had been gathered together and brought up to the deck. We, the passengers, drew together on the deck to get our first look Saratov and a portion of the region. So far, the area did not look any different then what we have been seeing since arriving in St. Petersburg. As the *Jessie* docked in Saratov, the same bible passages from Matthew came to my mind about being hungry, thirsty and a stranger. I wondered why the verses kept coming to my mind throughout our trip and, most especially, as we neared the end of this portion of our journey. Thinking back over the journey that we had made from Nauheim to Lubeck to St. Petersburg to the Volga River region, I thought about all that had taken place. They included:

- Encountering a cousin, named Anton, even before we left Germany. As it turned out, it wasn't Anton after all but a criminal named Andrew Koch. We could have been killed by Andrew but I could feel God's protection.

- Secondly, when the *Katherine* came across a ship wreck, we stopped to provide needed assistance. A lone man was rescued and brought abroad. I wonder what would have happened to him if we hadn't stopped. But more importantly, could I have lived with myself if we hadn't stopped to look for survivors?

- Lastly, I confronted the workers at the Chancellery office regarding the cheating of innocent immigrants and we provided food to the poor.

I feel that remembering the bible verse was a sign from God. I felt that God was telling me that I am living how he wants and expects me too. I know that I feel better when I look out for others.

August 1972

Tears were running down my face over Johann's and a female cousin dying during the last leg of the family journey to Saratov. How could the family bear to lose two family members, especially when they were both so young and had not experienced life to the fullest yet? The family was lucky to have escaped Germany without Anton / Andrew harming them. I wonder if I could have stood up to the ship's captain or the Chancellery workers like Conrad did. I am not sure that I could have in the past but am going to try to do so in the future.

Providing something as small as an apple made a huge difference in the lives of others. In addition, it really did not take away anything from what the family had; the family was still able to eat, sleep, to be clothed and would have enough money to continue the journey.

Could the bible verses that appeared to be following Conrad during the family's journey, change my life as obviously it had changed Conrad's life? I was willing to try but I knew that it might take time.

> *For I was hungry and you gave me food; I was thirsty and you gave me something to drink; I was a stranger and you welcomed me. Just as you did it to one of the least of these who are members of my family you did it for me. Matthew 25:35, 4*

Needing some rest, I closed the second journal, turned out the light and attempted to go to sleep. However, the thought of how I could help others kept swimming around in my mind. Over an hour later, I finally was able to fall asleep but had not come to a decision about what I could do to change my life for the better.

The next day when I opened the third journal, a map fluttered out. I sat the journal down, picked up the map and began to examine it. It was nice to see where Saratov was in relation to the larger Volga River region. I wondered where the family had finally settled and couldn't wait to find out what happened to the family in Russia.

German settlement map:
http://www.rollintl.com/roll/grsettle.htm

Journal Three

Arrival in Russia: 1765—1770

Once in Saratov, the German passengers were surprised to see how under—developed the region was especially since it had been advertised as a fertile region where crops grew in abundance. We reminded ourselves that the Russian representatives had stated that the Russian empire had great expanses of land available for settlement. However, I did not remember whether the representatives had stressed the fact that the majority of land in the Volga River region was largely uninhabited. Then, I recalled that one of the Russian men had said that parts of the Russian Empire were largely uninhabited and unused and had the potential to be very productive agriculturally.

Thinking aloud I wondered "if the immigrants only heard what they desired to hear: a fertile region where crops grow abundantly and they did not desire to hear about the region being largely uninhabited."

Looking at me, Uncle Herman simply replied that "we were tired of being politically suppressed, being conscripted into the military to fight in a war that we did not support, having no religious freedom, along with many other issues. I am positive that we did not want to hear about anything but what we wanted to hear about. We need to explore the entire region to find out what is really here."

"Correct as always Herman. Let's stay positive, see the entire region and give life a chance here." Dad replied.

Always interested in my surroundings, I saw that the fort was across the river from the town of Saratov; I contemplated why this was done. They should be on the same side of the river to provide the best possible protection. There were many residents willing to tell me about the history of their town. First off I was told that Saratov was founded in 1590 as military fort. Over the past 175 years, the fort remained in its current location due to it being an ideal centralized location. A town began to grow to aid in the development of the Volga River region and to house the fort's soldiers. In 1665, Saratov moved to its present location and began its growth as a civilian town. Over the next hundred years, Saratov remained small but grew in importance because of the region's fishing and salt trade.

In the early 1760s, Saratov was chosen by the Czarina Catherine when she started the Volga River expansion program. At the time, Saratov had approximately two dozen homes that were built close together, a church, a small school and a building that housed government offices. However, as migrants arrived the town grew and additional buildings were constructed. The streets remained a muddy mess due to the winter snows and to the heavy spring rains.

Conversations with the town's people told me that the hotel had recently been constructed along with a few other new businesses, including a restaurant and hotel. These businesses were established to accommodate the enormous number of foreigners migrating to the region. However, the hotel was never large enough to house the number of immigrants flocking to the area.

Just eleven months prior we arrived in Saratov the government ordered the region to be surveyed.[3] Surveying stayed on the western side of the Volga River because settlers were encouraged to stay on the west side. Settlement was discouraged on the eastern side of the river because the government did not want the immigrants to encroach on the land utilized by the nomadic people living in the east. Apparently, there had been conflict between the nomadic people and the Russians during the past month that had caused deaths of both the nomadic people and several Russian soldiers.

Even though the Russian government discouraged settling east of the river, the region still needed to be surveyed. Groups of surveyors were put together and sent out to examine the land in and around the region. Dad, his brother Herman, and I were placed in a group of six other men surveying the southern part of the region but we stayed to the west of the Volga River. The nine of us divided into three groups of three to exam the region quicker but were told to stay relatively close to the other groups. At this time, we were looking for any favorable spots in which a town could be established. Vassily Brezhnev, the leader of our nine—man group, said that we should meet back in our current location in an hour to discuss our findings.

Walking a short distance in a south—easterly direction Dad, Uncle Herman and I came to a place that could be a good location for building. Looking around at the slowly rising land, I suggested that we go to a high spot in order to get a better view of the region. Standing on what we thought was the areas highest spot, we looked over the river and surrounding land.

---

[3] Beginning in 1764, the surveying continued until 1768.

While discussing the pros and cons of this high spot being an ideal place for a town we heard a very soft rustling noise which caused Herman to turn and look behind us. Herman saw six exotic looking men with bows and arrows. Speechless Herman softly whispered that there were armed men behind us. Dad and I attempted to make a slow turn in order not to startle the groups of men and saw six men that Herman told us about. The men were intently examining us; they were probably as curious about us as we were of them.

Extending his empty hand in greeting, Herman said hello. However, the men did not speak German, they just pointed their bows and arrows at us and then pointed in a more westerly direction. I quietly said "I think that they are telling us to leave." Indicating that we were leaving caused the men to remove their arrows from their bows, they then turned and left. Quickly, we retreated to where we were to meet the rest of the surveyors; once the others joined us, we described our encounter to them.

Vassily said that the "group of men we encountered were from a nomadic group of people that were, probably, a hunting party looking for meat. Did they make much noise when they approached you?"

"A slight rustling noise was all that we heard," replied Herman.

"Nomadic populations that live in the area, have learned to stay downwind and move quietly as not to startle their prey. They have become quite good at surprise."

Quietly I interjected that "It is time for us to retreat before we become their next meal."

"Since they were hunting, I wouldn't worry so much about them. They haven't seen too many foreigners in this area and are probably more curious about us then we are about them. They understand that we are encroaching on their traditional hunting grounds. One day Europeans could be at war with these nomadic people over land. So just be careful and be aware as we survey the land. Besides if I were you, I would be more concerned about the Russians."

"You're Russian, should we be concerned about you?"

"No, largely because I don't live in this region; I am just here temporarily to do a job. If I lived in this region, I could view you as competition for resources and land. I feel that the development of this region is a way for the land to be turned into agriculture. More land under cultivation means fewer food shortages across Russia".

I then asked Vassily "Are your beliefs normal among Russians or are you unusual?"

"Well," began Vassily, "I would say that about half believe as I do but the other half probably don't want foreigners migrating to the area or into Russia at all. Let's move a bit westward and get back to work before those nomads decide that we should be their next meal." We all nervously laughed before we moved on to the next area.

I am not normally nervous in new situations but, recent incidents have caused me to wonder whether my life would be cut short. Will the next incident with an armed man be my last? Maybe I should ask not to be assigned with any group of surveyors examining eastern areas. On the other hand, I do not run and hide from life so, I decided to say nothing and continue going where the job took me.

Dad, Uncle Herman and I continued surveying the area with the other six men. We found several good locations for towns and farm land. Herman sketched the area out on paper while the remaining eight of us stacked it out. A larger stack with the number of the settlement was placed in the middle of the area. Upon finishing surveying the area our group returned to Saratov.

Once back in Saratov, our nine—man group was split up and reassigned with other groups. Uncle Benjamin joined Dad and I surveying an area surrounding the Medvelitza River, which was west of the Volga River. While Uncle Herman joined a group surveying about eight miles south--southwest of where we were located. Uncle Benjamin, Dad and I were surprised to see Nicholas and Alexander among our group of surveyors. We caught up on each other's travels from St. Petersburg to Saratov while we continued to survey the region. I noticed that the majority of the land surrounding the Medvelitza River was located on a bergseite. Earlier I learned that a bergseite is what I would call a hillside. The bergseite that we were on provided a wonderful view of the area. If a town was built on the hillside it would be protected from periodic flooding. The same periodic flooding could aid in agriculture. I knew that this land would be perfect for a settlement.

We decided that this bergseite and surrounding area would make an ideal place for a town and for farming. We paused to consider where and how the town should be laid out along with plots for farming. Vassily Brezhnev, continued to be our leader, said that we should stop and survey this hillside for a village and farm land. As we staked out lots for homes and businesses one of the surveyors made a sketch of how the town was to be laid out and its exact location. The sketch and lay out would be taken back to Saratov in order to be filed in a governmental office. The sketch would also be used for assigning home and business lots to migrants. We did not know it at the time but this site would eventually become Hussenbach and the family, including Nicholas and Alexander's branch of the Funk family, would eventually settle there.

Once the town was finished being laid out on the hillside, we broke up into three groups to work at dividing up the surrounding land into 81—acre parcels to be used for farming. Sketches were made of these lots for farming, once again, to aid the government in assigning acreage to people. Since the lay of the land was hilly and rolling, land for farms took on various shapes. The variations in the land parcels for farms added to the beauty of the region. Dad, Uncle Benjamin, Nicholas, Alexander and I agreed that the land to the north—northeast of Hussenbach was the best acreage; the land gently slopped, had water access and was not that far from where the town was to be built.

While surveying and marking the farm plots, several of us felt that we were being followed but could not see anyone. After having looked around, I tried to put aside the feeling of being followed. Since we were surveying agricultural lots Uncle Benjamin, Dad and I were further apart then when we laid out the town lots. As a result, the three of us were not overly close to each other. At this point, Dad was approached by two armed men. Looking at the men, Dad noticed that one of the two men was Andrew Koch. Shocked at encountering Andrew, Dad calmly asked "How did you escape the authorities in Germany?"

"I had a concealed gun that I used to kill the police officers. After escaping, my goal was to track you down and kill you. I knew that you and your family were moving to Russia. Once in St. Petersburg I asked around enough to learn that the majority of German migrants were moving to Saratov and the Volga River region. Once in Saratov, it was a little more difficult with so many Germans milling about. However, I did see your lovely wife having lunch with several other women. I considered intercepting her but my friend here," indicating the man to his left, "discouraged me from doing so. He said that after I killed you, I could go back for your wife."

By this time, Uncle Benjamin and I noticed that two men were near Dad and had guns pointed at him. Uncle Benjamin recognized Andrew after he got a good look at him. Immediately, Benjamin handed me a gun and whispered to stay there but to be ready to help when he shouted 'NOW!'"

Uncle Benjamin crouched low and made his way slowly in and around Andrew Koch and his friend. He hoped that Dad would keep Andrew talking long enough in order to get close enough in order to provide assistance. Dad was calmly talking to Andrew when he caught a glimpse of his brother Benjamin; the two brothers made brief eye contact just prior to Uncle Benjamin shooting Andrew in his right arm which caused Andrew to drop his gun. Hearing the shot, I did not wait for another signal; I shot and killed the man traveling with Andrew then pointed my gun at Andrew. Shaking, Dad had grabbed the gun that Andrew had brandished at him. He then pointed it at Andrew. Having several guns pointed at him, Andrew stayed where he was as the remaining surveyors rushed to see if they could help Dad, Benjamin and myself.

"Vassily," stated Uncle Benjamin, "We need to get this man to the local authorities; he attempted to kill Jacob."

Retrieving some rope and bandage material, we first tied Andrew up and then attended to his wound. Andrew's swearing and yelling caused us to gag him. We buried Andrew's companion on the other side of the river and marked the grave with a wooden cross; this site became Hussenbach's first cemetery. We had not finished surveying the farm land, we knew that we needed to tune Andrew over to the authorities. Dad, Benjamin and I told the remaining surveyors that we would be back to assist them as soon as possible. We then began our journey back to Saratov to turn Andrew over to the police and to give the police a detailed report. We were instructed to stay in town until Andrew could be brought before the judge. A week later Andrew Koch went before a judge and was sentenced to life in a Siberian prison. We, as recent immigrants, had heard of Siberia but did not have a clear picture of how cold and harsh conditions could be there. Dad thought that since Andrew had escaped once he could probably do so again. However, he could not live the rest of his life looking over his shoulder for Andrew. Dad prayed that Andrew would never leave the Siberian prison to come after him again.

During the week before Andrew faced the judge, I noticed that Saratov was overwhelmed with a large number of immigrants that were homeless. At this time, the government was having trouble keeping up with supplies needed to feed and house the migrants. Many of these new arrivals were provided a piece of canvas, a pole and some stacks. They were expected to use the canvas, stacks and poles as a temporary dwelling. Others were provided some rough looking pieces of wood to construct a lean—to. I wondered how the lean—to's and canvas tents would assist the people to survive an extremely cold winter, or even a normal winter that could dip into the single digits.

A tent / lean—to city had grown up on the outskirts of town. The streets of the makeshift 'town' were muddy and the entire area had a smell of unwashed bodies and raw sewage. I did not stick around the 'tent city' long enough to find out how they handled getting rid of their waste. Time would tell if it the waste was being handled improperly. Within weeks people began getting sick from inappropriate sanitation practices. I might not ever know how many passed away as a result of the inadequate sanitation but am positive that the numbers were high.

Since I was assisting with the surveying, I knew that a large part of the region was not ready for settlement. At this early stage, there were only a few places in the region that were prepared for people to establish a community. I wondered why the Russian government allowed immigrants to continue journeying into the region prior to having the surveying completed. I also didn't understand why those working in Saratov's Chancellery office couldn't see that there was not have enough timber for the building of homes, schools, or other businesses. Just looking at the few piles of timber, I can tell that there was enough to build between 230 to 240 homes. There was a need for more than 240 homes six months ago.[4]

Currently, there is a need for well over a thousand homes in order to accommodate the immigrant population already living in Saratov. In order to accommodate migrants already in Saratov and for the huge number of new settlers arriving daily, the region needed supplies to build an additional two—thousand to twenty—five hundred homes within the next month. I thought about how I might handle the situation if I were in charge of the Chancellery, I admitted that I was not privy to the governmental bureaucracy that the office has to deal with on a regular basis. Maybe the office staff had asked for more timber just to have it fall on deaf ears back in St. Petersburg.

Disorganization has caused families to spend a year or more in Saratov prior to being sent on to their final destination. Many have come to the realization that the settlement program had been opened up to Europe's population prior to

---

[4] Less than a year later, Saratov's officials finally reported to the main office in St. Petersburg that the region was in dire need for an additional 1.3 million planks of wood to build more homes. Within three years, an additional 4,560 homes had been constructed for 6,433 families settling in the region.

proper arrangements being completed. It did not help that the Chancellery didn't have a full picture of the region. Had people high in the Russia's government, including the Czarina, been to Saratov and the region before they went ahead with the immigration program? Probably not or they would have had the region completely surveyed along with enough building supplies ready and waiting in Saratov. Granted there was no way to know how popular the program would become, however, there should have been enough timber available for at least half the number of homes needed prior to allowing immigration to begin. If there had been lumber left over from the building of homes, I am positive that it would have been used for other projects such as outbuildings or businesses.

Even though immigrants were provided six months free housing, we still had to scramble for any kind of employment to help us survive temporarily in Saratov. Many men took jobs in the surveying industry while others entered the construction field and began the process of expanding Saratov. On the other hand, women looked for almost any type of employment. Several women took in sewing and found themselves so busy that they often had to turn down work. Sewing provided the women access to scraps of fabric that they used in making of new quilts.

Quilting wasn't a paid job but a job that needed to be done in order for the survival of any family. We had quickly learned that we needed more quilts in order to keep warm during the bitterly cold winter nights. The quilts that were in progress of being pieced when we arrived in the Volga River region were quickly finished. A second, third or fourth quilt was often completed prior to winter arriving. I noticed that the woman made the quilt tops by themselves but joined together to do the actual quilting. Working together made the actual quilting go faster and aided the women in bonding with other women.

When Saratov's lone restaurant was hiring for the breakfast shift, Aunt Elizabeth, my sister—in—law Molly and cousin Barbara were hired. Aunt Elizabeth, became the restaurant's breakfast cook while Molly and Barbara waited tables. All three liked the fact that work at the restaurant was steady so the staff was kept busy. A down side of waiting tables that Molly and Barbara did not like was that they often had their bodies pinched by men. This was a common problem for the entire wait staff and the owners of the restaurant attempted to reassure them that it meant nothing. They were told that if they tolerated the touching they would receive larger tips. The possibility of larger tips did not make the pinching or patting by random men any easier to take. Plus, the wait staff argued that the majority of men accosting them did not leave larger tips, in fact they usually left smaller tips.

One day a man in his late twenties reached out and pinched Barbara's behind; Barbara whirled around slapped the man soundly across his face. Amazingly, almost everyone in the restaurant applauded and cheered Barbara. Turning scarlet, the man laid money on the table and left in a hurry. The incident caused many customers to leave her larger than normal tips for several days. Many of the customers did not understand why the wait staff put up with the pinching and patting so, were ecstatic to see that Barbara had finally stood up to it. The incident caused word to quickly spread about how the wait staff did not like to be pinched and patted so it stopped. As a result of the incident, the staff noticed that business increased especially during the morning shift. Many customers just desired to see the waitress who had turned into a celebrity.

Besides the pinching incident, there always seemed to be a drama going on with the customers. The drama sometimes provided humor for the staff and at other times it made them realize that their own life was not so bad. The staff often laughed over some of the dramas. One such drama involved a young man who complained daily about his boss expecting him to arrive at his job by seven o'clock each morning. He argued that this was extremely difficult to do as that he did not get to bed before two in the morning. However, he did not add the reason he got to bed so late was due to his drinking and partying.

Another table of customers complained over the lack of a symphony orchestra, a ballet company, or English breakfast tea in Saratov. This trivial matter made the restaurant staff laugh uproariously as the majority of the workforce had never been to the symphony or ballet and they drank whatever was available, tea or not.

The women's favorite drama involved two groups of customers. Three women were being seated when they passed a table where a man and woman were having an intimate luncheon. One of the women stepped over to the table, picked up a glass of wine and threw the wine in the man's face before screaming that "this was the last straw; their marriage was over and he could take his whore to the bank as he would not get any more of her money." Jumping up quickly, he followed his wife apologizing as he went. The man's date was aghast that this was occurring because she had no idea that the man was married. The staff and the customers secretly cheered the woman for standing up to the cheating husband; several of the women had wished that they had exhibited enough nerve to stand up to their cheating husbands. These spectacles provided incredible stories to share with the family at the end of each day.

While traveling from St. Petersburg to Saratov several young Funk men had met and fell in love with young German women.

Numerous weddings began to take place in Saratov prior to the immigrants moving onward to their final destination. My brother, Henry, met a young woman named Elizabeth after both had arrived in Saratov. After a short courtship, Henry proposed to Elizabeth and they married in early October of 1766. The outdoor wedding took place in the garden of a local Lutheran Church that was close to being completed. An autumn wedding is always nice as that there was an abundance of yellows, golds, oranges, and reds in nature along with the vivid greens of evergreen trees.

During the ceremony, I considered those family members in attendance. I wondered if they would meet someone to marry, and where would they live if and when they married were just two thoughts that ran through my mind. I knew that being married meant that the new couple could stay near the husband's family but also could live close to the wife's family. Newly married couples could stay in Saratov, or any number of places scattered along the region's rivers If they choose to move fifty or more miles away it could be difficult for a family to stay close. Living in Saratov, or other towns close by could mean that we, as a close family, might see the couple only periodically or we might grow apart and never see each other again. At this time, I especially considered my brother, Henry, and his new wife, Elizabeth. I felt blessed that Elizabeth's family planned on settling in Hussenbach so we would not lose contact with my brother and she would stay close to her family.

At this time, I was considering whether Katherine and I might be lucky enough to have our own family. Both Katherine and I felt that we should have had a child by now. Having a baby during the long journey to Russia would not have been enjoyable due to rough seas, thievery, and not having a permanent home as yet. Hopefully, we will have a child when we get settled in our new home, where ever it may be.

As more of the land in the Volga River region was surveyed, the Chancellery began sending colonists outward from Saratov. The Russian royal family and the directors of the Chancellery reserved the right to name the villages. Often the villages would not given names when they were founded but at a later date. By royal decree in February of 1768, the village where we decided to settle was officially named Lake Linevo.[5] Lake Linevo eventually had its name changed to Hussenbach. Hussenbach came from the community's first mayor, Jacob Hussenbach.

Prior to the town officially taking the name of Hussenbach, many members of the Funk family began the final journey to our new home along the Medvelitza River region. By the time the family arrived in Hussenbach, we noticed that several houses and businesses were already being constructed. As we waited to be given the okay to settle our chosen parcels of land, the family made do in town but eventually went to the land we desired and set up a temporary camp. New settlers assisted in the construction of Hussenbach as they knew that when it was time to build their home and outbuildings others would help.

While I was helping with the building along main street, I began to think about the religious freedom that we were guaranteed. At this early stage in the Volga River region we were allowed religious freedom but I wondered whether we would be able to continue this religious autonomy in the future. I know that having a place to worship would aid the settlers with a small piece of comfort in our new home. Maybe we should help the Mennonites and Catholics build their churches. I am positive that they would return the favor and provide us, the

---

[5] The name was derived from the nearby lake.

Lutherans, assistance with building our church. Prior to constructing several churches, Hussenbach residents decided to first finish building the needed homes and outbuildings, to plow and plant their fields. As a result, the Lutheran and other churches were put on temporary hold. When the Lutheran Church was eventually constructed it was decided that it would have a high steeple; this steeple would tower over the one—story dwellings throughout Hussenbach.

However, prior to places of worship being constructed, religious services were held at the school or outside in the warm weather. When the weather was bad or the school unavailable, smaller groups would gather together in individual homes. These small groups would often have a bible study instead of a regular church service due to a lone minister would not be able to attend each small gathering at the same time. Even when the churches were completed there were not enough pastors in the Volga River region. At this time the majority of churches shared a minister; a minister was lucky to manage only five or six churches at a time. This could mean that a minister would come to a church only once every five to six weeks. Those of us settling in Hussenbach felt blessed that our church was able to obtain a minister that only had to manage three other churches. Our minister came to Hussenbach once every four weeks. During the other three weeks, teachers would help in providing religious training. To assist with the church services when the minister was not available, men would often step up to become a deacon.

At this time, I noticed that several of the younger German immigrants decided to go into the ministry. One of my cousins, Uncle Phillip's youngest son, decided he wanted to become a Lutheran Minister. Since the region was not fully developed yet, those seeking to become a Lutheran minister often had to either travel back to Germany for training or to do a form of training under a current minister. The majority of the men training for the ministry decided to train under a current minister because there was an uncertainty as whether Germany would allow them to return to Russia. As a result, my cousin obtained his training through the minister that had Hussenbach's church on his circuit. Once his training was complete, he was assigned to manage churches in Frank, Kolb and two other towns. The growth in newly ordained ministers caused a reduction in the number of churches that one minister was required to manage. Some pastors were assigned to two larger churches that were located in towns not far apart. This meant that the minister not to have to travel great distances between churches and towns. This allowed a number of ministers the ability to have their own home, the possibility of marrying and having a family.

I and others who had surveyed the area knew that the Volga River region was largely a wilderness that contained few trees with large expanses of three—foot tall grasses. Used to seeing and loving trees, especially in the autumn months, I noticed that German settlers planted various kinds of trees across the region. Years later, I would be amazed to note that many of Hussenbach's homes would be partially hidden behind a thick standing of cedar trees.

Clearing virgin fields and placing the land under cultivation was a task that many Europeans had never faced before. Clearing the tall grasses was tough because the grasses in the Volga River steppe region had a deep, deep root system. Clearing this land was vital as that we needed to build our homes, outbuildings, and to plant crops. Land clearing was slow but obtaining the building materials that the Russian government promised us was even slower. If the promised materials were not delayed, the supplies could be inadequate or totally inappropriate. Inappropriate supplies might be as simple as a lawn rake when we needed a garden rake. Just like the fact that there was not enough timber sent to the region, there was never enough hammers, nails and saws sent for the building of homes, outbuildings, or businesses. The tools and implements that we had in Germany for building and fixing things were sold before we began the journey to Russia. Items sold back in Germany along with the tools and implements not arriving when needed caused many migrants to regret the move to Russia.

Dad, Charles, Henry, and I each received eighty—one acres. We were lucky that the land we received bordered each other's land and lay on the north—west side of Hussenbach. Eighty—one acres per household was enough for us as most farmed about forty acres back in Germany. Benjamin, Herman, Nicholas, Alexander and other Funk's settled acreage to the north, and to the north—east of the property where we would live. We felt blessed that so many Funks lived so close together in Hussenbach.

During this early period of settlement, a group of renegades were robbing the region's immigrants, but especially women. Over a fifty—mile region, several women had been robbed, attached and left for dead. The population was never told exactly what the group of renegades did except rob their victims. We were told to keep an eye open for the renegades and not to travel alone. About fifty of the 20,000 Cossacks stationed in the Volga River region were called on to catch the gang of renegades but so far, they had been unsuccessful. Taking matters into our own hands, we decided to set up a make—shift group of 'law' men to help stop crime in and around Hussenbach. The group seemed to be successful as that the renegades have never appeared to come near Hussenbach until now......the day began as men in the area began constructing homes and out buildings. We needed to build homes and outbuildings for seventeen families. We were building the houses first and then we would come back to work on the outbuildings. This was due to the amount of building materials being available for the region[6] and that the homes were of higher importance than the outbuildings.

It was decided to build Dad's Homestead first in order to have a place for the entire family to live. An outbuilding was also constructed to store supplies. On one sunny but breezy Wednesday morning, I came back to my parent's home stead to gather a few items that was needed at one of the sites where we were building another family home. After obtaining the needed materials I paused and watched wash and rinse tubs being hauled outside along with scrubbing boards and soap. Several women started a fire for heating water. Then, I noticed that a large number of women, both young and old, brought water from the spring. They used buckets, pans or whatever container they could find in order to carry water.

The women had divided the chore into washing and hanging. The job seemed to be going faster as they laughed and talked. Being far enough away I could hear their conversation only faintly but could not make out clearly what was said. When their laughter rang out, I wondered what they talked about that was so funny. Whenever a man neared a group of women, the conversation always seemed to stop and then picked up once again after he left. I often speculated on what the women were laughing about; was it something to do with men? Probably, but

---

[6] Building materials was totally inadequate for the number of colonists. The colonists had to wait sometime before Saratov was able to get an additional 1.3 million planks of wood needed for home construction for the entire Volga River region.

I won't ever know for sure. No man will ever know what women talked about when we were not around.

During the washing process, one of Uncle Benjamin's daughters, Helen, was sent to our first outbuilding in order to retrieve some additional clothes pins. Helen was just out of sight of the family when she was approached by a group of three rough looking men carrying guns. Pointing guns at her, Helen was directed to quietly go inside the outbuilding. Frightened, she did as she was told.

However, once inside they instructed her to take her clothes off or be killed. Frozen, she couldn't move or do what was asked of her. One of the men stepped forward and began to strip off her clothing. She began struggling and screamed as loud as she could. The men panicked and started to beat Helen. Hearing members of the family approaching, the men quickly left. In their haste to leave they left behind one of their guns.

Mom and Helen's mother, Rose, found Helen sobbing and trembling on the floor of the outbuilding. Upon seeing Helen, Mom quickly ran inside the house to retrieve several quilts in which to wrap Helen. Returning to the barn, Rose was already holding the young girl. Helen was wrapped in several quilts and helped into the house. Mom told the other family members that Helen was hurt and that she and Rose would help her. She sent three family members with a gun and the family dog to get Benjamin. She then asked the remaining females to please complete the laundry.

The Cossacks were brought in to investigate but Helen had not recovered enough from the beating to describe those who had attacked her. Uncle Benjamin handed the gun that was left behind, over to the Cossacks. "Well," one Cossack said "this is the first time they left something behind. If the young woman is able to remember anything about the men please let us know. We will keep you posted if and when we have any new information."

Love and understanding aided Helen to slowly recover from the incident; she never completely forgot but the memory somewhat faded. She became shy around people she did not know and would not talk to any male except those in the family. In early November, a group of Cossacks returned to let the family know that the group of renegades had been captured and were awaiting trial. They asked Benjamin and Rose if they felt that Helen would be able to testify against the men.

Rose told them "Since the incident, Helen has been frightened, introverted."

Benjamin asked "Are there others who could testify against the men?"

"Yes, we have enough evidence and women testifying that the group will be found guilty and sent to prison. We just wanted to get as many people to testify as possible. Plus, we wanted you to know that they were captured."

During a year or two after this incident, the family's women were more careful about doing anything alone—they began traveling in pairs or doing chores with three or more people.

The family continued to be saddened by the incident with the rough men and Helen but knew that we had to move forward. During this period of family sorrow, building of Hussenbach and the region continued at a fast clip. Having twenty women, children and grandchildren in a relatively small house was often difficult but the women felt protected in the large numbers. "Besides," as Katherine pointed out, "chores seemed to be finished faster and can be more enjoyable when completed together." One of the other women indicated "that the chores might have been more enjoyable to get done but there was more of them to accomplish: more laundry, more dishes, more food to cook, etc."

Henry's wife, Elizabeth, did not mind the extra chores because when the tasks were done the women would sit around and do their darning, sewing, knitting or quilting. She remarked that she liked "learning to quilt from such a large group of skilled quilters."

Mom said "I am not sure how skilled we are as quilters; we just enjoy doing it."

Life appeared to settle into a pattern; certain days were continued to be set aside for various jobs. For example, the women did their baking on Mondays. On the first Monday, the women did not bake enough bread to last a week. Realizing their mistake, the group had to bake again on Thursday. It took several weeks of bread baking to get the correct number of loafs baked in order to last an entire week. In addition to baking bread, the women also churned butter and baked other items such as pies and cakes on Mondays.

Wednesdays were reserved for washing and mending but if it rained on Wednesday, wash day would be changed to another day. Tuesdays and Fridays were spent working in the garden. The remaining time was spent doing other chores around the property. Cooking meals, milking cows, feeding livestock, and collecting eggs all had to be done daily and often several times a day. In addition, the women began handling jobs that were normally done by men: plowing was one such job. Since the family needed food to sustain us. the women decided that they had to take on the chore of plowing and planting. The fields needed to be plowed and planted in order to grow the crops for market.

A vegetable garden was another vital planting that the women handled. The entire family would live off this one vegetable garden this first year. So, the women plowed and planted an area four to five times as large as what an individual family would normally use. Since several houses were nearing completion, the women discussed establishing gardens near these dwellings. It would be more work at this time to go to the newly formed gardens in order to water, weed, and to eventually harvest the vegetables. But, in the long run, it would help that a garden would be established virtually outside of the house.

Looking back at this last section of the journal, I realized that women do a lot of work; more work then what they often get credit for. Men work hard but not as much as women.

Attempting to conclude building as quickly as possible, the family's men ate, slept and worked at a property until a house was completely finished. As a group we would then go to the next property to erect the next dwelling. Fires would be built close to the building site for keeping a pot of coffee hot, for sleeping warmth and some meal preparation. The majority of meals were brought to the building site by the women of the family. Usually three women would bring a cold meal for us to eat at noon. The women would then stay to prepare the evening meal over the open fire. After dinner was finished, two men would take the women home, visit, sleep and return to the work site with the morning meal.

Four walls, a roof, a floor and a fire place would be built first to allow us to finish the interior of the house; this was especially helpful in cooler weather. When a house was completed, the family whose house it was would move inside. As each house was finished, Mom and Dad's house slowly emptied out and became unusually quiet. Mom had to feel somewhat lonely without so many people surrounding her. Even with living in their own homes, the family was still tied to Dad and Mom's place for livestock, and milk. Scrap wood was utilized to quickly construct chicken coops at the newly finished houses so when the family moved into their new house, some of the chickens also moved into their new coops.

Construction on eleven outbuildings began after a discussion of how to best utilize the material we had on hand. Since there was not enough timber to complete seventeen outbuildings, we decided that family members with adjoining properties could share an outbuilding temporarily. As the materials for the remaining six outbuildings did not arrive for several years we had to make do. However, the Chancellery office eventually provided each family with livestock and farm equipment but it was not always done in a timely manner. I noticed that some, including my family, were provided the allotted livestock and equipment when we only had one outbuilding, while others did not receive equipment or livestock for six months or possibly several years. This meant that the outbuildings that we had were temporarily crowded until we were able to gain enough material to complete the remaining outbuildings.

Many migrants felt cheated when it came to the condition of the region's soil. We had been told that the regions soil was deep black in color, fertile, and that it didn't need manure. The actual soil lacked humus, was not fertile and definitely needed manure. Obtaining manure was a hardship for many of us as the money we had was stretched about as far as humanly possible.

Somehow the majority of us managed to get the needed manure. If we managed to obtain extra manure, which wasn't often, we would share it with family or neighbors.

As luck would have it, the government finally saw its way clear to provide us the promised seeds for the first planting of the season. This was done just as the Funks had completed construction of the seventeen family homes. Other people were not so lucky. Not only were their houses not fully constructed but they had not tilled their land last year in preparation to planting a crop. These migrants had to stop building in order to till up their virgin land so they could plant the newly acquired seeds. Hmmmm….I wondered if they were experienced farmers?

Many of us received these seeds as we were celebrating our fourth year in Russia and the second year on our property in Hussenbach. Countless Germans, including the Funks, had brought enough seeds from Germany for our actual first planting. We had planted this seed last year, our first year in Hussenbach. So, I guess that we were blessed that our land had already been plowed up last year, so it made it easier this year. Plus, we were able to make some money off last year's crop.

We had been guaranteed that rice, beans, oats, and rye had been growing abundantly in the region so we expected these types of seeds to be provided. As it turned out we were provided a limited amount of wheat, barley and oat seeds. We had to purchase additional seeds to fully plant just half of our acres. Instead of buying more wheat, barley or oats, I purchased beans and rye seeds. The shortage of beans and rye in the region caused me to sell both of these crops for a premium price at harvest time. The first Sunday after this second harvest Dad and Mom decided that the family should have a pot—luck style celebration. The entire extended family was invited to attend which by now was well over a hundred people. A pig was placed on a spit and placed over a low fire. While tending to the roasting pig discussion ensued regarding the agricultural condition of the area.

While at the pot—luck celebration there were several conversations taking place. I walked up to several family members who were discussing the conditions here in Russia. Uncle Benjamin was stating that "We already know that Germans and other Europeans were not told the entire truth about crops being grown in this region. We should have known this was not true as the representatives stated that the area was largely uninhabited." Benjamin further argued that "In addition, we were told that the winters were mild; which they are not. The cold lasts longer than three months. What else have they lied to us about?"

Uncle Herman pointed out that they were guaranteed household and farming equipment "but we have not been provided half of what we really need to operate a farm. We still have not been supplied with adequate timber in order to build enough homes or outbuildings."

Then Uncle Phillip jumped in and said that "the Chancellery did not lie to the immigrants completely; they just omitted the whole truth. Yes, the Russian government desired to entice us to move here and to settle this region. And yes, they stated that we would have a mild climate, have fertile soil, be provided with seed and be supplied with needed equipment for farming and running a household." He continued by stating "If they did not live here, how would they really know about the climate? Climate can vary by a mere fifty miles and from year to year. Furthermore, if they had not attempted to plow up the soil how would they know what is really here? As we know the soil in Saratov is different than what it is like here."

Philip argued that his wife "constantly reminds me that she left behind half of what she really needed to run a household properly. I had to make her a new butter churn because she left hers behind and Russia did not provide one. I'm guessing here but, I feel that the Chancellery just provides migrants with the same standard equipment with no variations. And I'd wager that the Chancellery did not consult farmers regarding what they might need to operate a farm!"

With his anger dissipating, Dad calmly stated that "we do understand your points Phillip. We will just have to make the best of the situation as we cannot afford to move back to Germany." Furthermore, he stated that he was as mad as rest of us but knew that "we had to be realistic about the situation and work with it. Let's make a go of the farming here before deciding to move back to Germany or anywhere else."

Jumping into the conversation, I pointed out that "back in Germany we experienced droughts, crop failures, hunger, military conscription, political suppression and lack of religious freedom. Can we make an effort to build a new life here? If it does not work out then we can emigrate elsewhere. We moved once; we could do so again but do we want too?"

As we sat down to dinner, the men had finally agreed that it was better to be here in Russia, even if we were not fully supplied. Back in Germany we could still be experiencing war, starvation or worse. We came to an agreement that life in Russia was not that much different then what it was like in Germany. The exception being that we were guaranteed certain rights such as no conscription, freedom of religion and no taxes for a number of years. As far as we knew there was no other place that provided these freedoms.

After several years of hard work, all of our outbuildings were completed. Fam animals and farm implements could now be close at hand and we wouldn't have to go to share a family member's outbuilding. During this period, each farm was different but the majority of the family placed forty—five acres under cultivation; the remaining thirty—six acres were used for the home, the family vegetable garden, or for outbuildings. Our cattle were pastured on treasury land. The treasury land was often referred to as common land as it was for the good of the entire community. Much of the land set aside for farming did not have an adequate water supply needed for raising of livestock; there was enough water for growing crops but not quite enough for livestock. Around here the farmers are grateful or the common land and that there is sufficient water for the land and for the livestock.

With farms established and Hussenbach on its way to being suitably established, a school began to be constructed. Russia provided the land for the school at no charge but the actual building was constructed and paid for by the people of Hussenbach. While helping build the school, I suggested that we should take up a collection for the purchase of a stove to heat the building. Someone mentioned that "we should take turns supplying aged, split wood for the school." I could feel our community's commitment to learning since we willingly spent our time and money on building and maintaining a school.

Once built, we obtained the needed text books. Text books written in German were hard to come by here in Russia. Somehow, we obtained enough books in German for instruction to begin. We hired a teacher from Germany to teach all eight grades. I pondered on whether we would need to expand the school and hire additional teachers due to the growth of students in the near future. Or would we need to build another school on the other side of town. We will just have to wait and see....

Christmas of 1972

I could not believe that during the first years that the family spent in Russia they faced hardship and adventure. It is difficult to imagine living in a small house with over thirty other people, even if they were thirty family members. Granted, the majority of males in the family were busy building houses and outbuildings during the day and even throughout the week which meant that there were not thirty—five people in the one house at one time. It was hard to imagine that the females not only handled their every day—to—day household jobs but had also stepped up to complete the agricultural jobs such as plowing and planting. Plowing had to be a tough job, especially for women, but the job was done so the family would survive.

It appears to be normal for people during the mid—to—late 1760's to help others build, with their plowing and planting. For example, the family aided in constructing the town, the school, churches. and provided help to others where there was a need. I wonder if people around the world offered the same type of help to their neighbors today. People today seem to be skeptical of those they do not know and are reluctant to offer assistance. I honestly believe that there are still people that provide assistance to others with an open heart but I wonder where they are…..

Once again Conrad's favorite bible verse came to mind.

For I was hungry and you gave me food; I was thirsty and you gave me something to drink; I was a stranger and you welcomed me. Just as you did it to one of the least of these who are members of my family you did it for me. Matthew 25:35, 45

Looking the verse up in the bible, I found out that verse 36 through 39 discussed clothing the naked, taking care of the sick, and visiting those in prison. Would we have to do it all to help others in order for God to feel that we did it for him? Could people just do a few things like feeding others, clothing the poor or welcoming strangers? I don't know but it is something to consider.

Adventure seemed to follow the family, Conrad especially. Conrad, his Dad and Uncle Herman encountered several nomadic people with bows and arrows. They could have been killed but for some reason they were spared. Not long afterwards Jacob, Benjamin and Conrad were confronted by Andrew and another man with loaded guns. It appears that Andrew had every intention of killing Jacob but Benjamin and Conrad intervened. After being captured and tried, Andrew was sent to prison for a long time. Tragedy occurred to Helen as a result of the group of renegades terrorizing the region. Across my mind ran the bible verse from Matthew:

I was sick and you took care of me.   Matthew 25: 36.

Tears ran down my checks as I thought about Helen being nursed back to health but was never the same.

I wondered whether I could have survived two hundred years ago while attempting to build a new life in the wilderness. We are so spoiled with modern conveniences such as washing machine and dryers, television sets, and other items. When we need a loaf of bread, we go to a bakery or to a grocery store. I wonder how many people today would take the time to make bread by mixing and kneading the dough, allowing it to rise and then baking it; or would they take the easy way out by going to the market. I know that it is not a dying art as that I have seen Grandma make yeast bread several times.

Without electric lights and the hard work that people did every day, I did not wonder any longer why they went to bed at dusk. Sitting before a fire in the fire place with only kerosene lamps had to make it difficult to read or do handiwork in the evenings. What will happen to Conrad and the family next? Will they ever see Anton / Andrew again? Will they have additional encounters with the native population of Central Asia? Will their relationship with the Russians continue to be good or will it turn sour? Only time and reading will provide me answers to these questions.

I am grateful that Grandma brought the remaining translated journals with her when they came to Denver for Christmas. I cannot wait to finish finding out what happened to the family.

Journal Four

Early 1800s

Over the past thirty—five years since we arrived in the Volga River region, the population has dramatically increased. In 1798, over nine—hundred people now call Hussenbach and the surrounding area home. Artisans, including shoemakers, tailors, and blacksmiths, have opened shops on Hussenbach's main street. During the early spring of 1801, a few farmers and I gathered outside the town's general store. We began to discuss what it costs us to send our grain out to be ground. Karl Mueller pointed out that "I am tired of sending my grain elsewhere to be ground. The price for shipping the grain to these others places to be ground has doubled in price. The returned flour product has also doubled in price. I am considering not growing wheat or any type of grain in the future."

"I concur whole heartedly!" Karl's brother, Matthew argued. "However, instead of stop growing grain, I have considered building a mill of my own. The cost of the mill would pay for itself within a couple years."

With my hand on my chin, I thoughtfully said "Let's do it."

The men looked at me in bewilderment and said in unison "Do what?"

"Build a mill, of course." After a short pause, I continued "We have a perfectly good river where a mill could be built." Allowing the statement to sink in, I then added "As a group, we could share in the cost of building and operating a mill. Of course, as Matthew stated, it would pay for itself within a couple years. Plus, not one of us would have to provide a huge amount of money in order to build the mill."

"Owning the mill would mean that our grain would be processed faster at a lower cost." Interjected my brother Charles. "I'm thinking that any farmer wishing to be involved, could be and it could be called *Mill on the Medvelitza*."

After a moment of thought, Karl said "You know, after we get it built and operating, we could, for a price, grind grain for farmers in neighboring areas. That way it would be bringing in money and our grain would be practically free to grind."

Karl Mueller gathered a few famers together to look for a parcel of land along the Medvelitza. One day while the group was examining land about a mile south east of town, some men carrying weapons approached us. Although they were babbling at us in a language that we did not understand, we knew that they were angry about something. Maybe they weren't mad at us in particular but they were upset about something. Trying to remain calm, we attempted to get the foreigners to communicate with us about the problem. After much frustration, on both sides, we were able to finally convey that we wanted to retrieve an individual who might speak their language. Paul Miller went back into Hussenbach to locate Henry Hoffman. After what seemed liked forever, Paul returned with Henry. He told us that the men were from the Caucasus Mountain region, which was many miles south, south—west of Hussenbach.

"Aren't they a bit far from home?" Paul asked.

Continuing to talk to the men, Henry related to us that the group had tracked a man back to this region. The man was suspected of robbing several people in their homeland. "Please tell them that we will assist them in finding the man or men involved in the robbery." I wondered if it could be a neighbor that had just returned from what he said was a business trip.

Taking the men with us to town, we got the law involved. The sheriff did some poking around and found out that the neighbor in question was the only individual who had been gone for an extended period of time. He had come back with a tidy sum of money; however, he could not tell anyone what he had sold or service that he had provided to gain the money. When the sheriff brought the man to face the men from Caucasus Mountain region, he became nervous and stuttered when he said "I have never seen these men before."

One of the foreigners disagreed vehemently before stating that "this is the man who had robbed me, and the others, at gun point." Assuring the group from the Caucasus Mountains that justice would be served. Many of us provided room and board for the foreigners while our neighbor was brought before a judge. After a week of testimony and argument, the local man was found guilty, lost his land and possessions. He was then sentenced to ten years in a Siberian prison. The money that was found on the thief and in his house was given back to the Caucasus Mountain men. Thanking us, the group then began their journey home.

We then returned to the parcel of land where we met the foreigners and decided that it would be a perfect location for a mill. The mill was constructed within six weeks; we just needed to locate a pair of millstones. We were told that once the millstones were ordered it would take four to six weeks to be finished, transported to us and mounted in the mill. However, the mill-stones took not four to six weeks but fifteen weeks in total to be made, delivered and installed; hmmm—four to six weeks!

The cost of processing Hussenbach's grain was lowered. In addition, enough business was generated from neighboring communities that we were able to pay a small salary to a seasonal mill operator. Being interested in mills and how they operated, my brother Henry applied for the seasonal job as mill operator. Over the years, Henry didn't become wealthy working part time at the mill but gained a reputation as the best mill operator in the Volga River region.

Czarina Catherine's grandson, Alexander, decided to reopen the immigration program during the early part of the nineteenth century because he desired to encourage additional craftsmen to immigrate into Russia. Western Europeans were ready to move as a result of the Napoleonic Wars affecting the western part of the continent. However, many of us living in the Volga River region felt that additional immigrants would be a hardship for the current population.

I knew that there was still land available for new settlements but that land less accessible to water and was further away from the region's towns and villages. Distance from town would make it more expensive for people to bring their crops to market or to obtain services. No one desired to spend their crop profits on transportation costs to get these crops to market. This was the main reason why this land had not been settled during the last immigration period thirty—five years ago.

At this time, many Germans living in the Volga River region would like to gain access to more land. We were ineligible to gain virgin land that was set up for immigrants; we could only purchase land owned by Russians who were selling their property. However, Germans had to have cash in hand in order to purchase any property that was for sale. The question is how to obtain the needed cash for purchasing of the extra land. I knew that many, including myself, are barely making a living farming the eighty—one acres of land that we have access too. We would like to have twice as much land to farm. But, if memory serves me right, when we first migrated here, we were ecstatic to receive eighty—one—acres to farm. Eighty—one—acres meant more acreage then what we farmed back in Germany. I guess that I, and others, should count our blessings and not complain about what we think that we should have.

I, personally, began to think about what it was like for my family when we left Germany. We barely made it out of Germany before laws were implemented against migration to other countries. In addition, we ran into Anton / Andrew, encountered a ship wreck, experienced Russians cheating innocent people, had a brother and female cousin die and we were delayed in Saratov for almost two years.

If people here in Russia had tried to prevent us from migrating then where would we be today? We should welcome new immigrants to the region. Again, a portion of the verse from Matthew comes to mind:

> *I was a stranger and you welcomed me. Just as you did it*
> *to one of the least of these who are members of my family*
> *you did it for me.   Matthew 25: 35, 45*

I have come to the conclusion that this verse acts as a reminder that we should treat others with respect and to always welcome others.

Reopening of the immigration program caused an influx of new immigrants to flow into the Volga River region. As during the last arrival of immigrants, recent settlers were delays in both St Petersburg and Saratov along with a shortage of supplies. I wonder why the government had not learned from the past; they should have had more supplies available, land surveyed and money available before allowing a large number of people to move into the region.

As a result of the influx of new people into the area, many of the current residents have begun to consider how to make themselves and their children more employable. Higher education became the answer for the majority of us living in the Volga River region. Being a physician, a teacher or a minister has meant a guaranteed income and respect. Many males across the region have learned a trade or craft in which to support themselves on top of farming. Philip, Katherine's and my only child, learned how to do carpentry work by watching and helping me after the farm chores were done for the day. The region's Germans would often practice their trade during the day. Plowing, planting and harvesting was seasonal work and could be mainly handled twice yearly. Plus, we had many male hands in the family that accomplished the seasonal farm work quickly. We could then get back to our other businesses, like blacksmithing or operating a mercantile or being a carpenter.

Philip

As father said many, many times over the years, my skills as a farmer and as a carpenter were learned from him. This happened partly through just following him around and absorbing how he did things. Growing up along the Medvelitza River was great fun for me. Nicholas and Heinrich, my cousins, and I often went fishing together. We would bring our catch home with the idea that we would have fish for supper. Being gracious, our Mothers accepted the fish but they did not like cleaning them. As we got older, we were expected to clean and fillet the fish prior to bringing them home to our moms.

Nicholas, Heinrich and I got into mischief regularly but never over anything horribly bad. Although there were a few times we felt for sure that our Dad's would give us a good talking too, these talks were never overly harsh. As the three of us grew into adulthood we worked together in farming and in operating a carpentry business side—by—side. We produced German 'colonist wagons' that were purchased by many that lived in the region and by people living hundreds of miles away. Besides building wagons Nicholas, Heinrich and I produced benches, tables, rocking chairs and other household items. Our wives, mothers and many other women in the area enjoyed our rocking chairs. The rockers have roomy seats and broad arms that make them extra comfortable. The rocking chairs have become almost as profitable as our 'colonist wagons'.

My grandparents asked me to live with them in order to help them in their old age. Seven months after my moving in, the pair passed away in 1799. The farm that my grandparents operated was handed down to me. Lydia, my new wife of two months, and I are the second generation to farm this homestead in Hussenbach. My dad and mom continue to work and manage the property that borders this property. As I am their only child, I know that their acreage will come to me when my parents pass; I hope that they will not pass to soon. I often wonder how many more generations of Funks will live on and work this acreage on the fringes of Hussenbach. I may never know the answer to this question but can only imagine.

In 1800, as Lydia and I found out that we were expecting our first child. This caused us to discuss the need for more space. I suggested that we either add on to the back of the house or to add on to the second floor. We eventually decided to add on to the back of the house and to the second floor. We chose to do so as we might not be able to afford to do so at a later time as more children arrived. Several months into the addition to the house, Lydia gave birth to our first son whom we named George. Over the next six and a half years, we had three more sons and a daughter. At least Lydia and I know that we have four sons to take over the farming of the one—hundred—sixty—two acres.

Each year that we lived on the property, we expanded our garden. We planted typical crops such as beans and peas but added different varieties of squash, broccoli, pumpkins and many other types of vegetables. Back in 1775, Dad and Grandpa had taken a chance when they decided to plant a few fruit trees. In the beginning, the trees provided little to no fruit but as the trees matured enough fruit was provided for the family to make jam, preserves, and some pies. Over the years, many individuals inquired about obtaining cuttings from our trees to grow on their farm. Through grafting and rooting I cultivated fruit tree saplings. I sold these saplings to a select group pf people in Hussenbach and to other people along the Medvelitza. Within a few years, the Medvelitza River region became known for its fruit trees. By 1800, I slowed down in providing others with these saplings because I did not want the market to become saturated.

In 1817, our two oldest sons, George and Jacob, having finished their formal education, were now assisting me with the plowing and planting. From an early age, Jacob had always talked about becoming a Lutheran Minister. One evening after the farm work was complete, Jacob and I discussed the prospect his becoming a minister. The two of us discussed how Pastors married people, baptized new babies and preached weekly. However, they often had to travel extensively to cover a group of churches around the region. Extensive travel could be hard on a family so I asked whether he would like to have a family in the future.

"Maybe, but I feel that I would like to explore the possibility of going into the ministry. I know that I can make a difference in the region's spiritual life."

Early on I wasn't completely sold on Jacob becoming a minister because I knew that it could be a lonely life. On the other hand, I felt that my children had the right to decide for themselves what they did with their lives; I might not agree with it but it was their choice. Besides, if Jacob's faith was as strong as mine then I know he would make a wonderful minister. I told Jacob that he should visit Reverend Sachsen the next time the Reverend was in Hussenbach.

Jacob was finally able to meet with the Reverend a couple weeks later. The conversation between the two began with Jacob inquiring about the Reverend's life as a minister. The Reverend had known for a while that Jacob was interested in the church but did not realize the extent of his interest until now. Reverend Sachsen began by telling Jacob that the question was tough to answer. "Do you want to know about the training needed to become a minister? Or about the hectic traveling life of the rural minister? How about the lack of a family life that the rural minister experiences? What exactly would you like to know Jacob?" Reverend Sachsen asked.

"All of it!" Jacob replied eagerly.

"Where to begin, where to begin…..Since we will become friends during this exploration you might as well call me by my first name, Franz."

"I don't know if I can call you by your first name, Reverend. You're special and…"

Reverend Sachsen quickly interjected while holding up his left hand, "Wait! I am just a human being like anyone else; nothing special! I went through the same process that you are going though now in order to become a minister of God. God selects ordinary men to become extraordinary ministers so that his word may be spread among the people. Those chosen to serve the church have made mistakes in their lives and have human frailties. I have gotten angry many times; often I have desired a wife and a family.

"Years ago, I fell in love with a woman that I thought of marrying. I asked myself that if I had married her where would we live? I couldn't drag her from town to town to stay with a different family each night. We might not have a home of our own. If I provided her a home, I might only be able to return once every five to seven weeks, depending on how many churches I was asked to manage by the home office. If I was lucky, I might have three churches which means that I could settle down but there is no guarantee. There is nothing in the church rules that state ministers cannot marry. However, being a rural minister is a tough way of life and can be hard on a marriage.

"Now, can we start over? Since I do not have an immediate family, I do like to have a few close friends in my life. Please be one of those close friends, call me Franz."

"Okay, Franz! Like you, I have a few friends but none are close enough for me to tell my heart's desire too." Jacob said with a shy smile.

"Being a minister can be a lonely occupation. Like me, most ministers do not have a family, they travel extensively which creates many superficial friendships, and lastly," Franz stated with a twinkle in his voice and a small smile, "many people put me on a pedestal." Jacob grinned back at the reverend.

"When I trained to become a minister, I had to go through three years of theology education prior to training under another minister for two years. However, individuals studying to become a minister today must spend four years in a theology school. Students study theology along with courses on the bible, preaching and most importantly, how to deal with the congregation. Let's face it people are wonderful overall but you get them together problems can and often do arise. After the schooling, students will spend two to three years training under another minister. If you decide to do the four years of formal schooling, I would love to be your mentor and provide the two to three years of training. I could use the help and would love to have the constant contact of a good friend."

"Where are the theology schools located? How do I apply? And what else do I need to do?" Jacob inquired.

"A new school of theology is located in Saratov. Since my rounds will take me near Saratov during the next two weeks, I will pick up the applications that you will need to fill out and return. I think that you should be able to begin the schooling during the upcoming fall semester."

Thanking the reverend, Jacob and Franz parted and promised to meet in a month. At their next meeting Jacob would fill out the applications and Franz would write the required reference. Once completed, Jacob would return the documents to

Saratov's new School of Theology. Lydia was extremely proud that Jacob wanted to become a minister. As I knew that I would, I came around after putting aside my reservations, and totally supported our son's decision.

As I was plowing the fields for the spring planting, knowing that Jacob was going to become a minister, my mind wondered to George. I wondered what George desired to do with the rest of his life. I know that he had a genuine interest in farming and had become a great help to me in recent years; especially when I broke my arm while stacking hay in the loft area of in our outbuilding. Having George's companionship and assistance in working the land has made farming more enjoyable. However, since he is only fifteen years old, I knew that he would not continue working eighty—one acres with me. I wondered whether he might desire to take over my parents eighty—one acres in the future. I know that George still has time to figure out what he desired to do in the future so worrying about it did no good so my wonderings stopped, at least for the time being.

After finishing the plowing for the day, George and I unhitched our horses, led them into the outbuilding, rubbed them down and provided them with hay, oats and water. As we were working George decided that this was as good a time as any to talk to me about what was on his mind. "Dad," he began slowly "I wondered if you have noticed that the wine making industry is growing across the region? And that more and more farmers are planting grapevines?"

I told George that I had noticed an increase of grapevines in the region but knew little of the wine making industry. "Why do you ask?"

"Well, I think that we should add some grapevines to the property. Grapes can be highly profitable for the wine making industry but also as table grapes."

Rubbing my chin thoughtfully, I slowly said that "it was not a bad idea. How long do you think that it would take before the vines would begin producing fruit?"

"If we plant roughly a hundred plants, we should be able to harvest enough grapes for our own use within two or three years. Within five or six years the vines will have matured enough to produce sufficient grapes to sell to a winery. We will need some wire and a few stacks for the grape vines to grow upon."

"I guess that you did your research prior to talking with me."

"Of course, I did" replied George. "I knew that otherwise you would blow my idea out of the water."

"Okay, let's give it a try. Next time we go to town we can get the needed supplies and get started."

After dinner, with the dishes washed and put away, and the children were in bed, Lydia and I sat together near the fire place. Lydia was darning socks as I finished going over the books. Moving to the rocking chair near my wife, I told Lydia of George's idea regarding growing grapes. Smiling, Lydia looked up from the darning and asked me how I felt about adding a few grapes to the farm.

"As you know, fruit trees have been good for the family. The trees are not profitable, as we don't sell the fruit that we grow. But we have made some money by selling a few saplings. However, grapes would be an excellent way for us to make additional money from our acreage; even if it takes five or more years to develop. George says that there is a growing demand for grapes by those individuals in the wine making business. I know that the wine making industry needs as many grapes as possible. In addition, wine makers will pay a high price for what they purchase. I am unsure of the exact number of plants that we need in order to make it profitable. George seems to think that we need about a hundred plants to make it semi—profitable. I have to go to Saratov next week on business so I could enquire at the agricultural office about growing grapes."

"Whatever you decide, dear, is fine with me. My only concern is whether we have enough land available for the growing of grape vines. If we do, then do what you think is best. We don't have to plant a lot to vines; just enough to make a small profit." Changing the subject, Lydia then said that she "couldn't believe that George is such a wonderful help on the farm and is well on his way in becoming a master carpenter. Jacob plans on going to school for ministry. Before you know Anna, Friedrich and Johann will be grown and living on their own. Where has the time gone?"

Replying through my laughter "You were just too busy and did not notice that the children were growing up. How will you feel when George or one of the other children gets married?"

"Please, I am not old enough to have a married child or to have a grandchild."

"I did not mention a grandchild, now did I?"

Laughing softly, we settled into a comfortable silence; I began reading an agricultural journal while Lydia continued darning socks.

At the age of fourteen, Anna assisted Lydia with many of the household chores while finishing up her last year of formal education. Anna had a secret desire that we, as her parents, were not aware of; she wanted to become a school teacher. She knew that she would need additional education but had identified no other details about what it took to become a teacher. Anna had overheard that Hussenbach's lower school would need a new teacher the following school year; the current teacher, Miss Bedel, had decided to leave in order to live and teach closer to her parents. The entire town was saddened that Miss Bedel was leaving but understood completely.

As we sat down to dinner during one evening in late August, Anna approached Lydia and I about pursuing teaching as a career. Lydia suggested that she and Anna should approach Mr. Kern, the current upper school teacher about what Anna would need to do to become a teacher. Taking the children to school the next day, Lydia and Anna went in to briefly talk to Mr. Kern regarding an informational meeting about teaching as a career. He suggested that Lydia return after school that afternoon and they could discuss education as a career. Later that day, Mr. Kern, Lydia, Anna and myself gathered together in a classroom to discuss teaching. Mr. Kern began by telling us that the teacher program could be completed in one year at a college in Saratov. When we inquired about the housing he said "Females live in the same building where the classes are held and had several female teachers living with them. Male students board in a smaller building next door and have two male teachers with them. Meals were taken together and are included in the price of room and board."

Mr. Kern pointed out that "Anna has enough credit to finish her education here in Hussenbach in December. There is an application that needs to be completed and turned in along with the needed transcripts. If this is done in a timely manner, Anna could begin her teacher training in January."

Anna could not believe what she was hearing! Imagine, beginning to studying to become a teacher in four short months. Anna was somewhat frightened when she considered living in

Saratov instead of at home in Hussenbach. However, Anna was determined to fulfill her dream. Before thanking Mr. Kern, Lydia asked where she might get the needed application. Mr. Kern said that he had several on hand if we needed one. After taking the application, I told Mr. Kern that we would give him an answer tomorrow morning.

After dinner, the dishes were washed, dried and put away. Then Lydia, Anna and I discussed the possibility of Anna going to Saratov to attend college. Lydia wondered whether "the school board might be willing to wait a couple months for Anna." Looking puzzled, Anna considered what her mother meant. Lydia continued by stating that she was just pondering the idea of whether "Anna might be considered for the position Miss Bedel would be vacating. If the school board agreed to waiting for and then hiring Anna, she could live here with us, if she chose too. This would mean that she would only have to live away from the family for a year while she was studying."

Anna liked the idea of living at home but decided that she might change her mind after all that was a year—and—a—half away. If she chose to live with the other teachers' she would be on her own but close to her family. After Anna headed to bed, Lydia quietly said that she was "concerned about where we would get the money to pay for the schooling and Anna's living expenses? As it is, we have just enough money to pay our expenses, Philip, and to save a little. However, if we have Jacob and Anna attending school in Saratov how will we pay their expenses."

"Let's worry about that later, dear." I replied as I banked the fire, blew out the lamps and we went to bed. The next morning, I hitched up the team to the wagon in order for Lydia and I to take Anna, Friedrich and Johann to school. Lydia, Anna and I went inside to talk to Mr. Kern while Friedrich and Johann stayed outside to be with their friends. Of course, the other children were curious to know what was going on inside because fathers usually did not come to school. Mr. Kern was thrilled that Anna decided to pursue teaching and took the filled-out application from the Funks. He said that he would gather together a recommendation and an official transcript; both the transcript and recommendation would need to be sent in with the application.

"I will get them in the mail as soon as possible. But first I need to tell you that last night, at the school board meeting, I presented the idea of Anna going to the teachers' college beginning in January. The board members know Anna and your family's reputation. The board stated that they would be pleased to offer her the teaching position once she completes her education. The board is willing to locate a substitute teacher for autumn semester while we wait for Anna to finish her course work. The board is also willing to pay her tuition, room and board while she is studying in Saratov. But of course, she will need to maintain a 'B' average while there." Anna and her parents could not believe what they heard. Anna was thrilled about the opportunity. She heartily agreed and began preparations to finish school in less than four months and for the move after Christmas.

Mr. Kern asked if "Lydia or I could return that evening to retrieve the needed transcript and reference? If you fill out the application, have Anna sign it this afternoon, then you and Anna could mail the application, transcript and reference to the college this afternoon."

At the beginning of the New Year, Lydia and I took the excited but somewhat sad Anna to Saratov to attend the teachers'

college. Studying to become a teacher energized Anna but it was also distressing to think that she would not see her family daily for almost a year. Upon arrival at the school Lydia and I helped her to settle into her room. I then suggested that we get dinner at the restaurant a few blocks away. Finishing dinner, we leisurely walked Anna back to school with the promise to return to see her prior to leaving Saratov for home.

The nest day, Lydia went into a local shop that specialized in fabrics. As always, Lydia was looking for that special piece of fabric for a future project. She always said that the project would come to mind when she saw a unique bolt of material. If she saw the unique material, she might purchase several yards or maybe even the entire bolt. Sometimes, all Lydia needed was that scrap piece of fabric that the shop had left from a bolt and wanted to sell.

Noticing that the shop carried a small selection of yarns, Lydia was curious to see what kind they had. The shop did have some wool sock yarn which caused Lydia to select several skeins of the yarn. With five children and the two of us, Lydia was always knitting socks. After Lydia purchased the needed fabric and several skeins of sock yarn, we went down the block to a business that I wanted to visit. After talking to the owners, I was able to secure a new contract for the German 'colonist wagons' that my cousins and I made. I couldn't wait to tell Nicholas and Heinrich that we would be building an additional thirty wagons. We wouldn't have to add a delivery charge since the buyers agreed to come to Hussenbach to pick up the wagons when they were completed. "It might be best if you notify us as you complete two or three wagons." they said "It would be easier for us to retrieve two, three or four wagons then all thirty at once." We agreed to do so and thanked them for the business.

Arriving back at the hotel in time to get cleaned up, Lydia and I left to pick up Anna for dinner. It was a nice experience for Lydia to not have to cook the meal and then clean up afterwards. After being seated and then ordering our meal, Lydia asked Anna how her first day went. Anna told us about meeting Isobel, her roommate, and attending their first classes together. Tuning out the conversation, my mind wondered as to what life would be like back at home with just the four boys with no Anna. She teased the boys as badly as they teased her. Over the years, Anna had been a good sport as she had her feet stepped on as her four brothers learned to dance. Coming back to the conversation I said "We hope that you know that we both will miss you while you are here; we can't wait to be together again."

Anna smiled and indicated that she knew and would miss us also. Returning Anna to school, we hugged and said that we would be back in two or three months for a visit. Then, Lydia and I went back to the hotel, we started for home early the next morning.

Late summer of 1818, we began preparing to send another child off to Saratov to attend school. Similar to the earlier trip with Anna, Lydia and I took Jacob to the Theology School in Saratov. After settling Jacob's positions into his room, we decided that it was time to pick up Anna for dinner. Even though Jacob would not admit it, I knew that he had missed his younger sister over the past eight months. Now that the two were both in Saratov, Jacob intended on seeing her as often as possible. Over the next four months Jacob and Anna saw each other every Wednesday evening for an early dinner and then they attended a bible study class together. Each Sunday, the siblings attended church together and then would get a bite to eat at a local restaurant.

Being between childhood and adulthood, both Jacob and Anna decided to enjoy their special time together. The two knew it would end when Anna finished her course work and then returned home to begin teaching. Anna finished her schooling just before Christmas, Lydia and I picked her up. We had dinner with Jacob and then the four of us returned home for the holiday. After the New Year I took Jacob back to Saratov and Anna began her life as a teacher. Jacob knew that he would miss his sister but she had made the transition from home to being on his own easier to bear. Besides, he decided, it was only two and a half more years.... WOW! But he knew that he would make it.

Spring 1973

From reading this journal, I realized that the majority of Germans during this period were fair in their dealings with people in general. The men from the Caucasus Mountain region could have been told that there were no criminals in the Hussenbach region. However, Conrad had suspected his neighbor of not being totally honest in his dealings with the townspeople or foreigners. I, also, learned that there were many Germans forgetting why their families had moved to Russia thirty—five years before. If they had remembered why their family immigrated, they would not have attempted to prevent others from doing the same thing.

With the influx of new immigrants, it was interesting to see how those already living in the Hussenbach region began to look for ways to better their situation. Education or learning a trade seemed the way many attempted to improve their lives and their children's lives. This isn't any different than today even though we live half way around the world from Russia and it is a hundred and fifty years later.

I had left home for college approximately seven months ago, so could understand how both Anna and Jacob felt as they left home in order to gain more education. The main difference was that I was almost eighteen when I left for college while Anna was fourteen or possibly close to turning fifteen when she left for the teacher school. I know that I was not ready to leave home when I was her age; I began to wonder what gave Anna her strength.

Picking up the fifth journal, I began to leaf through the journal. Thoughts strayed to what else happened to my ancestors. I wondered what they experienced during the next couple of decades; what caused them to decide to make another move, this time to the United States. I had hopes that the fifth journal might hold a map or possibly some letters inserted between the journals page; unfortunately, there weren't any. I am looking forward to reading about Anna's teaching career and whether Jacob actually had become a minister.

Journal Five

Life in Russia—1820—1870

In January of 1819, Anna began teaching in Hussenbach's lower school. The early days of teaching was tough as many of the children remembered Anna as being a student in their school and not the teacher. Frustrated, Anna approached Mr. Kern about how to handle the situation. He was somewhat surprised that the children in the lower grades were being a problem. Usually the younger children were still excited to be in school and loved their teacher. Not that the students did not love Anna but they just wanted to test her. Mr. Kern gave Anna some suggestions about how to turn the children around; his suggestions worked well and Anna never had a problem with the students again.

After teaching for roughly four and a half years, Anna met a young man and fell in love. The two courted for a year before they decided to get married during the late summer of 1824. Of course, Lydia and I were unhappy over having Anna move away with her new husband but we were happy that she had found love. Of course, we saw Anna and her growing family regularly the first couple of years; but as time passed and responsibilities took over, we saw each other less and less often.

After four years of schooling, and interning three years under Reverend Franz Sachsen, Jacob became a minister and was provided his own group of churches to pastor. The group of churches caused him to move east of the Volga River. Missing his family, Jacob returned home as often as possible. On one visit home, Jacob asked Lydia and I whether we knew of a family named Koch. Lydia and I thought for a few moments but could not think where we had heard that name before.

"At the church in Eckheim there is a family named Koch. When I introduced myself as Jacob Funk on the first Sunday, there was a loud gasp from several people near the back. This group proceeded to rise and leave the church. After the service, when I was outside greeting members of the congregation, one of the individuals who had left the service had stayed behind; after a moment he stepped up in order to have a few words with me. The individual apologized for the family's rudeness; he said that about fifty years ago there was a Jacob Funk who was instrumental in having their father put in prison."

It was now Lydia's turn to gasp as she and I remembered the story of Andrew Koch. I began to relate the story of Anton /Andrew to those family members gathered around the dinner table. "Years ago, there was a man named Andrew Koch who was impersonating a relative named Anton. My grandfather, Jacob, was instrumental in having Andrew Koch arrested and put in jail as the family was leaving Germany about fifty years ago.

"After killing three police officers, Andrew had tracked the family to Saratov. He located my grandfather and great-grandfather in a region that they were surveying. As that Andrew Koch was threatening my grandfather, his brother, Benjamin, was able to wound Andrew. The group were able to take Andrew to Saratov where a judge sent him to a Siberian prison. That was the last we had heard about him until now."

Jacob did a little digging on Andrew Koch, a few weeks later, when he was able to return home, he had some news. "From what I was able to find out, Andrew spent about fifteen years in prison before being released. He was let go because of a mix up of prisoners. The prisoners that was to be let go ended up serving the rest of Andrew Koch's sentence. Apparently, Andrew decided to come to the Volga River region to look for Jacob (Great—Grandpa) or Conrad (Grandpa). In Eckheim, he met and married a young woman named Katarina; Katarina changed Andrew's life. When asked about his earlier life, Andrew told his family how he ended up in prison but he twisted the story to make himself appear innocent and Jacob Funk as the criminal. Andrew died about twenty years ago."

Lydia gratefully replied "The Funk's should be grateful that Katarina changed Andrew. The third time the family might not have been so lucky and someone in our family might have been killed."

George

Shortly after Jacob's visit, Dad quietly passed away in his sleep one night. I realized that Mom was suffering deeply even though she appeared to be functioning on the surface. For many months, I questioned myself what could be done to help Mom overcome her grief. I wondered if it would help if I and Elizabeth, my wife of eight months, moved in with her. I asked Elizabeth how she felt about moving in with my Mom; She loved the idea and asked whether I had asked my Mother about it yet. With a shy smile, Mom pointed out that she "did not like living alone since my brothers, Friedrich and Johann, had moved to town to be closer to their business." So, she welcomed the idea of having Elizabeth and I living with her.

Mom suggested that maybe we should add an additional room or two onto the house in order to provide Elizabeth and myself some privacy. Mom and I had a heavy discussion regarding an addition since the house had plenty of room. However, Mom won and two rooms were added onto the house. Nine months later, Elizabeth provided me with our first son whom we named Henry. Over the next five years, Elizabeth and I had two more sons and a really nice surprise: twin daughters.

Thinking about how fast my life had changed since marrying and having children, I realized that the town had also changed. The Church that the family attended had burned to the ground shortly after Elizabeth and I married. After a short mourning period, the congregation began to raise money to rebuild. We could not believe how other Hussenbach churches came together to offer monetary assistance along with the use of their buildings until a new building could be completed. Members of the other churches felt that it was their duty to help others in need. Plus, they hoped that if it they had lost their building, we would step up to assist them. So, our congregation accepted the many gracious offers from the other churches. We did so on a rotating basis as not to overwhelm any one church. A year later, we had money to purchase the needed wood for rebuilding of the church and metal for the roof.

During this period, I realized that the government continued to allow religious and political freedom for the Volga River Germans. However, I noticed that over the years the Russia slowly lost control of the schools; The Lutheran Church stepped up, and took control of the region's schools. Religious books began to replace the traditional text books used in the past. The clergy now did the hiring and controlled teacher's salaries.

In recent years, a growth in the region's population has meant more agricultural products being grown and needing to be processed for market. The *Mill on the Medvelitza* has become overwhelmed with the additional grains that needed to be ground. The mill found itself operating twelve hours a day Monday through Saturday and were considering operating Sundays in order to accommodate this extra work.

Those of us operating the mill saw the need to build and operate a second mill. The second mill would aid in handling the growth in mill work that had taken place over the past five years. I traveled to Saratov to seal the deal with a manufacturing company that would make us another mill stone. Carpenters across Hussenbach came together to build the new mill. Once built this second mill helped to grind the additional grains grown in Hussenbach, and for the additional grain grown in the surrounding area and from a few other regions further away. It feels good to know that we live in an area that has prospered over the past fifty years and that the German population played a vital role in this growth.

Henry

Many in Hussenbach consider me, Henry Funk, to be a wealthy farmer with an entrepreneurial spirit. This is due in part, that I take advantage of opportunities as they present themselves. Recently, I took advantage of the growth of the region's cotton, flax and wool. In the near past, sheared wool, harvested flax and cotton had been shipped to other parts of Russia for processing.

A large portion of these fibers were returned as yarn, thread and sometimes fabric. Feeling that the people of Hussenbach and surrounding area should not have to send their raw products elsewhere for processing and then pay a higher price for returned products made me consider operating a spinning mill and possibly a textile mill.

Research into spinning mills caused me to be torn between using the tried and true spinning wheels or the relatively new spinning machines. Spinning wheels have been utilized for spinning thread or yarn from wool, cotton or flax for hundreds of years. However, once people learn how to use the spinning machine, fibers can be processed faster. Spinning wheels are still widely used but are slowly being replaced by automation. I feel that both the spinning wheel and spinning machine could be used successfully in my business.

When asked why I did not use the new machines instead of the old-fashioned spinning wheel I would tell them that it was difficult to purchase enough spinning machines in order to operate a mill. Besides, it took time for many workers to learn how to operate the mechanized spinners while other workers learned to operate the machines quickly. In the beginning, spinning wheels were more efficient to operate because women already were quick making high—quality thread and yarns with the wheels. Within a few years of opening the mill, I tried using a new roller spinning machine that operated at different speeds. The rollers aid in making the machine work faster and more efficiently than the spinning wheel. The roller spinning machine produced a more even thickness to woolen thread and yarns.

The Medvelitza and Volga Rivers are being exploited in bringing raw fibers and for transporting finished products to other places outside the immediate area of Hussenbach. A cloth weaving company, located on the edge of town, was on the verge of closing due to the cost of bringing needed supplies from far off places. My spinning mill was able to completely supply the cloth weaving company at a fraction of the cost the company paid in the past. The cloth weaving company stayed in business and was able to make a profit each year afterwards. This helped me to decide that I really did not need to open a textile mill since the cloth weaving company was doing a great job of turning out quality fabric. The owner of the cloth weaving company argued that he was indebted to me for helping him successfully compete with other textile companies across Russia. I don't feel that he owes me a thing as that his company purchased my threads at a fair price.

Besides adding to the economy monetarily, I am able to provide jobs for twenty local men and women. Of course, the women are natural operators of the spinning wheels and the spinning machines. Men have kept the machinery operational and they carried the fibers to the spinning wheels and machines. Once the fibers have been spun into yarns or thread, the men would take the finished products to the area for boxing and for shipment. In order to produce a large quantity of fabric, cloth mills often purchased a hundred or more spools of one color of thread; this frequently resulted in thousands of spools of thread, in various shades, to be shipped to one textile mill.

By 1842, the spinning business was so successful that I had accumulated enough money to purchase property from a landed Russian estate owner. The 175—acres have enabled me to increase the number of acres used for growing cotton and flax in the region. Hussenbach families usually have no more than a dozen sheep at one time on their farms. However, the additional acreage enabled me to maintain several dozen sheep at any given time. The extra sheep has meant more wool for my spinning operation.

On the 175—acre property, I had a new home and several outbuildings constructed. With operating a business, and building a new home, I have been extremely busy but, have felt very lonely. I am surrounded by my parents, siblings and other members of my family but, at times, I still felt somewhat empty, alone and sensed that something was missing from my life. This loneliness occurs mainly in the evening hours. One day my Mother mentioned to me that she saw Emma Zinn at the general store the other day. Emma and I had gone through school together but I hadn't seen her in for many years.

"I wonder what she has been doing." I thoughtfully said.

"Well," Mom began "she told me that she had been teaching school over in Frank. But she missed her family so decided to return home."

"So, what is she doing here?"

"In the fall she will be teaching school here in Hussenbach's lower school."

"Hmmmm…." Was all that I could get out of my mouth before Mom continued telling me that "She asked about you. She is staying with her family. Go over and call on her."

"Mom, I don't know that I can do that."

"Yes, you can."

Through Mom's prompting over the next two weeks I finally called on Emma. At first, Emma and I were a bit shy around each other but it did not take long for us to feel extremely comfortable when we were together; we both knew that we had fallen in love. Christmas Eve of 1843, I proposed to Emma and we were married by the end of the following summer. I enjoyed having Emma's companionship whenever we were together. During the early days of our marriage, Emma established a large garden. She planted and grew the normal garden staples of carrots, beans, peas, squash and onions. She decided to try garlic, a crop that was relatively new to the region. If she was successful with this crop, Emma would plant more the following year. She found that garlic added a nice flavor to many of the dishes she prepared.

A year into our marriage, Emma approached me and said "You know that your Mom makes the best fruit pies in the region."

Wondering where the conversation was going, I replied "I agree."

"Do you think that we might plant some fruit trees on our property?"

Picking up my cup of tea, I looked over at Emma. "I could talk to Dad about getting a few fruit trees. How many would you like and what kinds of fruit trees should we get?"

With a twinkle in her eye she said "Definitely apple, and whatever else we could get."

"Okay, I will meet Dad this week and look at what we can do."

About two dozen saplings were obtained and planted well before the first freeze. Of course, it would take many years for the trees to mature enough to produce fruit. I knew that when the trees do produce fruit, our family would have a wonderful time picking the ripe produce together.

After some prompting from Emma, I finally found some time to build a chicken coop to house a couple dozen chickens. The eggs collected were more than what we could consume so Emma was able to sell some to the town's general store. The egg money was used to purchase material for her lovely quilts. Emma's Mom, my Mom and Emma became very close over various quilting projects. One day, as the three were making a wedding quilt together, Emma shyly asked how one knew that a baby was expected. Mom eyes glowed, Emma's Mom smiled and the three discussed all that was involved when expecting a baby. Six and a half months later, I returned home from work one afternoon to find Emma in pain. She looked at me through her labored breathing and asked that I go get her Mom and my Mother. As quickly as possible I found my Mom and sent her to my home. I then went to retrieve her Mom and then returned to assist Emma.

Mom quickly asked for "some clean towels and warm water, please." After I providing Mom with what she asked for, she proceeded to send me off to take care of the animals, to get my Dad, to get a meal, or to do any number of chores. I came to the realization that Mom was attempting to keep me busy while Emma labored. Finally, Emma presented me with our first son. I marveled at how tiny Christian was but more importantly, I thought about how Christian was the fourth generation of Funk's to live in Russia. Six years later Emma and I were blessed with a second son; the child was named George after my father. Another three years passed before we were blessed with a third son whom we named Adam.

Christian was unsure what to make of either of his brothers when they were babies. He stated that all they did was cry, sleep, eat and consume his mother's attention. Emma pointed out to Christian that his brothers looked up to him, especially George. George would benefit from spending time with him.

"But what could we do together?"

"Well, you could teach George how to tend the farm animals. You could begin by having him join you in feeding the chickens and pigs." And so, the mentoring began....eventually it developed into a friendship. As Adam grew, he was included in the mentoring process by both Christian and George.

Christian enjoyed spending time with his brothers but he took pleasure in the time that he spent in school. He found that he especially enjoyed math which played a large part in his father's business. Payroll, payments for suppliers, shipping costs, and payments received all involved facts and figures. When I first started my business, I was able to handle the bookkeeping myself. However, as my business grew, I had to hire a full—time bookkeeper. When Christian finished his formal schooling, I brought him into the business to work as the bookkeeper's assistant. The idea was to have Christian eventually take over as bookkeeper as the current bookkeeper wanted to start a new chapter in his life. This new chapter might be called retirement. He wanted to spend time with his wife, children and grand-children. I decided that I would provide the bookkeeper with a sum of money as a job well done bonus when he finally stopped working.

By 1864, eighteen-year-old Christian became my company bookkeeper. Knowing that Christian would be thinking of starting his own family one day, I was able to purchase fifty acres of land that bordered my property for him. I sent word out through the family grapevine that I would need assistance in building Christian a small two-story house. Two small bed-rooms would take up the second—story while one large room made up the first floor.

Consulting Christian regarding an outbuilding, it was decided to build a medium sized outbuilding that would be large enough for a couple horses, some milking cows, for storing hay in a loft area and for storage of the farm machinery. A wall was put up to separate the machinery from the livestock. A few days before the house and outbuilding was complete, I started a fire in our pit that we had dug for pig roasts; a pig was prepared for cooking and the slow roasting began. Lydia turned and basted the pig to slowly cook the meat. The side dishes would be prepared closer to the time that the pig would be finished. The house and the outbuilding were finished just as the pig was finished roasting, those assisting us gathered on my property to partake of the feast. Over the next few weeks, Christian and I worked at building enough furniture for the small but adequate home.

Christian

One day in early autumn of 1865, I stopped at the school to ask George and Adam if they wished for a ride home. Sitting in the wagon, I waited patiently for school to end. After a short period, I saw a beautiful young woman open the doors to the lower school. I knew that the young lady had to be the new teacher, Abigail Zinn. Running out of the lower school, Adam saw me. He rapidly approached me and climbed into the wagon. George exited the upper school and saw Adam and me waiting for him. Once George climbed into the wagon, I asked "What are you two doing?"

"We climbed abroad the wagon for a ride home is what we are doing." Both of my brothers said at the same time with smiles on their faces.

Casually conversing, I asked Adam and George the name of the young woman standing just outside the school door. Looking somewhat strangely at me, Adam said that her name was Miss Zinn.

Looking at Adam I asked "Is she related to mother."

"I don't know."

Overhearing part of the conversation, George began to tease me about my sudden interest in the new teacher. The teasing continued all the way home. Finally arriving at the family homestead, the three of us climbed down and my brothers ran inside while I unhitched Dad's horses. Taking the horses into the barn, I placed them in their stalls, rubbed them down and provided them with some food and water. Going into the house, I made some small talk with Mom before I inquired about the new teacher and whether she was related to the family.

"Yes, distantly; her great, great, great grandparents are my great, great grandparents. In case you are wondering, her name is Abigail."

"I do not remember ever seeing her before."

"Her family moved to a village south of here about twenty—five years ago. As the years have passed, her family returned to Hussenbach less and less until they finally stopped coming about fifteen years ago. She should be attending church services Sunday; do you wish an introduction?"

"Yes, I think that I would like to meet her. But don't get any ideas mother."

"What kind of ideas are you talking about?"

Rolling my eyes, I asked Mother what she was making for dinner. "The chicken stew is simmering over the fire and the bread is almost ready for baking. Did you want to stay?"

"Yes, I think that I would. Is there anything that I can do for you?"

"Abigail told me that Adam could use some assistance with his math. Could you assist him in understanding it better?"

"I will help him with his chores and then the two of us will tackle his math homework." Seeking out Adam, I assisted him with his chores, then we concentrated on his homework. After the family consumed dinner, I helped Mom clean up prior to heading home.

As usual on Sunday, I attended church services with my family. We sat a few pews ahead of where Abigail was seated, so, I was unable to steal glances at her. Smiling, George and Adam poked me throughout the first portion of the service. Mom told them to stop but it took a stern look from Dad before they stopped. Dad decided that after church he would have to have a serious talk with my brothers about how to behave in God's house.

As in the past, families gathered together around the outside of the church for lunch. About fifteen years before, men from the church built wooden picnic tables and benches for these lunches. Two years ago, Dad, I and a few other men built enough pergolas to form a shaded area around the tables and benches that are scattered around the church property. The pergolas were built with sturdy open lattice work at the top to support vining plants such as honeysuckle. The honeysuckle vines that were planted when the pergolas were built have grown to cover about a third of the lattice. The pergolas look wonderful with just a bit of sun peeking through the lattice.

Dad and I retrieved the family lunch baskets from the wagon while George and Adam started a game of ball with the other boys. Mom had invited Abigail to join the family for lunch earlier in the week; Abigail had gladly accepted the invitation and had brought cheese and homemade bread to contribute to the lunch. Mom introduced Abigail to Dad and myself. As our eyes meet, Abigail and I knew that we had an instant connection. After lunch was finished, people slowly began to head home. I escorted Abigail the short distance to the two—room house where she resided. Abigail and I sat on the porch steps getting to know each other for about half an hour before I returned to the church yard to rejoin the family.

"I think that I will make a pair of rocking chairs for Abigail's front porch," I said to no one in particular. I, then, missed the glance that Mom and Dad exchanged along with their smile. My parents knew that they had witnessed something special that took place between Abigail and myself.

Of course, on the way home, George did his usual amount of teasing me. Having enough of the teasing, I finally asked fifteen—year—old George if he was interested in girls. "Yes, I like girls." He began to think about Christina, a girl he liked. George, then, stopped teasing me.

Adam was unusually quiet on the way home because he was not sure he wanted his older brother courting the new teacher. Adam felt that it was a guarantee that his friends would hassle him about his brother and the teacher. If I married Abigail, Adam knew for sure that his friends would never hear the end of it. Pulling Adam aside when we arrived home, Mom wanted to know what was bothering him.

"Nothing is bothering me, Mom!" he replied.

"Now Adam, I know better than that. You became awfully quiet since George and Christian had words about girls and the new teacher."

"Okay, okay! I am not sure how I feel about Christian courting the new teacher."

"They just officially met today. I would hardly call that courting."

"But they looked at each other the same way that you and dad gaze at each other;" Adam argued "all gooey eyed and weak in the knee kind of look."

Trying not to laugh or crack a smile, Mom replied "I know the kind of look you are talking about. When two people first fall in love, it is hard not to have that look."

Having caught part of the conversation from the other room, Dad decided to join in the conversation. Entering the room, he told Adam that he still felt that way about his mother. "It is hard to understand relationships especially those that involve a man and woman. One day you will meet the right girl and feel the same way as your Mom and I do."

"I think that I understand what you are saying, Dad. There is a girl at school that I sort of like; I think that she likes me too."

"Give it time, Adam! Your awfully young and you will like many girls before the right one comes along. Christian and Abigail just met and it is too soon to say if anything will come of this relationship."

A year later, after I turned twenty—one, I asked Abigail for her hand in marriage. Upon her acceptance of matrimony, the two of us discussed when we would like to get married. After a very short dialog, Abigail and I set the date: October 14. Mom and Dad invited Abigail's parents for a visit in order for the families to meet and to get reacquainted. You could say that they just wanted to get acquainted since it had been a number of years since the Zinn's had moved away. Plus, Dad and Abigail's Dad, Charles, had never meet before. Abigail's parents, Charles and Hannah Zinn, traveled to Hussenbach several weeks later and stayed in the guest cottage that Dad had built several years ago for visiting clients.

Mom, Dad and I got along famously with Charles and Hannah Zinn. Mom and Mrs. Zinn talked about quilting, knitting, gardening and exchanged recipes while Dad and Mr. Zinn discussed farming. While examining the family garden, Mrs. Zinn suggested that Mom try growing parsnips; she explained that parsnips were similar to carrots but with an attitude. Both women laughed at this concept and Mom decided to give parsnips a try next year. Mrs. Zinn told Mom that she would send her some parsnip seeds.

After a short discussion, it was decided that the wedding would take place in Hussenbach since both Abigail and I lived here. Charles and Hannah were at a loss on what to provide us for a wedding present. Since the house had two bedrooms upstairs and a larger room on the main floor, the Zinn's decided to provide money for building an addition to the first floor. The gift was well received by Abigail and myself because we felt that having a slightly larger home would be nice when children, hopefully, began to come. The new addition was completed just a few days prior to the wedding. Abigail and I decided to utilize part of the new addition for our bedroom while leaving a small portion of the addition for a possible future nursery. At this time, the two bedrooms upstairs would be utilized for office space and storage.

Dad and Mom provided us with a matching pair of rocking chairs, just like those they had received years before. The pair of rocking chairs that I had made Abigail for the teacher's cottage were left behind for the next teacher. Mom and several women in the family gathered together to make several exquisite, new quilts for our home. The marriage ceremony was beautiful with many family members and friends in attendance. After the wedding we went home to begin our life together.

Late Summer 1973

During the first part of the 1800's I wondered why some family members, like George and Henry, did not write much in the journals. Was it because they felt that they were too busy? Or maybe they felt there wasn't much to relate in a journal. Could it be that they had forgotten about the journals? Were they reminded of the journals later in life? If so, is that why they wrote a few pages and passed them on to the next generation?

Whatever the reason, it is still nice to read about how the community came together when the church burned and was rebuilt. It was also interesting to learn how Henry had built a business that helped others in the community thrive. For example, farmers were able to sell their cotton, flax and wool without having to pay high transportation costs, and the cloth weaving company was able to profitably compete in the market place. In addition, Henry was able to employ twenty people from Hussenbach and the surrounding area.

Grandma and Grandpa returned to Kansas several weeks ago so I wasn't able to ask her in person about the spinning mill that Henry started; so instead I wrote her a letter. Grandma was as surprised as I was about her Great—Grandfather owning a spinning mill in Russia. Her Father or Grandfather had never mentioned the spinning mill or what life was like back in Russia.

I wondered if when Henry helped his community, he experienced God and found out that it was important to help others whenever possible. I know that when I spend time with the elderly lady that lives across the street, the two of us learn from each other but I learn the most. Besides I enjoy just being with her and hearing about her life.

According to what was written in the journals, I knew that Conrad and a few other family members lived their faith. I wondered if the remaining family members felt the same way about religion as Conrad did or his grandson. From the journals I had found out that my fourth time great uncle Jacob had become a minister roughly a hundred and fifty years ago. Religion is felt differently by different people, even within a family. I guess that is why my uncle William is a minister while Mom does not attend church. I have often wondered what caused my parents to turn their backs on formal religion.

In some church's babies are baptized while in other churches baptism is done when the individual is older. My siblings and I weren't given a choice as we were never baptized and we only went to church on Christmas and Easter. When asked why we did not attend church services on a regular basis, I wasn't given a direct answer so I eventually stopped asking. For quite a while, I have felt that something was missing in my life but I wasn't sure what it was. Reading these journals has made me think that maybe what is missing is not having a journey with God. It is something to think about and explore....

December 1973

Returning to college in late August did not provide me the opportunity to begin the sixth journal until the semester break. Two papers floated out of the sixth journal as I opened it. Picking up the papers, I saw that one was a photograph. Looking at the photograph I wondered who the five men in the picture were. Turning the picture over, I read the back which said that the men were representatives from the Volga River region sent to investigate land in the United States, 1874. Wow, a hundred years ago Germans that were living in the Volga River region decided to explore land in the United States. This had to be because Germans living in Russia were thinking about immigrating once again. If this was true why did my Great—Grandparents wait for another twenty—five years before they moved once again? Did they leave family behind in Russia?

The next item that had fallen out of the journal was a flyer advertising south—western Kansas. Could this item be a major factor in why the Funk's choose Kansas instead of other regions of the United States? It is interesting to see how the railroad advertised a temperate climate, abundant water, and good soil. This seemed awfully familiar to what Russians were saying when they were attempting to recruit migrants in the 1760s. Wondering where the remaining journals were going to take me, I picked up the translation of the sixth journal and began to read about the next period of my family history.

http://www.kshs.org/p/online-exhibits-from-far-away-russia-part-2/ 10680

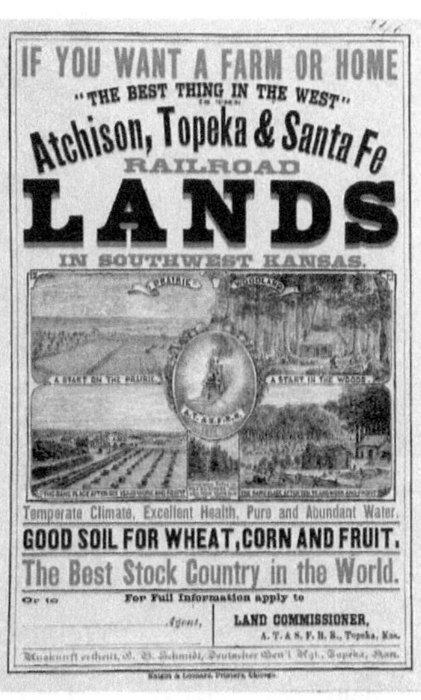

http://www.kshs.org/p/online-exhibits-from-far-away-russia-part-2/10680

Journal Six

Discontent—1870—1875

While love, marriage and life happened to people living in Hussenbach, good relations continued to flourish among the Germans and the majority of the population living in the Volga River region. However, a tension among the Russian nobility, politicians and middle-class intellectuals developed; many referred to this tension as Germanophobia. Germanophobia began as a criticism against German scholars. It was argued that German scholars neglected the Russian language and were publishing articles only in foreign languages while they received a pay check from the Russian government. Furthermore, it was suggested that any Russian citizen, including those of German origin, who did not speak Russian as their main language or follow the Russian Orthodox faith should be considered a foreigner. These feelings were not widespread and the movement quickly died out because of the Imperial family's German roots.

I, Christian, often wondered why this tension seemed to be only with those who had money or were in power. Normal, everyday people could care less that we do not practice the Russian

Orthodox faith or that German scholars publish in any language or whether they publish at all. Around this same time, the Russian government began in earnest to remove any and all of the special privileges that were promised to German emigrants a hundred years ago. There were many Russians that envied the special privileges that Germans were promised. In addition, they resented any economic success that citizens of German descent held.

The government began to treat Germans like Russian peasants. Despite relief programs existing in the various communities, the wealthier Germans were forced to contribute land and supplies for those less fortunate. Many of us do not mind helping others but do not like being forced into doing so. The remaining privileges that Germans were guaranteed began to disappear. In addition, our culture was being eroded away which caused dissatisfaction among the Germans across Russia. Germanophobia, being treated like a peasant, being forced to support those less fortunate, disappearing privileges and erosion of our culture made a large number of Germans consider leaving Russia.

The Franco-Prussian War along with the founding of the German empire in Europe resulted in the Russian government conscripting Germen males into the Russian military. Germans, living in Russia, did not wish to become trapped into fighting a political dispute that we did not support. Many Germans asked each other "Wasn't conscription one of the reasons that we left Germany. Weren't we promised that we would not have to be conscripted into the military?" We had to be reminded that being free of conscription was only for the first ten years. In 1874, Russia made sure that it would be mandatory for all men to serve in the military. I guess that we have been fairly lucky that we have not faced conscription until now: a hundred years after our ancestors had migrated to Russia.

In order to address the various issues that Germans faced while living in Russia during the 1870s, the German community convened a conference. The conference was held in Herzog, Russia in 1874. At twenty-eight years old, I was one of twenty Germans that attended the conference from Hussenbach and the immediate surrounding area. As I traveled to Herzog, I began to question how many Germans had actually moved to Russia a hundred years ago and how many currently lived in Russia. I wondered whether if the number of German's actually living in Russia had grown so large that the Russian government had no other recourse but to officially end any and all of the special privileges that had been granted to us?

Once the conference began and various meetings were held, debate slowly heated up causing several physical fights to break out between attendees. Many of the delegates became uneasy as the debate converted to an angry discussion of Germanophobia. A German delegate from Ukraine argued "that Germanophobia placed a bad light on Germans as a whole. Especially since the majority of German scholars spoke both Russian and German and those individuals published in both the Russian and German languages."

I heard one of the delegates say that "We were given the right to practice our own faith; this has been one privilege that the Russians have not taken away from us. But how long will it be before they take that away from us?"

Another delegate wanted to know "how many Russians have taken the trouble to learn German?" I wondered why this was asked because Germans moved to Russia not the other way around.

"Why does the Russian government feel it necessary to revoke our privileges?" shouted out a third delegate. "Is it to pacify a few Russians who have complained?"

"I have heard," another delegate stated "that our privileges are being revoked because many Russians are jealous of these rights."

"What is ridiculous is that even though many of these special privileges have ended years ago, Russians are still bringing them up."

A delegate sitting on the stage rose, walked over to the podium and asked the commentator if he could speak. After the audience quieted, Johann Pfeifer quietly said "Gentlemen, I did not think that we were here to attack those who criticize us. Russians attacking us do so out of fear. The economic success we have experienced is a credit to the German race and we have worked hard to achieve it. We should put our heads together over the next couple of days and come up with a viable solution and not add to the problem."

Many of the delegates felt ashamed as they had forgotten why we were really there—to lead. So, we began to discuss possible solutions to the problems at hand. Many were ready to leave Russia for good. I wondered whether moving was the right answer to settling our differences with other ethnic groups. We cannot keep 'running' away from the world's problems. My thoughts were interrupted when another delegate stood up near me and pointed out that moving could be an option for us. However, there was no prefect place to live. Plus, the majority of the delegates wanted more information prior to making a decision regarding moving.

Many Germans remembered being told by their ancestors that Russians had been promised that the Volga River region had abundant crops growing in the fertile soil. But no crops were growing in the region and the soil lacked humus. We have heard rumors that the great plains of the United States were looking for immigrants. Apparently, the plains of the United States were largely uninhabited and consisted mainly of grass lands. This was not that much different than in the Volga River region of the 1770s. I began to wonder whether the American were promising the same things the Russians promised a hundred years ago. The Russians promised no taxes for a period, religious freedom, no conscription and more land to farm then what we had access to in Germany.

Before making a decision on whether to move once again or not, the conference delegates decided to send a few representatives to the United States to investigate the land and conditions in Nebraska, Kansas and Arkansas. I am sure that like what happened in the 1770s, many will move to a new land while others would stay behind.. Johann Pfeifer was chosen as the leader of the five representatives being sent to investigate the land opportunities and conditions in the United States in the mid—1870s. One of my distant cousins, William Funk, was selected to travel with the group investigating Kansas.

Spring 1974

Picking up and looking at the picture enclosed in the journal again, I wondered which of the five men was William Funk, my distant relative. I cannot believe that a relative would be traveling with the group exploring the United States and, more importantly, the mid—western states. With what he and the other four men told the Russian—Germans about the United States would cause many to leave Russia.

The five men convened to plan their strategy for the trip to the mid—western region of United States. The men traveled Russia's waterways north—northwestward to St. Petersburg. From there the men booked passage on a ship that was heading for Hamburg, Germany. This was the first time that many of the Germans had the opportunity to visit their homeland. The men were surprised to hear a difference in how their language was spoken. As the five men did some traveling in and around Germany, they heard many different dialects. Sometimes it took as moment or two to fully understand what was being said. Those individuals living in Germany also had to listen carefully to fully understand the German spoken by those Germans that came from Russia. The five men began to realize that living in Russia for roughly a hundred years had affected how they spoke German. They also observed that the German culture was slightly different here than what was practiced in Russia. Obviously, Russia's culture had impacted the culture of the Germans living in Russia over the past hundred years. The entire group could not wait to relate what they had learned when they returned to Russia.

After a week in Germany, the group boarded a ship that would take them to the United States but would first make a stop in Southampton, England. After picking up additional passengers in England, the vessel began the next leg of the journey to the United States. Arriving in New York City the representatives traveled southward to the nation's capital to talk to governmental officials regarding settlement in the Midwest. Afterwards the group traveled westward to explore Kansas, Nebraska and Arkansas.

Once in the mid—west they found that the land was somewhat flatter than what we had in Hussenbach. The five men noted that there was enough rivers and streams to provide needed water for livestock and for growing crops. The men observed that western Kansas and western Nebraska seemed to be somewhat drier and flatter than the land in eastern parts of those states or in Arkansas. The group saw that there was a lot of land not being cultivated in western Kansas which was not much different than what the Germans experienced in Russia roughly a hundred years ago.

America's population had religious freedom and were not expected to be part of singular faith; this was very important to us. The representatives observed some prejudice toward other ethnic groups which was no different than what was occurring in the Hussenbach and other parts of Russia. The main difference seemed to be that in America there were many ethnic groups so no one group appeared to get the brunt of the harassment. The group visited various communities and farms across the mid-west. The men liked that the land was similar to the land of the Volga River region. The five men talked to the two railroads that were being built through the state of Kansas. They found that all three states would be good for emigration, but the group of five men favored Kansas.

Arriving back in Russia, the five men went back to Herzog in order to inform the Russian—Germans about their trip to America. For those Germans who were not able to return to Herzog to hear about the findings, the five men spent time traveling to select German communities throughout the Volga River region. There the Russian—Germans heard about Germany and the United States.

Back in Hussenbach, William Funk set up a town meeting to discuss America and the possibility of emigration. The meeting was held at the school on the first Saturday afternoon after William's return. The building was packed because a high percentage of the region's population were thinking of emigrating. William began the meeting by telling the community about his experience in Germany. The people were amazed that there were many different dialects of their spoken language. Those of us living in Russia do not notice the difference in our spoken language. Could it be because we, as Germans, have not moved around much across the region? Maybe pastors notice the slight differences in the spoken language since they travel the most while working their various churches.

Traditional German costumes had not changed over the years which made the people smile. However, William pointed out that the culture in Germany had changed, maybe slightly but changed, and was somewhat different then what we have experienced in Russia. William pointed out that just like here in Russia, German agriculture had also changed over the past hundred years due to mechanization which made farming easier. William stated that changes in culture is similar to how mechanization changed farming which altered our lives. Heads nodded in understanding this metaphor.

Discussion then began on what it was like in the United States. William told the group about how the United States government official stated that the constitution guaranteed religious freedom for all those living in America. Furthermore, he stated that money was all that was needed to obtain farm land. The delegates pointed out that in some cases the government opened up lands in the western part of the nation for settlement. When this occurred, men could claim up to 640 acres at no cost. However, people were required to live on and farm the claimed land for seven years before it would officially become theirs.

A member of the crowd asked if all land in the western part of America was free for the picking. "No," replied William, "this is just in areas where there are not as many people living and in areas that the government wished to populate. This is not much different than what our ancestors experienced here in Russia a hundred years ago."

"Free land just for living there and working it! This can't be true! Russia provided us land but we could not sell it because" interjected a voice from the back, "we do not own it."

"So, what proof do we have that the land will be ours?" another skeptical voice asked.

"All that I can tell you is that in traveling to the mid—western portion of the United States we were able to talk to the people freely. We were able to visit farms where we met people living their dream of land ownership. We were reassured that they obtained their 640—acre farm by living and farming the land for seven years. Correct me if I am wrong but, I think that a 640—acre farm in America is eight times larger then what we received a hundred years ago and is no larger today than what is was then. Let me reiterate that not all of the acreage in the region is free for the taking; a lot of the acreage is for sale by the owner and at reasonable rates."

Bedlam seemed to break out across the room. Many of the Germans were ready to move to America just on the land issue alone. I stepped to the front of the room to bring calm back to the meeting. "Remember," I began, "this sounds great but we have to have money for land in some locations, building a home, outbuildings and farm machinery. I am not saying that we cannot do this but just think about the big picture before jumping on the band wagon and leaving for the United States."

Stepping to the front, Dad asked the groups if they "had forgotten that if we leave, we will have to pay the Russian government ten percent of our wealth?" This ten percent 'tax' was implemented to discourage the population from moving and to reimburse the government for the use of the land, years of no taxes and many of the other incentives. Not everyone had remembered this point and some had conveniently chosen not to recall it. Quick calculations were done in the heads of many regarding what this could cost them. Would the cost outweigh the benefits? If the answer was no, a move would take place; if the answer was yes, the people would remain in Russia.

Thinking about what William was telling the group, many of the region's population contemplated the idea of moving to a foreign country. This could be frightening as none of us have moved even a short distance let alone half way around the world. This caused me to contemplate what our Great—Grandparents or, in some cases our Grandparents, could tell us about moving such a distance!

One thing on the minds of many was where would this opportunity take us? Others wondered whether if they would take the chance for a better life or would they stay where they knew that life would not change dramatically in the near future? In addition, we must consider the extended family. Most Germans came from close families and they desired to stay together. So, the question was should we move as a family or stay in the region? There was a lot to consider.

While contemplating whether to move or not, a voice in the crowd asked what else William had learned during his trip to America. William told the group about how a railroad was built during the 1860s and it cut through the state of Kansas. "Just think about what this could do for us as farmers?" William added that "After harvesting our crops they could be shipped by rail to markets in larger cities both to the east and further west. In the eastern portion of the United States, they were passing out a flyer regarding this new railroad. We brought back a hundred flyers apiece to share with everyone interested. Could I get some help in passing the flyers out?" William allowed about ten minutes for the flyers to be passed around and then another ten minutes for everyone to digest the information on the flyer.

Stepping up to the podium once again, William preceded to tell the crowd about the railroads. In order to afford the cost of building rail—lines the government granted some land.. They were given ten miles on each side of their rail lines. To encourage the growth of towns along the rail—lines, the railroads advertised that land for churches and schools would be provided at no cost. By 1872, both the *Kansas Pacific* and the *Atchison, Topeka & Santa Fe* railroads began land along their railways began to be sold off. Roughly every fifty miles, towns began to spring up along the railroad lines across Kansas, Nebraska and Arkansas. These new towns were built to accommodate cattle ranchers that were attempting to get their cattle to market. Ranchers drove their herds into Kansas from as far south as Texas.

William pointed out that "just like in Russia, people were moving to newly established towns to open blacksmith shops, shoemaker shops and general stores. Larger parcels of land enticed many Americans to move further west to farm full time." Furthermore, William said that "the railroad people told us that flyers were printed by the *Kansas Pacific* and *Atchison, Topeka & Santa Fe* railroads in many languages, including the ones in German that were just passed out. The company sent the flyers with agents to Europe and Russia to entice immigration to the great plains of America. About a year ago, Mr. Schmidt, an employee of the *Atchison, Topeka & Santa Fe* railroad, had traveled to Russia in order to recruit immigrants from among the Russian-Germans." William paused and then casually said "Did any of you ever talk to a Mr. Schmidt about moving to America? At our 1874 conference nothing was said about any representative from America being in the country to talk about immigration."

Bedlam reigned once again! When Dad and William quieted the crowd down Dad argued that "it sounds as if the government would not allow foreigners into Russia to solicit immigration. Think about it for a moment; would you wish to lose a large portion of your citizens to another country? And more importantly, would you wish to lose a portion of your citizenry that is very productive? Remember, many Russians resent the economic success that numerous Germans enjoy."

A voice from the crowd said loudly "You are correct in your thinking. But also remember that many countries across Europe banned Russian representatives soliciting for immigrants a hundred years ago! Well, its history repeating itself."

A loud cheer rose from the crowd; it took a while for control to be gained once again. William pointed out that the Kansas railroads were anxious to sell land to farmers. Land sale meant profit for the railroad, even after subtracting the cost of building the rail lines. Further profit was made by charging for shipping of grain, cattle or other merchandize on their lines. The newly constructed railroads lured immigrants to make the move by offering free sleeping cars on express trains leaving Kansas City for the farm lands to the west.

There were many in the room who wondered about the sleeper cars. What distance would justify providing immigrants with sleeper car accommodations aboard a train: two hundred miles, two hundred and fifty miles, three hundred miles? I wondered if it was just a tactic to entice immigrants to America to buy their land and use the railroad to ship their merchandize to other parts of the United States. Another question that came to my mind was what is an express train? How often would it stop to let off people? What good was an express train if it did not stop until California. Another thing that many questioned was the fact that 'some farmers' would be supplied with wheat seed for their first crop in Kansas. Could they define who 'some farmers' were and how it was decided who would receive the seed? William could not provide a good answer regarding why some would receive the free seed while others would not.

William's brother, Johann, stood and asked "Would you migrate to this region after what you learned and saw?"

"Without any hesitation, I would move tomorrow if I could! More land means more crops to sell and the land would be mine, not the governments. Yes, there is hate in the world and it is everywhere, even in Kansas. During my journey to the United States, I experienced individuals turning away Irish immigrants, just because they were Irish. It is a matter of what you do when faced with hatred that is vitally important. I chose to stand up against it and to make the world a better place."

Instantly there was a standing ovation for William! Blushing, William attempted to obtain order once again. He continued by stating that "it was now up to each individual and family to decide whether to relocate or to stay in Russia. Having talked to immigrants in Kansas and Nebraska I learned that often a few members of a family would migrate and settle into the new place. A short time after the first group moved, another family cluster would make the move to join the first family unit. The new members would have a place to stay while looking for and obtaining their own property. This migration would continue until everyone in a family who wished to move had done so. They call this principle 'chain migration'. This type of migration often results in ethnic groups being concentrated in certain areas across America."

The meeting ended with almost the whole community exploring the idea of moving. Not everybody was interested in moving but they were interested in the information provided by William Funk. Others thought that if they emigrated in smaller groups instead of all at once could it be easier to leave Russia! Maybe.....we'll see!

Early June 1974

It was interesting to read about how disappearing privileges caused Russia's German population to seriously discuss migrating elsewhere. Of the five individuals sent to explore part of the United States one was a distant relative: William Funk. On the word of William, many people felt that both owning land and more of it would be worth the move. I wondered why my Great—Grandparents had waited for another twenty—five years to leave for the United States? Was it fear of the unknown that caused the family to wait? Or was there an underlying issue that had kept them in Russia before finally leaving?

Picking up and leafing through the next journal, a map and two pictures fluttered out of the volume and onto my lap. Examining the map, I located Lane County where my Grandparents currently live. The back of the map stated that the counties bordered in black and shaded in pink and blue were where the Russian—Germans settled in Kansas. I noted that Rush and Ellis Counties, shaded in pink, were just a few counties east and a bit south of where my Grandparents lived in Lane County. So, if the family moved to these counties then Grandma did not move far from where she grew up. Interesting.....

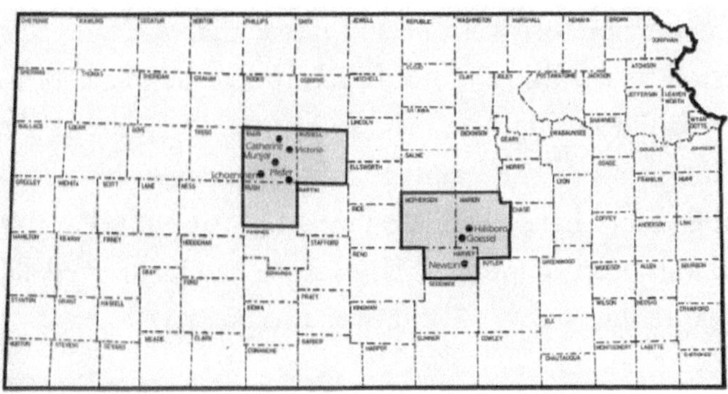

http://www.kshs.org/p/online-exhibits-
from-far-away-russia-part-1/15648

I then looked at the two pictures that had fluttered out of the journal. The first picture was of some sort of housing. Flipping it over to the back side, I noticed that it stated that it was of picture of some temporary housing located in central Kansas. I wonder if this means that many of the Russian—Germans lived in this type of building prior to buying, building and settling on their own property.

http://www.kshs.org/p/online-exhits-from-
far-away-russia-part-3/10681

The next picture was of a sod house that was located near LaCrosse Kansas. The sod house reminded me of a sod house that is located in Dighton. The sod house in Dighton always made me think of the Laura Ingalls Wilder's series of books. Over the years I have speculated on who had built it and lived in it. Had it been abandoned? If so, how had it survived all the years before the county took it over and preserved it?

http://specialcollections.wichita.edu/collections/
ms/95-20/sh-La_Crosse1.JPG

The Sod House in the picture looked like it was starting to fall apart. Did Rush County attempt to preserve the house? Or has it fallen into disrepair and finally collapsed? Why was this picture located within the journal? Had my ancestors lived in this house? Or was it just for an example of a sod house? Hopefully, the journal might answer my questions. I look forward to learning more about the family's history and the history of Kansas through the journals…..

Journal Seven

Kansas immigration begins—1876—1880

Thousands of Germans left Russia for America's mid—west during the mid to late 1870s. I have heard that some Germans first traveled eastward to Manchuria before heading southward across the China Sea. The vessel would hug the coast line as the journey took them around Asia and the Middle East. They would then travel westward across the Mediterranean Sea before making a turn northward towards England. Traveling by boast around Asia, through the Middle East and around Europe just seemed to be such a long, drawn out journey. The journey that sounded the best bet for me is the one where migrants traveled towards St Petersburg where they would board a ship. The ship would take the migrants across the Baltic and North Seas before making a stop in England. In England, the migrants would board a steamship for America.

After William Funk's 1875 presentation, a group of Volga River Germans, including several family members from the Funk clan, left Hussenbach to begin a new life. We received many letters from family members after they had arrived and established themselves in the United States. The letters informed us about the Germans being encouraged by the *Kansas Pacific Railroad* to settle on land in central and western Kansas. Some migrants settled in Nebraska because they thought that Nebraska had better land for a lower price while others decided to settle in Kansas.

The letters also educated us regarding how some Americans viewed Russian—German immigrants as being distinctive from other immigrants moving to Kansas because we migrated together in large groups and settled whole, entire areas. There is a grain of truth to what is being said. However, we, as Germans, like the support of family so it is natural for us to move together and to live close together. In Russia, we were encouraged to live in German settlements where our language was spoken and customs practiced. We wondered why it should it be any different in America.

Many of the Germans having left Russia began settling in central Kansas. As part of this migration, members of our family began settling in Rush County. Dad, Mom, George, Adam and I remained behind in Russia in order to see how the migration went. As more of the population left Hussenbach for the United States, there were fewer buyers for Dad's business which meant there were fewer, lower offers. Dad desired to get as much as possible for his business because we would have to pay the Russian government ten percent of our proceeds. We will just wait to see how things go.

Three years later, in April of 1878, Abigail and I continue to live and farm the same acreage that the family has lived and farmed on for over the past hundred years. Continuing to work as Dad's bookkeeper, I assist Dad whenever possible in farming his land. During this time of uncertainty, Abigail concentrated on the home, growing a garden, raising the two children and making quilts. She has become a master quilter and she has won prizes for her quilt designs. People have traveled from miles around to purchase her quilts; she even has had a few customers from as far away as Moscow, Kiev and St. Petersburg. Customers traveling to Abigail for a quilt would be taken to a fabric shop to select and purchase the needed fabrics for the quilt. They then would go to the Mr. Schneider's factory to obtain batting. The final payment for the quilt would be collected when the quilt was completed and picked up.

Abigail has more business than she can handle along with her regular chores of baking, laundry, cooking and taking care of the two children. One day I suggested that Abigail officially open her own quilting business in town. She could hire women to help her with the piecing process and in the quilting. Fabric and threads could be stocked for easy selection for her customers.

"I don't know Christian." Abigail began "I am used to making my quilts here at home. If I had a shop, I would have to be in town daily which would take me away from the children. I still have my regular chores to do."

"If you would prefer it could be a fabric shop for quilters. As I mentioned before, several women could be hired to assist you in the store. That way you would not have to be there all the time. You could continue quilting for others but would have a place for customers to come, pick out the fabrics and a quilt design. Mr. Schneider would probably give you a reduced rate if you referred quilters to him for the batting."

"I love the idea of a shop to encourage quilters, Christian. It is time that this town had a quilting shop. But I have one question for you; I thought that we were immigrating to the place called Kansas in the United States? If we are, why would we open a quilting shop?"

"We will be immigrating, just remember that we have not decided exactly when we will be moving. And we could use the extra money that the shop could provide us for the move."

"Okay, let's try the shop."

During the next few days, I looked for and found a small store front in which I thought was perfect for us to open a shop for quilters. The next morning, we left the children with my Mom so Abigail and I could go to town to view the building prior to renting it. Abigail thought that it was a perfect size and it had a storage area in back to hold extra stock or to possibly hold classes.

"We will need shelving installed to hold the bolts of fabric preferably in a vertical direction. That way it will be easier to pull a fabric bolt for cutting."

"This could easily be done. How would you like to store and display the threads?"

"With the threads lying down, customers would be able to get a better view of the thread's color. However, it would take more room than if the spools were standing."

Thinking for a moment, Abigail said that "Quilters do not need an industrial size spool of thread like what is produced for cloth weaving. It would be nice if the thread used for quilting was a little thicker and on a smaller spool. Is it possible for your father's spinning mill to produce a smaller spool of thread that is slightly thicker?"

"A smaller spool can be designed and the machines can be adjusted to handle the smaller spools. Also, I will see what can be done about making a thicker thread tomorrow morning. What else will you need to set up shop?"

"We will need a long, wide table in which to lay out fabric for cutting. It would be nice to have a form of a measuring stick adhered to the table. It should be a thirty—six inches long with the inches showing. Sometimes quilters need a half or quarter yard of fabric so we need to know exactly how much we are cutting."

"I am sure that my cousin, Charles who is operating a carpentry shop in town, would be happy for the business. In addition to the shelves, I think that the quilt business could use a table to hold a cash register. Also, it would be nice to have a stool for the clerk to sit on when there are no customers in the shop."

Abigail quietly replied that she thought it was an excellent thought. Abigail and I went home to have lunch with Mom and the children. After lunch I stopped at the spinning mill to let Dad know that I would return to work after I went to lease the building for the quilt shop. I had a moment of hesitation regarding getting into another business when we knew that we would be leaving the country. However, I knew that opening the business would ease the mind of those in the Russian government regarding additional Germans leaving the country. Besides, we cannot live our lives saying we cannot do this or that because we might do something else. We might decide to leave Russia next year or it could be in ten years. So, we have to live for today.

The next morning, I went to *Funk's Carpentry Shop* and was greeted warmly by Charles. "Long time no see, Christian! What's new?"

"I came to see you today regarding a building that is between the grocers and the savings and loan."

"That property just came on the market, didn't it?"

"Yes, and as of yesterday afternoon, I rented it,"

"Wow! What are your plans for it?"

"That is why I came to speak with you this afternoon. Abigail and I are going to open a shop. This building is a perfect location and size. The plan is to bring together fabric and thread for quilters. Where we need your assistance is in building custom shelving to hold bolts of cloth. We also need a custom table that has thirty—six inches carved in one edge for cutting of material. In addition, we need an L shaped table to hold a cash register, miscellaneous materials and have two or three under the counter shelves. We will need one chair for behind the counter along with three or four rocking chairs to be placed strategically around the shop. I will be working with Dad's shop regarding smaller spools of thread. When I get this worked out, we will need some type of special shelving made. Have I overwhelmed you yet?"

"No! But there is a lot to digest. Let me get a pad of paper and pencil. I will tell David that I will be gone for an hour or so and where I will be in case he needs me. I will need to measure inside the shop for the custom shelving units, the cutting table and the L shaped table. Chairs are standard height unless you want a very high stool for behind the counter."

"The table for the register should be high enough for a standing person to work comfortably. Staff will be sitting when there are no customers needing assistance so a medium height stool should work nicely." I replied after a moment of thought. Arriving at the building, Charles and I examined the space. Charles made some suggestions about placing shelves along the walls in addition to having several shorter shelves perpendicular to the wall shelves. The perpendicular shelves could be four feet in height while the shelves along the wall would work well at five feet tall.

On his pad of paper, Charles sketched out a rough drawing what the shop could look like. In the sketch, Charles placed the L table with stool near the shop's front door. A seventy—five inch by fifty inch cutting table could be placed in the middle of the shop; that way there would be enough space for the staff to maneuver around with bolts of cloth. Rocking chairs could be placed within the shop and moved around as needed. I loved the idea but wanted to consult Abigail since she understood the quilter's mindset better than I do and it was really her shop. Charles agreed to meet with me after I discussed his plan with Abigail. Within three days I told Charles that Abigail liked his ideas so the renovation began.

Within days of the renovation beginning, Abigail and I approached David Schneider regarding the cotton batting. Schneider was receptive to the idea about providing a discount on any batting she purchased for her use if she referred customers to him. Leaving the batting shop, Abigail and I drove the wagon over to a textile mill to see what kind of deal they could make regarding a large number of bolts of fabric, in various shades and patterns of course.

Within four months, Charles had built and installed the needed shelves, tables, stool and rocking chairs for our newly established quilt shop. The last item to be built was the thread cabinet as we wished to have a custom fit for the thread spools Dad's spinning company was able to produce. Once completed, the thread cabinet was filled with threads in multiple colors. The textile mill was able to produce about sixty—five percent of the cloth needed to operate the shop. The remaining colors were delivered to the shop in about two weeks.

The only thing left to handle was the hiring of three or four women who desired to work part—time. Hiring female help could be difficult because women had small children at home. It was easier to hire someone to work in the shop if a family's children were grown or if the children attended school during the day. This enabled the mother to work while the children were in school. Abigail understood this better than most business owners because both Jacob and Allison were under the age of six; both children were not in school yet. Abigail did not need to be in the shop all the time so she approached my Mom about watching Jacob and Allison from time—to—time. Mom agreed to watch the children whenever she was needed. Afterall both Allison and Jacob were old enough to assist her in the garden, with the chickens, gathering eggs or any number of other chores.

With selecting help for the shop, Abigail desired to hire women who were quilters. Quilting experience aided in figuring out the correct yardage that women needed for the back of a quilt or how much of a certain fabric would be needed for the flying geese pattern or any other pattern. Abigail was able to locate and hire two women who were quilters with different skill levels; Each woman was able to work twenty hours a week. An additional experienced quilter was hired to work thirty hours a week.

Abigail's quilt shop was an immediate success with Hussenbach's women. They appreciated that the shop provided a better selection of fabrics than the general store. Plus, the shop provided advice and in general, was the only place that women could gather to just sit and visit. An additional half dozen rocking chairs were purchased and placed in and around the store. Many women inquired about when Abigail might begin offering quilting classes. Abigail considered this request and thought that the shop would need additional space. The owners of the building agreed to add a room on to the back. The new room was a bit larger than either of the older rooms so it became the shops classroom.

Correspondence between the family in Kansas and those of us still living in Hussenbach flourished. These letters informed us about conditions and how the family was doing in Kansas. Early on the most popular topic included in the letters was the condition of the prairie. The letters informed us that the Kansas prairie was largely a grass land that had never been plowed up before. Hmmm....preparing this type of land for agriculture could be tough for farmers.

The letters also informed us of a grasshopper infestation that the family experienced the previous year. The family never elaborated about the grasshoppers so we don't know how big a problem the infestation was. I attempted to speculate on how much of the family's crops were actually destroyed due to the plague but found that it was impossible to figure out. I guess that I will have to wait until we make the move to America and ask the family then.

Relatives informed us that the early Russian-German homes on the Kansas prairies were often clustered together to form a village or town. This isn't much different than what happened here in the Volga River region. Letters further informed us that in Kansas, temporary structures were utilized until the settlers were able to construct and move into standard frame houses on newly acquired land. These temporary dwellings were later abandoned or used as storage buildings. Several families, settling in Kansas, constructed their first family homes out of sod. Sod houses have thick walls that made the home cool in summer and warm in winter. Eventually those living in sod houses would go on to build traditional homes that were made out of wood or brick.

Mid—Summer 1974

Now I understood that the large rectangular and triangular shaped buildings were used as temporary housing for the Germans in Kansas. Being new to the area and not having family or friends to stay with during the latter part of the 1870's and into the 1880's meant that many of those moving into the region needed temporary shelters. The sod houses provided the settlers with a home until a traditional house could be constructed. I am still not sure whether the picture of the sod house was a home where some of the family lived or to show what this type of house looked like.

I was surprised to learn about a quilt / fabric shop that the family started and operated in Russia during the last quarter of the nineteenth century. In an earlier journal, I had learned how my Great—Great—Grandfather had built a spinning mill that helped not only the family but also aided Hussenbach to thrive. I wonder if the quilt shop helped the community as well.

Did Grandma know of the new family businesses prior to reading and translating the journals? That very afternoon I wrote Grandma a letter asking her about the businesses. Within two weeks I received a reply:

> *Dear Dani,*
>
> *However, I can say that prior to reading and translating the journals I did not know that my Grandfather was so successful in Hussenbach or about my parents having a quilting shop in Russia.*
>
> *As you read the journals you will find out more about the family's spool and quilting businesses. I don't want to take away any surprise from the remaining journals, so read on!*

I hope that you are enjoying reading about the family. Grandpa and I are looking forward to seeing you at Christmas time.

Love Grandma

Mom, my brother and my two sisters inquired about what was in the journals. I told them that I was learning about Grandma's family. This seemed to satisfy them as they stopped asking. I realized that they were not at all interested in the history of our family; I wondered whether they would ever be interested in learning about our ancestors.

Picking up the next journal, a post card dropped out and landed in my lap. The back of the post card read Immigration station, 1892. I wonder why this post card was tucked into the journal. Did a portion of the Funk family go through New York City / Ellis Island when they immigrated to the United States?

http://en.wikipedia.org/wiki/Ellis_Island

When did Christian's brothers, George and Adam along with their families, migrate to the United States? Could they have sent them the post card? If so, why wasn't there writing on the back? Grandma's mother, father, and siblings came around 1901 so did they pick up the post card? Was the post card with the 1892 picture date still being sold in 1901 or 1902? Hopefully the journals would answer some of the questions running though my mind. In addition, several letters, written in German, fell from the journals. I know that Grandma had translated the letters for me and would be within the journal's translation.

Journal Eight

Immigration
continues—1890—1902

Early in 1891, Dad and Mom had quietly passed away within two weeks of each other. Having worked at the mill for a long time, I stepped forward to handle the day—to—day running of the mill. My oldest two children, Allison and Jacob, assisted me whenever and wherever possible with the mill operations. At the time, Abigail was busy with her shop and our two—year—old son named Philip.

George and Adam, took over the running of our parent's farm with the assistance of their older children. George's wife, Mary, had passed away five years ago due to bad case of influenza. Two years later, George married a second time to another wonderful woman named Mary. He and his second wife had two daughters, named Katherine and Mollie.

Since our parents passed on, George, Adam, and I discussed finally leaving Russia. Around Hussenbach there was talk about possibly forming a group that would travel together to America's mid—west. However, I never heard anything more of this topic, so am not sure if it took place; maybe it was just a rumor. I do know that those deciding to migrate choose to make the move after the first spring thaw of 1892. However, in order for our family to move we would have to dispose of our father's business and the 175—acre parcel of land which we owned outright. Knowing that we would have to pay ten percent of the proceeds to the government, the three of us wanted to get the highest possible price for both the the land and business.

After exploring all possibilities, we finally decided that Adam, George and their families would migrate to America now while my family would stay behind to sell Dad's business and Abigail's quilt shop. We decided to attempt selling our father's acreage and farm equipment first. We told people that with our parents gone their 175—acres were too much for us to handle along with our own acreage and operating the mill. The property sold quickly and the money was split three ways. Since we were disposing of Dad's farm implements, livestock, and household items, George and Adam decided to sell their items from their farms as well; the three of us hoped that the extra items up for sale would not be questioned. The money earned from the sale of livestock and machinery aided Adam and George in paying for their move to America.

George, Adam, Mary, Christina, and their nine children left Hussenbach for America in the summer of 1892. Waiting for the first thaw, allowed the family to travel along the region's waterways north—northwest. Once in St. Petersburg, the family booked passage on a vessel heading for Hamburg. Once in Hamburg, the family purchased third class tickets on a steamship that was heading for New York City Harbor. Third class tickets were often referred to as 'steerage'. George and Adam decided to purchase steerage tickets because they needed as much money as possible to settle in America.

Arriving in New York City harbor Christina sent us a letter that related how steerage conditions was poor and unsanitary. Furthermore, Christina argued that being located near the bottom of the steamship was horrible as steerage quarters were crowded and many of the family members, including Mary, spent a large part of the voyage in their bunks due to seasickness. Everyone in the family survived but many were very weak as they entered New York City Harbor.

The steamship docked at the East River pier to allow the first—class and second—class passengers to leave the ship and pass through customs. Christina's letter told that third—class passengers were transported by ferry from the pier to Ellis Island for inspection. Apparently if the passenger's papers were in order and if they were in good health, the inspection process could last between three to five hours. If the papers were not in order or the people were in ill health the inspection could go on indefinitely and there was a real possibility that they could be sent back to Europe. These inspections took place in the Registry Room (or Great Hall), where doctors would briefly scan every immigrant for obvious physical ailments.

Late Summer of 1974

One of the family members must have picked up the post card of the immigration station on Ellis Island while they were there in 1892. Migrants having to be examined by doctors and then to have their papers scrutinized seemed harsh to me. However, I have heard that officials of the American Government were trying to stop disease and epidemics from entering the country.

I wondered whether there was a problem with illegal immigration in the 1890's. During the 1970s the United States has had a problem with illegal's immigrants. Those people that do come to this country do so for better pay and better working conditions. Many of these illegal immigrants send as much money as possible back to their homeland in help support their families.

Part two of journal eight continued

From Ellis Island, the family had a wonderful view of the Statue of Liberty. A large number of the passengers had heard of the statue back in Europe but were amazed at its height of three—hundred and five—feet. Some passengers wondered whether they would have a chance to be closer to the monument before they departed New York harbor.

The next part of the family's journey was conducted by train. The family was surprised that it took so long to get to their destination. It took another seven to eight days of traveling for the family to arrive in west—central Kansas. This seven to eight—day travel included a thirty—six—hour delay in New York City prior to catching their train to Chicago. The family also experienced short layovers in both Chicago and Kansas City prior to boarding the *Kansas Pacific Railroad.* Adam, George and their families were met by other members of the Funk family at the train depot.

Both Adam and George were able to purchase and settle farms of over five hundred acres apiece. Family members assisted Adam and George in building of homes and outbuildings. Just before Christmas, we received a letter from Christina and Adam.

November 1892

Dear Abigail and Christian,

I am writing to let you know of that we arrived safely in Kansas. As you can tell by the picture of the huge temporary dwellings that is where we stayed until our house was built.

Our third son, named William, was born at the end of October. William was a wonderful surprise especially since Conrad and George are fourteen and fifteen. I am sure that you understand this since Philip came fourteen years after Jacob.

We are going to plant a small fruit orchard but have not decided on which trees to plant. The climate here is a bit warm for apple trees but we think that cherries would do well.

This past summer we grew many of the same crops that have been grown back in Hussenbach. Many varieties of squash that grow well in Hussenbach, grow well here in Kansas. One variety of summer squash that grows well here is called zucchini. Zucchini has grown so well that we cook it in stews, soups, have fried it, and sautéed it with a little oil and garlic. Enough zucchini grew that we even sell some at a local farmer's market. One of our new neighbors gave me a recipe for zucchini bread; it is quite good.

Hope all is well with you in Hussenbach. We miss you all and can't wait to see you.

Love Adam and Christina

Over the years many letters have passed between Kansas and Hussenbach. In 1895 a letter from Mary arrived informing us of a new baby.

February 1895

Dear Abigail and Christian,

We can't believe that it is already 1895 and that we have been in Kansas for more than two years. The family continues to thrive here. It is hard for us to believe that George and Henry are in their twenties now.

In December we added another son to our family; his name is Alexander. Katherine and Mollie are not quite sure what to make of Alexander. They say that all he does is cry, eat, sleep, but most importantly he takes up my time.

How is the family? We miss you terribly and can't wait to see you.

Love George, Mary and family

During this time period, George and Adam were making headway in placing half of their acreage into growing wheat, corn, hay and sorghum. As that there is no common land in order to pasture livestock, farmers have to put a portion of their land into grazing land. Farmers began to fence in some of their acreage that they desired to use for animal grazing. Adam finally was able to plant cherry trees on several acres. The family garden was larger than what they had in Russia plus they added several vegetable varieties that were not available in Hussenbach.

In later letters, Adam and George told stories about the range war that took place across portions of mid—Kansas during the late nineteenth and early twentieth centuries. Cattle ranchers desired an open range so they can drive their herds northward to the railroad. However, farmers are tired of having their crops trampled by herds of cattle being driven northward. At this time, many farmers increased the usage pf barbed wire and stakes to protect their fields and crops. Abigail and I hope that the ranchers and farmers will settle this dispute prior to us moving to Kansas. After reading the letters from George and Adam, I began to wonder whether they were experiencing this range war first hand. I assume so as that they provided us interesting insight to the problem. Maybe they had written us about this problem because nearby neighbors had lost crops due to cattle being driven across their land. I sincerely hope that this 'range war' ends prior to us moving to the region.

Both Abigail and I noticed that the population of Hussenbach was dramatically reduced due to migration that began in 1892. This caused me to worry that maybe Abigail and I made the wrong decision by not moving with George and Adam. However, by 1894, Hussenbach's population has rebounded. Hopefully with this growth in the population Abigail and I will make money when we sell our businesses prior to moving.

In early 1894, I was looking for a mechanic to aid in keeping the spinning machines in working order. We had many men apply for the position but I only interviewed four applicants. Out of the four candidates one, named Daniel Heller, impressed me the most and after some thought I hired him. In the beginning, Daniel kept the machines operating in excellent condition, was pleasant to the other employees and went out of his way to be a good employee.

Early on Daniel set his sights on my daughter, Allison, because, as I found out later, he thought that if he married Allison, he would be set for life and would never have to work again. He tried to con a co-worker, named Friedrich, to introduce him to Allison. Friedrich had seen the lazy, conniving side of Daniel and would not make the introduction. Daniel dug around to see if he could find some dirt on Friedrich in order to blackmail him to make the introduction. However, Daniel found no dirt on Friedrich so he made up some smut in order to intimidate Friedrich. Friedrich still refused to make the introduction and simply told Daniel that he was going to have a discussion with me. At first Daniel panicked but quickly this panic changed to anger and he once again threatened Friedrich. However, Friedrich refused to be bullied.

In the meantime, Daniel had finally caught the eye of Allison; she arranged for someone to introduce them. Once they officially met, they dated occasionally. Before I knew it their casual dating quickly escalated into an official courtship. Daniel asked my permission to marry Allison in September of 1894. With much hesitation before replying, I finally said "Daniel, I need to mull this over before I give you an answer."

Daniel began to worry that his plan could disappear but kept his calm as he replied "I understand, after all she is your only daughter."

Just before Daniel had asked my permission to marry Allison, I had begun to suspect Daniel of causing trouble at work. I noticed that other workers, including Friedrich, tended to stay away from Daniel. In addition, Daniel's work was not getting completed. On several different occasions I attempted to locate Daniel to no avail. After locating Daniel, I would ask him where he had been. Calmly, Daniel would say that he had been working on one of the spinning machines. Often it would be the last machine where I had looked for him so I knew that he was not truthful. Even though I knew it was a falsehood I did not call him on it but filed it with the other fabrications that Daniel attempted to pass as the truth. After a few more incidents of Daniel being missing, I decided to keep a written log of what was taking place in case I needed to let him go. His untruthfulness did make me wonder what else Daniel was lying about and what else he was hiding. But, more importantly, what was he doing if he wasn't working.

I was extremely worried about Allison's future if she continued on with Daniel. A short time later Daniel proposed without my permission and the pair set the date for their wedding: the 15th of January of 1895. Prior to the wedding Abigail and I decided to give the couple fifteen—acres from the 175—acre property that we had inherited. After a small two room house with a loft began to be constructed on the acreage, Daniel loudly argued that the house was way too small. He insisted that the daughter of the spinning mill owner should have a much larger house with more acreage. Angered, I told him that "I was not a '*wealthy*' landowner. If he wanted a larger house on more property then he could do so with his own money." Panicked, Daniel realized that he had stepped over the line; he quickly backed down and apologized. Construction continued on the home and was finished just after the 1st of January.

On the day of the wedding a light snow began to softly fall. I wondered whether the falling snow was a bad omen for Allison and Daniel's marriage; I might never know! But I did know that now that he was married to the boss's daughter, Daniel was spending less and less time at work. One day I stopped at Allison's house in hopes of catching my son—in—law in a lie. When asked where Daniel was, Allison replied "At work, of course. He left at his normal time." Thanking Allison, I left for the mill. At the mill I was told that Daniel had never arrived at work. I wondered where he gotten too but I had an appointment with a new client at the town's hotel so couldn't worry about Daniel for the time being anyway. While at the hotel's front desk, I asked where I might find my client, Mr. Keller. I was told that he was waiting for me in the restaurant. Thanking the clerk, I turned and saw Daniel and a beautiful young woman with their arms intertwined as they headed towards the restaurant. I then proceeded to follow Daniel into the eatery. The pair were seated at an intimate, secluded booth in a far corner. Prior to sitting down Daniel leaned closer and kissed the woman. I walked up to the table where they were seated and quietly stood there. Feeling a presence, Daniel ended the kiss and looked over at me. Horror crossed his face as he realized that his life had quickly changed for the worse. Looking at the young woman, I asked if she would excuse my son—in—law because he and I needed to have a few words. From the look on her face, I could tell she did not know Daniel was married; she jumped up, slapped him face so hard that there was a vivid red hand print across his left check. Before storming away, she yelled loudly "I hope that you rot in Hades! Never, ever contact me again."

Looking at Daniel sternly, I told him that I had a meeting but I expected him to immediately go to the shop, begin work and I would talk to him when I finished my business. About two hours later I returned to the mill and asked one of the workers if he could let Daniel know that I wished to talk to him in my office. A nervous Daniel quickly made his way to my office where I calmly told him to close the door and sit down.

"From what I understand you have left for work the same time as you leave for work each morning. However, you never made it to the mill until after I saw you with that young woman.

Am I correct in thinking that your idea of work is to escort the young women to the restaurant and then back to her room for sex?"

"I think that you misunderstood what you saw this morning. The young woman is my niece."

"Your tongue was down your 'niece's' throat. The relationship with her ends today! Do you understand? If I ever get wind of you being with another woman besides Allison, I will personally run you out of town. From now on you will be here at seven each morning; no later or earlier. In addition, you will work until six each evening; you will leave no earlier or later. I will be checking on you here at work and at home. You're dismissed, now get back to work."

After Daniel fled my office, I sat at my desk trying to calm myself and my heartbeat down. I knew that if I did not do both, I might have a heart attack and die shortly after. Who, then, would protect my wife and more especially Allison. While composing myself, I thought that I would never understand how a man can balance the needs of his wife against the needs of a mistress. Besides, who would want too? I love my wife and do not need anyone else. I do not want to injure her by being with another woman. I don't understand Daniel's need to have a woman or women on the side.

Shortly after Allison and Daniel's marriage, Jacob had begun to court Anna Hemel. Anna was one of the young women that had started working twenty hours a week in Abigail's quilt store. As Abigail's need for additional help increased, Anna went from part—time to full—time. Abigail stated that what made Anna an exemplary worker was that she was versatile! Her instincts on material were impeccable, she never made mistakes cutting material and her favorite thing to do in the shop was to teach classes, especially classes on piecing. Her most beloved quilt block was the log cabin pattern that began in America but somehow had made its way to other countries including Russia. Many women came in to learn how she made this block and how to put them together.

In town, on farm business in late April of 1896, Jacob met Anna for lunch. The two went to the church yard to eat their lunch under one of the churches pergolas. Shyly, Anna asked Jacob how the farm was doing. "The farm is producing better than ever. I plan on planting butternut squash this year."

"Butternut squash is not widely grown in this area, is it?"

"No, but it is grown by a few farmers near Saratov. Dad and I decided to try it here because we need to try different crops. In order to keep the fields producing, the crops need to be rotated."

"I am not sure that I understand what you mean by keeping the field producing."

"Well, if we continuously plant the same crop that depletes the nutrients from the soil it can lose its fertility."

"What you are saying is that a crop that takes one kind of nutrient from the soil it can be replaced the following year by planting a crop that is not similar."

"I cannot believe that you understood that so easily."

"It helps that I grew up on a farm. From what I remember dad would also leave a field fallow every six or seven years, in order for the soil to rest for a season."

"Yes! I think that farmers have been using this method for years. How do you like working at the Mom's quilt shop?"

"I love it. We are planning a sixteenth anniversary celebration beginning next week."

"It is hard to believe that mother's shop has been open for so long. I barely remember when she did not have the shop."

"Which reminds me, I better get back to the shop. Your Mom probably would like to go to lunch."

Jacob escorted Anna back to the quilt shop, he then headed home with his seeds and a new hoe. That evening, Abigail inquired about the long lunch he took with Anna. Jacob smiled at her inquiry but made no reply.

Later that summer I mailed a letter to Christina and Adam that Abigail had written. She couldn't wait to announce the birth of our Allison and Daniel's first child, first grandchild.

Spring 1896

Dear Christina and Adam,

This past spring, Allison and Daniel had their first child, a girl they named Heidi. We are so excited about the baby.

Because of his lack of farming skills, Christian assisted Daniel in planting a medium sized winter garden. We are concerned that Daniel does not seem to be knowledgeable about growing crops, even kitchen garden.

Jacob continues to grow and develop his farming techniques. He is trying new plants to see how they do in our soil. He plans on planting butternut squash next summer. He began courting a young woman named Anna.

Both businesses continue to do well. Our thread and yarn are being sent as far away as England. It will be nice if we expanded into America. Then we could legitimately ship thread and material to you and Mary.

We send our love,

Christian and Abigail

In September 1896 Jacob finally got up the nerve to propose to Anna; they planned to have a small wedding after Christmas and maybe around the New Year. Anna parents, Abigail and I helped the pair plan the wedding. The Hemels and Funks first discussed the possibility of immigrating to America. The Hemels had decided that moving was not an option for them. "If Anna marries Jacob there is a real possibility that they could move with us to America. How do you feel about that?" Christian inquired.

"We discussed this possibility with Anna and Jacob when he asked for her hand in marriage. Her mother and I are fully prepared to accept this and we will miss her terribly."

"We appreciate your feelings. Abigail and I put off moving until my parents passed away because we knew that they were too old to handle such a long move."

The four of us then discussed where the young couple should live. If the pair lived with either the Hemels or us for an extended period of time it might look suspicious to the government. So, we decided that we would set them up in a small cottage of their own. We paid for the construction of the home that was built on the Hemel property; that way when we left Russia, the Hemels would be able to utilize the house for other family members.

Light snow fell during the afternoon of December 31st but stopped several hours before the wedding. I felt that having the snow stop was a good sign for Jacob and Anna's future. I felt that the falling snow at Allison's wedding had been a bad sign because I felt that Daniel would one day hurt my daughter.

Jacob and Anna's wedding turned out to be beautiful. A light dinner was served at the beginning of the reception that was held in the church's adjoining social hall that had poinsettias scattered about. Everyone in attendance had a wonderful time. Going to their new home, the two found a traditional Funk family wedding present in their living area: a pair of rocking chairs. This brought tears to both of their eyes. In the bedroom lay the most beautiful quilt the couple had ever saw: a quilt made up of poinsettia blocks.

The family continued to grow during 1897. This growth included:

- Allison and Daniel's second child arriving and being named George;

- a letter from George and Mary announced two more family marriages that took place in Kansas;

- A baby was expected during the summer—George and Mary's first grandchild.

February 1897

Dear Christian and Abigail,

Henry and Katherine married in June of 1896. Katherine is expecting our first grandchild; the baby is due in August.

George married Anna in early September of 1896.

Charles is dancing around girls; being fifteen he thinks he likes them but is not totally sure. There is a young woman named Lucy Weber that he likes and you can tell she likes him too. They are a bit young to be serious, so we will see.

After this year Jacob will have one more year of schooling to complete. He has expressed an interest in becoming a Lutheran minister. We are happy that he has the interest so are looking for ways to pay for the tuition. Katherine, Mollie and Alexander are keeping me busy.

We are exploring adding more variety of fruit trees to our small orchard. Others have had successful with pears so might try them.

How is the quilt shop doing? I wish I were there to obtain fabric. There is not much selection of fabric here in Rush county. Hayes has a fabric shop that has a medium sized selection but it is a long trip there and back. Needless to say, we do not go there often.

George was unable to purchase a farm close by. The acreage George purchased is at the opposite end of the county from where we live. Henry purchased acreage on the southern side of Rush county.

The extended Funk family continues to graciously come together here in America to build family homes, for weddings, for baptisms and for funerals.

We miss you and can't wait to see you! We look forward to your family migrating here. Remember, we and others in the family have enough room for the two of you, your adult children, spouses and grandchildren for when you make a permanent move.

Love George, and Mary

After reading the letter aloud Abigail wistfully said "I miss them so *very much*. I wish we could join them tomorrow. After we are settled in America, I would like to open a smaller version of our current quilt shop. That way Mary, Christina and I will have an excuse to be together."

The thought of the three of them needing an excuse to get together made me smile. I then said "I think that is a great idea. Maybe we can bring some bolts of cloth and spools of thread with us to America in order to stock a shop in America. By the way, I have another letter here; it's from Adam and Christina. Do you want me to read it?"

Abigail stated that she hoped that Christina and Mary had received the letters she sent in December telling them about Jacob's wedding. I told her that "the letters probably passed in transit."

February 1897

Dear Christian and Abigail,

The weather here is lovely; we are buried under two feet of snow. We have learned that we needed to string rope from the house to the barn so that during blizzards, like the one we had last week. The rope is used to locate the barn and so we can return safely back to the house.

The first year here, Adam got stuck in the barn for two days when a blizzard suddenly came upon us. Luckily, he had hay to sleep under or he would not have made it.

Conrad is a great help with the farm, is serious about a young lady named Lydia and is looking forward to purchasing his own land.

He is fast becoming a master carpenter and is working part-time at a shop in town. George is apprenticing at a blacksmith shop in Dodge City. He will be finished in the summer of 1898. His plans are to return home, buy a farm and open up a small shop on the property. That way he can run the farm and earn some extra money during the off season of farming.

How is the quilt shop? The spinning mill? The children? We can't wait to see you.
Love Adam and Christina

Early March of 1899, Jacob and Anna had their first child, a son whom they named John. Just over a year later a daughter, named Elizabeth, joined the family. Abigail, Jacob, Anna, Allison, Daniel, Philip and I came together shortly after the birth of Elizabeth to discuss joining the family in America.

Being in total agreement, arrangements were made to sell both the spinning mill and the fabric businesses; selling the two businesses wasn't as hard as we expected. The farm owned by Abigail and myself sold easily but the smaller property owned by Daniel and Allison took longer to sell due to its size. The hardest items to leave behind were the beloved rocking chairs. We decided that when we settled in Kansas new rocking chairs would be made.

In June of 1900 six adults, one eleven—year—old and six younger grandchildren left for America. We planned on taking a path similar to that taken by George, Adam and their families eight years ago. The difference is that we did not plan on stopping in Germany. I silently said a prayer that the family would have a safe journey, good health and God's protection. We began our travels to America by taking the regions rivers in a north, north—westerly direction to get to St. Petersburg.

This time the journey was different than what is was a hundred and twenty—five years before when the family had migrated to Russia. Russian crews were pleasant and they were as interested in the Germans as the Germans were interested in the Russians. This time the Russian crew expressed extreme hostility towards the Germans, making the journey very un-comfortable. Once in St. Petersburg, we could not wait to leave Russia. We booked passage on a smaller steamship that would take us directly to Southampton, England, which meant that we would bypass Germany.

Prior to booking passage, the group discussed whether to travel third class or second class. Both Mary and Christina had written about the horrors of 'steerage' and how many of the passengers had been sick the entire voyage; several people had not survived the journey. So, we mulled over whether we should spend the extra money for second class tickets or save the money! Steerage would cost each passenger twenty—five dollars; this was equal to about three week's wages for an average coal miner in Russia. We found out that immigrants traveling steerage were provided a numbered metal berth that had a burlap mattress stuffed with hay. A life preserver doubled as the berths pillow. This did not provide any privacy for married couples. Plus, six small children could bother other travelers with their playing, crying or fighting. One of the six children was barely two months old and Anna would need privacy in order to feed the baby.

Second class cabins cost an additional twenty dollars per ticket; for a total of forty—five collars per person. This would mean that we would spend an additional 260 American dollars for the voyage. By traveling second class we would not have to be ferried from the East River pier to Ellis Island once we arrived in the harbor of New York City. Abigail and I both remembered reading in a letter from either Mary or Christina that an immi-grant's paper work would be inspected and passengers would be examined by a doctor. George, Adam, Mary and Christina had all seen people being delayed from entering the country. Some of these passengers had actually been sent back to Europe because of ill health or incorrect paper work.

The money from selling the spinning mill would be split three ways between George, Adam and myself when we arrived in Kansas but the profit from my farm and Abigail's quilting shop was ours to spend as we saw fit. Deciding to spend the extra money on upgraded accommodations was an easy decision for me; I purchased second class tickets for our passage to America.

We were lucky as the ship crossed the ocean: we did not experience sea sickness. I wonder whether sea sickness could be linked to steerage accommodations alone. Could individuals in first or second accommodations also experience sea sickness? We spent time in our rooms but a lot of time walking and sitting in the fresh air. I am told fresh air helps people not to fall ill. Once we arrived in New York City, we left the ship and passed through customs quickly. The trunks that we brought with us were retrieved after we cleared customs. Besides the basics, we had brought a couple of cases of quilting threads along with some extra spools. Abigail had brought three dozen bolts of fabric packed away in several trunks. We were provided assistance in taking our baggage to where transportation could be obtained.

At the train depot, the ticket master stated that the best route was to take the train that traveled from New York City to California. The train made stops in many large cities, such as Cleveland, Chicago, Kansas City, and Denver. In addition, the train stopped in some smaller places for passenger convenience. We booked passage on this train with the idea that we would get off in Kansas City. The train was scheduled to leave New York in two hours which meant that baggage had already begun to be taken abroad. Meanwhile, the family was directed to the lobby to wait for the boarding call. We decided to ask the ticket master where we might get a bite to eat, we were instructed to go down the hall and on the left we would find a food stand that sold sandwiches, fresh fruit and various types of drinks.

Once in Kansas City we would obtain passage on the *Atchison, Topeka & Santa Fe* Railroad heading westward and going through Rush county. After booking passage, a telegraph was sent to George and Adam regarding the time we were scheduled to arrive to in mid—Kansas.

August 1974

The letters written by Mary and Christina were very interesting as it provided a glimpse of what was important in the lives of the family during the late 1890s. Christian and Abigail learned from George and Adam's steamship experience and had decided to travel second class instead of steerage. It would cost the family more money but it was felt that it would be worth it. The family managed to live and flourish during their time apart. The group kept in touch regularly and would be together again shortly.

I am not sure exactly how I feel about Allison's husband. I know that he's not a nice person, a cheater, and a blackmailer. But Allison must have seen some redeeming qualities in him or she would not, hopefully, have married him. Although, I have heard that love is blind, I often wondered how true that was. However, Daniel has proven himself to be a cad by flaunting his 'girlfriends' around Hussenbach. I wonder if he will continue his wayward activities in Kansas.

I thought of the bible verse that Conrad seemed to live his life by:

Just as you did it to one of the least of these who are members of my family you did it for me.   Matthew 25: 45

I wondered if Daniel ever felt that what he was doing to Allison was wrong. If you want to have multiple partners then why make a commitment to a single person and cause them pain? All Daniel seemed to care about was having enough money to pursue his own desires. That is such a sad commentary about how someone lives their life. I might never know what eventually happens between Daniel, Allison and their family but, am interested in finding out.

Picking up the next journal I began to leaf through it hoping to find pictures or anything else loose in it. About the middle of the journal I came across a photograph that was labeled on the back: wheat framing in Kansas. Not being a farmer, I wondered what the equipment did to help the wheat farmer. From the picture, it looked like it assisted with wheat harvesting.

http://www.kshs.org/p/online-exhibits-from-
far-away-russia-part-4/10682

I do know that mechanization has made farming easier than plowing and harvesting with the help of horses or oxen. I could not wait to read about the how my Great—Great Grandparents and family lived in Kansas at the turn of the twentieth century.

Journal Nine

Kansas—The early nineteen hundred's

As we traveled across eastern Kansas on the *Atchison, Topeka & Santa Fe,* I sat looking at the scenery flying past. Wheat, corn and other crops were gently blowing in the wind. The skies were a beautiful blue with a few clouds that looked like white, fluffy cotton balls. I couldn't wait to get to our destination and start the next chapter in our lives. Five minutes prior to the next stop the train's conductor announced that we were approaching Rush County. Once the train stopped, we, along with several other families, exited the train. Porters assisted the departing passengers in unloading their baggage. At this point, I wondered how exciting it would be to work as a train porter or engineer. Doing the job for several years, would enable the employees to view the growth and changes to America firsthand. But on the other hand, it could be tiresome to always be traveling.

I was brought out of my day—dream when I saw my two brothers waving at us. Smiling broadly, I waved back and began walking towards George and Adam. The pair, along with several of their sons, had been waiting for the family for about an hour. The group had brought several wagons to accommodate us and any baggage we had brought with us. We could not believe how big George and Adam's sons had become since we saw them last. Eight long years does wonders for growing young people.

Growing up together, Jacob and his four oldest male cousins had been close friends while living in Russia. The five were still good friends even though they had not seen each in eight years. I introduced Anna and Daniel to George, Adam and my nephews. Everyone warmly greeted both Daniel and Anna then hugged the rest of us.

While the wagons were being loaded with our baggage, Abigail, Allison, Anna and I briefly told Adam and George about our trip. We did not want to tell everything about travels because we knew that Mary, Christina and the rest of the family would want to hear it also. Having finished loading the wagons, the young men came back to retrieve Abigail, Allison, Anna, Adam, George and myself. It was exciting to get a view of the country—side as we rode from the station to George's home. Upon arrival at George's homestead we were slightly overwhelmed at the number of people gathered waiting for us. It seemed that there were hundreds of people around the house but there weren't hundreds, just closer to two to three dozen people. Hugs, kisses and introductions took place over the next half hour.

The family decided to quickly let us know the temporary housing arrangements that would be until Jacob, Daniel and I found acreage to purchase and houses built. Abigail, Philip and I would stay with George and Mary while Jacob, Anna, and their two children stayed with Conrad and his wife. I noticed that Daniel, Allison and her growing family would stay with Adam and Christina. At this point, my nephews took the appropriate baggage to the homes where we would be staying.

Upon returning to George's house, Jacob pulled me aside and preceded to tell me that "Anna and I noticed that Daniel was more than slightly uncomfortable with the family, in fact he was very uncomfortable and it showed."

"I noticed the same thing. I was hoping that he would get over it quickly." I replied "I think that we might have to wait to see what happens and how he adjusts."

"Okay," began Jacob "I just hope that it doesn't come back to bite us." I nodded in agreement while I wondered whether Daniel would ever feel relaxed around a family that were virtual strangers to him? Why did Anna fit right in and was perfectly comfortable with the relatives she had never met before but Daniel couldn't? Was it because the two were totally different personality—wise? I am just grateful that I only have one individual like Daniel to deal with; I just wished I didn't have one to deal with.

After the meal, Daniel seemed to relax somewhat. I wonder why? Was it because he knew that Allison, their children and he would be staying with Adam and Christina? If this was true, then why does he feel so uncomfortable around individuals closer to his age? Was it possible that maybe Daniel felt that people around his age could see through him easier than older people? I am not sure how true this is because I have grown to see right through him.

That afternoon, our large family gathered together to get reacquainted. The youngest children were laid down for a nap while some of the older children scrambled off to play together. Watching the children for a few moments, I realized that children in our family always seemed to graciously accept other children, even if they had just met. They didn't always get along but they always come to an understanding and accepted each other's differences. I wondered why adults often became quite cruel and unaccepting of differences. Saying my name, George brought me back from my thoughts and we began to swap 'war' stories about migrating to America.

The family was anxious to hear about what was different in Hussenbach, about our trip across several of Europe's waterways, an ocean voyage and then a train trip across the United States. Half of George and Adam's family had been seasick during their 1892 voyage across the Atlantic. As a result, many family members had limited memories of that part of the journey. Their memories of the journey seemed to begin with first viewing the Statue of Liberty.

I began to tell the family the changes in Hussenbach over the past ten years. "There are rumblings of a civil war, some are calling it a revolution. Many argue that the royal family is out of touch with the people and feel that the Czar should abdicate his throne. Economic conditions have not improved over the past ten years. The poor still do not have access to their own land. Industrialization has caused more and more of the population to move to the city where they are exploited. As a result, workers have become ripe for radical ideas. This has caused Russia to be broken up into different political groups. One political group that seems to be attracting the majority of the poor is being referred to as the Socialist Revolutionary Party."

I continued by telling the family that "a majority of Russians were expressing more of their hate and prejudice than ever before. As you remember from your leaving Russia there is a lot of traveling by river before actually leaving Russia. We traveled along the Volga and other rivers as we attempted to leave Russia. The Russian crews did not attempt to hide their hatred towards

Germans. I wondered if it was because we were German! Or was it for some other reason. I guess that we will never know the answer. As we left the last river vessel in St. Petersburg, the crew shouted at us *'good riddance'*. We never responded back to their hatred but were glad as the steamship, we had booked passage on, left St. Petersburg behind."

"For us, leaving Russia about eight years ago, it was almost as bad but not quite. Overall, Russians did not wear their hatred on their faces, like they did for you," stated George "but the voyage across the Atlantic made up for it."

Wishing to change the conversation somewhat, Abigail said that the family "really enjoyed seeing the Statue of Liberty when we finally arrived in New York harbor. Your letters told us that it was tall but it still did not prepare us for what it really looked like." Many heads nodded in agreement around the room.

Christina injected "that it was getting late, that we should consider preparing dinner." So, the women went to begin making dinner for the family.

Deciding that this was a good time for a talk about the sale of our father's mil, I initiated the conversation by saying "I have the money that we made from the sale of father's spinning mill. If my calculations from Russian Rubles to American dollars are correct then we made a profit of 2000 dollars; we had to pay the Russian Government 200 of that $2000 in order to leave Russia. So, by my figures we should each receive 600 dollars."

"Wait a minute," Adam jumped in, "from 1891 to when the mill sold you had extra work and you did not take any extra money for a salary. Plus, you put forth the effort to get the mill sold so I feel that you should get more than a third of the profit."

George stated "I agree with Adam." Eventually, I came away with 800 dollars while Adam and George each receiving 500 dollars. The extra money would help me pay for a farm and farm implements in Kansas. Adam and George saved some of their share and used the rest for their farm operation.

The next day, George and Adam showed me, Jacob and Daniel several farms with acreage that were available for purchase. The first property was in the northern portion of Rush county. The 400—acre farm had a small two—story house, a barn, several other small outbuildings with several fields fenced for use as pasture land. The farmer owned and operated a steam-powered threshing machine that he was willing to sell for an additional price since he was moving to Kansas City. Daniel appeared to like this farm. Jacob and I knew that he liked this property because the crop was already growing in the field. We also knew that if he and the farmer reached an agreement on the threshing machine, he would hire the threshing machine out during harvest time.

Late August 1974

I now know that the machine in the picture must be a threshing machine. I wonder how long that type of threshing machine was in operation or is it still in operation today, seventy—five years later?

Journal continues

The next property that George and Adam took us to see had 480—acres and was located in the eastern part of the county. The property had a house, barn, outbuildings, but there were no fenced fields. The property was being sold with all of the farm machinery due to the owners having died without any heirs. The main drawback of the property, for me, was that the railroad line ran through the northern part of the acreage. A third of the land was north of the railroad line while the remaining lay to the south.

Having the railroad run across a portion of the property could be helpful if there was an official stop on the property or near the property so that the crops could be loaded on the train and sent on to market more quickly. But George stated that there was no official stop on the property, the owner had to take his crops to the train depot where the grain elevators stood. The depot was half a mile as the crow flies but a mile and a half by way of the county roads. Adam interjected that "that he wouldn't want a stop on his property due to neighboring farmers tramping across his property to access the train. How much of your arable land would you lose for grain elevators, access road and whatever would be needed." After thinking about what George and Adam had said I agreed that an official stop was not necessary but the property was worth considering.

Shortly afterwards we decided to head to George's home to eat lunch and discuss the first two properties. By the time we arrived, Abigail was finishing preparing our lunch. While we were looking at land, the rest of the family had eaten and headed back to work or to play. Abigail returned to bread making with Mary and Christina while we ate. The three women were just grateful that the entire forty-five-member Funk family were not living and eating under one roof. Having so many people gathered together meant much more work for those who had to cook, clean and do laundry.

After finishing lunch, George, Adam, Jacob, Daniel and I set off again to look at several more properties. Pulling up to the first property of the afternoon, the third for the day, Jacob commented that "it's interesting that here in America outbuildings are often referred to as a barn. The majority of barns seem to be painted a bright red, why is that?"

"Remember how in Russia we would seal the wood on out outbuildings with oil?" began Adam "Sometimes a linseed oil was used with milk and lime added to make a long—lasting sealant; the sealant dried and hardened quickly. Well, here in America there are two theories about why barns are painted red.

"The first one says that wealthy farmers add blood from the slaughter to the oil mixture. They say that as it dries it turns from a bright red to a darker burnt red. While the second theory argues that farmers add rust to the oil mixture. Rust is poison to many fungi, including moss and mold. Moss and mold trap moisture in wood which increases decay. So, adding rust to the oil and placed on the barn helps to prevent the growth of fungi."

"Well, they both make good stories but whatever the truth is, a red barn is fashionable here in America. Plus, the contrast between a red barn and a white house is striking, don't you think?"

Jacob and Daniel smiled or nodded in agreement while I added "You were always a good story teller Adam."

Adam feigned injury as he replied "Me! A story teller? I don't know what you are talking about, Christian."

George told us about a 640—acre property with nice buildings on it. This property is located on the west side of the county. Arriving at the property he said "As you can see, there is a two story, three—bedroom house that recently had running water installed. In the kitchen a pump had been mounted at the sink along with a drain to take the waste water to a septic system. A small room off the kitchen was built on to accommodate a bath tub with a drain system attached to the same septic system that the kitchen is connected too. Water still needed to be heated but having water pumped into the house makes the chore of obtaining water for the household less demanding for women."

"Recently I read a newspaper article that reported that a typical housewife carried water from an outdoor pump, a well, or from a spring up to a dozen times daily. Washing, boiling and rinsing one load of laundry used fifty gallons of water." George continued by pointing out that the "article argued that in one year a woman walked 148 miles just to convey water to where it was needed. The toughest figure in the article stated that over a course of a year a woman carried over thirty tons of water."

"That is amazing; no wonder women are tired." Jacob interjected.

"I think that I read the same article," Adam said. "If I remember correctly it went on to state that homes without running water lack a way to dispose of waste; women, then, have to rid the house of the waste water."

"That is a plus for this house; Abigail would love having running water in the house plus drains ridding the house of waste water." I asked "What else can you tell us about this property?"

"As you can see there is a barn and two additional outbuildings." Stated the property owner. "Several of the fields are fenced and each field has large tins in which to hold water for animals."

Prior to heading home for the day, Adam offered to take me, Daniel and Jacob to look at two additional properties tomorrow. I wanted to talk to Abigail about the properties we saw first. Adam stated that he would come by in the morning to see if I wished to see the other properties.

During dinner Abigail, George, Mary and I discussed the properties that we had looked at that day. I liked the last house we looked at; this causing Abigail to ask what I liked about it. "Well," I began, "the property has 640—acres. The house is a two—story building with three bedrooms. I think that the best part is that the house has running water."

Abigail's eyes grew large with thinking about running water in the house. She began by saying "No more going outside for water, especially in cold weather! That would be heaven." After a pause she asked if "it possible that we could go to see the inside of the house?"

"I will contact the owner first thing tomorrow. In fact, why don't the two of you come with me to see if we could view the house then?" George asked.

The next day George, Abigail and I went to the property to talk to the owner. Knowing how much Abigail desired to see the interior of the house, I deliberately waited to tour the barn and outbuildings. Having water in the house delighted Abigail and she absolutely loved the alcove that held the bathtub.

Feeling so very comfortable in the house and with the owner that Abigail offered to play hostess and to make a pot of tea for the four of us. The tea kettle was filled with water and set on the stove to heat while she located the sugar, cream, tea, tea cups, saucers and spoons. George, the property owner and I began to discuss the price for the property. After about an hour the widower and I agreed on a price for the property that in-cluded the new kitchen stove and most of the farm implements. The widower was moving in with his daughter and her husband in Gray County so he and his son—in—law did not need all the farm equipment.

The widower seemed to take a liking to Abigail so offered her the pair of rocking chairs that were located in the living room, near the wood stove. Abigail got up, hugged and thanked the elderly gentleman. If acceptable to us, the widower said that he could be moved out by the end of the month. We told him not to rush that we would wait as long as necessary.

We arrived home at around three-thirty that afternoon with the good news that Abigail and I had purchased the property. Mary told us that Jacob and Anna had come over about four hours before and said that they were going out with Conrad to view a few properties. In addition, Mary quietly inquired about Allison's husband, Daniel. Abigail and I looked at each other, and then asked if there were a problem.

"No," Mary replied hesitantly, "it's just that when Adam and Daniel came over earlier, they asked where you had gone. After I told them where you had gone, Daniel became horribly upset."

Abigail and I again exchanged looks prior to my stating that "Daniel is somewhat difficult to get along with, he has a bad temper when he does not get his way. Experience tells me that Daniel desired that property for himself. Did they say if they would be back or just going back to Adam's home?"

"Adam said that he and Christina would return after dinner for a visit. That way Daniel and Allison and their children could have some private time."

"When Adam and Christina arrive, I will go to their house to have a conversation with my son—in—law."

Reaching out for my hand, Abigail said "Now Chris, remember do not be overly harsh on Daniel for Allison's sake."

"I will be short, to the point and not rip his head off. He has been a problem for us since just before he married Allison. The bad thing is that Allison truly loves him which means that she cannot see his bad points."

Within an hour and a half, I arrived at Adam's house on one of George's horses. Slowly walking up to the house, I was attempting to gather my thoughts so I would not lose my temper with Daniel. Allison had seen me arrive so opened the door as I climbed the porch steps. Allison greeted me and asked "What brings you here this evening? Have you eaten?"

"I have already eaten, thank you Allison. I have come to have a discussion with your husband. Hopefully, he is here."

"He just stepped out back to check on the animals. He thought that there might be some wild animals hanging around the chicken coop."

"Maybe I should go outback to see him then."

Just as Allison was asking if there a problem, Daniel came inside and greeted me. Looking at Daniel, I asked about the children before suggesting that we have a seat in the parlor. I began the conversation by saying "I understand from Mary that you came over earlier."

Daniel replied that he and Adam had stopped at George's house. "Adam and I were told that George had taken you and Abigail to the house with running water."

"From what I understand you lost your temper at Mary."

"Wait a minute…"

Raising my hand to stop Daniel, I continued "Adam verified that you lost your temper when Mary told you where George, Abigail and I went. Are you still going to deny it?"

Stuttering some Daniel asked "What negative things did Mary and Adam say about me?"

"They didn't! Mary hoped that she was not out of line by telling you where we went. This family has provided you many opportunities. For example, a house was built for you in Hussenbach and you were provided a second—class passage on a steamship bound for America at no cost to you. But all you have done since marring our daughter is to be negative and to complain. Abigail and I have overlooked your temper and bad manners because of Allison. However, there is no excuse for your display of bad temper today."

"I was interested in purchasing that property for Allison. You knew this but you couldn't wait to scoop the house out from under me." Daniel stated angrily. Allison was deeply embarrassed because she knew that her father would not have done what her husband was saying.

"You showed extreme interest in only the first property yesterday because it was the smallest farm. You liked the fact that the current farmer had already planted the fields this season which meant less work for you. Plus, there was that threshing machine that you could rent out without any extra work on your part."

Indigently Daniel replied "Are you implying that I am lazy?"

"I'm not implying it; I'm saying it. Remember that back in Hussenbach you worked for me in the spinning mill. You looked for ways to get out of work. Once you married my daughter, I finally saw your true self! Your co—workers knew long before I did that you were lazy and conniving but none of them would complain because you courted and then married my daughter. Should we talk of the hotel incident?"

Turning brilliant red, Daniel quickly shook his head no. "I didn't think so," I retorted.

"There was no indication that you were interested in the 640—acre property that had the house with running water. You became interested in it once you thought I was. Also, nothing was said about my purchasing the property when George and I returned to view the house with Abigail this morning. But just so you know, you couldn't afford the property. It was way out of your price range."

"I don't have to stand here and take this from you or anyone else. My family will be leaving first thing in the morning."

Daniel stood up and left the house; as he left, he told Allison that he would sleep in the barn.

Standing, I said "I am sorry that it came to this Allison, but Daniel has to control his temper. He cannot continue to think that everyone is out to sabotage him. Plus, he needs to get a better work ethic and not be so lazy. No one owes him a living! You do know that you and the children do not have to leave with him, don't you?"

"I know father but, he is my husband. I did say that wherever he went I would follow. If I left him then the children would be followed with 'you're the kids with no father' for their entire childhood. I love you and Mom. Where ever we end up, I will try to send word to you and mother. However, I will attempt to calm him down prior to us leaving."

Saddened, I hugged Allison and then left with the thought that I might never see my beloved daughter again.

Back at George's house I slowly began to stable the horse; I knew that I was killing time. I did not relish the thought of telling Abigail and the rest of the family that Daniel was taking Allison as far away as possible. Because it was taking me a long time, George came out to the barn. "Obviously, it didn't go well with your son—in—law."

Looking up, I shook my head in a negative motion. "Let me give the horse some oats and water then we can go inside to talk before Adam and Christina return home."

Once inside, Mary handed me a cup of hot coffee and Abigail inquired how it went with Daniel. However, everyone in the room knew that it had not gone well. I proceeded to relate how Daniel denied losing his temper; he tried to turn it around and to blame Mary. I stopped him in his tracks by stating that I believed Mary but Adam verified what Mary had said. "What it boils down to is that Daniel assumed that I purchased the property even though I supposedly knew that he wanted to buy it."

George interjected "How were we to know that he wanted to purchase that property? He never showed any interest in it."

"I told him exactly that plus that he expressed interest in the first property only because it was the smallest farm and that the fields were already planted with this season's crops. Abigail, you know Daniel well, does he like to work or not? Does he just want everything handed to him?"

Abigail was shaking her head in agreement, saying that it was true. "What else did you tell him?"

"Well, I told Daniel that he was lazy."

"Oh Chris, you did not really tell him that did you?" an exasperated Abigail asked.

"Unfortunately, that is what I said in a nutshell. The icing on the cake was when I told him that he could not afford the property."

George agreed that I had paid quite a large sum for the property but "it included the house with running water and a bathtub, several barns, and fenced in pasture land. The widower was including the livestock and machinery because he was moving in with his daughter and her family. However, did you tell him that you purchased the property?"

"When I told him that he couldn't afford the property I am sure that he took that to mean that I had purchased the property. Anyway, Daniel totally lost it and told Allison to get ready to move; he plans on moving Allison and the kids first thing in the morning. After Daniel stormed out, I told Allison that she did not have to leave with him. She said that she made a vow to stay with him through good times and the bad times. Where ever they end up, Allison said that she would let us know where they were and that they were okay."

"Christian," Abigail's voice trembled as she said "I need to see Allison and the grandchildren before Daniel takes them off and we never see them again. Adam or Christina, would you please tell Allison that I will be over to see them first thing in the morning." It was always a bad sign when my wife called me Christian instead of Chris so I agreed to whatever she wanted.

Early the next morning, George brought the horse and buggy around to the side of the house. Mary and Abigail climbed into the buggy with assistance from me. My heart was broken about the idea of Allison and the grandchildren leaving. There was a real possibility of never seeing them again. Arriving just in time, Abigail, Allison, grandkids and I were able to say their tearful good-byes. While hugging, Allison whispered that she was sorry about the entire situation. Abigail slipped a packet of money into a pocket of Allison's dress and said "The money is for you and the children don't let Daniel know you have it."

Insisting that it was time to leave, Daniel placed the children into Adam's wagon and Allison climbed abroad and the wagon pulled away from the house making a sad song with its wheels. Christina offered us coffee or tea. George asked Christina "Did Daniel indicate where they might be headed?"

"He didn't say exactly. However, he did ask the time the next train would be leaving the station." Abigail looked puzzled by Christina's response so she continued "Everyone living in the area knows that the first train to leave the station on Wednesday mornings is heading west. The train passes through Denver on its way to points further west."

Understanding shone in Abigail's eyes as she replied "Daniel is not flush with cash so the furthest he could go is Denver."

George stated that "In Denver, he could get employment long enough to earn the money needed to take his family elsewhere."

"But," began Abigail "we know that he is lazy so it could be hard for him to obtain or to keep a job."

"Did you know that Allison is expecting another baby?" Christina asked Abigail.

"Yes, she told me during the train ride from Kansas City about the baby. She is hoping for another son." Abigail was saddened that she might never see the newest addition to the family.

Later that afternoon Adam and George took Jacob and me to look at a property that adjoined the land that I had purchased the day before. The four of us stopped to see the owner, William Schmidt. Mr. Schmidt told us that the property was 480—acres; forty of the acres were wooded and followed a wet creek bed. Walking closer to the creek the group looked to see whether the creek was indeed wet or if it was dry. The creek, gently sloping westward, had a steady stream running through it and looked roughly a foot deep. Mr. Schmidt stated that sometimes the flow of water was three times that deep and on rare occasions, it was barely a trickle. The creek would provide water for livestock and could be tapped to help with irrigation of crops if needed.

Several fields that surrounded the creek were fenced in as pasture land. Mr. Schmidt stated that the fencing dipped down one bank to the creek, went across the creek and then up the other side. "I did the fencing this way so that the livestock could access the running water and that I would not have to worry about them straying. I keep large tubs in the field for those times that the stream is lower."

Mr. Schmidt stated that in mid—spring he had planted corn, wheat, and soybeans. Pointing at a field to the left of the house, Jacob asked what crop was planted there. "New to this area?" Mr. Schmidt asked.

"Yes, we just moved from Russia. Why do you ask?"

"People living in Kansas for even a year have seen fields of sunflowers growing. This field was planted with oilseed sunflowers in mid—April. When harvested in the fall, the sunflowers will be converted to oil. Children love to watch sunflowers grow because the bud of the sunflower follows the movement of the sun from east to west. Once the bud opens, the flower mainly faces east."

"I noticed that the house is only one—story; how many rooms are there?" inquired Jacob.

"There is a parlor, a kitchen, and three rooms that we use for sleeping. There is stair case that goes up to an attic space that I made into a small sleeping area for my sons when they were younger."

George, Adam, Jacob and I thanked Mr. Schmidt for showing us the property. "We need to discuss the properties that we saw the past couple of days."

In the wagon, Jacob stated that he liked many things about the property. Looking at Jacob, I asked what exactly he liked best. Jacob began by stating that it was next to the property I purchased the day before. "A creek running across a portion of the property does not hurt either," added Jacob. "I think that I like this property most and am willing to make an offer."

Adam inquired "Do you think that Anna would like to see the house prior to you making a decision?"

"She has said that whatever I like, she will love," replied Jacob, "but I still want her to see the house first." The next day Jacob purchased the property; Jacob, Anna and their two children moved into the house a month later. It did not take long for our family to settle in our new homes.

Christmas 1974

After exchanging words with Christian, Daniel took his family further west. I had heard that Allison and her family had moved away but no one seemed to remember exactly when it had happened or why. Could this be the incident that caused Allison and family to leave the family fold? Many families have words over trivial matters and sometimes over more serious issues. Several members of my Dad's family had words with his older brother many, many years before. Angry, Dad's brother and his family left and the rest of the family never heard from him again. Dad and the rest of the family never discussed what caused the split within the Keller family. However, I don't feel that this is the case with my great—great—grandfather, Christian, and his daughter's family. Christian, Abigail and the family became separated from Allison unnecessarily because of Daniel. However, deep down I know that my ancestors will see Allison once again.

On a happier note, I know that both Christian and Abigail felt that it was wonderful that Jacob and Anna had located and purchased an adjoining property. I am positive that they felt it was wonderful having them live next door. This enabled the children to visit their grandparents on a regular basis. I have learned, from personal experience, that grandparents are God's way of providing children unconditional love and acceptance. Over the years, both of my mother's parents have taught me different things about life. Grandma taught me how to knit and crochet but also instilled the love of doing any handicraft in me. Grandpa, on the other hand, has provided me understanding and to be quietly happy within myself.

Picking up the tenth journal, I began to look for any flyers or pictures that might be inside. A letter written in German was inserted near the beginning of the journal which I am sure that Grandma had translated for me. I hoped that the letter was from Allison telling her parents where she and her family landed.

Journal Ten

Kansas 1902—1904

In the spring of 1902, I stopped at the post office and was told that there was a letter for me. Taking the letter, I felt that it had to be from Abigail but did not open the letter until I arrived home.

22 March 1902

Dear Mom and Dad,

We have settled in Denver; which Daniel says is temporary but I am not so sure. He goes out everyday looking for work but does not seem to have any luck.

We are living off our savings which is slowly being depleted. We live in a second story apartment near down-town Denver.

Our landlord has graciously allowed me to clean the common areas of the building along with the front stoop and sidewalk in exchange for the rent. I am able to keep the children near me while I work.

*Our fifth child arrived last week and is named
Henry. He looks like dad. Please do not worry about us,
we will be okay. I will write again.*
Love Allison

After finishing reading the letter aloud, I looked up to see tears running down Abigail's cheeks. Getting up, I went over to Abigail and knelt beside her. We made eye contact and gave each other a hug. "Abby," I began, "It will be okay. God is with Allison and the grandchildren."

"I believe God is protecting them. However, I worry about how Daniel is treating her; especially after his many 'girlfriends' in Hussenbach."

Shocked, I asked "What do you mean 'girlfriends'?"

"Come on Chris, do you think that I live in a bubble? People talk, especially women in a quilt shop. Do you remember the day you encountered Daniel with his Flossie in the hotel? A few women were in the shop talking about the incident."

"The women did not tell you about the incident, did they?"

"Well, no but, I overheard these women discussing the incident when I was in the next room preparing for a class. Coming out from the back room caused these women to blush and to stop talking. I had heard enough to know that Allison is getting a raw deal. How come you never told me about it?".

"I could not break your heart. I also did not wish to tell Allison about the episode but, I suspect Allison knows."

"Chris, I know for a fact that there were at least three different women that Daniel was seeing."

"Three? Wow! I knew of only the one; guess women are more intuitive then men."

Smiling, Abigail agreed before she asked "Do you think that we could travel to Denver in order see Allison?"

"I am not sure that would be wise because Daniel might be around which would cause trouble for Allison. But we should not close any door. Whatever happens we can get some money to her."

"That would be good." Abigail replied.

Several weeks later as I was examining the corn, I began to consider opening and operating a spinning mill in Kansas. If I do not open a mill of my own, I would at least like to work with a mill regarding producing smaller spools for holding thread for quilters. After much research, I found out that there was a medium sized spinning mill operating in St. Louis, Missouri. Being about seven—hundred miles away made working with the company in Missouri virtually impossible. Further exploration caused me to find another spinning mill operating in the Denver area. Being about three hundred and fifty miles away, I felt that it was close enough for me to work with. Besides it is an opportunity for Abigail and I to travel to Denver and to see Allison. For the time that we would be in Denver, Philip could be left behind to manage the farm and livestock. Abigail made arrangements for Philip to stay with Jacob and Anna when we traveled to Denver.

While discussing the trip to Denver with Jacob and Anna, Abigail asked if the pair were expecting another baby. Anna replied that she was and "that the baby was expected in mid—August. Jacob and I did not plan on telling you quite yet because we lost a baby last year. Plus, you and Dad are concerned about Allison."

"But dear this is good news! I am really happy for you and Jacob."

A couple days later, Abigail and I boarded a train headed for Denver. Once there, a driver took us to the Brown Palace Hotel in downtown Denver. Our motive for staying at the Brown Palace was because we knew that it was close enough to where Allison lived so we could 'accidently' run into her. Prior to leaving Kansas, arrangements had been made for me to visit the spinning mill the day after our arrival. Luckily, the mill was located not far from the downtown Denver area. Joseph Becker, the mills owner, met with me and Abigail in the hotel's restaurant for breakfast at eight the next morning. During breakfast Mr. Becker said "Please call me Joseph. Whether we do business or not, I think that we will become good friends."

"Please call me Christian and this is my wife Abigail. I look forward to a long relationship. After breakfast, we would like to invite you to our room in order to show you the smaller spools that we designed to hold thread for quilters."

"I can't wait to see them; for a long time, we have been attempting to make the perfect size of spool with the right amount of thread for quilters. We also are attempting to make smaller spools for the new sewing machines that are being produced for the general public."

After we finished breakfast, the three of us went to our room where we had left the trunk with a selection of spools. "Interesting!" Joseph said, "This small size makes it easy to handle. How much thread do you put on each spool?"

"We put 547 yards on the larger of the two spools and 222 yards on the smaller spool."

"I like the fact that both ends of the spool are flat instead of the traditional cone shaped spools that are used in the textile industry. You used maple for the spools?"

"Yes, we felt that maple was still the material of choice to make sturdy spools that last. In Russia, we encouraged shops selling our thread to give customers a percentage off their next spool of thread in exchange for returning empty spools. In turn, we provide stores credit for every empty spool that is returned to us. The customer benefits, the shop owner benefits, and we have to purchase fewer new spools so we as a manufacturer benefit."

"That makes great sense for everyone." Joseph admitted, "Customers and stores save money and the mill spends less on production. Why didn't we think of this?"

"When we started producing the smaller spools for quilters, we did not know how big it would become; we could not keep up with the demand fast enough. So, reusing the spools just made sense. I thought that if you liked the idea of the smaller spools then maybe we could make a business deal. Why don't we go to your shop to discuss the details?" Joseph and I gathered up several spools to take to Josephs mill. Once there, we found out that only a few minor adjustments would be needed for the spinning machines to accommodate the smaller spools.

While Joseph and I discussed business at the mill, Abigail decided to stay in our hotel room to rest prior to taking a walk. We both knew that she really desired to see Allison and the grandkids. I reminded Abigail that we planned on going to see Allison tomorrow. She nodded in agreement but just wanted to go anyway to see where Allison lived.

Later that afternoon, I returned to the hotel to freshened up before Abigail and I went to dinner. As I tidied up, Abigail told me that she had walked by the building where Allison and her family lived. Even thought she had hoped to see Allison or the children but did not. She told me that the building where they lived looked nice. On the way downstairs to the restaurant we began to discuss the deal that I made with Joseph. Once seated and dinner ordered, I told Abigail that Joseph and I had tossed around some ideas regarding spool production. "Since

Joseph produces quality thread we could eliminate the thread part of the operation and just produce spools. One idea that Joseph proposed is that we build a small shop on our acreage to produce wooden spools." Thinking aloud, I wondered "where I could obtain enough wood, specifically maple, to make quality spools."

Abigail looked at me and said "Maybe you should ask Joseph for suggestions prior to our leaving Denver."

As we began to eat our steaks, potato wedges and salads I told Abigail that "Joseph and I also made a deal regarding purchasing thread. Joseph said that he will send you any amount of thread that you might need for your quilting projects. Just send a number of empty spools to him along with letting him know what color of thread you would like to have. He will have the spools filled with the color of thread you need and send them back to you."

Abigail's eyes widened and asked "Why would he do this for me?"

"Well," I began, "maybe because he likes you. He also likes my idea of the smaller sizes of spools; the spools will make his business boom. Plus, if people see your spools full of thread they will enquire where you got it. In addition, he said that if you do open a quilt shop that he would provide us thread at wholesale pricing. Of course, this will mean that you can sell the spools of thread at a lower cost than other shops."

The next morning, Abigail and I walked the short distance to where Allison and her family were living. Luckily, George, Heidi and Melissa were outside playing when we approached the building. Seeing their grandparents caused a commotion among the three children as they were excited to see us. As the children drug us inside to see their mother, I asked if their father was around. Heidi told us that "Daddy is working" which caused both of us to be relieved that he was not there. Once inside the apartment, Allison looked up from diapering Henry. Seeing us caused her face to light up with joy. She encouraged us sit down while she finished up with Henry. When the diapering was complete, Allison handed Abigail her newest grandson. Abigail was thrilled to hold our newest grandchild for the first time. The children gathered as close around us as they could get while Allison some coffee for the adults and cookies for the children.

Abigail and I told Allison that her brother, Jacob had purchased the property to the west of our acreage. As we told Allison the particulars of Jacob's newly acquired property the three older children went out to play. Abigail told Allison that "Anna was expecting her and Jacob's third child in late summer." And then asked Allison when her baby was due.

"If my figures are correct, the baby will arrive in late October or early November."

Shaking my head, I softly said "I have often wondered how you have gotten five lovely children and now a sixth on the way when he is gone so often."

"Father," Allison said shyly and somewhat quietly, "it happens in the normal way. It's the same way you came into the world. Please remember that I am his wife. I pretend that I don't know about his whores…"

"You know about them?" I was in total shock to hear that she knew even about one of Daniel's friends.

"Yes, I know all about them" she replied. "The first one that I knew about was back in Hussenbach, just after we were married. The loose woman knew all about me and did not care. She told me that he was good for an expensive meal and a roll in the hay."

"I am so sorry that you had to find out about them." Abigail told Allison.

"I am too Mother! I am just sorry that I did not know about the other women before I married the cad. At least I found out early what kind of man I married; I no longer have any expectations of him. Supporting the children will always fall to me because his money is spent on his girlfriends. I am grateful when he does not often come to my bed demanding his rights as my husband. I suspect that he has a wealthy mistress here. I can't prove it but he is often gone over night and has even been gone for four to five days at a stretch."

"You can still come back to Kansas with us."

"You don't know how often I have thought of catching a train for Kansas. It would be quite difficult with five young children and another on the way."

Firmly, I said "It would be easier if you came back now since your Mother and I are here to help you."

"Can you give me overnight to think about it?"

"Yes, we will be back tomorrow morning to get your answer. How about we take you and the children for lunch tomorrow? I have heard about a place that the children will love." Abigail and I hugged and kissed Allison and the children good-bye.

Back in our hotel room, Abigail and I freshened up and went downstairs to join Joseph and his wife for dinner. While enjoying a leisurely meal, we saw Daniel at the bar having a loud and very heated discussion with another man. Shaking my head, I looked at Joseph and said "I would introduce you to our son—in—law but I don't think that this is an appropriate time to do so."

Surprised Joseph replied "I am sorry to hear that he is your son—in—law. However, it does not affect our relationship; just remember we can pick our friends but we can't pick our family."

Hearing gunshots we all looked over to see a smoking gun in Daniel's hand and two men lying crumpled on the floor. Going over to the bar, I asked that the police be notified as quickly as possible. Hotel security quickly came into the restaurant to maintain order and to retain Daniel. After the police arrived, the Hotels security assisted with the investigation.

Abigail asked Joseph and Marie if we could postpone our dinner until tomorrow evening at six o'clock. Abigail talked to the wait staff regarding the meal. She was told that the other couple already paid the bill and to keep our meal warm until Christian was finished with the police.

I was allowed to stay during the investigation because I told both security and the police that I was the father—in—law of the shooter. During the questioning Daniel admitted that he and one of the dead men, Francis Gregory, were rivals for the affections of a Denver socialite. The socialite was also the wife of a wealthy Denver businessman who had political ambitions. The second man killed was an innocent bystander who happened to get caught in the cross fire. In a soft voice, I said to Abigail "That explains where Daniel has been and with whom he spends his days." Abigail nodded in agreement. The police told us that they were taking Daniel to the police station to be booked. Under the circumstances, they said that he would be in jail until the trial was completed. I told the officers that I would let Daniel's wife know what was happening with her husband. But, prior to leaving for our room, I asked an officer if it would be okay for us to take Allison and the children back to Kansas to live.

"That's fine," replied the officer. Handing me a business card he said "Please put your address on the back of this card which I will take back." He then handed us another card and said to keep it for future reference. The officer then stated that "since Daniel admitted his guilt the trial will happen quickly. He will most likely spend a long time in jail. From what Daniel has told us, he has had several other dalliances since arriving here in Denver."

"We don't know about here but in back home in Russia he had at least four different mistresses' that we know about."

The officer shook his head and replied that he couldn't "understand men like Daniel! However, it takes all kinds of people to make the world go around." He handed us another business card before continuing "You might wish to utilize this attorney regarding a divorce for your daughter." As the officer walked away, I looked at the business card that he had handed to me. The card was for an attorney and I assume the name on the card was for a divorce attorney.

The next morning, Abigail and I went to see Allison and to tell her the bad news about her husband. We provided the children with the cupcakes that we brought from the hotel's restaurant. The goal was to keep them occupied while we talked with their mother. After greeting and hugging us, Allison asked how we liked the Brown Palace and how the business deal went the day before. I was delighted to have something else to talk about with Allison so told her about the business deal. After I briefly told her about the business deal Allison said "How exciting for you, Dad. This should help the economy of Rush County tremendously."

"To tell the truth, I could use some office help running this business; are you interested?"

"I am but how will I convince Daniel? He might not want me or the children returning to Kansas."

Looking at each other, Abigail and I both dreaded saying what we had to tell her next. "Allison, I don't think that it will matter much to him."

Allison immediately had a surprised look on her face but before she could say anything, I said "We saw Daniel last night at the restaurant's bar."

I paused to allow Allison to digest what we were saying before continuing on. "Daniel got into an argument with another man, he pulled out a gun and shot the other man dead. He also shot and killed an innocent bystander. The police have arrested and interrogated him. He was taken away to jail to await trial."

I paused once again, before I proceeded to tell Allison what the police recommended. Apparently I took to long because Abigail jumped in and said "The police recommend that you obtain the services of a divorce lawyer."

Not believing what she just heard, Allison stared blankly at the floor. Henry crying startled her back to reality. Allison then stood up, gripped her stomach and awkwardly fell to the floor. Both Abigail and I jumped up to help her and noticed that she was bleeding. "Christian, I think she is losing the baby. We need to get her some help."

I managed to get Allison to the hospital while Abigail stayed with the children. She packed bags for the children and managed to get them to our hotel. After I made sure that Allison was resting comfortably in her hospital room I returned to the hotel. "How is she?" Abigail inquired.

"The doctor said that she did lose the baby but will be fine after a few days rest. He plans on keeping her for another day or two; after that he said that we can take her but recommends that she rest in the Denver area for a few days before we return home."

"Hopefully we can pack up her belongings prior to her being released from the hospital. We can rest here an additional two or three days before catching the train for Kansas."

"By the way, I arranged for us to move to a suite since we now have five children with us. The hotel will send a bellboy to help move the baggage to the other room within a few minutes. I also asked the hotel to recommend a woman that could stay with the children while we have dinner with Joseph and Marie tonight."

"But Chris, we have not met this woman. How do we know that she will be okay?"

"Abigail, I met Mrs. Turner before I came up here. She is a widow who has been working for the hotel for over twenty years taking care of customer's children. She showed me a special children's menu and recommended dishes for the children's dinner. The two of us agreed on the menu for the children's dinner. Mrs. Turner will be here in about an hour and dinner will arrive shortly after. I am sure that the children will love having a new dish called macaroni and cheese, along with green peas and ice cream for dessert. Mrs. Turner said that the ice cream could be brought to the room when the children finish their dinner."

Moving rooms was exciting for the older children because there were three rooms instead of just the one. The boys thought that the large cart that the bellboy used to transport the baggage was thrilling; they wanted one for home. Mrs. Turner arrived and began to get acquainted with the children. Their dinner arrived about ten minutes later. As Henry was enjoying his bottle of warm formula, Mrs. Turner assured Abigail that the children would be fine.

Once again, I told Mrs. Turner that we were going to the hotel's restaurant to meet a client and we wouldn't be late. If she needed us for whatever reason to please contact the restaurant. We went downstairs to join Joseph and Marie. The two were waiting at our table along with a bottle of white wine cooling in an ice bucket. Joseph poured each of us some wine and rose his glass "I would like to purpose a toast to our new partnership."

"To our partnership," I chimed in. I added as we clinked glasses "may it last a long time."

"How did it go last night?" Joseph asked

"Not good. Daniel docilely handed his gun over to the police. He admitted that he had been seeing a socialite who was married to a wealthy Denver businessman. She rarely was seen with her husband but was seen about town with many different men. When Daniel found out that she was also seeing another man, named Francis Gregory, he went a bit crazy. He came to the bar with the intent to kill Gregory if he did not agree to stop seeing the woman. The two argued and Daniel shot Gregory along with an innocent bystander; both men died instantly."

Marie quietly stated "I wonder if he ever thought about how your daughter felt every time he pursued another woman; I know how I would feel." Joseph reached over to squeeze her hand and Marie continued "I guess that I am lucky to have married a man who has never looked at another woman like he looks at me."

"Why would I need too? I have loved you since the first time I saw you. So Christian, how did you daughter hold up to the news?"

Just then the waiter came to the table to take their order; after ordering our meals I told them "It could have been better. Yesterday morning she had told us that she knew about all about Daniel's affairs but tried to overlook them. However, she finally had reached her breaking point and was thinking about coming home with us. We went back this morning for her answer. When we told her, what happened with Daniel this morning she collapsed; we rushed her to the hospital where she lost her baby."

"I am so sorry!" both Joseph and Marie sorrowfully stated in unison.

"It's probably for the best since she already has five children to care for." Abigail replied. "I hope that one day she will find a man who really loves her, who will care for her and the children."

"I am sure she will. Prior to meeting Joseph, I was in a marriage very similar to the one Allison is in." Marie began. "Not only did my first husband have multiple 'flossies' or 'whores', whatever you want to call them, but he would beat me. He claimed that it was all my fault that he beat me so horribly. He also declared that I was the reason that he needed other women to be satisfied. Finally, a husband of one of his 'women' shot him dead just before he killed his wife then himself."

"How terrible for you!" Abigail quietly said.

"Yes, at the time I never thought that I would recover. Joseph was the police officer who came to my house to break the news about my husband's death." Marie shyly smiled and then said "He was a blessing for me then and continues to be a blessing in my life."

"I am sorry to hear such a tragic story but one that turned out to be wonderful for you. I am so glad that you found someone who treats you wonderfully. It gives me hope that one day Allison will find her Joseph." replied Abigail with a smile and wink in Josephs direction. Joseph smiled broadly in return.

The evening was very relaxing and it helped to give Abigail and I hope for the future. Since we would be in Denver for an extra few days Marie suggested that we take the children to the Denver's newest attraction: the zoo. The all agreed that going to the zoo would help them get over missing their mother while she was in the hospital.

After the zoo, Joseph told the group about how P. T. Barnum had purchased land in Denver twenty years before in order to have a respite for his show during the off-season. While in town they usually did a show or two for the locals. "The troupe will be performing the next day; do you think that the children would like to go?"

"Of course, the children would be interested. They heard about Barnum's circus being in town for a rest of sorts. Allison told us that they have asked her to go see the circus animals for some time. Especially interested in elephants, George has been asking why Jumbo is not traveling with Barnum's circus anymore."

"Didn't I read somewhere that Jumbo died a while back?"

"I read in a newspaper a few years back that Jumbo was killed by a train as the circus was unloading the animals and equipment somewhere in New England."

Attending Barnum's show was amazing for Allison's older children while the baby slept through the entire performance. Barnum's circus made such an impression on five-year-old George that on the way home he claimed when he was older, he was going to run away and join the circus. The adults all smiled at the thought of George being a circus performer. Melissa, on the other hand, claimed that "George can't join the circus! Who will take care of him?"

After Allison recovered enough, I took her to the police station to find out about Daniel. We were told that he was despondent and wouldn't eat; they were worried that he might commit suicide while in jail. I finally asked "What can be done for him?"

"We are providing him a counselor but he won't talk. We will probably send a minister in to talk to him. In the meantime, we are keeping sharp instruments away from him. We will not let him have anything that can be used to hang himself."

Tears began to run down Allison's checks as she thought about how her husband had deteriorated so quickly. I put an arm around her shoulder and told her that it would be okay before asking the police "When is the trial scheduled?"

"The trial has been placed on the court docket and will begin in about six weeks. If you plan on attending, I can have the court send you a notice a week or so before the trial begins so that you will have enough time to make arrangements to get here."

"Yes, we plan on coming to the trial. Thank you so much for the assistance that you have provided. It would be nice to have meet you under better conditions."

A few days before we planned on leaving town, I took Allison to see the attorney that was recommended to us regarding a divorce. The lawyer told us that under the circumstances Allison would not have a problem with obtaining a divorce and gaining sole custody of the five children. The paper work was begun that day; we were told that the divorce should be final in six months time. The legal documents that Allison would need to sign would be mailed to the court house in Rush County; After obtaining the signatures the court would then send the documents back to the Colorado court in Denver.

Joseph and Marie took us to the train station. We were very sad to leave our new—found friends but it was only for a short time. Both couples knew that we would see each other often. Arriving back in Rush County was a mixed blessing for Allison. She was sad that her marriage had failed but was so much happier to be home with loved ones. Her brothers, Jacob and Philip, were ecstatic to see her again. Anna absolutely loved the children and felt that the cousins would have a great childhood together. Anna wanted to tell Allison about her pregnancy but knew that it might hurt her since she had just lost a precious baby. However, Allison knew of the baby and congratulated Anna.

Temporarily, Allison and the children would be living with Abigail and me. Sitting down with Adam, George and Jacob, I began the discussion about building of a home for Allison and her children. Abigail was thrilled that it would be on our property so that she and Allison would be able to walk to each other homes in a relatively short period of time.

We laid out the floor plan on paper before marking it out on the land with stakes and string. As a surprise for Allison, we made sure that the house had running water to the kitchen and to an alcove for a bathtub. Off to one side we dug a root cellar to be used for storage of canned goods and for shelter when tornados threatened the area.

While the house was being built, I was contacted by the court in Denver regarding Daniel's trial. The letter stated that the trial was set to begin in thirteen days at eight in the morning in courtroom four of the Denver County Judicial Building. Since there was a lot of publicity regarding the trial the courtroom would be closed to the public. If the family planned on attending the trial, we were asked to please notify the office of the court system so that the judge and bailiff would know to expect us.

Abigail and I discussed telling Allison about the trial being in less than two weeks; both of us felt that it would be better if she did not attend the trial. The next day we told Allison about the letter from the court system in Denver and asked her if she wanted to attend. Fortunately, she told us that she had no desire to go or to ever see Daniel again.

Deciding to attend the trial, I wanted to make sure that Daniel spent a long time in jail. The trial took just under three days and the jury deliberated for just over two hours before returning with a guilty verdict. The jury recommended life in prison without any possibility of parole. The judge thanked the jury for their time and pronounced that sentencing would take place the following morning at nine. The judge banged his gavel and rose to leave the court room.

The next morning the judge stated that he was "saddened about the lack of morals not only across the western part of the United States but most especially with Daniel, the cohort that he killed, and the Denver socialite." Looking directly at Daniel he asked "Do you feel any remorse for killing an innocent by-stander? Do you ever think about what you have done to your wife and children?"

Not able to answer, Daniel could only drop his eyes to the floor. "I did not think so," the Judge continued, "You will have plenty of time to think about your crime and what you have done to your family. I hereby sentence you to life in prison without the possibility of parole." He banged his gavel, the courtroom rose, and the judge quickly departed the courtroom.

Turning to look at me, Daniel gave me a look of utter ha-tred. Was I imagining it or was he blaming me for his being sent to jail for life? Thanking the prosecuting attorney, I shook his hand and left to see Joseph and Marie before I returned home.

Four and a half months later, a staff member at Rush County court house notified me that a package of papers for Allison to sign had arrived from Denver. Knowing that this would bring up bad memories, I reluctantly told Allison about the notification after dinner. I knew that she had to sign the papers in order to end that part of her life forever but I still dreaded bringing up the topic. However, with five children and two looking just like Daniel, this part of her life would never be completely forgotten. As expected, crying ensued as the papers were signed. Abigail reminded Allison that she and the children could finally move on with their lives. Allison's mind understood this but her heart still needed healing.

After Daniel's trial, I finally arranged to separate an acre from my 640—acre property in order to build a spool business. In a loft area, a room would be enclosed to house an office where Allison and I would work harmoniously together. Allison was able to work part—time because the business did not require a full—time office person and it enabled her to be home with the children as much as possible.

In 1904, I hired three men to work in the mill producing wooden spools. The men hired were farmers, so would need time off to plant and harvest crops. This worked well for me since I was a farmer first and foremost. Philip was a great help with the operating of my farm and assisting with handling of the company's shipping operation.

In January of 1904 Jacob and Anna's family grew to include a fourth child. Jacob decided that the time was right to help make Anna's life easier by purchasing a new cook stove for her use. He also had running water brought into the kitchen and into an alcove that would house a bath tub just like what we had at our house. At that time new cabinetry would be built and mounted in the kitchen to hold dishes, pots, pans and whatever else Anna might use them for.

Just like back in Germany and Russia women in America canned fruits and vegetables to be used during the winter months. Women across the county gathered together to preserve as much of their harvest as possible. Abigail, Mary and Christina's kitchens were utilized to preserve vegetables and fruits. When finished, the group shared the canned goods equally among family households. Plus, the women helped each other by loading the canned goods into root cellars located with each house. I noticed that ninety per—cent of the time the younger members of the family were conscripted into taking the newly canned goods into the root cellars. One of the women would remain in the cellar to make sure that like goods would be stacked together on the shelves while the other women supervised the unloading from the wagons.

Combining chores made them go faster for the women. For example, baking once a week freed up other days for other chores. For some reason that I can't figure out, Thursdays became baking day. I was told that Mary, Christina, their daughters and daughters—in—law, Abigail and Anna would gather at a different house each Thursday to do the week's baking.

Each woman would bring flour, yeast, and other needed ingredients along with loaf pans, bowls and spoons to the house where they were baking that week. The bread had to be completed in stages because the oven could only hold a limited number of loafs at a time. Mixing and kneading the bread would be followed by ninety minutes of rising and then the baking took place. While the first batch was baking, the second batch would be rising and a third batch would be mixed together and kneaded. Enough bread would be baked each week to last each household a week. Of course, there were weeks that one or more household ran short of bread and additional bread needed to be made. This was okay with the children and men because they preferred the bread warm with melted butter.

Butter churning was not a particular favorite of the women but needed to be done. Jacob had made Anna two churns so the butter making would go faster for the women. He contemplated making an additional two churns because the family was growing and needed more butter. Baking day was interlaced with gossip, laughter and knitting. Allison appreciated taking home several loaves of bread along with some butter when she picked the children up from Anna's home or from our home. However, Allison expressed to both Abigail and myself that she felt that she missed out bonding with other female family members when she worked but knew that she had no choice.

Handling laundry was easier as that Anna, Allison and we had water already pumped into the house. From inside the house, water would be pumped in buckets, heated, utilized for laundry and disposed of down the drain in the bath—tub. On Friday's, laundry could be seen waving in the wind hanging in neat rows from clothes lines. Allison was able to join her mother and sister—in—law on laundry day because she did not work Fridays. As Jacob, Philip and I worked, we could hear the women's laughter from the shop or from the fields; it was like music to our ears. Laughter was so much better than crying. Laughter and keeping busy allowed Allison to heal and eventually Daniel's memory faded, never forgotten but faded.

Spring 1975

I noticed that how the women completed the chores was almost identical to how it was done in Hussenbach. Guess that things change but really do not change much.

I was stunned to learn about what had happened to Allison and her family while living in Denver. Surviving in a strange city with five small children and expecting a sixth had to be tough. In addition, working at cleaning the common areas of the apartment building aided Allison in providing a place for the family to live. This scenario reminded me of a book by Betty Smith that I recently read. Taking place in New York City, *A Tree Grows in Brooklyn* tells the story of a woman, like Allison, cleaning the common areas of a tenement building in order to support her family. The story differs in the that the man of the household has trouble finding work and he was often intoxicated.

Having Daniel stand trial for killing two men at the Brown Palace Hotel had to be the hardest thing of all for Allison to bear. However, moving back to a loving, caring atmosphere had to be wonderful for Allison. With five children, I am positive, that she would not completely forget Daniel; however, being close to the family had to help her to forget about the unpleasant interlude in her life that had begun in Hussenbach and ended in Denver.

Again, my thoughts went back to the bible verse in Matthew:

For I was hungry and you gave me food; I was thirsty and you gave me something to drink; I was a stranger and you welcomed me. Just as you did it to one of the least of these who are members of my family you did it for me. Matthew 25:35, 45

Joseph and Marie Becker went out of their way to make Christian and Abigail, my Great—Great—Grandparents, feel welcome in Denver and into their lives. My heart sang with joy that my relatives had met a couple like the Becker's. I hoped that the friendship between the Becker's and my Great—Great—Grandparents would last a long time to come.

I know that friendship can make life's rough spots bearable. I have a good friend that made my time in high school tolerable. The two of us got together at every possible chance during High School. For the past several years we studied at different colleges but have remained very close.

Still considering how I could welcome strangers, feed the hungry or provide clothing for the poor, I decided to volunteer at a local thrift shop. One morning a week I sorted donated clothing for display in the shop. While working in the shop one morning, an armed gun man entered the building with the intention of robbing the establishment. Seeing the robber waving a gun the manager tripped the silent alarm. The robber did not get far as he tripped over something on the floor and his gun was sent flying across the shop. Quickly getting up, he fled the store without his gun but was stopped by police. The officers quickly cuffed him and took him to jail.

This was not what I wanted to remember about my college years but, I learned something about myself that I did not know before: I could remain calm under pressure. I wonder if Conrad and the other men felt that way when Andrew / Anton came at Jacob with a loaded gun while they were surveying land in the Volga River area. Under extreme circumstances, such as a robbery, people find out what they could do and what they thought they could never do; Maybe it has to do with the idea of self—preservation.

Picking up the next journal, I looked for any pictures, post-cards, flyers or maps that might be placed within the journal. Once again there were several letters written in German. The letters are a wonderful thing in that they provided me an insight to what was important to the family and to what friendship means.

Journal Eleven

1905—1909

Change seemed to occur slowly during the early part of the twentieth century. The family had quietly settled into what seemed like an ordinary, everyday life. George and Mary had thirteen grandchildren when they had their last child in September of 1905; they named her Lydia. Adam and Christina became grandparents for the first time in 1904. In the spring of 1905, Anna and Jacob added a fifth child to their family. They named their son after Abigail and my friend, Joseph Becker. Continuing to farm his own 480—acres, Jacob assisted me in farming my property.

Our youngest, Philip, was working hard on my farm and helped out in the spool shop whenever he was needed. During the time in the spool shop, Philip realized that he enjoyed doing carpentry work. By the time, Philip was twenty he had become a master carpenter. Just like many other men at the time, Philip farmed and operated a successful side business. Like many other family members, Philip's specialty was making quality rocking chairs. Word quickly spread throughout western Kansas about Philip's rocking chairs. People came from as far away as Colby,

Garden City, and Dodge City to purchase rocking chairs. Before he knew it, people were coming from southern Nebraska, the Oklahoma pan—handle, extreme north west Texas and eastern Colorado to purchase a single chair, a pair of rocking chairs or a half dozen or more of his rockers. Many purchased six or more rockers to sell in their business in Nebraska, Texas or any where home might be. They told Philip that they knew the rockers would sell well back home and that they would be back for more rockers. They asked for Philip's contact information so that they could contact him regarding future orders.

Mary, Christina, Anna and Abigail sat down to discuss the possibility of opening a quilt / fabric shop in town. If a quilt / fabric shop was opened, Abigail wanted Mary and Christina to be equal partners with her; that way the women could share the responsibilities of running the shop but would also share in the profits. However, Abigail desired to operate a smaller shop than what she had in Hussenbach. But a shop where women could purchase quality fabric and threads locally. Abigail knew that women did not want to travel fifty miles for just one spool of thread or a single fat quarter.

In order to make the work easier for everyone, Christina, Mary, Anna, Abigail and a couple of the daughters and daughter—in—laws of both Mary and Christina could each work a single shift at the shop. Abigail thought that "the shop should be closed Sunday and Mondays. Being open Tuesday through Saturday from nine to four should be enough time for any quilter to obtain needed supplies."

George, Adam and I went to town to look for a suitable building. A two—story building was located next to the grocery store on Main Street. I thought that classes could be held on the second floor while fabric and threads would be set up on the first floor. Four hundred square feet did not leave lots of room for a few rocking chairs to be scattered around. So, George, Adam and I thought that three or four rockers would be sufficient for the shop. I'll have to ask Abigail how she feels about it. Maybe an additional three rocking chairs could be placed on the front porch.

The remaining bolts of fabric that Abigail brought from Hussenbach could be utilized in this Kansas shop. Needing additional fabric for the shop, Abigail and I planned on a trip to Denver. Last time we were in Denver, Marie had told Abigail about a textile mill that produced the most exquisite fabric. So, Abigail wrote Marie asking her about arranging a tour of the textile mill.

May 1905

Dear Joseph and Marie,

How is everything with the two of you? Allison has adapted well without Daniel. The children hardly seem to remember him. There are lots of men in the family that are spoiling them.

I have decided that it is time to open a quilt / fabric shop here in Kansas. Home life keeps us busy but the women in the region have argued that there is not a good place to purchase quilting material here. The shop in Hayes closed last year because the owner passed away. So Christian and I are planning on coming to Denver to purchase some fabric. Can you arrange a tour and put me in touch with whoever I need to talk too about buying material?

> *We look forward to your reply before we book passage on the train and get a hotel room.*
> *Love Abigail and Christian*

Marie was excited to hear that we were coming to Denver for a buying trip. Of course, when writing back to Abigail, Marie insisted that we stay with them. Besides going to the textile mill, Marie had several ideas for the four of us to do while we were visiting.

> *June 1905*
>
> *Dear Abigail and Christian,*
>
> *We are ecstatic to hear that you will be coming to Denver. Yes, I will arrange a tour and for you to talk to a member of the textile mill's staff.*
>
> *Of course, you will stay with us here in our townhouse. There is a Broadway play opening in two weeks; it will be here for three weeks. Please tell me that you will be here then, I will get tickets for the play. Also, we will arrange for tickets for the symphony orchestra.*
>
> *Love Marie and Joseph*

Abigail sent Marie a letter saying that they would love to go the theatre and the symphony with her and Joseph. In the letter she stated the date, the train number and the time that we would be arriving in Denver. Abigail and I figured that staying five days should be enough time to tour the textile mill, order fabric, go to Joseph's spinning mill for ordering thread, and to attend the symphony and theater.

The morning after arriving in Denver, Joseph, Marie, Abigail and I went to the textile mill. We viewed how the fabric was produced in America; I noticed the fabric being produced here was done exactly as it was in Russia. Going to the executive office suite to have a catered lunch and to discuss the type of fabrics Abigail wished to see in her shop. She told them that she wanted to use cotton fabrics because she felt that cotton did well not only for dresses and shirts but, also, for quilts; it lasted longer than other type of fabrics and was easiest to work with.

Back on the display floor we looked at the various fabrics that were being produced at the mill. Touching a violet calico, Abigail said "I love these calicos that you are producing; I would like to order four bolts of each in pink, blue, violet, green, red, brown and this buttery yellow. I feel that the small check patterns will also do well in the shop, no matter the color; well maybe not in pink because men do not wear pink shirts."

"Wait a moment," interjected Joseph, "I would wear pink." We laughed at the thought of a big man like Joseph wearing pink.

"A pink plaid could be utilized by women for dresses for girls and for themselves." argued Marie.

"Have you noticed that the Russian—German women tend to wear a lot of very dark colors?" Abigail said.

"Yes, I noticed; I think that it is time to change that habit." replied Joseph. Smiling, both Abigail and Marie agreed. Change would take time but Abigail was willing to provide colorful fabrics in order to help the change along.

"She will take some of the pink plaid along with the other plaid fabrics. Do you want three bolts of each color; maybe less, maybe more?" I asked.

"Okay, okay! I will take four bolts each of every color of the small plaids. The plaids will add to any quilt made but also make great shirts, dresses or quilts. Also, I would like to purchase three bolts each in every solid color that you produce except no black. Could we get three bolts of this fabric," Abigail said touching fabrics as she moved about the display floor, "this fabric, this fabric, this fabric, this fabric and finally, this fabric."

"Will we be able to take any of the fabric with us?" I asked.

"We have enough of the last six fabrics selected to send twelve bolts now; the remaining six bolts can be produced and sent to you. We could send one bolt of each solid color with you now; again, we will produce more solids and have them shipped to you. The same thing with the calicos and plaids; we can give you half of the number bolts you want now and ship the remaining bolts after they have been made. How long do we have to box up the bolts of cloth to take home with you?"

I told the textile mill staff that we would be in Denver three more days. Jumping in Joseph told the staff that "The boxed materials could be delivered to my house." He gave them his home address for the delivery over the next couple of days.

I stated that "since we live in rural Kansas the textile mill could send the later shipments to me in LaCrosse, Kansas. I will ask the train station worker to notify us when the boxes arrive and the family will pick them up to take to the shop." Then, I paid the mill owner for the entire transaction and thanked him for his time.

The mill owner sated "We cannot tell you how much we appreciate your business. I hope that we have a long and successful relationship."

After leaving the textile mill, the four friends headed for Joseph and Marie's home to relax before attending the theatre and having a late dinner. Over dinner the friends discussed the play and how much they enjoyed it. After dinner, we were enjoying a leisurely cup of coffee when Abigail said that she felt so "guilty because she did not have to cook the meal or clean up afterwards. I could get used to the idea of not cooking or cleaning up afterwards."

"It did not take me long to adjust to this life style after Joseph and I married."

Just then Abigail gasped and as she clutched my arm. "What is the matter dear?" I asked.

Following the direction of her eyes I saw Daniel. I immediately jumped up to intercept him. Touching him on the shoulder caused the man to turn and look at Dad. Thinking that he must be mistaken and intercepted the wrong man. "I am sorry, I thought that you were…".

"Daniel Heller?" the man asked.

"Yes, I thought that you were my son—in—law, Daniel."

"My name is David. May I join you for a cup of coffee?"

Being puzzled, I indicated the table that we were sitting at, I said "Please join us" as I motioned to the waiter for more coffee and another cup.

"I am sorry, I did not realize that you were with a group of people. Are you sure that it isn't an inconvenience?"

"Please have a seat." I said. Pulling another chair over to the table, while the others made room, we sat down, I began making introductions.

"This is Joseph and Marie Becker, and my wife, Abigail; my name is Christian Funk. I am sorry, David I did not get your last name."

"My last name is Heller." David replied and quickly interjected "Daniel and I are identical twins with a few slight physical differences. We were born and raised in Rosenheim, Russia. Being raised with seven children total, including the two of us, there never seemed to be enough to go around, that is according to Daniel. He was unhappy as a child. Whereas our other five siblings and I had happy childhoods. We knew that there was enough love, food and anything else we needed to go around.

"The six of us realized that we did not have to be rich to be happy but all decided to better ourselves with higher education. Both of our sisters have become teachers; two brothers studied to become doctors while another became a minister. In order to study agriculture, I moved to Saratov to attend the agricultural school.

"Daniel was the only sibling that did not seem to understand that money does not bring happiness. Growing up, he always felt cheated because he had to share our parents, the house and everything else with six other people, his siblings. Ever since he was a small child, he was lazy. By saying he did not understand his homework; he would get me to help him. As an adult I realized that I actually did his school work for him.

"Once he was old enough, he set out on his own. As you know he became a mechanic but a lazy mechanic. His ultimate goal was to marry into wealth and never work again. As he traveled around, he learned how to romance women to get what he most desired; a life of leisure."

"Just like what he did to our daughter, Allison."

"Unfortunately, that's true. If he truly loved her, he would never have had numerous affairs or treated her badly."

Quickly interjecting, Joseph asked David "to join us for dinner."

"If it isn't an inconvenience, I would love to have dinner with you." David replied. A menu was brought for David and we all ordered. While waiting for the meal to arrive we continued our discussion regarding Daniel.

Abigail asked "How did you learn of his extramarital affairs?"

"The family was able to keep track of what he was doing through an extensive family network in the Volga River region. We knew that he often had numerous affairs going on at the same time; sometimes he would never see a woman again after he spent an evening in her bed. Other times he would dump the woman after being threatened by an irate husband.

"While he courted your daughter, he had several women on the side but only one that lived in Hussenbach. However, Daniel knew that if you heard about an affair prior to his marrying Allison that the marriage would never take place. So, he laid off other women long enough to marry Allison."

Dinner arrived, so we paused the conversation until the waiter was finished. We then continued the conversation while we ate.

"Once your family left Russia it has been difficult to keep track of him. We found out that you were moving to America and Kansas in particular. I was able to move to Topeka about the time that Daniel murdered his rival and the innocent man here in Denver. I heard about the murder from the desk clerk at the hotel where I was staying."

Shocked, Joseph said "The news went as far as Topeka?"

"From what I understand, the story even made newspapers in New York City. Anyway, I arrived in Denver a couple days before the trial."

"Please call me Christian. I am surprised that I did not see you at the trial."

"That could be because I did not want to be noticed. I wanted to be there incognito, to attend the trial without causing a scene since most people cannot tell us apart. I wanted to make sure that for once he was paying for his crimes."

Dad replied "Yes, I agree that he needs to face the consequences of his actions."

"I wanted to meet Allison but as that I look just like the man that wronged her, I decided that it was best not to pursue it."

"What have you been doing since the trial ended and Daniel went to prison?" Abigail asked.

"I was able to get a teaching job at a new school called Colorado Technical College. I met a young woman named Mary. We married and we are now expecting our first child."

I congratulated him and then said "Thank you for letting us know about the childhood and early adult life of Daniel. We would love it if you kept in touch with us." Scribbling quickly on a piece of paper before handing it to David, I said "Here is our address in Kansas."

Finishing his coffee and dinner, David thanked us, said that he would keep in touch. Quietly, David paid for the entire meal prior to leaving the restaurant for his room. He left for his home early the next morning before we had the chance to say our good—byes.

Waiting at the train station, Philip and Jacob discussed whether they should plant cucumbers in the family garden this year. The brothers had been told that cucumbers grew well in Rush County and in other parts of Kansas. Jacob pointed out that we could have a small standing of cucumbers to see how it grew for ourselves here in Kansas.

Philip and Jacob were happy to see the train pull to a stop at the station and waited impatiently for us to make our grand exit.

Upon exiting the train, we hugged our sons then waited for the baggage and boxes to be unloaded. We placed the baggage and boxes into our wagon, climbed aboard and then asked the young men what they had been discussing prior to the train pulling into the station. They told me that they were kicking around the idea of growing cucumbers. Immediately, I thought that I vaguely remembered that cucumbers might have been grown in Hussenbach but could not remember for sure.

Abigail then asked if we could stop at the shop in order to drop off the boxes of threads and material. Philip asked "did you bring back a lot of material and thread?"

Of course, she smiled and told Philip and Jacob that "I bought out the store." They were shocked before realizing that she was 'pulling their legs'. "We were very conservative in our purchases. We were able to bring back about half of what we ordered; the rest will be produced and shipped to us." Unloading the boxes of what Abigail considered half of what we ordered caused our sons to roll their eyes. Jacob asked him mother whether we needed to unbox it today?"

"No," Abigail said "it can wait until tomorrow or the next day." I noticed that while we were in Denver, Adam, George and several of the cousins had built the needed shelving and tables. The floors had been refinished and the shop cleaned. Seeing that the shop was now complete, except for the displayed fabric and thread, brought Abigail to tears. She was thinking of all the responsibilities that would not all be hers but shared with others. Knowing this made owning a fabric / quilt shop far easier especially since she knew that she was not getting any younger. Not wishing to see his mother cry, Philip hugged her and said "What's for dinner?" We had a good laugh and decided to head home.

Arriving home, Abigail went inside to the smell of a hearty stew cooking slowly on the stove, bread cooling on the counter and Allison and Anna were setting the table. Since it was almost seven thirty, the grandchildren had been fed about two hours before. Jacob and I carried in the baggage while Philip took the horses and wagon to the barn. He unhitched the pair of horses, fed them and provided the horses water.

Over dinner the family heard about our trip to Denver, except how we met Daniel's twin brother, David. After telling our children about the play we saw and about the music we heard made me realize that we were both glad to be home but, we missed the fairy tale life that we led with Joseph and Marie.

Over the next month the women worked on getting the shop set up. The cutting table was placed near the large window in front of the shop. A pair of rocking chairs were placed between the thread cabinet and the cutting table. The placement of rocking chairs was so that the ladies could sit while the fabric was being cut in the natural light coming through the front windows.

Fabric was grouped according to color but, in some cases, were placed together according to the fabric pattern. For example, plaids might be altogether or within each color group: violet, yellows, etc. Over the next four weeks, we received three different shipments of fabric.

Upstairs, Abigail, Mary and Christine had decided to hold quilting classes like I thought that they would. For these classes they set up several smaller tables where pieces of fabric could be cut into various sizes and shapes. Then they would be sewn together into quilt blocks. There were two irons and ironing boards set up for pressing the seams of the quilt blocks. A stove was set up to keep the room warm and for heating the irons for pressing. They had six rocking chairs set in two groups of three for those taking quilting classes.

After much discussion, Mary, Christine and Abigail decided that they wanted to purchase a Singer sewing machine for use in the shop. But they asked themselves whether they could afford it? Considering the possibility, Jacob approached me about the two of us purchasing the sewing machine for the shop as a gift for his mother and aunts. We got together the money, purchased the machine, put ribbon around it, placed a bow on top and put it in the shop early one Monday afternoon. Abigail and the other women were pleasantly surprised to see the sewing machine when we brought them to the shop later that afternoon. They couldn't wait to try it out.

Some women preferred using a machine for sewing as opposed to doing it by hand. They argued that it was faster and that the stitches were more uniform. However, not every woman could afford the purchase price of a sewing machine so many of them tried the sewing machine at the quilt shop. Women liked that they could sew a twelve—inch block together in under fifteen minutes. Twenty blocks could be pieced and sewn together over a month. Often the quilt top was completed entirely by use of the shops sewing machine. The women would then hand quilt their newest creation at home. Over the years, the majority of women would save their egg money in order to purchase their own sewing machine.

The sewing machine remained popular because they might see a new pattern that they liked but did not know how to as-semble the pieces together. So, the shops staff would assist them in cutting of the pieces and then assist the quilter assemble the block before taking it home. Once one block was complete the women appeared to grasp the pattern and would then run with it.

Women from across Rush County used the fabric shop for producing quilts but also for purchasing fabric for clothing. The shop sold enough fabric and thread to stay in business but it never made a huge profit. Working one small shift each week, enabled the family's women to complete their chores at home and to take care of their children. Of course, owning the shop meant more than one shift at the shop for Abigail, Mary and Christina. Once a month, the three women conducted an inventory of the shop after they closed at four o'clock. Twice a year, Abigail and I traveled to Denver to select additional fabric from the textile mill. In between the trips to the mill, Abigail attempted to place orders through the mail. However, she found that ordering through the mail did not replace selecting the fabric in person but it was too expensive to do the trip four times a year.

July of 1907, a daughter, whom they named July of 1907, a daughter, named Hannah, became the sixth child in Anna and Jacob's growing family. Elizabeth and Molly were both ecstatic to have another sister, especially after having three brothers. Elizabeth and John both attended school while five—year old Molly, and three—year old David had farm chores to do close to the house. Molly and David fed the chickens while only Molly was allowed to collect eggs. They had tried to have David collect eggs but he broke too many. Molly and David assisted with weeding the family garden along with their mother. Molly, David helped Anna picking ripe vegetables. Anna decided that two—year old Joseph was now old enough to learn how to pick ripe vegetables without destroying the plants in the family garden. Each of the three children had their own baskets in which to place their hand—picked vegetables. Hannah would be brought out doors in a basket while Anna worked in the garden with Molly, David, Joseph and their cousin, Benjamin.

Life was good in Kansas, but there didn't seem to anything exciting going on at this point in our lives. Throughout my life I have figured out that life does not always have drama and excitement. Sometimes, life is just a series of 'boring' things strung together. No one can handle being robbed at gun point, or beaten up, or anything else daily. In fact, I figure that a normal, happy person needs a bit of boring in their life. I guess that Abigail and I have a ton of boring because we are as happily married as we were when we first married.

Also, during this summer of 1907, fourteen—year old Pauline Wagner caught the eye of my eighteen—year old son, Philip. Since Pauline was four years younger, Philip took his time in getting to know her. While helping to build several pergolas between the church and school grounds Philip would say hello to Pauline as she went to school or when she headed home after school. After about a year of dancing around his feelings, Philip was ready to make his first official step in courting Pauline by asking if he could walk her home from church each Sunday. To his disappointment, Pauline was not at church that week.

Having figured out that Philip was attracted to Pauline, Mr. Wagner stepped up to him and said that "she had left for Salina's teacher college two days ago. Pauline could be gone for one or possibly two years." Philip was disappointed that he wouldn't see Pauline several times a week but was happy that she had decided to become a teacher. Looking for any excuse to see Pauline, Philip arranged with her dad to bring her home for the Christmas holiday. Three quarters of the way to Salina, it started to lightly snow and the temperature began to fall dramatically. Upon arrival in Salina, the snow had tapered off but only temporarily. Philip went into the building where the school's office was located. After greeting the head master, he told him that he was there to take Pauline Wagner home for the holidays. Philip was told where the stables were in order to water, feed and bed his horses down for the night.

"After you take care of the horses," the head master instructed Philip to "come in and I will show you to a room." At the room, the head master told Philip that "dinner was being served to those still at the school in half an hour. This will leave you enough time to get cleaned up before returning downstairs. Meet me in the lobby in twenty—five minutes and we will go into dinner together."

At six o'clock, the dozen students that were still at school were seated in the dining hall. The kitchen staff waited patiently for the head master to arrive before serving the evening meal. The students wondered why there was an extra place setting at the table. The school often had potential donors, board members or prospective new teachers visiting so the students were not overly curious on who would be joining them for dinner. Pauline was happily surprised when Philip walked into the dining hall with the head master. Jumping up to hug him Pauline exclaimed "Philip, I am so happy to see you. What are you doing here this close to Christmas?"

Smiling, he replied "To retrieve you of course! I could not imagine what you were feeling when you knew that you would have to stay at school during your favorite holiday."

"Let's sit down so we can eat, shall we?" the head master said with a smile.

Slowly Pauline, Philip, and the head master sat down as Pauline said "Dad said he had too many obligations during this week to come for me."

"That's because I had asked if I could come for you. Your Dad said that I could. Your parents agreed not to tell you that I was coming because I wanted to surprise you."

"Well, you surprised me alright." She said while she gave him a shy smile.

The next morning the pair joined the group of students and head master for breakfast before they began the journey home. The kitchen staff had packed a lunch for the pair to consume on their way back to Rush County. Handing the basket to Philip, the cook said "You're lucky that the snow stopped yesterday and has not started up again."

"I am grateful that it has stopped because traveling in an open wagon while it is snowing can be very hazardous! It can be very hard to see where you are heading, especially after becoming a snowman." The head master wished them safe travel and a Merry Christmas. "By the way," Philip said as he handed a small box to the head master, "Pauline's mother sent this for you; she said to tell you Merry Christmas."

"Please tell her thank you!" Philip shook the Head Masters hand, then he assisted Pauline into the wagon before he climbed abroad. Philip told Pauline to adjust her coat, muffler, hat and gloves before he placed two blankets around Pauline and then several across her lap. Philip climbed up onto the wagon's seat where he adjusted his heavy coat, muffler, hat and gloves. He then spread two blankets over his lap, and then let the horses know that it was time to go.

About a half hour west of Salina, the snow began to fall again. The snow began to fall heavier the further west the pair traveled. Philip decided to follow the train tracks in order not to become lost. Even with following the train tracks he almost missed the train station due to the white out conditions that the snow storm was causing. Philip stopped, assisted Pauline down and escorted her into the station. Luckily, the man who worked at the station was there and had a fire blazing. The station worker invited them in and offered them some hot tea. Grateful for something warm to drink they accepted but Philip asked if he could first stable the horses. He also wished to give the team of horses some oats and water. The station worker directed Philip to the stable and where to find some oats and fresh water. Upon completion of settling the horses, Philip returned and gratefully accepted a cup of hot tea. Staying at the train station until the snow let up allowed the couple and the horses to warm up and rest.

When the snow stopped Philip and Pauline immediately proceeded to the Wagner farm. Upon arrival, Mrs. Wagner hugged Philip and asked Philip to stay for dinner. He declined the invitation as he wished to make it home before it got too dark or started to snow again. As he was leaving for home, the Wagner's thanked him profusely for bringing Pauline home. A week and a half later, Philip returned to take Pauline back to Salina.

In early June, Philip was excited to return to Salina to retrieve Pauline. He knew that she had decided to get the one—year teaching certificate instead of the two—year diploma; this was due to not having enough money for an additional year of schooling. Besides, she told Philip, she missed her family and had been offered a teaching position at the school in Ness City. They needed her to begin teaching at the beginning of the new school year.

Schools were beginning to change from what they were in the past. This was due to the increased number of people living in the mid—west and the far—west of the United States. Of course, this meant that there were more young people attending school in these regions. Schools had to hire additional teachers in order to educate the young. Schools in larger cities might have one teacher per grade and often had multiple schools.

Pauline had been offered the position to teach the first and second grades. Another teacher taught the third, fourth and fifth grades and a third teacher taught the sixth, seventh and eighth grades. Ness City's school board was considering adding teachers and building either another school or to add several class—rooms on to the existing school in order for students to take classes beyond the eight—grade.

Pauline settled into the four—room home that she would share with the other two teachers. Since she was close to home, Pauline often traveled to her Wagner farm on week-ends. She felt blessed having Philip to take her to the farm in time for the evening meal on Fridays; he would then return her to the teacher's house late Sunday afternoon. In addition, she felt fortunate that she was able to bring enough seasonal vegetables, homemade breads, butter, eggs and can goods back to Ness City help feed herself and her fellow teachers.

Late spring of 1909, Anna and Jacob had their seventh child, they named their newest son Peter. Jacob had learned some English since moving to America but learning new languages were never easy for him. However, he wasn't overly worried about his lack of English language skills because the majority of those that both he and I dealt with in and around town spoke German. Besides Jacob's children are learning English in school which is helping Jacob learn enough English to assist him with business.

Jacob's oldest son, John and his cousin, George, have become quite close and do just about everything together. This often includes getting into trouble at school. Of course, Jacob and George's siblings do not pass up the chance to tell their parents about the mischief that Jacob and George are doing.

After school the older girls, Elizabeth and Molly, assisted Anna by bringing in the clean, dry clothes inside and fold it. The only thing that they had trouble with was how to tell the difference between John's clothing and their fathers clothing. Or Joseph's clothes from David's clothing. For some reason all male or female clothes that are close in size were hard for the girls to tell apart and who they went too. Anna is just grateful that Jacob did not find diapers mixed in with his shirts and socks. On baking day, the girls helped churn butter. Because the boys thought that churning butter looked like fun they would occasionally offer to do the churning. The younger children, that were too young to attend school, assisted Anna by doing a number of easy but time—consuming chores. These shores included gathering eggs and feeding the chickens and pigs.

Tuesday mornings were hectic because Anna was scheduled to work in the quilt shop from nine to twelve—thirty. Jacob would bring David, Joseph, Hannah and Peter to our house for Abigail to watch. Allison's five children would join John, Elizabeth and Molly in Jacob's wagon and be taken to school.

Orange, brown and yellow leafs were slowly drifting to the ground one sunny Tuesday morning in the autumn of 1909. This day was not any different than most Tuesday's except that there was an armed robbery next door at the grocery store. The crooks happened to run from the grocers directly into the quilt shop. Clutching their bag of money, the two masked men told Anna that everything would be fine as long as she did what they told her to do. Trembling, Anna tried to stay calm and agreed to cooperate.

At gun point they told her they just needed a place to hide while the 'cops' looked for them in and around the grocery store. Anna indicated that they could hide upstairs in the classroom. She told the men that "If the police come in asking if I have seen anything, I will tell them no." The men, hoping that they could trust her, quickly retreated to the second floor. Anna quickly picked up a pad of paper and wrote:

The robbers are upstairs!!

Within five minutes two deputies carefully came into the shop and quickly did a scan of the shops first floor. "Mrs. Funk," began one of the deputies, "We are looking for two men who robbed the grocery store next door. Did you see anything?"

Anna said "I am sorry that I did not see anything" as she held up the pad of paper. Nodding their understanding, the deputy said "Thank you! If you see anything please let us know." One of the deputies opened the door and helped her outside. They whispered that she should go to the grocers next door. Once back inside the deputies closed the door behind themselves to indicate they had left. They drew their weapons and waited patiently for the men to come downstairs. Within few minutes the men quietly came downstairs. They were surprised that the deputies were waiting for them with their guns drawn and pointed at them. The robbers were captured without further incident.

Within ten minutes the deputy returned to the grocery store to give the grocer back this stolen money. In addition, he thanked Anna for her quick thinking and for aiding in the robber's timely capture. Turning to the deputy, Anna asked if they could inform her husband what had taken place. A deputy was sent to the farm to inform Jacob about the robbery. Jacob hurried to the grocers only to be informed that she had returned to the quilt shop. Entering the quilt shop, Jacob found a calmer Anna but he knew that she was still upset by the entire incident. Sitting down, Jacob asked Anna what happened even though he had heard about it from the sheriff's staff. He wanted to hear Anna's version of what had taken place. After which he asked Anna if she wished to continue working in the quilt shop after the robbery incident.

"Well, Jacob, I cannot deny that it was scary. But it ended safely with no one getting hurt."

"Next time it might not end as well. I could not bear to have you harmed by an armed gun man."

"We cannot live our lives wondering what is around the bend, Jacob. If I do not return to the shop next week I never will again. So, I must work in the shop next week. If I decide that I can't do it anymore then at least I faced my fears."

"Okay! But how do you feel about me coming with you next week?"

"Now what would you do for three and a half hours in a quilt shop?"

"I'm not sure but I am willing to try it." He said. After a moment or two he finally asked "How about I paint the shop?"

The next week Jacob went to the shop with Anna even though she appeared to have adjusted to the incident by then. She said that she would be okay in the shop alone but was glad that he was there. "If you plan on being here, where is your paint?"

"Paint? What are you talking about?" he asked innocently.

"Well, I talked with your mom regarding your offer to paint. She said that a fresh coat of white paint would do the shop good. With the crops in the field, do you have some time to handle the painting."

"Okay, okay I was pulling your leg." Jacob told Anna. "Did you want me to do the painting when the shop is closed on Monday or on Tuesdays? If during business hours we could leave the doors open to help air the shop of paint fumes."

"Well we thought that it would be better to do the painting on Mondays since we are closed but Tuesdays would probably be okay. Whatever day is good for you would be okay with us."

"Okay you've got a deal. I'll purchase some white paint from the general store and begin today. It might take a few Tuesdays to complete the job but since I am free, I don't think the owner and staff will have many complaints." Jacob headed off to the general store for the paint and brushes. Within an hour he opened the second—floor window and began painting. Two weeks later the entire shop had been painted. Anna was amazed how the newly painted soft white walls could make a difference in the shop's business.

The majority of the Funk women knew that it was not the new paint color on the walls that brought in more women; the increase in business had to do with Anna capturing the robbers. The rise in curious women meant an upturn in the shop's revenue. Business did not drop off as one would expect when the novelty of the robbery wore off. In fact, business became so good that more fabric and thread needed to be stocked. This caused Abigail to plan and make an additional buying trip to Denver. After talking to me, Abigail invited Anna to come with us on the buying trip.

"I would love to come with you," began Anna, "but with seven children under ten I don't see how I could."

"I already thought of that and asked Allison to help out. Christian has agreed to allow Allison to stay home in order to take care of the younger children during the day. Allison can assist Jacob with preparing meals during the week that we will be gone. Heidi is old enough to help her mother after school with child care and the cooking. Granted Jacob does not normally cook, clean, or other household stuff but can mange the kids at night, can't he? So, is it settled?"

Smiling Anna replied "Can I talk to Jacob first before I give you a yes or no answer?"

Abigail sent Joseph and Marie a letter telling them about the additional buying trip and that they would be bringing Anna with them. Abigail and I wanted to make the trip special for Anna since she was instrumental in catching the robbers.

> *Dear Abigail and Christian,*
>
> *We are excited to hear of your extra buying trip and we look forward to having the three of you stay with us. Joseph has notified the textile mill that you will be coming to purchase more fabric.*
>
> *There will be a new Broadway play in town beginning next week. We will go ahead and purchase five tickets. Just let us know when to meet you at the train station.*
>
> *We look forward to seeing you and meeting Anna.*
>
> *Love Joseph and Marie*

Anna's buying trip to Denver with Abigail and me was a wonderful success not only for the shop but it helped Anna further forget the robbery. Touring the textile mill and selecting fabrics was a marvelous experience for her. Anna selected several fabrics and shades that Abigail knew that she would not have chosen but felt that they would make a wonderful addition to the shop. Abigail felt that in order to keep the shop viable she needed a stock a wide variety of fabrics and colors.

July 1975

According to the last journal, life in Rush country seemed to settle down somewhat after the excitement of a grocery store robbery. I couldn't believe that Anna, like me, had an experience with someone who was desperate enough to rob a store. Innocent people cannot predict when others will be desperate enough to commit a crime that involves the use of a gun. Those being held up at gun point need to keep a cool head to survive the incident and in order to assist the police track to down the criminal.

It was nice to read about Philip's romance with a young woman named Pauline. I wondered what caused attraction between two people. I have noticed that people often fall in love with someone they have known their entire life whereas others travel far and wide before they meet the right person; sometimes people never find the right person.

Pauline's studying to become a teacher made me wonder when the education system changed from where the majority of children stopped attending school after the eighth grade to where many completed high school. My maternal Grandma finished her education with the eighth grade whereas, even then, some attended high school. Within thirty years the number of those attending and graduating high school increased dramatically. Of course, this didn't mean that every person graduated high school then or even today. Many individuals have dropped out of school after the tenth or eleventh grade.

Picking up journal number twelve, I caressed the leather binding. I couldn't believe that it had remained so supple after all these years. Once again, I hoped for some letters, a map or pictures to be inserted inside. This time there were nothing loose inside to slip out onto my lap. I can't wait to find out what happened next with my relatives. With my Grandma alive, I might find out about her early life before she was a mother or a grandmother.

Journal Twelve

1910—1917

In November of 1910, Anna and Jacob added a fifth son to their family; the new baby that would be called William. Two months before, David had joined his three older siblings in attending school. Hannah and Joseph became quite close as siblings often do; they would get into trouble together as they explored the family farm.

During the early autumn months of 1910, Edward Howard moved to Rush County from the pan handle of Oklahoma. He was able to locate and purchase a hundred—and—sixty—acre parcel of land a short distance from my acreage. The acreage had been broken off from a larger parcel of land so it did not have a barn or a house. Edward planned to build a two—story house along with a large barn.

Being neighborly, several men volunteered to assist Edward in building his house and outbuilding. As we were constructing the home and outbuildings, we got to know Edward better. We found out that he was a widower with no children who needed a fresh start. I noticed that from his exceptional work on his house, Edward was a tremendous carpenter. Wanting to ask Edward how he felt about coming to work for me, I began a conversation by stating "As you probably heard by now, I operate a type of carpentry business on my farm."

"When I was looking for property in the area, I heard about your business. Correct if I am wrong but I understand that your business makes wooden spools" replied Edward. "Before moving here, I worked for a small carpentry business. I set a high standard for myself to produce quality work. I was hoping to work as a carpenter here once I got settled."

"I have noticed your excellent work on the interior of the house; I especially like your crown molding and book shelves. I haven't advertised yet but a worker will be leaving within the next month and I will be hiring another worker. Would you be interested?"

"As a matter of fact, I would." Edward replied "Could you tell me a bit more about the pay, the hours and the job?"

After telling him a bit about the job, Edward and I came to an agreement about wages and when he would start work. He desired to complete his house and barn prior to beginning a new job. Edward finished building on his property in early December of 1911, so he was able to begin work in mid—December. As instructed, he came to the office to fill out paper work prior to being shown around and starting work. "Excuse me," Edward said to the young women behind the desk, "I am looking for…"

Turning around and looking at Edward, Allison and Edward's eyes met causing sparks to fly and lightning bolts to flash between the two. If there is love at first sight, which many do not believe in, it happened at the moment when Allison and Edward made eye contact. After what seemed like a long pause Allison quietly said "Are you Edward Howard?" After receiving a positive reply, she continued to tell Edward that "father is expecting you this morning. He told me to have you fill out some paper work. Dad will be back by the time you fill out the paper work." While talking to Edward, Allison had stood up, picked up the paper work, walked over and handed it to him. After handing him a pencil, she said "please sit down here at father's desk. If you have any questions please do not hesitate to ask."

"Well, I do have a question. You have the benefit of knowing my name but I don't know yours. Besides we need to be properly introduced if we are going to work together."

Blushing slightly, Allison dropped her eyes to the floor and replied "I'm sorry, my name is Mrs. Allison Heller."

Disappointed that she was married, Edward extended his hand and said "Nice to meet you Mrs. Heller."

Please, call me Allison."

"Okay, but then you must call me Edward."

Just then, I walked in and greeted Edward. "I am glad that you made it. Have you two introduced yourselves?"

He said "Yes, we have introduced ourselves." He then began to fill out the papers. When finished, he handed the paper work back to Allison and said "It was nice to meet you." Allison smiled shyly at Edward.

I asked Edward if he was "ready for the tour, your tools and work station?" We set off for the shop; Allison stood up and walked over to the office window that over looked the shop. She couldn't believe her eyes; Edward was the handsomest man that she had ever seen. She wondered if he was married or if he had children. It doesn't matter she told herself; I was in love once and what did it get me: a cheating husband, five children and, eventually, a divorce!

While courting Pauline, Philip spent quite a bit of time in Ness County visiting her. Both Pauline and Philip liked the gently rolling landscape in the extreme western part of the county so when a moderate sized property came available in the autumn of 1910 the couple discussed purchasing it.

A week later, Philip took me and his future father-in-law, Paul Wagner, to examine a three—hundred—acre property. The property had a large red barn that was in some disrepair, two smaller outbuildings that were in the first stages of dilapidation and a two—story—house that needed some minor repairs along with a fresh coat of paint. It also looked like it could stand a new roof. It appeared that the fields had not been plowed for several years.

"What's the story about the property?" Paul Wagner asked Philip.

"Apparently, the owner's husband died several years ago and the widow could not keep up with the farming or maintaining of the buildings by herself. There was little money left to buy seed the next year. By the time she figured out how to plow the fields and plant the seed it was too late in the season. With no crop to sell, she had no money for fresh seed or to pay someone to help her the following year. She decided to sell the property and to move to California to be closer to her sister."

"Considering the repairs that need to be made, she won't be able to get the price that she is asking for." I said. "I think that you should offer her thirty—five hundred dollars below her asking price."

"I totally agree" Philip agreed. "We can see what is wrong with the buildings but if the machinery has just been sitting, who knows what repairs need to be made. It could take the entire thirty—five hundred dollars just to make repairs to the buildings and to the machinery. Plus, I will need some money for my first planting."

Philip and the widow came to agreement at thirty—eight hundred dollars less than the asking price. Repairs were made to the house and Philip moved in just after the New Year. He then, began making repairs to the barn, other outbuildings and to the fencing.

Philip traveled extensively between Ness and Rush Counties for building supplies but mainly for household supplies. After moving to the property, Philip realized that he knew nothing about cooking and how much he depended on his mother for his every day survival. Feeling appreciated, Mom provided Philip with bread, butter, fresh and canned vegetables whenever he came to visit. The only stipulation she made was that Philip return the canning jars and lids.

Mid—spring 1911, Paul and Martha Wagner, Abigail and I came to his Philip's property in Ness County to help Philip and Pauline establish a family vegetable garden. Manure was added to the overgrown garden plot, tilled, enlarged, and finally planted. Poles for support were placed where peas, pole green beans and tomatoes were planted. In addition, corn, onions, parsnips, green peppers, carrots, and parsley were planted in groups and according to height. Cucumbers, zucchini, and squash were planted off to the side of the garden. An area was manured and plowed in preparation for pumpkins to be planted in early to mid—summer. As we finished planting the garden, Pauline had arrived from school and begin to prepare dinner. Paul, Philip and I put the farm equipment away. We got cleaned up and then joined Martha, Pauline and Abigail for evening meal.

Pauline was grading papers at the kitchen table while the meat loaf and potatoes were cooking in the oven. After dinner, while drinking coffee and having dessert, discussion began concerning Philip and Pauline's upcoming nuptials. Pauline stated that she "always wanted a summer wedding and desired to have the ceremony held in the church garden."

Martha agreed that "having it under an arbor with all the flowers in bloom would be picturesque. Depending on which month you choose for the wedding will affect what is in bloom in the church garden."

"I love lilies, so was thinking about July" said Pauline. So, planning a July wedding began in earnest. The pair decided that they wanted to have a small wedding with only family and a few close friends in attendance. Following the ceremony, the couple wanted a reception consisting of a cake and iced tea to be held in the church garden. In case of rain, the wedding and reception would be moved into the church and its social hall.

Desiring a dress similar to the one worn by her mother thirty years ago, Pauline and Martha Wagner asked Abigail if she might make Pauline a wedding dress. "First of all," began Abigail, "I will need to see your wedding dress, Martha. Could you bring it over to our house Tuesday?" From Martha's dress, the three women came to an agreement regarding Pauline's wedding dress.

Abigail then asked Martha and Pauline if they could come to the fabric shop one day after Pauline finished school in order to pick out the fabric. Once at the shop, Pauline stated that she wasn't sure she wanted a traditional white wedding dress; she was intrigued by a very, very pale mauve fabric that Abigail had just gotten in the shop. Abigail asked Anna to pull all bolts of pale mauve that the shop had. Retrieving the bolts of material, Anna lay them on the table. Abigail asked Pauline "Is this the color of fabric that you are referring too?"

"Yes! I think that it would make a lovely wedding dress. But am in love with this fabric in particular." Pauline said as she touched one of the bolts of fabric. She then continued by asking "What do you think Mom?"

"Well, it is lovely material! I guess that I am just used to picturing a wedding dress in white fabric. Things are changing and women are wearing more colorful shades. So yes, let's go with this fabric."

Abigail proceeded to make the dress from the pale, pale mauve. As customers watched the dress being made and Pauline trying it on at various times, many changed their opinion about only wearing a white dress. As a result of Pauline's dress, many women approached Abigail about designing and sewing a wedding dress for a family member. Abigail turned down all requests mainly because she did not want to get into this business. Besides having worked most of her life and being in her early sixties, she wanted to have some time with me, to relax and to do things that she enjoyed doing.

Jacob

The July wedding of my brother Philip and Pauline was beautiful and the guests seemed to really enjoy the reception. Mom, Dad, and the Wagners were happy that Philip and Pauline were married and all the wedding hoopla finally ended. The couple settled into their refurbished farm house in western Ness County. Of course, the couple traveled to Rush County often to visit family. Mom and Dad frequently visited Philip and Pauline in Ness County. Fifteen months later in the autumn of 1912, Philip and Pauline had their first daughter whom they named Theresa.

March of 1912, brought a fourth daughter to Anna's and my family. We named her Lydia. Thirteen—year old, John was excelling in his school work. John secretly desired to become a doctor but he knew that he or his family could not afford to pay for a doctor's education. So, John began to learn as much as possible about his second interest: horticulture. He borrowed many books on the subject from his teacher or from any other source possible. When he wasn't in school, John was experimenting with rooting and grafting of many different types of plants. His biggest experiment was with tree saplings. John developed a mini green house to use in growing trees. He grew many distinct tree saplings within the green house. As people heard of John's 'green house' they approached him about purchasing some of his saplings.

Elizabeth and Molly enjoyed school and, like their brother, they were avid readers of anything non-fiction. As a result of their reading, their education benefitted and both girls were at the top of their classes. Like John, Molly was interested in horticulture but her interest lay more with vegetable plants and flowers as opposed to trees. Interest in vegetable plants helped the family with growing vegetables for our garden. Experimenting with different varieties enabled more types of vegetables to be tried in the garden. Extra vegetables always seemed to be grown in the garden so we had a surplus to sell. The different varieties of vegetables went over well with the towns people; many asked the mercantile when he would be getting more in stock.

Now that Joseph was in school, he and Hannah spent less time together and she became more independent. Realizing that Hannah was interested in learning handicrafts, Anna began to teach her to knit and crochet. Before long she had the basics of knitting and crocheting down and she was making beautiful scarves, caps, and mittens. Hannah was intrigued about how her mother and grandmother knitted beautiful socks. At five years old she was determined to learn how to make socks.

My sister, Allison and Edward Howard continued to dance around each other and their feelings until October of 1912. At that point, Edward finally asked Dad why Allison's husband wasn't around. Dad replied that he was no longer in the picture. "Edward, I know that both you and Allison have feelings for each other. Why don't you ask her about Daniel, I am sure that she will tell you about it! All that I will say is that I'd rather have you for a son—in—law then the one I had before. Ask her!"

Being a bit shy, it took Edward a few more weeks before he finally approached Allison and inquired about seeing each other outside of work. "I would like the children to get used to me before I put it out there that we are officially courting."

"Edward, I am not sure that I am ready to be with another man."

"But why? I am attracted to you and I know that you're attracted to me. Please if you are going to 'dump' me I need to understand why."

"I guess that I am ready to talk to you about what happened in my past but it has to be between us and no one else." Edward nodded in agreement before Allison continued on "Almost twenty years ago a man began working for my father while we were still living in Russia. Daniel romanced me, making me feel special. Once we were married, I found out that he really did not love me; his true motive was to find a wealthy woman to marry so that he would not have to work for a living, or so he thought.

"Apparently, he thought that we were wealthy since father owned property and had his own business. The property that we had access to in Russia's had been purchased by my Grandfather Funk. When Grandpa passed, the property was handed down to my Dad and his two brothers. When the property was sold, the three brothers split the proceeds three ways; none of the three men became wealthy over the proceeds from the property.

"In addition, Daniel correctly assumed that the business my Grandfather Funk began did earn a profit. However, what he did not know was that the majority of the profit was put back into the business. If we needed something and our parents thought that it was important then we got it. Otherwise we didn't get it.

"I knew about several of the women that Daniel had relationships with prior to our officially courting. Thinking that Daniel had ended any and all of the relationships he had prior to our getting married caused me to be shocked shortly after our marriage when a woman approached me. This woman proceeded to tell me in graphic detail about the relationship that she was currently having with my husband."

Pausing for a few moments before continuing, Allison said "that over the years, I have heard about the numerous affairs that Daniel had along with many one—night stands. I began to look forward to when he wasn't home so he would not expect his husbandly rights. Although he was home enough that we had five children. About eleven years ago we moved from Russia to America. On the voyage across the Atlantic I realized that I was pregnant with our sixth child. While looking for property Dad and Daniel had words; in a childish tantrum, Daniel dragged the children and me off to Colorado.

"While living in Denver, I obtained a position that involved cleaning the common area of the apartment building where we lived while Daniel pretended to look for work. He took up with multiple wealthy socialites who paid him well and took him to fancy places. The end finally came when he killed two men over a wealthy socialite. Daniel was sent to prison for life and I lost our sixth child in my sixth month. Mom and Dad aided me in obtaining a divorce. My parents and I brought the children back to Kansas live. Do you now understand why I am shy about getting into another relationship?"

"I can understand but you are surrounded by many happy marriages. The majority of men are not like your first husband.

I am definitely not like him. Please can we start fresh with each other?"

"Yes, I think that we can; come over for dinner tonight and we will let the children know that we will be seeing each other from time to time. But please we will need to take the relationship slow."

"If that is what it takes, then so be it."

The relationship between Allison and Edward blossomed and grew until they announced their engagement in the summer of 1913; they planned to be married sometime in late 1913 or early 1914. Allison and the three youngest children would move into Edward's home once they were married. Allison's two oldest children was busy building their own special lives. Back in April of 1910, Heidi, Allison's oldest daughter, had received an acceptance letter from the teacher college in Wichita; she was given a full scholarship that included room and board. Completing the program in mid—June of 1912, Heidi spent the summer at home. In August, she would leave for Hayes to begin teaching at a private school. Hayes was far enough away for a certain amount of independence but close enough for her to be close to the family and to visit often.

For as long as George, Allison's oldest son, could remember he had desired to become a writer. So, he explored all possible ways that he could write for a living. During the spring of 1912, George's teacher told him about a job opening at a newspaper in Topeka. George was intrigued enough that he applied for the position and was hired immediately. In August, fifteen—year—old George moved into a boarding house in Topeka and began to work at the city's largest newspaper. He would be working as a researcher with an occasional chance of writing a special story. While researching for other writers, George did a bit of research here and there for his own novel. He hoped that within a few years he would be able to have enough information to write his book. Within three years, George was promoted to journalist and wrote stories for the paper. Liking research, George tended to do his own research whenever possible instead of using the newspapers research staff.

The remaining children still lived at home with their mom. Allison's second daughter, Melissa, began her last year of formal schooling. Enjoying books, Melissa thought about becoming a librarian. In 1910, Dodge City had received funding through an Andrew Carnegie grant to build a library. Other communities in southwest Kansas followed Dodge City's lead and received Carnegie funding to build a library. Our community applied for a Carnegie grant in 1923. We'll see if the town receives the grant.....

Library science became an accepted area of study at institutes of higher education. In 1912, the college in Wichita, began a program in library studies. Melissa and her teacher discussed what she would need to be accepted into the college in Wichita and into the newly formed library program. In the spring of 1913, Melissa sent in her application and was accepted with a small scholarship for the following fall term. She applied for other grants and scholarships to help pay for her education but also, for her room and board. Realizing how important this was to Melissa, Edward offered to pay her college room and board as long as she maintained a 'B' average. Gladly accepting Edwards' offer, Melissa completed the college program in library studies.

LaCrosse did not receive the Carnegie grant. While Melissa was in college, Allison and Edward secretly looked for property in town that they could purchase and use for a library. Taking classes year around, Melissa was able to complete her schooling by the end of the summer semester of 1916. Returning home, she planned on taking a short rest prior to looking for a job. Allison and Edward were waiting at the train depot to pick her up. They greeted her warmly and as they climbed into Edward's new car he said "Do you mind if we swing by a new building in town before we head home?" As they pulled to a stop at the corner of Elm and First Avenue, the three climbed out of the car. Melissa was amazed at the quaint, brick building and she asked "What type of business is going into the building?"

"Well," Edward began as he dangled the keys in front of Melissa, "let's go in and look around."

Once inside, Melissa saw tables, chairs, lamps, a counter and shelves with some books. Not quite comprehending the entire truth Melissa said "This looks like the beginnings of a library but…"

"We decided that the community needed a library. So, your mother and I brokered a deal with the county. Your mom and I bought the property and had the building constructed. The community is responsible for the building's maintenance, the purchasing of books and paying the librarian's salary. If it is okay, the human resources office would like to interview you for the position next week. By the way this package was left for the new town library."

"I wonder what it is and who it is from."

"I don't know, we can open it to find out."

Opening the package revealed a book entitled *Circus Performers also known as Circus Animals* by George Heller. Pleasantly surprised, but thrilled Melissa exclaimed "How exciting for George! Couldn't he tell anyone about getting published?"

"He did but your Mom and I were sworn to secrecy until the book came out."

Of course, Melissa was thrilled for her brother and about obtaining a job so easily; mainly she could not believe her luck in step—fathers. Edward had supported her in her selected occupation but also assisted her in gaining a job. Over the years,

Edward helped all five of Allison's children because he considered them his own.

After officially completing his schooling in 1914, John decided to pursue horticulture as a career. He thought about obtaining a small property of eighty—acres or one as large as one—hundred—and—sixty—acres. An eighty—acre property would probably be enough for building several medium sized greenhouses in order to expand his sapling business. Besides growing trees, John also thought about growing additional plants, such as scrubs or herbs. Several years of selling saplings had enabled John to save enough money for a down payment for a property. He planned on approaching the bank to obtain a loan for purchasing the land and building of additional greenhouses. At this time, my Dad contacted John. "I understand that you are looking for some land on which to build a home and business. Can you tell me about your plans?"

John began to tell his grandfather about his idea to build a horticultural business that would sell saplings locally. "As you know, my business is mainly local but I have decided to expand my sapling business to other parts of the Kansas and surrounding area. I will need to figure out how to successfully package and ship saplings. I have attempted to ship a few packages to your friend, Mr. Becker in Denver. I have had mixed results with the first couple of shipments; none of the saplings in the first shipment made it to Mr. Becker alive. I changed the packaging which resulted in just over half of the saplings arriving alive in the second shipment. Changes were made to the packaging once again and the entire third shipment made it alive. So, I am ready to expand the business. To do so, I need to a larger property and to build several additional greenhouses in which to grow saplings year—round."

"I have a business proposition for you. The house where your Aunt Allison lived is empty," John's Grandfather began "and I am willing to sell you the house along with thirty acres for a small token. I was thinking about a penny per acre. In order for you to expand your business, I will finance the building of three medium sized greenhouses. You would need to pay me back within five years. What do you think? Do we have a deal?"

John agreed to the proposition, utilizing the saved money to supply his business. Within two years, the sapling business was supplying trees across the mid-west. Within five years, John had paid his grandfather back in full.

While in the general store, sometimes referred to as the mercantile, in early 1916, John was surprised to see new people operating the business. He knew that the previous owners were considering retirement but he had not realized that the business had been sold. Introducing himself, John told the owners that he operated the greenhouses outside of town.

The new owner introduced himself as William Boxberger; calling his wife over, he said "This is my wife Lydia. Lydia, this is John Funk he owns the greenhouse business just outside of town."

Extending his hand John replied "It is nice to meet the two of you. Welcome to our lovely town and Rush County. I came into the store today to order some landscaping trays."

Retrieving the catalog from under the counter, John and William went through the section dealing with seed trays. John ordered enough landscaping trays to handle his booming tree business for several months.

"While I am here," John continued "I will need some rooting hormone."

"This is a first for me; In all the years in business I have never had anyone ask for rooting hormone before."

While William leafed through the catalog, John told him that he had several lilac bushes on the property that he was interested in propagating in order to sell.

Locating the rooting hormone in the catalog, William handed the book to John. John ordered the rooting hormone that he needed, and thanked William for his time. William got John's contact information and said that the items arrived, he would contact him.

A week later, John journeyed into town to pick up and pay for the items that he had ordered at the general store. He was startled to see a beautiful young woman behind the counter. After introducing himself, he told her that he was there to pick up an order of landscaping trays and rooting hormone.

"Aw yes, you are the gentleman that father told me owned the greenhouses outside of town."

Not knowing what else to say he just said "That's me."

"If you want to pull you vehicle around back to the loading dock, I will have Matthew bring your items out."

Pulling his truck around back he saw a young man placing a box on the loading dock. Climbing out of his truck, John said "You must be Matthew."

"That's me. Here is part of your order; I will be back shortly with the rest of it." As the boxes were loaded into the back of the truck, the two men talked about the weather, living in Kansas and the general store. John found out that Matthew was the son of the owner and that the Boxberger's had moved to LaCrosse from around Abilene, Kansas. He wanted to inquire about his sister but did not know how to do so without feeling awkward.

Sensing that John was interested in his sister, he simply stated "Her name is Emily."

Startled, John replied "Excuse me?"

Chuckling softly, Matthew said "Other men have expressed interest in my sister but have been rebuffed. Telling me that you were pulling around to the loading dock to pick up your order, she said that you were 'sort of cute' which means she is interested. Don't tell her I said so or she'll have my hide. Would you like me to introduce you?"

"I don't want to scare her off; how about you introduce us the next time I come to the shop?"

Back at the greenhouses with the landscaping trays and rooting hormone, John took several cuttings from a mature lilac bush, dipped the cuttings in the rooting hormone and placed the cuttings in the prepared nursery trays. The cuttings needed to be kept warm, have the correct humidity and have the right amount of air circulating so the sapling wouldn't rot. Many people had failed to successfully root and grow lilacs. John was able to be successful the first time out. Eventually his lilac saplings outsold the majority of his regular tree saplings.

During the late spring of 1917, Anna and I had our tenth child; we named the child Benjamin. Thinking about being the father of ten kids made me feel old. When Dad turned seventy—one he began to seriously consider having Allison, Philip and I take over the spool making business. At this time, Dad wanted to relax more and work less. With this thought in mind, Mom arranged for Philip, Pauline, Allison, Edward, Anna and I to come over for dinner one evening in early June. Dad began the conversation by stating he "wanted to slow down and enjoy his remaining time with mom."

A panicked Allison jumped in to say "Wait a Moment, Dad. Are you sick or dying?"

Waving his hands to indicate for her to stop, Dad said "NO! I just know that I am over seventy. I would like not to work every day for the rest of my life. Besides, I would just like to enjoy the time that I do have left. I desire to spend some time with my brothers, George and Adam. I would like to spend some time with the grandchildren so they will have some memories of me. I was hoping that I could pass the business on to the three of you. I understand that all three of you might not wish to work in or keep the spool business operating. Philip might feel that distance he would be required to travel could prevent him from the day to day operation of the mill. In that case, Jacob and Allison could keep the business operating. If none of you want to carry on the business then I can sell it. So, let's discuss the situation."

Allison jumped in to state her interest in keeping the business going. "The business has been good at providing employment for not only me but for a few others across the county. The five men who work for the company depend on the income from us to supplement their farm income. Besides, over the years we have not only provided quality spools for Joseph's spinning mill but also for ten other mills across the mid—west. If we close where will these mills obtain their spools?"

"Allison's right in stating that other companies depend on us to supply them spools at a reasonable price. The amount that we charge for shipping is minuscule compared to what spinning companies will have to pay if they are forced to get their spools from Cleveland or Atlanta."

I further argued that "We may not be a wealthy company but we provide employment and add to the economy of Rush County. I vote to keep the business open."

Philip shaking his head stated that he "understood how both Allison and Jacob felt. However, since I live forty some miles away, I am less impacted by your company, Dad. Living where I do, I could not actively assist Allison and Jacob in running the mill."

"Yes, you could!" Allison jumped in and then said "Dad has always acted as the bookkeeper and I don't feel that I know enough to keep the books. You could easily do the books from your home. We could take turns providing you with what is needed for the books."

"What do you mean?"

"Well at the end of the first week you could come to the shop and handle the book—keeping here at the shop. The work could probably be completed in about two hours if it were done weekly. Then you and Pauline could have dinner with us. The next week, Jacob and Anna could bring you the needed materials and then have dinner with you and Pauline. The third week, Edward and I could bring want you need and then stay for dinner. The books would get done and we would have a chance to keep in touch with each other."

"Dad, how long do you spend on the books each week?" Philip inquired.

"Maybe two or three hours; it depends on how often I get interrupted when I am working on the books."

"I could easily handle that from my home office."

Smiling, I interjected "Home office? Wow, you have come up in the world. I do any paper work from the table where we eat our meals. Guess that you are more important than me." Philip shot back at his older brother with a grin. "Really, I just placed my desk in a corner of the parlor."

"It sounds like the three of you are willing to take over the business so I can retire or at the least to semi-retire. Now if we could get your Mom to slow down some."

"Hey! If I got any slower, I would be dead. Remember I stopped doing shifts in the fabric shop about a year ago. The only thing that I still do for the shop is the twice a year buying trip. I won't give that up because it is my chance to visit with Marie and Joseph."

"You're right about enjoying the buying trip. I, like you, enjoy the train trip and the visit with our oldest and dearest friends here in America. I won't be quitting work tomorrow; I will ease the three of you into taking over."

"Can we have dessert now?" Mom inquired, "I made a German chocolate cake."

Over dessert, the family discussed the revolution that was taking place in Russia. We were all happy that we had 'escaped' Russia when we did. We recently heard that Germans living in Russia had been scattered to parts of Siberia, Kazakhstan and other regions of Central Asia. We were saddened to hear about the abdication of Czar Nicholas and that the royal family had been imprisoned. By the end of summer, we heard that the Czar and his family had been brutally killed. Over the next few years we learned that the individuals that had taken control of Russia were just brutal dictators and that the population did not receive any of the freedoms that they or we had hoped for.

After much reflection, John finally got around to being formally introduced to Emily Boxberger. I was amazed that it took John another six months before he asked Emily if he could escort her home from church services the following Sunday. Once the ice was broken the two quickly became exclusive. The pair often went on Sunday afternoon picnics, they took leisurely horse and buggy rides in the early evening, and often had dinner with the us or with Emily's family. After six months of discussing almost everything from the past, the present and their future together, the pair announced their wedding plans for the summer of 1918.

The usual wedding plans took place regarding the exact date, the location, the type of reception, the size of the guest list and the wedding dress. However, in the beginning neither John nor Emily expressed their desire to keep the wedding small and or simple. This resulted in both Anna and Emily planning a medium sized wedding that bordered on being colossal. Being concerned, John came to talk to me. "Dad, I think that Mrs. Boxberger and Mom are not planning a wedding but a royal coronation."

"Did you and Emily tell your mothers what size of wedding that you would like to have?"

"We discussed the date, the location, type of reception, the wedding dress but not the size of the guest list."

"Which means that you or Emily actually told your mothers that you wanted a small wedding. In fact, I'm still not sure what size of wedding that the two of you want. Did you only generally discuss who you would like to attend the wedding? Have the invitations already gone out?"

"No, the invitations have not been made yet."

"So, it's not too late to tell your mothers that Emily and you really want a small wedding with maybe fifty guests. Do you think that the two of you can tell that to your mothers?

"Yes, we can; can you and Mom come to dinner at my house tonight?"

"What time do you want us to come?"

"Around six would be great. I am going over to invite the Boxbergers."

After inviting the Boxbergers, John stopped at the new bakery on Main Street to purchase a cake or pie for dinner. He then proceeded home to do some cleaning before Pauline arrived to prepare dinner. After dinner, we settled in the living room with coffee and cake. Some small talk led John to broach the subject of the wedding. "I was wondering if we could discuss the actual guest list for the wedding."

Mrs. Boxberger agreed pulling out a list of who they wished to invite. Looking at the list John did a quick count. He began by saying "Mrs. Boxberger…"

"Since we are going to be family, I think that it's time that you call me Lydia."

"And please call me Will" said Mr. Boxberger.

"Thank you! Emily and I have discussed how large we would like our wedding" began John.

Emily jumped to help her future husband "Mom, Dad and Mr. and Mrs. Funk, John and I would like to have a small wedding."

"When we say small, we mean roughly fifty or maybe sixty guests. That includes immediate family and a few close friends."

"Mom, you have fifty-eight people on your list alone" said Emily. "What if the Funks have fifty—eight or more on their list? That makes the guest list twice as large as we would like. How can we reconcile our wishes with your lists?"

Both Lydia and Anna looked at each other prior to bursting into laughter. Confused, Emily and John looked at each other and then their fathers. Both of us shrugged our shoulders as if saying I don't know. Anna began by saying "Of course we can cut the guest list down."

"We were trying to make the guest list larger so the two of you would tell us exactly how many you wished to invite."

"By the way Emily, please call us Jacob and Anna." Emily thanked my wife, hugged her and then me.

Relief crossed both Emily and John's faces. The group then seriously made up a guest list that included twenty friends and forty-six family members. John and Emily were happy with the guest list of only sixty-six people. The August wedding was intimate and beautiful. The pair settled into their life operating the greenhouses and farming the remaining twenty—five acres.

In 1918, a co-worker came into the shop's office. He told Allison that she had a visitor. Allison told him thank—you for letting her know and began the climb down the stairs. However, once on the landing that was just outside the office, Allison saw Daniel. Horror stricken, she stepped backwards into the office. All she could say is "Father, its Daniel."

"What!" Dad said jumping up. Dad opened his desk drawer and pulled out a pistol. "It can't be Daniel; he was given life in prison. Stay here and I will confront whoever it is." Of course, Allison did not stay in the office, she was directly behind her father as he left the office. Dad realized that indeed, it could very well be Daniel but it also might be his twin brother, David. Downstairs, Dad said "Daniel?"

"Well, well after all these years you remember me. It is nice to see you after all these years Allison. Where are the children; all grown up and scattered to the wind?" Daniel said sarcastically.

Dad demanded to know what he wanted after all these years.

"I just came back for my wife and children."

Looking around at the staff, Dad asked them to take an early lunch. Leaving the building casually, one long time worker and friend, named Thomas, left the building but then rushed to my house. He asked Mom if he could use their telephone. "Of course, is there a problem?"

"I will explain after making the call." Picking up the receiver, he used the hand crank that alerted the operator that an individual needed to make a call.

The operator asked "Whom may I connect you with?"

"Sally, this is Thomas Kelly out at the Funk Spool Mill, please connect me to the sheriff's office."

There were no questions asked and the connection was made instantly. "Sheriff's office" said the individual in the police station.

"Henry, this is Thomas Kelly over at the Funk Spool Mill we need assistance immediately. There is a man here claiming to be Allison's husband. Christian has his gun drawn and pointed at the man."

"Right! I will send the sheriff along with an additional squad car immediately. If it is possible, have the others stay clear of the situation and seek shelter."

"Hurry" was all that Thomas could say before hanging up.

Looking at Mom, Thomas said "Christian seems to have the situation under control; Allison was safely behind her father when I left. The sheriff said that others were to stay back so as not to aggravate the situation; he is on his way. The man is a lunatic but, don't worry Abigail."

"You do not understand, Thomas. Was the name Daniel used during the exchange?"

"Yes, that is the name Christian used to refer to the man."

"Allison's first husband's name is Daniel Heller. After an argument with Christian, Daniel took Allison and the children to Denver about fifteen years ago. While in Denver he killed two men and was sentenced to life in prison without the possibility of parole."

Calmly, Thomas took Mom's hand and had her sit down at the dining room table. He proceeded to make a pot of coffee while talking to her. Within a few minutes that felt like several hours, three patrol cars arrived with no sirens or lights flashing. Quickly the officers surrounded the mill and entered through three different access points with guns drawn and pointed.

Daniel was determined not be taken into custody again, no matter what. With his eyes and loaded gun never leaving dad, Daniel claimed loudly "One way or another I will kill the man who took away my life."

The sheriff calmly replied "Could you put the gun down and tell me why you think that Christian took away your life?"

Keeping his gun pointed on Dad, Daniel looked in the direction of the voice talking to him. Dad took the opportunity to quickly push Allison behind some boxes stored under the staircase and indicated for her to stay down. Waving his gun at the sheriff Daniel angrily stated "Christian was responsible for my being arrested and jailed in Colorado."

"What did Christian do to cause you to be arrested and jailed?" the sheriff asked as one of the deputies quickly and quietly shepherded Allison out the back door; the other deputy kept his gun on Daniel.

Oblivious to the movement behind him, Daniel preceded to tell the sheriff how Dad and he had gotten into an argument at the Brown Palace bar. Two innocent bystanders had been shot and killed during the argument. When the police arrived, Daniel stated that dad had twisted the story so that he was arrested and sent to jail for the killing. According to Daniel, Dad had convinced his wife to file for divorce; a corrupt attorney obtained the divorce and "sent me notification of the divorce while I was in prison."

The sheriff asked whether we could "rationally discuss the situation without anyone getting harmed?"

"I have already been harmed; I have spent the last fifteen years in prison." A shot rang out from outside the mill, Daniel fell to the ground and David, along with several Colorado police officers, entered the building. Looking up, Daniel angrily shouted "How could you shoot your own brother?"

"I didn't shoot you but how could you get me and others to take the blame for anything and everything you did? Being notified of your prison escape, law enforcement asked me where I thought that you might go. There was only one person who stood up for what was right and just, your ex—father—in—law! And here you are attempting to kill him and to forcibly take Allison."

The Colorado police officers thanked Dad, David and the Rush County Sheriff's Department. They took Daniel into custody and began their journey back to the prison in Colorado. Allison was aghast to see two men that both looked like her ex-husband Daniel.

Dad hugged Abigail while making introductions. "Allison, I would like you to meet Daniel's twin brother, David."

Almost speechless, Allison stepped forward to hug David and then said "I do not know what to say except thank you! I can't believe that I never knew about any of Daniel's family let alone a twin brother."

"We have a lot of catching up to do, then don't we?" replied David, taking her arm and asking Abigail if they could have some coffee. Once inside we sat down to talk while we waited for a fresh pot of coffee to brew, Dad and Mom finally were able to tell the family about how they had met David years before. David began to explain to the family the story about his and Daniel's childhood as twins along with five other siblings. Of course, he brought the story up to date regarding how Daniel escaped from prison and his journey to Rush County. "Allison, I wanted to meet you years ago but could not bring myself to do so since Daniel has caused you such heartache."

"I feel that I have missed out on knowing members of the Heller family. It is important that you meet the children while you are here."

"I would love to finally get to know my nieces and nephews. I am sorry that mother and father never got the chance to know you or their grandchildren."

After meeting and spending a few days with the Funks and the three youngest children, David prepared to head back to Colorado. He exacted a promise that they would visit him and that he and his family would visit the following summer in order to finally met Heidi and George.

Allison said "I sorry that your wife was unable to come with you. We can't wait to meet her and the children. David, please remember that just because Daniel and I are not married anymore, you are still family." David smiled and told her thank—you. Allison felt that her family had grown to include part of the Heller family and thought that it was vital for her children to know a part of their father's family.

Prior to boarding the train David turned and said "Remember that there is more to life than money; money can always be replaced but family can't be." Stepping over to Allison he reached out, taking her hand he brought it up to his lips and kissing it lightly. "Allison, I am sorry that Daniel has brought so much grief into your life. I also regret that I did not meet you before Daniel; you and I would have had a glorious life together." Allison knew that it was David's way of telling her that he loved her. She had developed a special love for him but knew that, because both David and Allison loved others, their love for each other would remain platonic.

Before the First World War, there was a period of economic and political reform in the United States. As the nation's population grew, more and more people moved westward in order to obtain land or a better job. Those of us in rural western Kansas wanted the people moving westward to keep going further west. We did not want our small towns to become a city. However, many of those moving westward wanted to leave the large city with its high crime; these people desired to live in a small town.

Several of these small towns grew out of necessity. Rural southwest Kansas and north western Oklahoma had plenty of cattle ranches and large farms. It was a natural progression that businesses handling meat packing and food processing would spring up in rural areas where the meat and food were grown. I heard that Garden City, about seventy—five miles from our town, grew dramatically as a result of the meat packing industry. Many easterners and many of the young people living in western Kansas moved to Garden City for the job opportunities.

While discussing Dad's possible retirement and before we began planning John's wedding, America was semi-divided about entering the war in Europe. Many wanted to keep a policy of isolation and neutrality while small groups of Americans were in favor of some sort of involvement in the war. The majority of people that I knew supported President Wilson's approach to staying out of the war.

However, the United States officially entered the war in the spring of 1917. In order to raise military manpower for the war, Wilson relied primarily on the draft rather than voluntary enlistment. From what I read in newspapers the Selective Service Act of 1917 authorized a discriminatory draft of men between the ages of twenty—one and thirty—five. Later drafts considered men who were between the ages of eighteen to forty—five. During the years of 1917 and 1918, twenty—four million men were registered for the draft but only about three million were inducted into the various branches of the military. At this time, the draft was universal but I read in a newspaper that southerners seemed to raise the most objections because they felt that the conscription practices across America were unfair to the poorest of America's population. These practices often exempted the upper class and industrial workers from serving in the war. It has been claimed that the poor were considered to be the most expendable.

Due to the first Selective Service Act, John Funk and his cousin George Heller were too young to be drafted but Twenty—eight—year—old Philip could have been conscripted. Fortunately for Philip, his poor eye sight kept him out of the war. Several Funk cousins, related through our Great Uncles, George and Adam, were drafted. About a third of those family members going to war did not return. All of those returning from any war, have felt that whatever the cause of that particular war did not justify the huge loose of life. One Kansas veteran argued that war gives men a license to kill someone you do not know. Although the men agreed that tyrants or dictators needed to be stopped and people should be allowed fundamental rights, but war and killing was not necessarily the way to stop injustices. Many have asked the question of how to stop tyrants without killing innocent people. We might not ever have a good answer to that question.

Because the war involved many countries fighting Germany many German—Americans faced harassment across America and were accused of spying for 'the enemy.' Numerous people of German descent had never been to Germany and had lived in the United States their entire life so being accused of spying for Germany hurt deeply. At this time period, German—Americans were not allowed to live near military instillations, airports, Washington DC or in port cities. German—Americans were forced to fill out registration forms and were fingerprinted. Those who did not do so were considered to be dangerous.

Really? That is all that I could say about that negativity. It is no different than what we faced in Russia. Guess hatred is the same everywhere in the world.

Late August 1975

So much was packed in this one journal. Daniel Heller entered the family's life once again and he attempted to harm both Christian and Allison. Once again, he was stopped and taken back to prison. Allison finally had the opportunity to met David, Daniel's twin brother. David was thrilled to find out that Allison had finally found true love, married and had another child. It was nice to learn about several of Grandma's cousins through her Aunt Allison. It was amazing to find out that one of her cousins had become a teacher, one a writer and a third a librarian. Furthermore, it was interesting to know what Grandma's brother, John, chose a career as a horticulturalist, and to find out how he met and married Emily Boxberger. My Great—Great—Grandfather was finally thinking about retiring or at least to semi—retire.

It was interesting to learn about changes in the United States around and after the First World War. Apparently as America's population grew, it was a natural progression for people to desire to move westward where fewer people live. Reading about history through family journals is much more interesting than reading chapters from a history book. Maybe it is because my family were involved in what happened. For example. taking part of the mass migration from Germany to Russia, and facing conscription to fight in a war against Germany.

What was the hardest to read about was that many German—Americans faced harassment from both the American government and its people. Harassment that included spying, being forced to register and fingerprinted, and not being allowed to live where they chose too. I remember that a family member once told me that having a German last name would be enough for harassment to begin.

I am anxious to find out what else happens to my family in the upcoming journals....

Journal Thirteen

1918—1925

In 1918, Dad was able to completely turn the business over to Allison, Philip and myself. Mom and Dad began to spend quality time at home with each other. In addition, Mom and Dad spent time visiting with Adam, George, Christina and Mary. My parents still made their twice-yearly fabric and thread pilgrimage to Denver; they continued to stay and visit with Joseph and Marie. Instead of the usual quick four—or—five—day trip, they might stay for two or possibly three weeks.

On one buying trip in late spring 1919, Joseph passed quietly away during the night. Not wishing to leave her alone, Mom and Dad began a conversation with Marie about moving to Kansas with them. Making an argument about not moving, Marie began with stating that "who will run the business Joseph left me."

"The manager," I argued "that Joseph hired a few years ago. He is doing an excellent job. He can be in touch with you through mail and through the use of the telephone. Remember, Joseph had the telephone installed at the mill several years ago.

Being that we are country bumpkins doesn't mean that we don't have one of those newly fangled telephones." Dad smiled before continuing "Phone lines were finally strung across Rush County. So, we were able to have a telephone installed at the house and next door at the spool mill.

"That's right, I forgot. Guess that there is no excuse for me not come with you, is there?"

Mom jumped into the conversation to state emphatically "NO!!! You and Joseph have been wonderful to the two of us over the years; it is now our turn to repay you."

Marie agreed to move in with Mom and Dad but she insisted that they keep the townhouse in Denver for use in future buying trips. Making arrangements with the housekeeper and her husband to leave their rented apartment and to move into the townhouse. Marie felt better about moving because she did not desire to leave her home unoccupied. The housekeeper, her husband, Dad and Mom lent a hand in selecting and packing items that Marie wished to take with her. We had to remind Marie from time to time that we couldn't take everything—some things needed to be left in the home for use when we returned to Denver. Two weeks' worth of picking and then packing items finally meant that we were ready to book passage on the train leaving Denver for points eastward. Marie's possessions would be shipped to Kansas on a freight train within the week of us leaving Denver.

Once in Rush County, Mom showed Marie around the house. Mom asked which of the two spare bedrooms Marie would like to use. Realizing that the three of them were getting older, Mom decided to broach the subject of adding two bedrooms onto the first floor to Dad. Dad loved the idea of having two bedrooms on the first floor; upstairs bedrooms could be used for visitors and closed off when they were not needed. The question remained on when the addition could be done.

As they waited for me to arrive in order to discuss the addition, Dad stepped out onto the porch and noticed a funnel cloud kicking up in the distance. At the moment I arrived and quickly got out of my vehicle, I confirmed that it was a funnel cloud and it was coming our way. Swiftly, we got Mom and Marie, and headed for the root cellar. As we pulled the door closed, we heard what sounded like as freight train roaring past. As I locked the door, Dad lit the lantern and we sat down to wait out the storm. When the storm passed, we were finally able to leave the root cellar. Luckily for the family, the funnel cloud passed through without causing major damage. A few crops were damaged, a watering tin or two had been tipped over and a few fences broken. Other portions of the county were not as lucky as that several homes were leveled and seven people died as a result of the storm.

Before getting down to business, I contacted Anna to make sure she and the children were okay. Mom, Dad, Marie and I then sat down to discuss the addition. Dad stated that they wanted to build two bedrooms on the first floor. He wanted a sitting area and closets in each room. Understanding what was needed, I drew up some plans that had both rooms side-by-side off the living room. I placed equal sized closets located between the two rooms. Small sitting areas would be located on an outside corner of each room: one on the left side of a bedroom and one on the right side of the other be.

I decided to make the porch a covered porch that would be placed between the two sitting areas and would be accessible through French doors from both bedrooms. Since the addition would be facing west, I suggested that three rockers should be placed on the porch, the trio could then watch the sun setting together each evening. Loving the idea, Dad asked me if I could handle the addition. Marie insisted on paying for the addition since Dad and Mom were making the changes because of her. We thought that the addition could be completed by the end of October but weather caused delays so it wasn't completed until just before Christmas.

Eight months later, like Joseph, Dad passed away quietly in his sleep. Mom was devastated but it helped that Marie was there. Being strong women, the pair continued to remain active but stayed close to home. Buying for the shop changed at this point due to the next generation of Funk women not wishing to leave their young children for as long as a week. Marie arranged for the textile mill staff to bring samples to Rush County twice a year. Shortly after Dad had passed away, Marie had consulted a lawyer to make adjustments to her will. She desired to make sure that the spinning mill, the townhouse, and a portion of her wealth went to the Funk family upon her death. The remaining wealth would be left to a distantly related cousin of Joseph and an orphanage that was located in Denver.

Jacob

By 1919, the staff of the fabric shop had changed somewhat. Aunt Mary and Aunt Christina were both in their late sixties, and Mom was in her early seventies; the three wished to slow down and play a less active role in the shop. Cousins were marrying, moving away, and having babies which left fewer women to operate the shop. Anna, Elizabeth, Allison's daughter Lydia, and Mary's oldest daughter Katherine were the four that mainly kept the shop operating.

Aunt Mary, Aunt Christina, and Mom came in to teach popular classes. Not realizing their popularity, the three never noticed that every class they taught was popular, filled to capacity and had a waiting list. Anna and Elizabeth stayed late on Saturdays to handle the shops inventory. Usually the pair would have lively conversations about what occurred during the shops many quilting classes. They would laugh over customers complaining about this, that or the other thing. Having 'girl' time made life more enjoyable for

One Friday afternoon Katherine and Elizabeth were working the shop together. Katherine was upstairs working with a group of women learning how cut and put together a block called card trick. Preparing for a class on how to make a log cabin quilt, Elizabeth was downstairs cutting strips to place in a prepackaged packet. Each packet contained a red square for the blocks center and there would be enough light and dark strips to make one block to be completed during the class. The remaining blocks would be done with fabric of the quilter's choice and as time permitted. Elizabeth planned on showing a scrappy log cabin so the students could see what the quilt looked like with each block made with different lights and darks. Students would then be able to utilize scrap material that they had at home or they could purchase enough material to finish a log cabin quilt.

In the process of cutting dark strips, the bell at the door dingled to indicate a customer had entered into the shop. Elizabeth called out "I will be right with you" and finished cutting the strip.

Turning, Elizabeth saw the handsomest man that she had ever seen. She stammered "How can I help you?"

"My name is James Wolf. I came to purchase some material for my mother."

"Having a man buy material, even if it is for his mother, is a first for me," Elizabeth said with a smile. "What color are you looking for? Do you want a fabric with a pattern or solid fabric? By the way, my name is Elizabeth Funk."

"I'm sorry there is much more to selecting fabric then I thought. Could you show me a few different fabrics to help me decide?"

"Of course!" Elizabeth said as walked over to the shelves, pulled several bolts from different spots in the shop and placed them on a corner of the table. "We recently received these calicos from the mill in several different shades." Indicating one of the bolts of fabric in pale green, Elizabeth continued "this is my favorite of the group. What will your mother be making?"

"Well, it is for her birthday so am not sure what she will make. What do you suggest?"

"If she made herself a dress, I would need her height and her dress size?"

"I am not sure of her dress size but do know that she is about your height. I think that I would like to buy some of the green fabric that you like."

"Liking a fabric is the easy part. Is she slim or...." began Elizabeth.

Laughing softly James responded by saying "Besides being your height, she is about your build."

"Now we are getting somewhere. She will need six yards to make a dress."

"Sold! How much is the fabric?"

"This fabric is thirty-five cents a yard; six yards will cost two dollars and ten cents." Elizabeth replied as she began measuring and cutting six yards. James thanked her and left with his package of fabric.

Over the next week, Elizabeth and James ran into each other almost every day. Ten days after they first met, the two saw each other outside a local diner. James asked Elizabeth if she would join him for a cup of tea. Elizabeth hesitated for just a moment before agreeing. The two went into the diner, were seated and ordered a pot of tea. As they waited for the tea to arrive, Elizabeth casually asked where James was from.

"Originally I am from Kentucky but moved to Kansas for the prospect of having more land. A couple weeks ago I was able to purchase eight hundred acres to the east of town."

"The Hoffman property?"

"Yes, how did you know?"

"The Hoffman property is the only acreage for sale in the county that large. To be honest, it has been on the market for a while due to the property's size and the price. I heard that the Hoffman's were willing to negotiate on the price but…."

"The Hoffman's and I negotiated a price that I could afford and they were still able walk away with what they thought was a fair price."

"What are your plans for the property?"

"Back in Kentucky I saw how much people paid for beef cattle in the east. After my parents died, I decided to sell the property and head west to try the cattle business."

"Didn't you purchase material last week for your mother?"

Blushing a brilliant shade of red, James said "You've caught me! Purchasing material for my mother was an excuse to become acquainted with you. I am not sure what I would do with the fabric I acquired. But meeting you was worth paying two dollars and ten cents."

Now it was Elizabeth's turn to blush. It was flattering that a man would go to such lengths to meet her. "James, I'm speechless. A man has never gone to such extremes to meet me before. Why didn't you just come into the shop and introduce yourself?"

"Would you have thought that I was crazy?"

"Well…probably but…."

"Let's start over then. Hello, my name is James Wolf and I am dying to know the most beautiful woman in Rush County."

"Okay, okay! You're the craziest man in Kansas and possibly even in America. How about meeting me at Church Sunday and you can escort me home."

So began the courtship of Elizabeth and James.

The 1920s has often been referred to as the 'Roaring Twenties.' Following the First World War and the Spanish flu epidemic many countries around the world experienced economic prosperity. Some countries did not enjoy economic prosperity but faced a severe economic downturn. This was due to the country having a large war debt and to the Treaty of Versailles. Germany saw the devaluation of their currency early in the 1920s which lead to economic problems and a rise in the Nazi party.

During this period more and more people had expendable income, including us. This created a growth of consumer goods such as home appliances and ready-to-wear clothing. I noticed that women's hem lines were slowly rising and many women began to wear trousers. People began to purchase ready-to-wear clothing which caused fabric shops to sell less material and to eventually close. However, the majority of Rush County's population continued to make their own clothes because they could get the clothing they wanted, in the color they desired and for less then what ready-to-wear cost. In order to help increase sales, the fabric / quilt shop began to be open on Mondays.

Hannah was asked to work Mondays in the shop. Hannah assisted with the cutting of fabric for customers. Besides working in the fabric shop Hannah cleaned the town's school after school five days a week. She started work at four at the school so would need to leave the quilt shop fifteen to twenty minutes before closing. Hannah's duties at the school included dusting, sweeping the floor, and cleaning the chalk boards; she finished the work in an hour. Tuesday through Friday mornings Hannah helped Mom in the garden, canning, baking or any other job that needed to be completed.

Reading the newspaper told me that for the first time in the history of America there were more people living in urban areas than on a farm or in a rural area. Economic prosperity along with urban living, aided in the demand for new products across America. Beginning in the mid—1920s, talking movies caused silent films to slowly decline. I heard it argued that by 1930 more than three-quarters of Americans would go to the movie theater each and every week. I thought that this was an odd fact since Rush County did not even have a movie theater. If we wanted to see a moving picture we would have to travel to Hayes. I don't know anyone in the county that travels to Hayes to see a moving picture.

In 1925 a new process for frozen food came on the market which caused an increased demand for frozen foods. This, in turn, caused a larger demand for vegetables grown across Kansas, Nebraska and other mid—western states. Of course, to take advantage of frozen foods people would need the new—fan-gled refrigerator. Which means that more people needed to be connected to electrical power.

I had gone to the power company with the argument that the power lines were running down the main road. My property runs parallel to the main road and these lines. "Why can't you just run some lines three hundred feet to my house?" Of course, the power company refused to do so because of the high cost of running the lines to my house. They argued that it would probably take five years to recoup that cost from my monthly bill. I finally gave up arguing with them about connecting me to the power grid.

The number of radios and radio stations have grown in numbers throughout this period. However, many people living in rural areas still did not have electricity so, how could they utilize a radio? If you lived in town, you probably had electricity and could have a radio, a refrigerator or many of these new conveniences. Radios and movies brought the outside world into homes like a newspaper never could.

Over the next decade, the lives of women became easier because of the rise of home appliances. These appliances helped make all—day chores being accomplished in a quarter of the time. One day the power company let us know that rural areas would now have access to electricity. I was extremely curious about 'why now' but did not ask. But I suspected that the corporations that produced appliances, radios, etc. pressured the power companies to electrify the nation as a whole. So, holes were dug, poles set in place and electric lines strung across the county so that the people would finally get electricity. We were now able to get electric lights and a few of those newfangled appliances. The one that most women in Rush County seemed to like best was the electric stove. That way they did not have to have to keep stoking their older stoves with wood. Stoking the wood cooking stove during the sizzling summers months could make the house unbearably hot while during the winter heat from the same stove was wonderful; guess there's no happy medium. The second most popular appliance in the region was the washing machine. Many washing machines ran with a portable gas generator; I have been considering purchasing this type of washing machine along with the gas generator in order to make Anna's life easier

Recently I read in a local newspaper that migration to the United States began to be restricted as a result of the Immigration Act of 1924. The act limited the number of individuals emigrating to the United States from any eastern and southern European countries. It also enforced the ban on immigration from Africa, East Asia and South Asia. Many Germans remember our own emigration process so, we are sad to see immigration being restricted.

The same newspaper reported that many companies had aided in the war effort during the First World War; the wood products industry was no different. Wood manufacturing businesses saw an increase of orders for lumber, construction materials, furniture, or many different items. After the war ended, companies reverted back to peacetime production, including those producing wood products. After the war ended, many companies had trouble locating enough raw materials to supply their needs. This was no different for the wood products industry. As a result, many companies went out of business. However, Dad's Spool Mill not only stayed afloat but quadrupled in its business.

Around this time, David began working in the mill after school and on Saturdays. After finishing his formal education, David went to work full time in the mill. As a side line, David built quilt frames, rocking chairs and chests. Within a few years, David had become a master carpenter and a handy man.

During this time of transition, the 1920s, John and Emily discussed adding vegetable seedlings to their business. Emily asked John what kind of vegetables he was thinking about and who would they be sold too. "Well, to begin with, I was thinking about starting with tomatoes and maybe a few herbs. As you know more and more are leaving rural areas and living in urban regions. A large portion of those living in towns and cities still desire to have a small vegetable garden but might not have the time or the patience to germinate the seeds."

"I like the idea. As a woman doing the cooking, cleaning, raising children and often working outside of the home having vegetable seedlings ready to plant would be a wonderful help. I think that we should also try peppers, cucumbers, and eventually some bush green beans. These vegetables along with tomatoes and herbs are best when picked fresh."

"How do you feel about asking Molly to assist us with the seedling production?" John stated "She has always been good at getting garden vegetables to grow in any condition and any soil."

"Great idea!"

John approached Molly within a few days about working with him in his horticultural business; she agreed and went with him to the General Store to order the seedling trays and seed packets. Lydia Boxberger, John's mother-in-law, suggested that John and Molly "add onions to the seedlings that you grow and sell. Women always use onions in their cooking."

The seedling business boomed due to, as John thought it would, urban living and people desiring home grown, fresh vegetables. Within a year, vegetable seedlings from the Funk Greenhouses were selling from Abilene, Kansas to Kit Carson, Colorado and southward into the Oklahoma panhandle. John eventually hired a driver to assist him in getting the saplings and seedlings to market quickly, while maintaining the plants freshness.

Living and farming next door to Philip Funk in Ness County, a new neighbor asked Philip where he got his saplings. Philip replied that "My nephew owns a greenhouse in Rush County that sells a wide variety of saplings and seedlings."

"Do you know what kind of saplings he sells? Is he selective in what he grows and sells?"

"I am not exactly sure that he sells everything but I don't think that he is overly selective. He has had excellent results with lilacs and maples. I heard through the family grape vine that he is experimenting with rose bushes at this time."

Philip's neighbor thanked him for the information and obtained directions to the John's Greenhouse. A few days later the man made a trip to the neighboring county to check out the greenhouse. When the neighbor arrived, John was busy attempting to propagate fruit trees in one of the greenhouses. He was experimenting with both rooting and grafting. He knew that the simplest way to propagate trees asexually was through rooting. He made a cutting from the parent tree and placed it in soil.

To aid in his success, John decided to use some of his favorite artificial rooting hormone. If the cutting did not die from dehydration first, roots will grow from the portion of the cutting buried in the soil. John knew that the most common way to propagate fruit trees was through grafting. The grafting process involved ensuring maximum contact between the tissues lying just below the bark. This enabled the two plants to grow together successfully. John had found out that the best time for grafting to be carried out was in the spring when the sap rises but prior to the plant sending out their buds.

In growing seedlings, Molly had a routine where she prepared the trays with soils and planted the seeds usually on Mondays, Wednesdays and Thursday afternoons; she kept the seedlings moist at all times to ensure growth. At a certain height, the seedlings were ready to be sold to locals for planting in their vegetable gardens. While Molly and John were occupied with their individual projects, Mom was getting out of her vehicle with John and Molly's lunch, Philip's neighbor pulled in behind her.

Climbing out of his truck Philip's neighbor said "Hello! I am looking for John Funk."

"He should be in one of the greenhouses." She replied as she tooted her vehicle's horn. "That is our signal that lunch has arrived. Would you care to join us for lunch?"

"I don't wish to be an inconvenience and besides, you weren't expecting me."

"There is no such thing as an inconvenience; we have plenty to eat. By the way my name is Anna Funk, I'm John's mother."

"I'm Philip Hemel…"

Interrupting Mom quickly asked "Are you related to the Hemel family that lived in Hussenbach, Russia?"

"Family legend states that a branch of the Hemels left Germany for Russia during the 1760s. My branch of the family immigrated to the United States from the Frankfort area in the mid—to late 1860s. You sound as if the name Hemel plays an important role in your life."

"You could say that the Hemel name has played an important role for me; My maiden name is Hemel. There is a very good chance that we are distantly related; my family left Germany in the 1760s and settled in Hussenbach, Russia which matches your family legend."

Mom and Philip were hugging which surprised John and Molly as they came out of their perspective greenhouses. Molly inquired if "there was something we need to tell dad?"

Mom and Philip chuckled as they told the pair of their finding. "By the way, I am from Ness County and I live on the property just west of Philip Funk. I guess that he is related to you as that he told me that his nephew owned and operated this greenhouse."

"Yes, Philip is my uncle" John said. "Let's sit down and have lunch." Settling down at the picnic table, Mom and Molly began to unpack the basket. "By the way, my name is John. You came all the way from Ness for a reason; how can I help you?" Between eating sandwiches, carrot sticks and potato salad Philip told them that he was interested in obtaining some maple saplings for his property. Before lunch was completed Philip had purchased a dozen maple saplings and half dozen lilac bushes.

Throughout the meal Philip kept darting quick glances at Molly; Molly being shy kept her eyes averted but knew he was watching her. Understanding Philip's interest in Molly, Mom said "Molly, why don't you tell Philip what you do here at your brother's greenhouse?"

"Mom, it isn't as exciting as what John does. But here goes....utilizing seedling trays I turn seeds into vegetable plants. It seems that the majority of my seedlings sell to people living in towns and cities who desire a garden in their back yard. I have had a few people inquire about how they could grow a few vegetables when they don't have a yard."

Interested, Philip asked "So what do they do?"

"I have had success with container gardening."

"Container gardening?"

"It is where you would take a large pot with a hole in the bottom for drainage, place a few small rocks in the bottom of the pot and fill the pot with soil. Plant the vegetables selected in the pot, tapping them in gently and water. Large containers could be placed on a porch or step just outside the house. Smaller containers are good for growing herbs and can be placed in a kitchen window."

"That is a great idea. Do you have some herbs that I could purchase in order to try this container gardening idea at home?"

"Why don't you come with me in to select your herbs for a small container garden. I will then make up the container while you look around a bit. Or you could continue visiting with Mom."

"I would really like some basil, thyme and dill. Those are the herbs that I mainly use in my dishes. Having them growing fresh right in the kitchen would be wonderful."

Amazed, Mom said "Wow, a man who cooks! What are your favorite dishes?"

"I cook a mean beef stroganoff and when I can obtain a good piece of lamb, I make Swedish lamb with dill sauce."

"Both dishes sound delicious!" Molly said before she excused herself to prepare a small container with dill, basil and thyme. "Parsley is also good for a quick garnish and adds a nice flavor to any dish."

Mom went with Molly into the greenhouse to assist in making the herb garden for Philip. Pulling out two pots and small plates to catch the excess water Molly began to assemble the two containers with rocks, soil and plants. The larger of the two pots she made into an herb garden while the smaller pot she planted some colorful primrose.

Sitting down on a stool, Mom said "I can't believe that after being separated by almost hundred and fifty years and several countries, two Hemels, possibly but most likely are from the same family, accidently meet in Kansas."

"That's amazing; I wonder if he is married? Most men do not admit they cook."

"You're right, it is hard to guess whether he is or isn't married. He is handsome," said Mom with a twinkle in her eye, "but most Hemels are good looking."

Laughing, Molly replied as she looked at her mom "A bit conceited, aren't we?"

Molly placed the larger container in a card board box. Then the smaller container was placed next to the larger one inside the box. Then the Molly and my wife headed outside to load the box into Philip's vehicle. John and Philip were just finishing up loading the saplings in Philip's truck as the two women joined them. Molly placed the box in his truck bed. Philip asked "How much do I owe you for the herb garden and flower garden?"

"The flower garden is our gift to you; the herb garden is seventy—five cents."

So began the relationship between Philip Hemel and the Funks; more importantly this was also the beginning of the courtship of Molly and Philip. Finally, he asked Dad for Molly's hand in marriage late in 1924. Mid—April 1925, Molly and Philip had a small, intimate wedding with a few family members and friends; Molly moved to Ness County and became a farmer's wife. Philip built Molly a small greenhouse so that she could continue producing seedlings for her Brother John's business. John provided her the needed seedling trays, soil, and seeds; Molly planted and nurtured the seedlings. Every two weeks, the delivery man that worked with John would bring more trays and to pick up the trays full of seedlings ready for market.

Shortly before Molly and Philip's wedding, Elizabeth and James announced that they were planning on getting married during the summer of 1925, preferably in August. While in the midst of planning the wedding, an opportunity arose for James to purchase a thousand acres in southeastern Colorado. The property in Colorado was flatter and had access to several streams and the Arkansas River. It was also better suited for cattle ranching than the Kansas property. Discussing the situation with Elizabeth, the two decided to sell the Kansas property and purchase the Colorado acreage.

The property in Kansas was split into two 400—acre parcels to make it more affordable and for it to sell faster. While waiting for the two properties to sell James contracted a company to build a house and outbuildings on the Colorado acreage. By mid-June both properties in Kansas were sold and James moved to Colorado to make sure that the new house would be completed in time. During this time before the wedding, Elizabeth handled the remaining last-minute details. Changes needed to be made to her wedding dress and another location had to be found for the wedding. A tornado had developed and hit the southwestern side of town. The tornado leveled the Lutheran Church along with five houses, caused eight people to die and twenty people to be injured. Not only did Elizabeth need to find another location but out of respect to those who had died or lost everything she wanted to downsize the wedding dramatically.

"Elizabeth, you don't have to make the wedding smaller. People understand that you have been planning a wedding for several months now."

"But mother, I would not feel right in having a large celebration when people lost their home, their business, were injured and eight people lost their lives." So, the wedding was moved to Grandma's yard due to her lovely flower garden. An arbor was quickly built, chairs were brought in and set up, and a small table was set up to accommodate a punch bowl, cups, plates, forks and the wedding cake. Announcements were sent out that stated:

James Wolf and Elizabeth Funk
Announce their wedding on
August 8 1925 at two o'clock
Place: garden of Abigail and Jacob Funk

Due to the recent tragedy please no gifts

Although a somewhat subdued affair, the wedding was beautiful. The next day Elizabeth and James left for Colorado where I know that they will have a long, happy marriage and their cattle ranch will be successful.

Weddings can be expensive and stressful at the same time. With Molly and Elizabeth have married four months apart, I am a happy man that the nuptials are over for the time being. I just glad that Hannah and Lydia are a bit young to be married, at least for a while.

Since Grandpa had passed away about six years ago, the 609—acre property was too much for Grandma to manage alone. So, Dad stepped up to work both his mother's property along with his own 480—acres; he found that operating over a thousand acres while assisting in operating the spool mill was overwhelming.

Once Joseph was finished with his formal schooling, Dad had him assist in operating both properties; by the end of 1925, Joseph had completely taken over the operation of Grandma's farm. My younger brothers, Peter and William, assisted Dad and Joseph in farming both properties. Before school, my thirteen-year-old sister, Lydia, and eight-year-old brother, Benjamin, fed the chickens, gathered eggs and helped to milk the cows. After school the pair aided with weeding the garden and gathered vegetables.

October 1974

It was sad to read about not only my Great—Great Grandfather passing but also that his good friend Joseph had passed. It was nice to read about how Marie and my Great—Great Grandmother were there for each other during their time of loss. Friendship is a wonderful thing!

I have never experienced a tornado but have heard from Grandma that they can devastate an area. Not only had the county been hit by a tornado once but a second time within a short period of time. The first tornado that was written about did not hit the town; the second one damaged the church and several homes in town. The family survived both tornados with only minor damage.

It was also interesting to read more about how the 'roaring twenties' affected the nation as a whole but also the small area where my ancestors lived. The increase of frozen foods caused farmers to sell more of their crops at a slightly higher price. The rise in ready—to—wear clothing did not seem to affect the family fabric shop during the early part of the twenties. However, in a few years I am positive that the shop will be affected by more people buying ready—to—wear and the depression.

Movies, radio and prohibition caused changes to the nation. But as that much of the rural population still did not have electricity. Residents in rural Kansas were not as affected by the growth in radios yet. A little research revealed that a movie theatre did not come to Dighton, where my grandparents settled, until the early thirties. Talking to my mother, she said that during the forties and very early fifties she would go to the theatre every Saturday that a new movie was being shown. I remember going to see movies at a local theatre in Denver during the mid—sixties. It was exciting to see Disney movies on a big screen in a movie theatre.

Both of Grandma's older sisters met and married during the nineteenth—twenties. Finding out that Grandma's sister, Elizabeth had moved to Colorado explained why I had never met her growing up.

Once again as I was ready to begin reading the next journal, I picked up the book and fingered the supple leather. However, as I opened the volume, I found that the journal was blank. When asking Grandma about this she said that life got in the way for members of the family; they were overly busy and did not have time to continue the tradition. How will I continue to find out about the family? Grandma said that we would have to get together and we would pick up the story. The following summer, I planned on traveling to Dighton to have the conversation with Grandma.

Grandma's story

During late summer of 1975, I was finally able to travel to Dighton to visit with Grandma. Grandma brewed a pot of coffee and we sat down at the dining room table. Grandma began by stating that in July of 1925, when she turned eighteen—years old, she knew that she "would never meet a husband working as a school janitor or in a fabric shop. I realized that my sister, Elizabeth, had met her husband in the fabric shop but, I knew that I wouldn't. Besides, did I want to continue working as the school's janitor for the rest of my life? I was not sure what I wanted to do with my life, I just knew that I needed a fresh start."

Continuing on with her narrative, Grandma stated that when her older sister, Molly, was visiting the family in 1925, she looked at me and asked "what did I want to do with my life." A shrug of my shoulders caused Molly to ask me to "come to Ness City and live with her and Philip for a while. Of course, it would just be until I decided what to do in the future. Besides," she said that "I could use some help taking care of our daughter while working on the seedling project." I heartily agreed and moved with her to Ness City.

Roughly nine months later, David stopped in Ness City to see Molly, Philip and myself on his way to Lane County. Over dinner, we reminisced about our childhood. Even though Philip had not grown up with the Funks, his childhood memories were not that much different than ours. We laughed over how our mother would sometimes say with a smile on her face "look at Mr. so—and—so's wheat. It is so much taller than your wheat." Dad would start to get mad, turn, see her face and then would burst out laughing.

David asked Molly and I if we remembered "playing hide and seek in the corn fields. Remember how Dad would become angry when we were playing in his fields?"

"I remember playing in the corn fields but don't remember why dad got mad at us." I replied thoughtfully.

Both Molly and David chimed in together "Because we were trampling his blessed corn stalks."

Heartily laughing, Philip stated that he could not believe that he had married into such a wild bunch of hooligans. He then asked "By the way, David what takes you to Lane County?"

"A while back, I heard about a carpentry shop needing someone to run the day—to—day operations. I applied for the position, was contacted regarding coming to Dighton for an interview. The woman conversing with me stated that her husband had died several weeks before and she needed to either sell the business or get a man to run the shop. As it turned out, she really wanted to sell the business. So, we came to an agreement on a purchase price."

"How did you come up with the money?" asked Molly.

"I had half of what she wanted for the business saved up; the remaining half will be paid to her over the next several years. I stopped in Ness on my way to Dighton because I wanted to see the three of you. But I have ulterior motives." He looked at me before continuing on "Knowing that you have an adventurous spirit, I was hoping that you would move to Dighton with me."

"But what would I do there?"

"First off you could help me as I am helpless around the house! I could probably get by with my cleaning abilities for awhile. But I know that I will quickly die due to my lack of cooking skills."

Thinking of David cooking for himself caused Philip, Molly and I to laugh hysterically to the point where Philip fell off his chair. With dramatic indignation but with a smile David said "I do not see the humor in this situation!"

Philip apologized through a trembling voice that threatened to erupt into laughter again. I agreed to move with David because I knew that I needed a paying job; a job that would some provide purpose in my life. Helping to care for my niece was a good purpose but I could go days and not see anyone but Molly and Philip.

"What happened when you and Uncle David moved to Dighton, Grandma?" I asked.

"Lots of things! It just takes awhile to tell the story" Grandma replied. Before continuing on, she looked at the time and stated "We need to start making the evening meal? Your Grandpa will be home in about an hour expecting some food on the table. Come on, we will prepare dinner as I continue telling you what took place early in my life." In the kitchen, Grandma asked me to get a sauce pan, a loaf pan and medium sized bowl from the cabinet. Grandma mixed the ingredients for a meat loaf while I scrubbed and pealed several potatoes.

"Now, where were we?" Grandma began "Oh yes, as I packed the few items that I brought with me to Molly's home. I realized that I was sad to be leaving Molly and Philip but was a bit worried about starting over once again." I wondered whether

I was making a mistake going with David on his journey to Lane County. I could be making a mistake, but I will never know for sure if I don't take the chance. If it is a mistake, I can always return to Molly's home or go further and return to Rush County and live with Mom and Dad again.

As David and I drove westward along state highway 96 towards Dighton, David and I examined the crops being grown, the barns and the houses. "I am almost nineteen years old and this is the first time that I am doing something without dad's permission. I sort of feel that I need to go back to see if it is okay with him."

Smiling ever so slightly, David said "Prior to my leaving, Dad, Mom and I talked about this move. Dad suggested that I stop at Molly's and see if you wanted to make the move with me. They both felt that you were looking for a new adventure and a new life."

"They are correct in that I needed a change but am surprised that they knew before I did."

"What do you mean?"

"Well, I knew that I have felt restless; unlike John, Elizabeth or Molly, I do not know what I really want to do with my life. Almost a year ago, Molly asked if I would stay with her and Philip to aid in caring for their new baby. Within hours, well maybe days, Mom suggested that I might consider moving to Ness and live with Molly and Philip for a while. "As you know I made the move to Ness and aided with the cate of Arlene. It was easy to fall into a groove and continue to do odd jobs around their farm. Don't get me wrong, I love Molly and Philip but I was beginning to wonder how I was going to get 'a real job' that would allow me to support myself."

"I understand completely! Think about it, John is married and operating a successful greenhouse; Elizabeth is happily married with twin daughters, Molly is running a farm with a daughter; Joseph is operating grandmother's farm; need I go on?"

"But, David, you are taking over a successful carpentry business. You were able to pay for half the business up front with the rest payable over the next several years."

"I know but I have felt that dad expected more of me and that at twenty—two, I should be more settled."

"Guess we are cut from the same mold. Dighton is going to be the place where we both excel."

On that note, I noticed a road sign up ahead; once we were close enough, I read that we were entering Dighton. In smaller letters the sign also informed us that the town's population was 503. David quietly said "make that 505!"

Stumped, I looked at David and said "505?"

"Yes, the population is now 505." David replied with a smile before saying through laugher "five hundred and five people is the perfect size for a small town."

I thought so too but I wondered what kind of jobs would be available for a single girl in such a small town. "Since agreeing to accompany you to Dighton, I forgot to ask whether you have a place to live or not; I hope that we do."

Laughing again, David replied that "of course we have a place to live. Before returning to Rush County to pack my be-longings I rented a small two—bedroom house. Luckily for us the house came furnished." Arriving at the house, we unloaded our belongings and began settling in. Within the hour of ar-riving at the house we decided to go to the local grocers to do our food shopping for the week.

Over the next few weeks, David and I got to know the town while David prepared for the grand reopening of his carpentry shop. I cleaned, cooked and looked around for businesses that had 'help wanted' signs in the window. After a week of looking,

David came home for lunch and told me that the town's hotel needed a part—time maid; applying for the position, I was hired to clean rooms five mornings a week. Cleaning rooms took me roughly two to two and a half hours each day. As I cleaned a room, I would take the sheets and towels to the wash room in the basement where the owner's wife would wash them and leave them for me to hang on the lines located behind the hotel. When the last room was cleaned, I left the last load of sheets to be washed then retrieved the dry sheets off the lines and folded them. I would leave for the day after the last load of sheets were hung out.

Overall, I was satisfied with the job but I wondered if I would ever find someone to love that would love me in return. I felt positive that it would happen but as each year passed, my concerns grew. However, I knew that if God meant it to happen, it would happen. I just had to relax and be confident in myself.

Since arriving in town, David and I became active in Dighton's Lutheran Church; David as a reader of the Word and I taught Sunday school. Teaching young people about Jesus was a wonderful experience for me partly because the children were so eager to learn. Sometimes they asked the toughest questions but it kept me on my toes. Work and church helped David and I to meet people.

Many of those that we meet at Church helped David's carpentry business grow. Women were tired of asking their husband to fix a squeaking door, a drippy facet, a loose floor board, or any other number of jobs. Often the husband was busy during the day working a full—time job and didn't have time to handle the odds jobs that needed to be completed around the house. Desiring for the odd jobs to be completed, Dighton's women thought of David. Even though he was a carpenter it was just a simple jump from carpenter to 'handyman'. So, David Funk, the handyman was born.

After being in Dighton for about a year an incident occurred that was scary for the entire town but especially for David. In the spring of 1928, David was approached by the towns doctor, Dr. Weinenger, to look at his wobbly examination table. He wasn't sure what the problem was, he just knew that when he had a patient sit on the table, it tended to lean to one side and wobbled slightly. David told the doctor that he "would be happy to come in and look at the table that was giving the doctor problems."

Arriving at the doctor's office the next Monday morning he approached the doctor's receptionist, who immediately said "Dr. Weinenger told me to expect you. Have a seat. I will take you back in a moment." Upon finishing up with a patient, the receptionist stood up and said "Mr. Funk! Please follow me."

Standing, David followed her to one of the doctor's examination rooms. She indicated the table that needed to be fixed. "Dr. Weinenger will be with you in a moment or two."

Thanking her, David preceded to examine the table and to think about how fix it. The table was solid and well made. He knew that the doctor would not want to purchase a new table that was not as solidly built as this table. Just then Dr. Weinenger walked in, said hello and proceeded to ask David if the table could be fixed?

"Well, doc," he began, "it is fixable." He then proceeded to tell Dr Weinenger what would be needed to fix the leg properly. As the pair finished discussing the table, the nurse came in to inform the doctor that there was a medical emergency.

"Excuse me David, I have to go. Do whatever is necessary to fix the table and provide me a bill." As the doctor hurried out of the examination room, the nurse was telling him that a man in the waiting room needed the doctor to assist a boy who had a foot crushed by a tractor. As Dr. Weinenger grabbed his bag he briefly wondered why he asked to go to the boy instead of them bringing the boy to Dighton's hospital for treatment.

Arriving at their destination, the doctor discovered that he had been deceived as there wasn't a boy with a crushed foot but a wounded man. Looking closely, he realized that the wounded man was Howard 'Heavy' Royston. The doctor quickly understood that if the man was Royston, then the group of men must be part of the Fleagle gang. Worry about his safety slowly overtook the doctor because he knew that the men were notorious killers. After Dr. Weinenger finished treating Royston, two of the men bound and blindfolded him. They placed the doctor in his Buick, drove him off the ranch to an area north of Scott City and then shot him in the back of the head. The men then rolled the doctor's body and his car into a ravine. The doctor's car and body were spotted within twenty—four hours by a group of men looking for the Fleagle Gang.

"Grandma," I interjected "that is terrible! Who could kill someone especially after they assisted you?"

"Well Dani, sometimes life is hard to understand."

Continuing on with what happened, Grandma said that "prior to abducting and killing Dr. Weinenger, the Fleagle gang, had robbed the First National Bank in Lamar, Colorado." Ralph and Jake Fleagle, George Abshire and Howard Royston had scoped out the bank at several different times before actually doing the robbery. They knew the layout of the bank and had maps of the county where Lamar was situated.

The gang carried license plates from Kansas, Oklahoma and Colorado in the trunk of the car. The plates would be changed in order to confess witnesses and to throw the police off their track. The gang left their Kansas ranch at around three in the morning and headed towards Lamar. Their plan was to rob the

Colorado bank in the early afternoon. Realizing that the bank was being robbed, the bank's president, A. N. Parrish, ducked into his office to grab his forty—five. He shot at the closest robber to his office, which just happened to be Royston, hitting him in the jaw; Royston then slumped to the floor. The robbery and shooting created chaos and a struggle ensued between the robbers and customers. As a result of the struggle, the bank president and the bank president's son, were killed.

The gang took over ten thousand dollars in cash and twelve thousand dollars in liberty bonds. Originally, the gang had planned on taking the bank presidents son hostage. The robbers felt that the bank president would not risk his son's life by pursuing them. That way they could easily escape and then ditch the bank president's son. Plans changed as bank president and son had been killed. On the way out of the bank, the gang had to take hostages. Edward Lewis and Everett Klinger became the hostages that the gang fled Lamar with in a 1927 blue Buick Master Six. Pursuing the gang, the sheriff's car sputtered to a stop at Sand Creek, northeast of Lamar.

The hostages pleaded with the gang to be released but the bandits refused. Everett Klinger was taken to a shack near Liberal, Kansas and shot by the Fleagle brothers; his body was found three weeks after the robbery. The other hostage, Edward Lewis, was killed as the gang attempted to make a quick escape after they killed Klinger.

It was reported that the four men split the loot and separated. It took over a year for the police to track down the entire gang. Jake Fleagle was killed in a shootout in rural Missouri, Royston was captured in California and Abshire was detained in western Colorado. Ralph Fleagle was taken into custody in Illinois where he confessed to the crimes of bank robbery and murder. He plead guilty in exchange for the release of two of his other brothers who were in jail for petty crimes. Ralph Fleagle, George Abshier and Howard Royston were tried in Lamar in late 1929 and the three men were all sentenced to hang.

"I am sorry about the deaths of the doctor, the hostages and the bank employees. But I am glad that the entire gang was captured and held accountable for their crimes." I then asked if "the town able to hire a new doctor?"

Thinking for a moment before answering, Grandma finally stated that "it was tough for the town to locate and to hire another doctor. The robbery and killing had been widely reported in newspapers and on the radio across the region and across the United States. This caused several candidates to withdrew their applications before the selection process could take place. A few that did come for the interview ended up withdrawing their applications after they heard about the killing. Those on the search committee decided not to mention the incident because we had never had a doctor killed before and hopefully, it wouldn't happen again. If asked what happened to the previous doctor, the committee decided to just state that he had died and cross our fingers. Six months later, the town finally obtained a new doctor."

December 1975

Checking the potatoes, Grandma asked me to drain them and then mash them. She took the meat loaf out of the oven and quickly heated up some green beans. Grandpa came home and we ate dinner. Grandma and I decided to take a break and pick up the story in the morning.

Grandma's story continued

The next morning Grandma and I sat down after we finished breakfast, cleaned and put away the dishes. This morning,

Grandma began telling me about a new family, named Schwartz. that had moved to town. The family had moved to Dighton from Hutchinson, Kansas with plans of opening a restaurant that specialized in German—American food. Back in Hutchinson, Mr. Schwartz operated a restaurant with two of his brothers. Besides being known for their German food, the three brothers were known for their Hungarian Goulash and Swedish meatballs. Business was so good that the trio wished to expand their business. The brothers decided to open the same type of restaurant in two other places. One brother stayed in Hutchinson while one of the brothers moved to Topeka and the last brother moved to Dighton.

Mr. Swartz purchased a building that the family felt was the perfect size for their restaurant but the building needed work to accommodate the business. The Swartz approached David regarding refurbishing the building to fit the needs of the business. As he began working on the building, David caught sight of a beautiful, young woman whom he assumed was the Schwartz' daughter but was not sure. The pair would catch each other's eyes but both were too shy to talk. Mr. Schwartz finally introduced the two. "David, this is my daughter, Susannah, but we all call her Anna. Anna this is David Funk."

Shyly they both said hello and went their separate ways. Over the next several weeks they became more comfortable with each other and David finally asked Anna out on a date. At home, I teased my brother about being so shy around 'girls'. As David and Anna began to see each other more often, I was thinking about getting my own place but was not sure that I made enough money to do so.

Early summer of 1928, the hotel owner told me that they would be closing the hotel for a short period because her mother was ill and they needed to return to the Texas panhandle. "We will let you know when we return from Texas" the owner said. For the remainder of the summer and early fall, I took many odd jobs to earn money.

One job that I did was picking crops at several farms on the outskirts of town. On one day, as I was part of a group picking a field, a man with the county road crew smiled at me. Walking over to deposit the vegetables picked into a larger container, I stopped to get a drink of water. Luckily the road crew was stopping for lunch when I was getting a drink of water which provided the young man the opportunity to approach me and say hello. I said hello and asked if he wanted a drink. Over the next few minutes I learned that his name was Lawrence Anderson and that he was in the county to work temporarily on a road project. "And yes," said Grandma "this is the same man that I would eventually marry and he would become your Grandfather."

Getting back to work, I gave Lawrence fleeting glances throughout the rest of the day. It took two weeks for Lawrence to gain enough confidence to ask me out and it took another couple of days for me to say yes. As Lawrence and I got to know each other better, we occasionally went to dinner or just for a walk around town. Over several months of seeing each other, I related how the family had moved to Rush County from Russia in 1901. In addition, I told him bits and pieces about my life growing up on a farm and working in my grandmother's fabric shop.

I learned about how Lawrence's widowed grandmother had moved from Sweden to Kansas with her only child, Andrew, in the early 1860's. Working to support her son and herself left Andrew enough time to explore the streets of Abilene. Lawrence related stories of how his father came upon many of the legends of the Wild West. Lawrence told me was about how his Dad encountered Wild Bill Hickok. In 1871, the town of Abilene Kansas hired Wild Bill Hickok to be the town's marshal. While working as the marshal, Hickok had an ongoing dispute with Philip Coe, a local salon owner. At one time, Hickok attempted to arrest an outlaw named Hardin for wearing his pistols in Coe's saloon. Many felt that the incident was a result of Coe and Hickok's dislike for each other. In October, Andrew witnessed Hickok attempting to break up a street brawl. At this point, Mr. Coe stepped out of his saloon and fired two shots. Hickok decided that Mr. Coe needed to be arrested for interfering with the law. Hoping to finally kill Hickok, Mr. Coe quickly turned his gun on Hickok. However, Hickok was faster and Coe was killed instantly.

Lawrence and I continued to exchange stories about our youth and growing up as we got to know each other better. Lawrence began to attend services with me every Sunday morning at the Lutheran Church. While I taught Sunday school, Lawrence would wait for me outside. During the time that I was getting to know Lawrence, my brother, David, was seriously courting Anna. By Christmas, David and Anna announced their engagement and about their plans for a wedding in 1929. I was so excited for David but was seriously worried because I knew that I could not afford the rent on most houses in town; Dighton did not have apartments at the time. Plus, what would I do with an entire house to myself. Besides, after growing up in such a large family I was not sure that I desired to live alone.

The county road project was completed in late September, 1929. This meant that over three—quarters of the crew were let go. Lawrence felt lucky that he was kept on by Lane County Road Department permanently. He would be working on repairing roads during the warm weather and in the winter, he would assist in keeping the roads clear of snow and ice. Having Lawrence stay in Lane County was a blessing for me as that I knew by then that I was in love with him.

In just the short time that David and I lived in Dighton, the town's population has grown by over fifty percent; there were now over eight hundred people living in the town alone. The growth in the population caused a boom in house construction along with an increase in businesses opening their doors. During this period, the town gained a second grocery store, a car dealership and a pool hall. There was talk that Dighton would finally gain a movie theater. Furthermore, David's carpentry and handyman business literally boomed. He had mare home repair jobs that needed to be completed then he could handle. David also assisted in the building of new homes.

In early spring of 1929, the Schwartz' needed additional help. They hired me to wait tables and to wash dishes for the evening meal. As part of the deal, I was able to eat my evening meal free at the restaurant. By this time, the hotel had reopened and I began to work again. After completing my hours in the hotel, I would rush home and prepare dinner for David. I would leave dinner simmering over a very low heat and then rush off to the restaurant to wait tables. David would arrive home within a half hour of my leaving to eat his meal. Working the dinner shift, having dinner provided and cleaning hotel rooms helped me make enough that I could afford to look for a place of my own, a small place but, a place of my own.

Throughout the remaining months of early spring of 1929, David and Anna's wedding plans progressed. Some of the decisions seemed to be blown out of portion. Decisions such as where the wedding should take place. For example:

1. The Schwartz' felt that the ceremony should take place in Hutchison because that is where the majority of Anna's family lived;

2. But, maybe the wedding should take place in Dighton since they lived there;

3. David thought that it might be nice if they held the wedding in LaCrosse but really wanted to have the wedding where they now lived.

Dighton won the wedding would be held there. They just had to decide whether to have the ceremony at the Lutheran Church or Methodist Church. I secretly thought 'who cares' as long as the wedding took place in a church. Besides, I was glad to see David and Anna quickly agree on the church and everything else dealing with the wedding.

Everyone was happy to see May 29th finally arrive; the wedding was beautiful. Both families attended the wedding, filling the hotel to capacity. In addition, many of the Funks just drove to Lane County from their homes in Rush County; the drive was about eighty miles one way which could easily be accomplished. Having purchased a house on the western edge of town, David had enough room for a few family members to stay the evening before the wedding. Several of the Funks had driven to Ness City the day before the wedding and stayed with either Philip and Pauline or Molly and Philip.

Luckily, a month before the wedding I had found a small one—bedroom house to rent. The house was within three blocks from everywhere I needed to go on a regular basis: Hotel, post office, Restaurant and grocery store. The only thing further away was the church. Other than that, the house was in the perfect location for a person that needed to walk everywhere. The house provided me with a large enough backyard to set up a clothesline and establish a garden.

When attending David's wedding, Molly and Philip brought several trays of vegetable seedlings for both David and me. In addition, Molly brought me several Irises. "As you know, Dani," Grandma interjected "Irises are my favorite flower. In recent years, Irises fill the largest portion of my flower garden."

"Yes," I replied "irises are my favorite flower too. But I also love lilacs and jonquils."

Getting back to the family story Grandma stated that "at David and Anna's wedding reception, Lawrence asked Dad for my hand in marriage." However, since Lawrence was not German, Dad was reluctant to consider the proposal. My parent's left Dighton for home without Dad giving Lawrence an answer.

"But you got married anyway" I argued. "Did your Dad ever give his permission?"

"Patience Dani," Grandma began, "by mid—June, Lawrence decided to propose to me with or without my dad's consent." I answered yes and we decided to get married quietly in a small, private ceremony in January of 1930 at Dighton's Lutheran Church. Hopefully before January 1930, Dad would get to know Lawrence and agree to the two of us marrying. If not, we decided that we would get married without his permission. Dad never did give his permission but came to accept Lawrence as my husband.

At the beginning of our marriage, Lawrence and I continued to live in the small house that I had rented in town. I gave up working at the restaurant once we were married; the following summer I also stopped working at the hotel when I realized that I was expecting our first child.

December 1975

Grandma and her brother, David, had moved to Dighton to start a new life. They both found love and married but I am still not sure why Grandma's father was adamant about marrying only a German. The most interesting but sad aspect of my conversation with Grandma was the killing of the town's doctor. He was an innocent bystander who was doing what is expected of doctors: helping those in need. Without a doctor, the town's people would have to travel an average of fifty miles to the next town in order to get medical attention. Fifty miles is a long distance especially if you are having a heart attack or anything else major.

I wonder what else has happened to Grandma and Grandpa! After retrieving some papers, Grandma handed several photographs to me. This first photograph was an excellent one of the dust storms that I have heard a little about. I can't believe that the clouds were so dark and ominous. I read somewhere that it was hard to estimate the actual number of individuals that died as a direct result of these dust storms. Some died because of dust pneumonia while others died attempting to flee the storm.

http://www.livinghistoryfarmorg/farminginthe30s/water_02.html

Next, I picked up the map that showed the area that experienced the majority of the dust bowl. It seems amazing to me that Dighton was virtually in the middle of the area impacted by the dust bowl.

http://www.pbs.org/wgbh/american
experience/films/dustbowl/

Finally, the last picture that Grandma handed me was of a family. I immediately asked who the people in the picture were?

"Dani," Grandma began "it is of my Aunt Allision and her family."

I was speechless! After all that I had learned of Allision I could not believe that I got to actually see what she looked like.

Grandma asked that "we pick up the story again tomorrow; I'm a bit tried."

"Is everything okay, Grandma?"

"Everything is fine! I just need a break."

Grandma's story continues

The next morning, we began to have a conversation again after I finished cleaning up after breakfast. Grandma plunged right into the story by stating that "during the early years of our marriage, the nation was experiencing a depression. Farmers in Lane County and across the nation suffered as crop prices fell dramatically, causing many farmers to default on their bank loans."

In efforts to help America get out of the depression and to assist the people, President Roosevelt implemented a program called the New Deal. "I am sure that you have heard of the New Deal, Dani" Grandma said. "The New Deal was intended to provide jobs and relief to those suffering the most.

"One New Deal program that helped put the population back to work was called the Civilian Conservation Corps (CCC). The CCC provided employment for thousands of young men during the thirties. The employed men were provided shelter, clothes and were fed. Eighty—per—cent of the paid salary was to be sent home to help support their family. The CCC aided in the planting of over three billion trees, built shelters and trails in more than eight—hundred parks across America.

"Here in south—west Kansas we were not affected by the CCC as there were no large national parks located nearby. However, several young men from the area joined the CCC in order to assist in supporting their widowed mothers and families."

The policies of the New Deal focused on the '3Rs': relief, recovery and reform. Grandma argued that "Many Lane County families renamed Roosevelt's 3Rs as the 2Rs and MD."

I asked "What are the 2Rs and MD?"

"Repair, reuse and make do. During the depression, my sisters and I repaired clothing, patched holes, and passed clothing down from child to child and often from one cousin to another cousin. Younger children often never saw a new piece of clothing and made do with hand—me—downs."

I interjected that "I read in a local paper that yesterday's 3Rs are todays reduce, reuse and recycle. Reduce, recycle and reuse began because of the movement of being environmentally conscious. Many Americans feel that water quality needed to be improved and that waste products, like tin and plastic, should not just be dumped into a land fill, that they should be recycled and reused."

Grandma stated that she had "heard the same thing about recycling of tin and plastic. Many feel that glass should also be reused or recycled. Women who preserve, which as you know is also called canning, reuse their canning jars over and over again. Many of us take care of our tin lids so that they can also be reused."

Grandma argued that Roosevelts policies were never aggressive enough to bring America's economy out of the depression completely. "In Roosevelt's defense, I knew that he had tried to implement many programs to get people back to work. But FDR's early programs were primarily geared towards men.

It was done so because it was assumed that men were the family's provider. If a man had a job then the entire family benefited from the governmental programs. This wasn't necessarily true. It soon became evident to those in Washington, D.C. that the government needed to also help women. This was due to many women being widowed which meant that they had become the principle bread winner for the family."

Grandma went on to explain how the Works Progress Administration (WPA) was established to directly assist women. The WPA hired single women, widows or women with a disabled or an absent husband. Women were hired for school lunch programs and were assigned sewing projects. Often women made clothing and bedding to be given out to hospitals and to charities. Many women across Lane County, who were widowed or home alone because their husbands were elsewhere looking for work, benefited from programs of the WPA. It aided them in getting through the tough periods created by the depression.

The depression caused many people, including your Grandfather and I, to have a shortage of money. Without having money or little money, we made do with what we had. Those of us that quilted were often found sewing patches on older quilts instead of making a new one. Of course, this caused business at the fabric shop to dramatically drop off. Eventually, my grandmother had to close the quilt / fabric shop in 1930. The year before, Marie had passed away quietly in her sleep which caused the family to decide to close her spinning mill. The family sold her Denver townhouse shortly after the spinning mill was closed.

Supplies needed for making wooden spools became scare and companies still in operation were not buying new spools, they were just reusing more and more spools. Just like the families spinning mill did back in Russia, mills in America provided a percentage off new purchases if the customer returned older spools. Dad, Aunt Allison and Uncle Philip decided to finally close the spool business in mid—1931. It was a sad day indeed when both the fabric shop and spool business closed.

Farmers of Lane County continued to grow a wide variety of crops, and to harvest fruit. The people of Dighton just made their gardens larger and grew more and more of their own vegetables. During this period, women continued to bake their own bread, make their own noodles, and increased what they could preserve. Canning enabled families to save money but it meant long hours over a hot stove during steamy summer months.

Self—sufficiency became a part of our social life. Church pot—lucks and one—dish suppers was a vital way for the community to share what food we did have. Those taking part in pot—lucks or one—dish dinners experienced fun and their relationships deepened. Those living in Dighton, knew that the majority of people did not have extra money so many of us turned to bartering. For example, David's clients might give him a crate of sweet corn or a portion of a butchered hog in exchange for him repairing a broken window or repairing a piece of furniture. Bartering did not work when an individual needed to repay a bank loan or to pay an electric bill.

While still working for the county road department, your Grandpa and I had moved to a farm house south—west of Dighton by the summer of 1931. The five acres around the house enabled us to have a larger garden and to have a few chickens. The owner of the farm had moved in with his son and daughter—in—law after his wife had passed away. Since he had moved two counties away, he had rented out the remaining land to a neighboring farmer until he and his son decided on whether they should sell the farm or not.

We, as other people living in western Kansas, were always busy. Chores still had to be done daily and sometimes twice daily. Gathering eggs, tending the garden and filling a wood box would have to be done daily. While milking the cows or feeding livestock had to be completed usually twice a day. Gardening, raising chickens, collecting eggs and taking care of your Uncle William, made me sort of glad that your Grandpa and I did not have to worry about milking a cow or several cows. The milk would have been nice but....

When I was a child, I helped with the milking each morning and late afternoon. My siblings and I would each take a three—legged stool along with a bucket and work our way down the line of cows. When the bucket was full, we would take the milk and dump it into a larger container. Milking was a time for us, as siblings, to have fun together. As an adult, milking could be a time to contemplate life and to wrestle through problems.

"I, along with other women, spent a lot of time mending and washing clothes" Grandma simply stated. "Several women had been given automatic washing machines prior to the depression. The majority of these machines were powered by electricity but with the onset of the depression, many could not afford to pay the electric company. Some utilized generators to power washing machine but how could poor people afford to run a generator. Cost of electricity and or a generator and running it caused laundry to be largely done by wash tubs and wash boards. Laundry in the thirties was not done differently than how it was done two hundred years ago. Hmmm progress...."

Changing the subject slightly I asked Grandma "about the dust bowl and the droughts that took place on the plains. Denver County did not experience the dust bowl first hand so the

School System did not elaborate much on the topic. Did you experience these conditions?"

Grandma thought for a moment and then said that "yes, Grandpa and I had encountered the great dust bowl during the early thirties. Also, we lived through several periods of drought like conditions. Years before the two of us began living in Lane County, natural prairie grasses grew on the plains for thousands of years. These natural prairie grasses acted as a groundcover, trapped moisture causing the land to withstand a drought or drought like conditions. The grasses had been plowed up to accommodate the growth in the numbers of farmers living and working in the region. Each year, farmers living in Lane County would plow their fields and plant crops in hopes of reaping a sizable cash crop. It was said that one good wheat crop could bring the monetary equivalent of ten years of raising stock.[7] This caused more and more farmers to contemplate growing wheat. However, by early 1930, there was a glut of wheat on the market. Because there was so much wheat on the market, the price for this crop had fallen to twenty—five cents or less a bushel; this was about half of what it cost a farmer to plant the seed and grow the crop."[8]

Grandma continued by stating that "as droughts became more frequent during the early thirties', crops had this uncanny ability to not grow. Or if it did grow, the crop would wither and die before it had a chance to fully mature. This left soil exposed to the mercy of high winds, low humidity and little to no rain. Winds that crossed the open plains whipped up the loose soil. Slowly these winds and dust increased causing billowing clouds of dust to rise and blow across the region.

[7] Duncan and Burns. *The Dust Bowl*, 29.

[8] Ibid, 37.

"At first," Grandma continued, "the region's population did not know what to make of these storms. Animals and birds scurried ahead of these storms while the people just stood there watching it approach and finally over taking us. When the storms arrived, we would be covered in darkness. It was so dark that when we were inside, we had to light a lamp. As the days and weeks passed, the horrible winds were persistent and the dust storms continued. Between the dust storms, life became as normal as possible: we would sew, read, and handle indoor chores."

One evening while reading the Hutchison newspaper, Lawrence told me that the paper said the soil was being blown in an easterly direction and that the wind caused the dust in the air to blacken the sky. This was not new fact to us or for those living in the area where the dust storms were occurring. Another evening, Lawrence looked up from the paper and said that "the dust storms were blowing the prairies most fertile soil all the way to the east coast." Looking back at the paper he stated that "the soil was being deposited into the Atlantic Ocean." He looked up and said to me "a lot of good the soil does in the ocean."

Late one day, as Lawrence returned home from work, he said that many across Lane County were forced to wear a gauze mask over their mouth and nose. When I asked why, he said that he was told it was to prevent the dirt from going into their lungs. That same evening, as Lawrence was once again reading the newspaper, he looked up at me and said that "the paper declared that the gauze masks were being handed out to school children across the state." He said that the paper claimed that "these masks have become totally clogged with dirt within an hour."

People contracted dust pneumonia in Lane County, in western Kansas and parts of eastern Colorado. This type of pneumonia caused body aches, shortness of breath, and wrenching coughing spasms. The people became nauseated and were unable to keep food down. A week or two later, Lawrence once again looked up from reading the evening paper and told me that the paper reported that hundreds of residents that lived on the Great Plains died as a result of this 'dust pneumonia'. Of course, I worried that Lawrence, William or I would come down with this type of pneumonia. I kept William inside the house, away from others and had him wear a mask when the dust storms were blowing. All these things helped to keep him from getting sick.

It was harder to keep your Grandfather healthy since he had to go out to make a living, be around more people than William or I did and because he worked outside most of the day. Each morning your Grandpa would be inside the shop for about half an hour handling paper work. At the end of the day, he faced an hour of paper work. The remaining six—and—a—half hours in his work day were spent outside. I just hoped that a dust storm would not blow up and cause problems for the road crew. Many times, the day would start clear with beautiful blue skies but would end with black skies and dust flying. Often workers did not have time to seek shelter. The majority of men carried cloths to cover their eyes, nose and mouths to prevent the entire brunt of the dirt from attaching their internal organs. The men would often seek shelter in the cab of their road machinery; if the machinery did not have a cab, they would crouch beside the machine opposite the blowing wind. The road workers prayed that the storm would pass quickly and not bury their machinery or themselves. However, a few men died due to being buried under what looked like a ton of dirt. Once the storms passed, often the men had to dig out the tractors they used for their work.

August of 1933, your Grandpa contracted dust pneumonia which caused him to spend two weeks in the hospital. He spent an additional month at home recuperating. Through a smile, Grandma asked me if I knew "how hard it is to keep a grown man in bed for a month while they recuperated?"

The regions newspapers reported that fourteen dust storms occurred during 1932 and that thirty—eight dust storms occurred in 1933. Farmers began fleeing the mid—west for the San Joaquin Valley of California. Once in California, these farmers sought out migrant work until they could find permanent work or to save enough money to purchase their own land.

In 1933 Lawrence and I started to look for a larger place to live. West of Dighton, a small farm house with 200—acres became available for sale or rent. The previous owners had defaulted on the farms loan because of the dust storms. We approached the bank about renting the house along with a few acres. We were told that the bank wished to keep the entire property together. However, they would consider renting the house along with ten acres as long as we knew that when the bank found a buyer for the land and buildings, we would have to move. We agreed to this arrangement. Three days later, as we were moving into the house, the bank came out to the property and told us that they had talked to the farmer next door. This farmer had agreed to rent the remaining 190—acres until the entire farm sold. This arrangement worked well for the bank, the neighboring farmer and for us for several years.

Your Grandpa and I planted seven and a half acres of the land with a cash crop. We figured that planting, harvesting and then selling a cash crop would help us survive the depression.

When the cash crop sold the money earned could assist us in paying the rent for four to seven months. The entire time that we lived there we never lost the entire crop due to the dust storms—guess that we were blessed. Each year that we lived on the acreage, I was able to successfully plant a medium sized garden with the help of seedlings from my sister Molly. There was a year or two that a small percentage of the vegetables either died or did not grow so well due to insufficient rain.

I had good luck with growing cucumbers which I turned into pickles. Both my dill and sweet pickles won blue ribbons at the county fair of '34, '35 and '36. The drought affected the sweet corn that I attempted to grow the first two years of living there; by the third year I stopped planting corn and planted green peppers and more carrots. As William grew, he helped me to weed the garden and eventually pick the vegetables.

"In June of 1934," Grandma continued "your mother was born. As you know we named her Elaine. Your Uncle William was not sure what to make of the new baby. First of all, he expected a brother that was close to his age and not a baby that took up my time. Within a six months William adjusted to your mother being part of the family."

As the dust storms began to diminish farmers in Lane County and the rest of Western Kansas began to be plagued by black—tailed jackrabbits. Reminiscent of the grasshopper infestation that western Kansas experienced sixty years before, the rabbits ate everything in their path. Jackrabbits could quickly eat an entire green plant including its roots. Making it worse was the fact, that adult jackrabbits could produce up to eight offspring every thirty—two days. Warm weather and lack of rain eliminated many of the natural conditions that could kill young rabbits so they survived into adulthood.

At this time, the state estimated that there were roughly eight million rabbits in the thirty counties of Western Kansas. "If a farmer was able to get a crop to grow through drought conditions, hot temperatures, and blowing soil" claimed Grandma "they faced jackrabbits. The jackrabbit infestation caused us to totally lose the wheat that we planted in 1934."

"How did you pay the rent that year?" I asked.

"Well," began Grandma "with no cash crop to sell we had to scrimp. Some of the rent came from my selling a larger portion of my eggs. We bought less, saved more and had to use a percentage of your Grandpa's salary for the rent. It was a tough time for us but we survived."

Grandma looked at me and said "Getting back to the jackrabbit nuisance. Several counties offered a bounty of one to four cents for each rabbit killed. Hodgeman County was forced to stop paying the bounty after forty—four thousand rabbits had been turned in for the bounty money. This alone threatened to bankrupt the county's budget.

"Wow!" interjected Dani, "It is hard to imagine that eight—million jackrabbits were living in western Kansas. Forty—four thousand would barely make a dent in the rabbit population. How did the region's population get rid of the annoyance?"

"Well," began Grandma "to aid in the controlling of these rabbit's, we attempted Sunday afternoon drives. Some of these drives would begin on Saturday and go through Monday. These drives would be held usually in late winter to early spring; the months of February and March were the most popular. They would be advertised in local newspapers, such as the *Dighton Herald*. The largest and most successful drive that took place in Kansas was held here in Lane County."

In late 1935, a planning meeting was held one evening in Dighton's high school auditorium. Over seventy percent of the county's population attended the meeting. Discussion began with when the next Sunday drive would take place. We needed as many people as possible to aid in the removal of the jackrabbits so, the second part of the meeting involved how to get the word out about the event. The *Dighton Herald*, agreed to advertise the drive during the month prior to the event at no cost. Newspapers in surrounding counties picked up on the story and placed an article about it in their papers for two weeks prior to the actual event. The goal was to get as many people involved as possible to capture as many rabbits as we could.

Thirdly, we discussed where would we house the large number of people that potentially could come to Dighton in order to help us rid the county of the jackrabbit nuisance. The town's hotel could only house a limited number of people. Everyone at the meeting agreed to make their homes available to anyone coming to assist in the rabbit drive. Someone suggested that we could use the gymnasiums in the grade and high schools. So, it was decided to use the schools and homes whenever possible.

Then we discussed how to feed such a large group of people that we hoped would help us. Those farmers in attendance said that they would share what food they could to those willing to cook and serve the meals. The grocery store also volunteered to provide food at no cost, bag it and deliver it to the women as needed. Women signed up to cook and to serve the food. To make it easier on the women and the grocer we decided that the High School's cafeteria would be used to cook and serve meals. The cafeteria already had a large kitchen, lots of silverware and dishes so was a natural choice for meals. Plus, we would use the gymnasium as a make shift dormitory for as many people as possible to be housed.

Overwhelmingly, this idea was agreed too. Since it was December and school would be still open, it was decided to close school for a day or two while the hunt for jackrabbits took place. Prior to ending the meeting, we discussed the most important aspect: how to capture thousands of jackrabbits. Grandma paused a second which caused me to jump in and ask "so what was decided?"

"Patience, Dani!" Grandma said prior to continuing with the jackrabbit story. "The evening before the first drive began, Dighton's residents were pleasantly surprised to see almost nine—thousand people gathered to aid us with the drive. On the morning of the drive an additional twelve hundred people came to town to assist us."

It was awesome that over ten thousand people had come to Lane County to aid with the rabbit hunt. Many of those ten thousand people were also having a problem with jackrabbits or they knew of someone that was being plagued by the irritation. So, taking part in this jackrabbit drive it was felt that a drive could be replicated in and around their county with help from others. Hopefully, in no time western Kansas would be free of the jackrabbit nuisance. Your Uncle David and Grandpa were just two of Dighton's male population that took part in the rabbit roundup. Anna, half of the town's women and I handled the cooking, serving and child care. Other women assisted with ridding the region of the jackrabbits.

The plan was to cover eight—square miles on the first day. The drive began with the people lining up about every ten feet in the shape of a square; we would have multiple squares. The people were told to make as much noise as possible as they walked towards the center of the square. Sometimes men would have their wife and children behind them. The women and children would blow car or truck horns, or pound on pans to scare the rabbits. The idea was to force the rabbits to continue towards the center of the square. As the people got closer together near the center all possible routes of escape would be blocked off. The men carried sections of fencing to put in place at the center in order to prevent the rabbits from escaping.. Within the fenced enclosure the rabbits would be clubbed to death. Firearms were prohibited due to the risk of the participants injuring themselves or others. This three—day drive captured over thirty thousand rabbits. We arranged for another rabbit drive to be held in two weeks. That drive netted an additional fifteen thousand rabbits.

Stories about the drive in Dighton along with other drives appeared in newspapers across the Midwest. These drives caused an outrage across the nation as many people thought that the rabbits were being hunted for sport instead of attempting to control the population. As we knew, these drives were not for sport; the rabbits were very destructive. Residents of Western Kansas attempted to spread the word of how damaging these rabbits were to crops and livestock. Those places that did not have an issue with pests, such as rabbits, did not understand the problem.

Eastern Kansas was one place that did not have a rabbit problem, so they were some of the most vocal critics of killing the jackrabbits. Some people from Eastern Kansas felt that the killing of rabbits gave a bad name to the state. However, someone in western Kansas proposed that instead of killing the rabbits that they should be driven to the eastern part of the state. Of course, farmers in Eastern Kansas did not want the rabbits but would not admit that they might be wrong. However, the suggestion caused the residents of eastern Kansas to stop being such vocal critics. Several farmers attempted to ship live rabbits to states in the eastern part of the United States, but these states realized that the jackrabbits were very destructive; the rabbits were refused but it is unclear with they did with jackrabbits. The bad press of the jackrabbit drives ended quickly.

"Did this two drives completely rid Dighton of rabbits?" I asked.

"No," Grandma replied, "but it was a good start. A few more drives across western Kansas caused the infestation to finally end."

As the dust storms slowly ended and after the jackrabbit infestation ended, a rare, out of season, tornado hit extreme south—central Nebraska and a small portion of northern Kansas. Rural north—central Kansas did not experience much damage. However, a town in south—central Nebraska was devastated. Eighty—five percent of the town was leveled and over thirty people lost their lives. The population of Lane County and other parts of Kansas came together to aid the town in Nebraska. Churches across Kansas and Nebraska began clothing drives and non—perishable food campaigns. A group of quilters from Dighton's Methodist Church had been working on two quilts that were to be used for an upcoming church raffle. After discussing the tornado, the quilters decided to donate the proceeds from the quilt raffle to the victims of the Nebraska tornado. The raffle made more money from these two quilts than they had ever made from a quilt drawing before: HURRAY!

It's funny how people will come out to assist others in need. Could it be that they knew that it could have been them needing help? Could it be they were living a Christian life?

Just as you did it to one of the least of these who are members of my family you did it for me.   *Matthew 25: 40*

As it was not the season for growing and harvesting crops, farmers came together to give as much of their stored food as possible. Women provided as much of their canned goods that they could spare. Several trucks were loaded with fresh and canned food, clothing, and other items that had been collected and driven to south—central Nebraska. Once the trucks were unloaded, the men decided to stay and to assist in the rebuilding of the town. Other communities brought timber and supplies needed for the rebuilding of homes, schools and businesses.

Church leaders from Nebraska gathered the people together to pray. Praying took place each and every morning during the rebuilding of the town and surrounding area. The ministers usually began the prayer with the verse from Matthew:

> *For I was hungry and you gave me food; I was thirsty and you gave me something to drink; I was naked and you gave me clothing; I was sick and you took care of me; I was in prison and you visited me; I was a stranger and you welcomed me. Just as you did it to one of the least of these who are members of my family you did it for me. Matthew 25:35—36, 45*

The prayer and bible verse helped center the volunteers from Kansas and Nebraska. Many of the Nebraska residents had lost everything except their family, which they were most grateful for. In addition, they were very grateful for what they had and for the assistance they received from others. Many of which were complete strangers.

"It doesn't seem that people today help each other as much as when you were young, Grandma." I quietly said before stating "Why is that?"

"You're not looking hard enough or in the right places, Dani!" Grandma replied.

"What do you mean?"

"Well," Grandma began "people still reach out to aid others in need. For example, a monetary collection might be taken up for a family that can't pay a hospital bill. Or food gathered for the poor living in poverty. There are countless ways to help others, it just is not as concentrated as it was for the tornado victims. Wait and see, when a major tornado or hurricane occurs here will be a larger out pouring of aid."

Between the droughts, the dust bowl, tornados and the jackrabbit infestation we, and many of the region's population, began to live normal, quiet lives. We learned how to further repair, reuse and make do. Anna, David's wife, and I got together to can vegetables and to share fabric scraps for quilting. Sometimes Molly would come to Dighton to can with Anna and myself. Other times, Anna and I would travel to Ness City to help Molly can what she had grown. Molly, Anna and I each had a daughter born between the years of 1933 and 1935 which enabled us to stretch our budget by sharing clothes between the girls.

Our younger sister, Lydia, married Rex Clouston in 1932, and had moved to a farm in Finney County. Lydia had a son in 1933 and a daughter in 1936; Molly, Anna and I blessed Lydia with some girl's clothing that our daughters had outgrown. It was harder to exchange boy's clothes as boys are harder on clothes. We patched clothing to make them last but eventually when the boy outgrew the shirt or pants the clothing usually had to be thrown away or cut up in order to patch other clothes.

The depression caused many of the nation's population to learn how to do many different jobs. For example, Allison's husband, Edward, worked as a mechanic in the family spool business. Once the spool business closed, Edward transitioned to being a part-time mechanic and learned more about agriculture in order to farm full—time. However, with the drought conditions, blowing soil, and people making do caused Edward's mechanical business to blossom and for him to do better at being a mechanic than as a farmer. Business was so good that Uncle Edward and Aunt Allison decided to rent a building in town. That way Edward could operate the mechanical business in a place that would be easy for customers to find. The building did not need much renovation because it had previously been a service station.

In the spring of 1936, Allison came to town at around noon to bring Edward his lunch. As the two were sitting down to eat in Edward's office, someone entered the shop and called out hello. Edward stood up, walked to the office door, and said "How can I help you?"

"Are you Edward Howard?"

"Yes! What can I do for you?" he asked again.

"I am Daniel Heller…" Choking on her sandwich, Allison let out a loud gasp. "Ahh, so she is here with you."

Realizing who the man was, Edward angrily stated "What are you doing here?" as Allison slowly rose and approached Edward from behind.

"Don't worry; I did not escape this time. I was released from prison due to 'good behavior'. I know that you can't imagine me getting out of jail due to good behavior."

"The judge gave you life without the chance of parole. How did you get out?" Allison asked.

While Daniel attempted to think of an answer Edward angrily said "You're not welcome here."

"Relax, I am not here to harass Allison; I just want to visit my children."

Allison interjected "Daniel, the children are grown, have families of their own and are doing well. Please, just let them alone."

"Don't I have the right to see my children?"

"After all the flossies you subjected them too? And what about the two men you killed in Denver? You now want to see the children? Heidi is 41 and has children older than she was when you were sent to prison. At 34 years old, Henry, has no memory of you whatsoever. The three that are between Heidi and Henry have varying degrees of memory of you; why do you want to disturb their lives?"

"Allison, I am a changed man. I realize that what I did to you and the children was wrong. I am sixty-nine years old and I would like to make amends for all the wrong that I did."

Edward jumped in to say "Give us a couple days to think about it. Where are you staying?"

"I am renting a room at a hotel in Hayes. I will come back at the end of the week."

After Daniel left, Aunt Allison and Uncle Edward sat down to discuss the situation. "Edward, over forty years of experience tells me that he hasn't changed in the least. I don't want to subject the children to him and his lies."

"I understand perfectly, darling. I feel blessed that the children view and accept me as their father. I don't wish to disturb that as I love them dearly."

Allison squeezed his hand tightly saying "I know! I also feel that the children and I are lucky to have you in our lives. The children have had a better life without him in it. But there is a side of me that wants to give them a chance to know their father."

"Let's think about this over night and discuss it again to-morrow."

Over the next couple of days, Aunt Allison and Uncle Edward discussed allowing Daniel in the children's lives. Heidi now lived in Dodge City with her husband and four children. So, Allison made a long distant phone call to Heidi in order to ask her how she felt about seeing her father again.

"I have mixed feelings about seeing him again, Mom. Memories of him have faded somewhat but from what I remember he was hardly ever there. When he was home, he didn't seem to care one way or the other about us." Heidi thoughtfully continued "I seem to remember that he just wanted us to be quiet because his head hurt. As a child, I thought that he had an illness and was dying; as an adult I realized that his headache was really a hangover from alcohol. I know that he is my father and I should see him but my dad is Edward. So, no I really don't want to see him."

Aunt Allison and Uncle Edward approached the other four children about seeing Daniel; they received the same negative response. Edward talked to the sheriff about the situation with Daniel and how they felt that he might attempt to kill them. Explaining to the sheriff about Daniel and prison, the pair wanted to know how he got out. The sheriff made a call to Denver and found out that Daniel had escaped once again. The sheriff agreed to come to the garage to help the couple with Daniel. When Daniel returned at the end of the week, the sheriff was with Aunt Allison and Uncle Edward when they broke the news to Daniel.

After introducing the sheriff to Daniel, Allison said "Daniel, we talked to the children about your wishes to see them. The children have no desire to see you."

Looking sad but very angry, Daniel replied "I do understand because it has been almost thirty—five years since they've seen me; but I am still their father..."

"Then be their real father and leave them alone. They all are adults now and don't need a father like they did thirty to thirty—five years ago."

Daniel pulled a gun out as he claimed in a loud voice "it is your fault Allison; you turned them against me."

With his gun drawn and pointed at Daniel, the sheriff stepped forward and said "Daniel, give me your gun."

Wildly waving his gun around, Daniel replied "I am going to kill Allison for ruining my life."

"Tell me how she ruined your life?" the sheriff calmly replied.

Daniel proceeded to tell a tale of how it had been Allison who drove him to other women and to eventually kill the men in Denver. Allison jumped in by saying "Twenty years ago you blamed my father for ruining your life. Now you say that it is my fault that you chased other women."

Pointing his gun at Allison, Daniel pulled the trigger shooting Allison; in turn the sheriff shot Daniel dead. The sheriff arranged for Daniel to be taken away, buried and all reminders of blood were cleaned up. Aunt Allison was taken to the county hospital to have the bullet removed and to repair the damage. Weakened by the bullet wound and the surgery afterwards, Aunt Allison never completely recovered. Within six months, Allison contracted pneumonia and died within a week. Her children, grandchildren, family and especially her husband Edward, mourned her loss deeply. Her family felt blessed that they had a family portrait taken several weeks before her death. Edward made sure that each of her children had a copy of the portrait.

December 1975

So, this explains why Grandma had included the Howard family portrait; I know that the family is extremely happy that they have it as a remembrance of their mother, Allison, and Edward had a photograph of his wife.

I felt a deep sadness about how Dighton had lost their lone doctor so tragically. I was even more surprised to hear about the jackrabbit infestation that seemed to cripple western Kansas. It was nice to read about how my Grandparents met and eventually married during the late twenties. I learned about the dust bowl in school but it really did not teach the students about the human cost of the dust storms. I couldn't wait to continue the conversation with Grandma in order to find out what happened next in the life of my Grandparents.

Conversation continues

My eighty—seven-year-old Grandmother was never able to completely reconcile herself to how Allison died. As a result, her health declined and she passed away in early 1937. During Grandma's lifetime she had divided the 609—acre property between Joseph, Peter and William. Peter and William had each built a modest home for their families. Joseph and his wife, Helen, and their two daughters had moved in with Grandma after Marie had passed away.

Grandma was able to leave each of her other grandchildren a small sum of money to help them pursue their dreams. The sum of money was not large but it helped Lawrence and myself with expenses of having a third child. Your Grandfather and I had your Uncle Gerald in March of 1937. At this time, William was in his first year at school while your mom was three—years—old. Your mom pretended that her baby brother was her personal doll. Of course, I had to keep a watchful eye on Elaine and especially Gerald. Needing a larger home now that we had three children, Grandpa and I rented another farm house that was two stories, had twenty acres, and a small barn.

Continuing to work for Lane County Road Department, your Grandpa was working forty plus hours a week. Each year that we lived on the farm, we planted a cash crop on the fifteen to sixteen of the twenty acres. Acreage closer to the house was utilized for a family vegetable garden. I had a green thumb when it came to growing vegetables. Close to the house, I planted iris, daisies, lilies and snap dragons. Near one portion of the fence that surrounded the back yard, I planted some hollyhocks.

While telling the children, especially Elaine, stories I would take two hollyhock flowers and make a doll out of them. William spent many happy hours in the vegetable garden assisting me with planting, weeding and harvesting the crop of vegetables. In 1940, William spent his first summer in Rush County aiding my brothers with the many chores involved in operating their large properties.

Having lost a few relatives and many friends from the first war, I was grateful that our sons, William and Gerald, were too young to be drafted to fight the Second World War. During the war, Kansas farmers responded dynamically to the governments call for more wheat, corn, hogs and cattle for the war effort. "I have been told that there were almost 180,000 men" stated Grandma "and about 3,800 women working on farms in 1940."

'Wow!" I said "That doesn't seem like a lot."

"Just remember this was 1940, not 1975! So, having a 183,800 people working farms for the war effort was a relatively large number. What little we grew and harvested on the sixteen acres we sold to the government for the war effort."

Continuing with her story, Grandma said "Your Grandpa, still an avid newspaper reader, would tell me how the newspapers argued that Kansas was becoming a place where the Air

Force and Army trained their pilots and aircrews. Kansas had been selected for the training due to having excellent flying conditions year around."

After reading another newspaper story, he would argue that Kansas was an ideal place for gunnery, bombing and training ranges because of the state being sparsely populated. The training obtained at Kansas airfields provided the airmen the skills and knowledge needed when they entered combat and helped in defeating of the Nazi's and the Japanese.

Like the rest of America, western Kansas saw many of their young men drafted and sent to Europe or the Pacific. One hundred and ten local men from Ellis, Rush, Ness, Lane and Finney counties died or were missing in action. However, many of the Funks were either too young or too old to be drafted so did their part at home. Entire towns would recycle needed materials, people would do without whenever possible, and many moved to the city in order to obtain a job to aid the defense effort.

Having these airfields or military bases so close brought the reality of war to small rural towns across Kansas, including Dighton. Besides military training, the bases provided civilian jobs in the field of office work, maintenance and repair. Many of Dighton's young people moved eastward for one of the jobs offered at the military bases in eastern Kansas. The majority of those moving to eastern Kansas were attracted to the aircraft industry that had developed in and around Wichita during the 1920s. As a result, Wichita had become known as the Air Capital of the World. This could explain why nearly seventy—percent of all new war plants dealing with aviation were located in Wichita.

"I heard that better pay was the key that attracted skilled men to the aviation industry and other types of manufacturing for the war effort needs" continued Grandma. "However, not every man had enough skills or the right kind of skills that was needed in order to obtain a job in the aviation filed; training was emphasized for those unskilled farm boys applying for jobs.

"In 1941, Allison and Edward's son, Robert, headed to Wichita to obtain training and then took a job in the aviation industry. Robert was lucky that he was hired, trained and then began work at Beechcraft. During his early years at Beechcraft, Robert helped produce the Model 18 'Twin Beech' aircraft that had begun to be produced in 1937."

At the end of the war many of the military and aviation industry airfields were considered surplus and were sold to the general public. Sometimes these airfields would be turned over to the local community and would be used as a general aviation airport. During the second world war, many people moved into manufacturing, construction, the food industry, printing and publishing in order to assist in the war effort. Better pay was the key that attracted many skilled men to the aviation industry and other types of manufacturing for the war effort.

After the war, manufacturing, construction, food industry, printing and publishing businesses continued to operate after shifting gears. "For example, the food industry shifted from servicing the military to producing convenience foods or frozen foods for working women." Grandma stated that "Many of Dighton's young people moved to Garden City to find work in the food industry. Due to the increase in food companies having been built in Garden City, the city saw an increase of feedlots and grain elevators. The feedlots and elevators were located in and around the city but were mainly positioned near the rail lines.

"I heard that eighty—percent of the young people stayed in their new, chosen field once the war ended. This meant that the young people leaving Lane County for jobs that supported the war effort did not return."

Grandma said that "Grandpa and I remained living on the twenty—acre farm that we rented. We also continued planting cash crops on the acreage. Cash crops assisted us in making extra money that we needed to make ends meet."

The children continued to grow and to do 'normal' things that kids do. Being a typical older brother, William teased his younger siblings but most especially his sister. Elaine took most of his teasing in stride but after one bout of teasing she was so angry that she grabbed a butcher knife and threw it at William. The knife missed his head by inches. As a result, Elaine was grounded and William curtailed his teasing for quite a long while."

Within two weeks of graduating high school in 1949, William moved to Denver to live with my brother Benjamin for the summer. William assisted Benjamin with his dry—cleaning business. At the end of August, William began taking classes at the University of Denver but continued to work for Benjamin on Saturdays. Like other freshmen, William lived in a dormitory. After registration William went back into his room and was slightly startled to see someone unpacking. He knew that he would have a roommate but was still surprised to see a 'stranger' in the room. Extending his hand, William introduced himself. Turning around, the young man shook hands with William and then said "Jeremy Collins. It's nice to meet you. What are you studying? I am studying English literature. Where are you from? I am from rural Nebraska......."

As Jeremy continued to talk, William could not believe that a male could talk so much without taking a breath; if he talked like this on a regular basis William wondered how he would survive? Finally slowing down, William was able to tell Jeremy that he was studying philosophy and that he was from rural Kansas. As the semester progressed the pair got used to each other. Jeremy seemed to talk less and William opened up more.

Being strapped for money, neither of the young men could afford to go home for Christmas. The dorm closed for two weeks between Christmas and New Year's so William had invited Jeremy to stay with him at his Uncle Ben's home. Being the first Christmas since his divorce, Ben was happy to have the company. William and Jeremy each gave Ben a small, thank you gift for letting them stay.

A few days before Christmas, Ben took William and Jeremy to hear the Denver Symphony Orchestra perform a selection of Christmas music. On Christmas morning they went to church and then spent a quiet day remembering the reason for the season. Even though the college was closed, Ben still had to operate his dry—cleaning shop due to people needing their clothes cleaned. William and Jeremy helped out whenever possible in Ben's shop. The two weeks spent together were wonderful for the trio but William and Jeremy were anxious to return to their studies.

Jeremy was able to return to Nebraska for the summer while William remained at the university and took several classes. One day while William was helping out at the dry—cleaning business a beautiful, young woman came into the shop to drop off some suits for her father. William was smitten by the petite, dark haired woman! Over the next several weeks he made sure that he waited on her instead of Ben whenever possible. Conversing with the young woman, William found out that her name was Marilyn Eriksson; she lived at home and worked as a secretary for an attorney. As he was waiting on Marilyn one day, Ben told her that he had an extra ticket for the symphony and preceded to ask her "if she would like to join my nephew and myself for the concert?"

Marilyn agreed because there would be the three of them, not just one or the other as that she was not ready for a serious involvement yet. By the end of the concert, Marilyn had become infatuated with William. The pair began to date each other and by March of 1951 they were discussing marriage. Since both their birthdays were on the seventeenth, one in June and one in February, they decided to be married on the seventeenth of December. Lawrence, Elaine, Gerald and I drove to Denver a few days before the wedding and stayed with Ben. Ben's home was cramped but the five of us made do.

During the summer of 1950, Lawrence and I finally moved into town. We rented a house that still enabled us to grow a garden, not a huge garden but one nonetheless. We planted cucumbers, green beans, tomatoes and a few herbs. I continued to make pickles from the abundance of cucumbers grown not only in our garden but also in her sister—in—law, Anna's garden. Anna did not make pickles from cucumbers but every year planted them to support my effort. I always provided Anna and David several jars of my pickles. Anna saved the canning jars and lids for me to use for the next batch of pickles or any other food that was being preserved.

Beginning her junior year in High School, Elaine could not wait for high school to be finished as she wished to get on with her life and get a job. Fourteen—year—old Gerald was enjoying life; he did not have any desire to leave rural Kansas for the city. Often the four of us would spend evening's together playing cards. At times Lawrence would overbid his hand which caused him and his partner, usually Gerald, to go set. Lawrence would then say "If I only had a partner."

Calmly Gerald would simply say "I'm not the one who bid."

"Years later, Grandpa and I played cards with you and your sister. Your Grandpa was still overbidding his hand and losing.

You and your sister came to expect him to say "if I only had a partner!" Being his partner, your answer was always the same as your Uncle Gerald's "I'm not the one who bid."

I took a job in the grade school's lunch room during the late fifties. Dighton's children knew that my name was Mrs. Anderson but often referred to me as the lunch lady. I liked the job because I enjoyed seeing the town's children. Plus, it enabled me to be off summers so I could have the grandchildren come stay with us.

Like in the forties, those graduating from rural high schools in the fifties and early sixties would often move to larger cities for employment. In June of 1952, Elaine felt that there were no employment opportunities in Dighton. So, she decided to move to Denver in order to find employment. Upon arriving in Denver, Elaine stayed with my brother Ben while she looked for a job. On her first job interview she was offered a job as a typist and would be part of the secretarial pool at *Denver Fire Clay*.

A wholesaler, *Denver Fire Clay*, provided a wide variety of services and products to hospitals, upholsters, restaurants, and many other types of businesses. The shop foreman, Thomas Keller, knew that the company was expanding and was in the middle of hiring an additional fifteen warehouse workers and two office workers. One of the new hires for the office was a replacement worker while the second new office worker would be a totally new hire due to the company's expansion.

Being a womanizer, Thomas made a point of introducing himself to each new office worker. Within an hour of beginning work, Thomas was in the office with invoices for the bookkeeper. Of course, the invoices could have waited until the end of the week but he wanted to be the first man to 'hit' on the new office workers. Both of the new office workers were young and would be flattered with the attention from an older man or so Thomas thought.

This was not the first time that Thomas had misjudged women. One new hire, Diane Farmer, was not impressed by Thomas at all. Past experience had taught Diane that womanizing men did not make great boyfriends or, from what she had heard, not great husbands either. But, Elaine, being just eighteen, was flattered by his attention. The seven women who worked in the office ate together in the lunch room. While eating, Diane casually asked the other women about the warehouse workers. The five women that had worked there longer chuckled before one of them answered "If you're asking about smooth talker Thomas, our advice is to stay away from him."

Not having picked up on his womanizing ways, Elaine looked puzzled. Diane jumped in to ask the other ladies about their experience with Thomas. "Where to begin…" Mary Benson started and Belinda Allen continued "He likes to sweet talk women in hopes of getting them in bed."

"Once he gets a woman in bed he will 'dump' them." Susan Miller pointed out.

Elaine asked "How do you know this?"

Karen Turner replied that "two and a half weeks ago an office worker left because Thomas had romanced her, got into her bed and then acted as if he did not know her. Visibly upset, she told us what happened. Obviously, Thomas told the other warehouse men about her being 'easy' so all the single guys and even a few married ones started flocking around her. Not being able to do her job and tired of being harassed, she looked for and obtained another job, she then left in a hurry."

"Elaine, did you notice that when he was attempting to do his flattery routine with me that he gave up?" asked Diane as Elaine shook her head no.

Diane continued by saying "Experience told me that Thomas is not sincere in what he said to me so I ignored him and continued to work. He noticed this and stopped talking to me. He concentrated on flattering you. Please be careful and don't get caught up in his womanizing ways."

Not working at *Denver Fire Clay* very long and not having been approached by Thomas, Virginia Wright did not feel comfortable adding her opinion. However, she had picked up on the ways of Thomas early on and had steered clear of him. The co-workers felt that they did their part in warning Elaine; they could not stop her from seeing him outside of work.

Of the seven women working in the office, Elaine was the youngest and most inexperienced around men so Thomas continued hanging around and asking her out. Having received a pay check, she was able to look for an inexpensive place to live close to work. She settled into a furnished efficiency apartment in a building reserved for single women. Elaine either walked or rode the bus to and from work. Thomas noticed that she was not being dropping her off at work anymore by Ben so figured out that this was the time to push harder for a date.

Living by herself was lonelier than she thought so Elaine finally agreed to go to dinner with him the following Saturday evening. Asking where he could pick her up, she gave him the boarding house address and told him that she would meet him in the building's lobby. Picking her up, Thomas opened the car door for Elaine. During the car ride to the restaurant, throughout dinner, and the ride home, Thomas was exceptionally polite and attentive to her needs. After arriving back to Elaine residence, the pair decided to take a walk in the park that was across the street from where Elaine lived. A half hour later, Thomas made sure that she was safely inside before he left for home. Elaine began to wonder if the women in the office could be wrong about him. However, she decided that she needed to be careful until she knew him better.

The following Monday, Thomas was less obnoxious and obvious about his womanizing ways when he thanked Elaine for a nice time. The next couple of days he made an attempt to be the perfect gentleman. However, all the ladies in the office were not fooled except Elaine. On Thursday Thomas finally asked her out again for the following Saturday evening. Thomas had decided that he liked Elaine and not to scare her away. But mostly he wanted to prove the office staff wrong.

By late—July, only six weeks after meeting, Thomas asked Elaine to marry him. Since she was head—over—heels in love, she readily agreed. Having been married previously, Thomas was not thrilled about having a church wedding but Elaine wanted one. They finally decided to have a small, church wedding. They chose to have the wedding at the church Elaine, William, Marilyn and Ben attended. They set the date for the 5th of September 1952; they invited family and a few close friends. Lawrence, Gerald, and I once again drove in from Kansas and stayed with my brother Ben.

Both your Grandpa and I felt that since they had known each other for less than three months it was too soon for a marriage to take place. Plus, she was just eighteen! Being forty—one, he was old enough to be her father! Beyond asking her if she was sure about this marriage we did not say much because we knew that it was her life! If we pushed too much, she could still marry him and we might not see her again. "Hmmm, this sounds vaguely familiar, doesn't it?" Grandma asked me.

Thinking a moment before I finally said "Do you mean what happened to Allison and Daniel?"

"Yes!" Grandma replied. "Nine months to the day after the wedding, Elaine gave birth to a daughter that they named Sharon. Fifteen months later, they had you."

January 1976
Dani

Grandma did a good job bringing the family into the late 1950's, about two hundred years after the family considered leaving Germany and finally moved to Russia. Also, she mixed it well with what was going around the nation as a whole. It was interesting to read about both Uncle William's and Mom's early years in Colorado. Experience told me that my Grandparents and my Dad did not get along. Nothing was ever directly said by either my Grandparents or Dad but I just knew.

Back in Colorado and college, I contemplated about what happened after this point. During the late fifties, Grandma and Grandpa had purchased a two—bedroom home on East Annabelle Street. My Great—Uncle David assisted his sister by building her a chicken coop that was placed near the garage. The chickens provided Grandma and Grandpa with the occasional meal of meat but also an abundance of eggs.

Two weeks each summer Sharon and I spent two weeks in Dighton with our Grandparents taking swimming lessons, having tea parties with two neighbor girls, named Cindy and Cathy, and riding our bikes around town. Every afternoon Sharon and I would walk the two blocks to the post office in order to retrieve our Grandparents mail. The Anderson mail box was located on the very top row so when we were young, we had to go to the window and ask for the mail. The post mistress lived next door to our grandparents so she would give us the mail after briefly conversing with us.

Being a very small town, everyone knew when anyone came to town for a visit. *The Dighton Herald,* the town's paper, had a weekly column that discussed who was visiting whom, about marriages in and out of town, and other items of interest. The Wednesday before Sharon and I arrived, the newspaper stated that Elaine's daughters would be visiting their grandparents, the Anderson's.

By 1966 life was not easy as for Mom as she had four children under the age of thirteen and a husband who liked the bottle a bit too much. More and more often, Dad would stop at the local bar and have a drink prior to coming home. Sometimes he would just have a slight buzz but as the years went by, he drank more and more before coming home.

Mom began to understand better what her co-workers at *Denver Fire Clay* had been attempting to warn her about back in 1952. Dad was a womanizer back then and he continued his womanizing ways by flattering women, especially after he had a few drinks; unlike Daniel Heller, Dad never actually did anything beyond flattering the women. Mom worried about Dad's drinking. She also wondered what would happen if she became widowed at an early age because of Dad's alcohol abuse. If that happened, she felt that she had no means to support herself and four children. So, Mom arranged to go to a local technical school in order to gain the skills she needed to earn a living. Within a year, she finished school and had obtained a job with a major department store working in the billing department.

Six months later, Mom decided to leave my Dad and sought out the services of an attorney. The divorce became final during the spring of my I sophomore year of high school. For the first time in years, Mom thanked the Lord for allowing her to get training and be prepared for a better life.

At times, life seemed idyllic without any major incidents like what happened with Anton / Andrew or with Daniel. I am just grateful that life was quiet the majority of the time. However, at times I wished that my life did not seen so boring.

In August of 1972 I went to college to study journalism. Within a week of beginning college, I started working as a student assistant in the library. While we worked in the same library department, I met James, my future husband. When we first met, I wondered why James seemed to have more internal peace then what I had. Over a period of months and getting to know each other better, I soon realized that his peace came from having a relationship with Jesus. During the next two years I attended church with James, went through RCIA and officially entered the church just prior to the two of us getting married.

Shortly after getting married we began our journey of moving around the United States because James had joined the Coast Guard. At different duty stations, I would explore various classes held at each catholic church that we attended in order to learn more about Jesus and the church. Over the years, I have grown in my faith and have found the same peace that my husband always seemed to possess. Being active in the church my faith further developed and grew. I thought about the favorite bible verse of Conrad's:

> *For I was hungry and you gave me food; I was thirsty and you gave me something to drink; I was naked and you gave me clothing; I was sick and you took care of me; I was in prison and you visited me; I was a stranger and you welcomed me. Just as you did it to one of the least of these who are members of my family you did it for me. Matthew 25:35—36, 45*

Over the years, this verse became my favorite and I have attempted to live by this verse. I have helped with feeding of the hungry, collected clothing for the poor, and took part in other ministries. However, I know that there were times that I have slipped and fallen short of what the verse has asked of me.

As the years passed, I contemplated what I learned about the family from the 1760's through the twentieth century. During the 1760s, Germans, and other ethnic groups moved as a result of forced labor, military conscription, wars, foreign occupations, political oppression, religious suppression and drought conditions. From my journey into the family's history, I learned that Russia sent representatives to Germany and other part of central Europe to entice people to colonize under—populated areas of Russia. The people were guaranteed certain rights and were promised that they would be able to maintain their own language. Life in Russia was better for the Germans because they were able to practice their own religion, would be able to keep a hundred percent of the profits from their farming efforts, had the ability to purchase land that came available for sale by Russians, and were able to live in German communities within Russia.

However, after a hundred years the Germans were ready to leave Russia due to Germanophobia, conscription, being forced to support the less fortunate, and having many of their guaranteed privileges disappearing. In 1874, Germans living within the Russian Empire faced being drafted into the Russian Military. Forced conscription was the last straw for many Germans who began exploring migration elsewhere; many looked at moving to the United States. Just like other places around the world, the

United States experienced droughts, outlaws, wars and other issues that were not always good. But many felt that life had to be better than what they currently were experiencing in Russia. Hmmm....I wonder! Seems to me that the family experienced similar things in Germany, Russia and the United States.

I found it interesting that by 1900, the majority of Germans living in Hussenbach or in America did not know where their ancestors came from or why they migrated from their homeland. In addition, those who moved to America did not communicate to the younger generations why the family left Russia. Over the years, this also was forgotten and the younger generation had unanswered questions. Families left behind were never heard from again; for example, after the first world war, Anna Hemel Funk never heard from her German family in Russia again.

The family experienced having to deal with Andrew Koch; the danger of the native peoples of Central Asia; the renegades who were rapping, robbing and sometimes killing people in the Volga River region; facing robbers in the fabric / quilt shop; Dighton's doctor being killed; and dealing with Daniel Heller, Allison's first husband, not once but at least four times—twice at gun point. The family also faced natural disasters such as drought, dust storms, grasshopper infestations, and jack rabbit infestations. I guess that I am from a family of survivors!

Late—1990s

During the mid—1990s, I was able to travel to Frankfort, Germany to do some independent research on ethnicity. When I finished gathering the research material, I took a quick trip to Nauheim to see if I could collect more information on the family. Going into the town's record office, I began to search their holdings for any records or books regarding the family. One employee was assigned to assist me with the materials that I needed to examine. Near the end of the day, another employee came into the reading room, looked at me, smiled and said in heavily accented English "I understand that you are researching the Funk family." I replied that I was and as I looked at the employee closer, I realized that he looked somewhat like my Uncle Gerald.

"My name is Wilhelm Funk. From what I know about my family and from my own personal research I am related to the Jacob, Herman, Benjamin, Phillip and Elizabeth Funk that immigrated to Russia during the 1760's. The five siblings were cousins of my seventh time great—grandfather."

I am positive that my chin dropped and mouth fell open because Wilhelm grinned, laughed softly and then we hugged. He invited me to join him and his family for dinner that evening. I spent an extra—couple—of—days in Nauheim to get to know more about the Funk's that had stayed in Germany over two—hundred years ago.

After I left Nauheim, I continued my journey to the Volga River region and, in particular, Hussenbach. Standing on a bergseite just outside of town, I had a good long look at the beautiful, gently rolling Medvelitza River. Just beginning to change color, the autumn leaves shimmered and reflected off the water. Turning slightly, I then took a long look at the town. Overwhelmed at being where my ancestors lived, I felt a tear roll down my face. Having given me a few minutes, the translator and tour guide joined me. The translator asked me if I was ready to walk along the main street. I replied that "yes, I was ready to walk the same streets my relatives walked a hundred years or more ago."

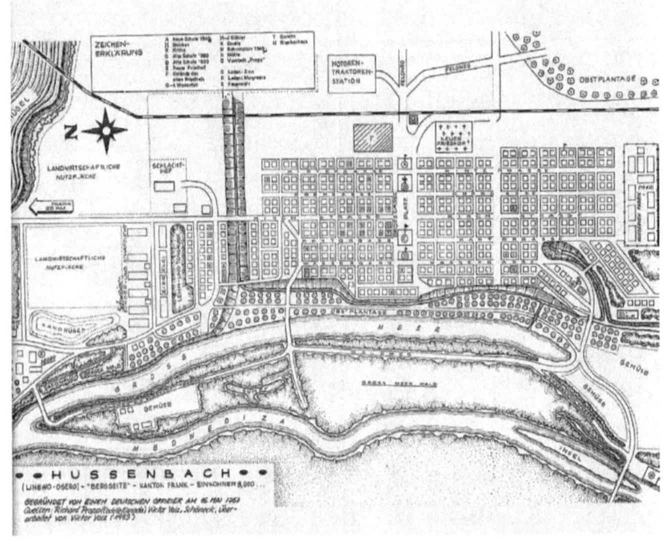

http://cvgs.cu-portland.edu/settlements/
mother_colonies/colony_hussenbach.cfm

Walking down the main street, we paused in front of the first building we came too. The translator told me that this was the first school built in Hussenbach. My hand went to my mouth as I thought of my ancestors attending this school. The tour guide asked the translator if he and I would like to go inside the school to look around. Once inside, I saw two maps on the wall. They were of the same map but they were in different languages. The first map was in Russian while the second map was in German. I was told that this map was how the town looked in 1940. If I wished for a copy of the map, they might have a copy of the map in English at the local mercantile. I lucked out, the mercantile had one copy of the map left that was in English. After purchasing the map, it was rolled up and put it in a tube. Once again, we were walking down the main street of Hussenbach, I asked "Will you be able to show me the property where my family lived?"

After the guide said something to the translator, he then turned to me and said "that he couldn't tell me the exact location of the land where the family lived and farmed. You said that your family probably planted the first fruit tree orchard in Hussenbach and the surrounding area. Since many fruit trees have been planted since that time, we cannot tell you exactly which property had the first orchard. This was because the birth, death, marriage and land records had burned in a fire that took place thirty years ago. We could get in the general area but, the guide, would not be able to say for sure which property."

Further down main street. We went into many of the same stores that the family had patronized. We stopped at a store front that the tour guide said once housed the fabric shop operated by my Great—Great—Grandparents. I asked "How do you know if records were burnt?"

"Because the store was so popular," began the guide "that everyone knows where the fabric store was located."

The store was now a clothing store which I though appropriate since fabric had once been sold there. How wonderful that my ancestors had been so memorable. I could not stop the smile that spread across my face.

We then stopped to view the Medvelitza River. From this vantage point I could see a building that looked like it was in bad shape. Pointing at the building I asked "What type of business was housed in that building?"

I was told "that it had been a mill. About forty—five years ago the mill had closed. The building did not sell so had fallen into disrepair. The mill stone and parts of the water wheel remained within the dilapidating building." The mill that was built later had also fallen into decline but there was nothing left there except the buildings shell.

I asked about the Spool Mill that the family operated. I was told that many in Hussenbach still remembered the Funk's Spool Mill and where it had been located. I was told that the building still stood although it was falling apart. The guide, translator and a few towns people took me to where the mill quietly stood. I was able to carefully go inside the mill and look around the empty building. Cob webs, rusty machinery and a few wooden spinning wheels brought tears to my eyes. Somehow, I was also able to obtain a spinning wheel that had been in the mill. Two of the men that came with us were asked to take one of the spinning wheels out of the buildings shell and have it crated with lots of padding. They were told that we would retrieve the carton when we were finished touring the town.

Asking when the mill had closed, the translator asked the tour guide who then told me that the mill had closed about the time of the 1917 revolution, when communism took over. I couldn't believe that the mill had been closed for over eighty years but the building continued to stand, dilapidated but still standing. The wooden sign on the front of the building stated:

Spinnerei von Funk

"I assume that Funk is the family name but what else does it say?" I asked. The interpreter said that it said "Funk's Spinning Mill." I asked if it was possible for me to obtain the sign to take home.

"What sign?" was the reply that I received and after a few words to the same two men the sign was taken down. The translator said that once again we should meet the men at their shop to retrieve the boxed—up sign when we finished.

After the tour of Hussenbach, the translator left the guide and myself at a park bench that overlooked the river and parts of the town while he went to get us some sandwiches and several

Journal One

Germany—1764

Recent talk around Nauheim indicates that more farmers than ever have chosen to move away. I, Conrad Funk, am positive that the main reason farmers are leaving is due to the droughts that are plaguing the region. With fewer farmers selling their harvest at market you would think that those left to sell their crops would make more money. However, we are being offered less money for the produce we are selling. At the same time, the general store charges higher prices for flour, seasonings, coffee and other commodities. Without the money earned from the crops that I am selling, where am I to obtain money for needed supplies?

About the Author

The author, **Marta Lee**, lives in southeast Virginia with her husband James. They have two children and four grandchildren. Due to her husband's thirty—year Coast Guard career Marta and her family have moved to and lived in the great lakes' region, the mid—west and the mid—Atlantic states. Marta began attending college in her early—thirties while living in Virginia. During the next twelve years they moved to Wisconsin, Michigan and eventually back to Virginia. To help pay for college, Marta worked at the Mariners' Museum library, in the fast food industry, and Macomb Community College as a geography tutor. Eventually she obtained a bachelor of science in geography, a master of arts in humanities, and a masters' in library and information science. After becoming a librarian, Marta has worked in the library at the Census Bureau, Washington Theological Unions' library, Regent University library, Yorktown Public Library and been a volunteer librarian at the Colonial National Historical Park. While working at Regent University Library, Marta wrote on the topics of library services to distant students, inter—library loan, reference services, mentoring and the public library system of south west Kansas. Currently, Marta is semi—retired and enjoying researching and writing.

bottles of American Coca—Cola. As I thought of the many thousands of miles that I had to travel in order to drink an American beverage caused a smile to cross my face.

While sitting on the bench waiting for the translator, I thought that it was it was important to write about the family's journey from Germany—to—Hussenbach—to—western Kansas and other points further across America. It has been a nice circle to return to where the family had lived and loved for hundreds of years.

I somehow managed to bring the sign and spinning wheel back to the States with me on the airplane. Once home, Jim had a sign made up that read Funk's Spinning Mill to hang with the sign that read: *Spinnerei von Funk.* Both signs were hung on the outside of my husband's two-story barn. Periodically people ask where I got the signs and one or two have asked if I would sell them. Of course, I will never sell either one but especially the one that I brought back from Hussenbach. My husband and I managed to get the spinning wheel to Dighton, where it has been put on display in a museum near Dighton's Sod House.

2011

Looking back on my journey with my family, I realized that things change but have not really changed? During the 1770s, Germans endured droughts, conscription, crop failures, and had no religious freedom. These problems caused large portions of Germanys population to think about and to eventually move to Russia. While the family lived in the Volga River region the Germans faced conscription, were forced to contribute to the less fortunate, Germanophobia, were criticized for not speaking Russian and for not following the Russian Orthodox religion.

These items triggered a strong desire within many Germans to begin the migration process once more.

Was life any different or better in America? Deep down I do not think so. Like in Germany and Russia, America has had the draft, droughts, crop failures, ethnic discrimination and religious discrimination. The most important thing that I learned from my family journey was the need for people to be loved and accepted. I thought of Conrad, my six—times Great Grandfather, and contemplated his favorite bible verses:

For I was hungry and you gave me food, I was thirsty and you gave me something to drink, I was a stranger and you welcomed me, I was naked and you gave me clothing, I was sick and you took care of me, Just as you did it to one of the least of these who are members of my family you did it for me.   Matthew 25:35—36, 45

According to Conrad's journal writings, the verses in Matthew played a prominent role in his life. As time wore on and others wrote in the journals the bible verses did not seen to play as prominent role; the verses were not written down. However, the family still aided those in need by feeding, clothing and taking care of the sick.

The birth of my first grandchild, a granddaughter who was named Hannah after her great—great—grandmother, caused a desire in me to relate the story of the Funk's journey from Germany—to—Russia—to—America. I did not want future family members to wonder where they came from and why they left their homeland. Quietly opening my laptop, I launched my word processing program and began writing….